# PRAISE FOR *BLITHEDALE CANYON*

"*Blithedale Canyon* is a compelling and lively debut with a narrator I won't soon forget: a deeply flawed young man who longs to be more noble and honest, a person who is at once full of so much love and tenderness, and yet also capable of such deceit, too. With this riveting novel, Michael Bourne gives us a vivid portrait of Northern California at the turn of the 21st century: the complicated signifiers of wealth, the crushing inevitability of gentrification, and that old California, part myth, part memory. A story of love, addiction, regret, and hope. I couldn't put it down."

– Edan Lepucki, author of *California* and *Woman No. 17*

"Michael Bourne's debut novel is an ode to the pleasures and pains of the return to the familiar, to the gravitational pulls of addiction, old friends, and Springsteen on a car stereo, but mostly of home. *Blithedale Canyon* is a tenderly nostalgic and page-turning portrait of a man who can't control his worst impulses, written by an author in full command of his own tools."

– Teddy Wayne, author of *The Love Song of Jonny Valentine* and *Loner*

"We are surrounded by stories about winning, but where are all the great modern novels about failure? *Blithedale Canyon* is about Trent Wolfer who has lost almost everything. He moves back home to start fresh and quickly finds himself at risk of losing it all again. Bourne is brave enough to be honest and honest enough to write an unvarnished truth. This novel brims with humor, it's cathartic, original, and lonely. It's a wild ride."

– Claire Cameron, author of *The Last Neanderthal* and *The Bear*

"Trent Wolfer is a screwup, but one so smart and observant and oddly self-aware that we can't help rooting for him – and noting the ways in which we're a little like him. Trent wants more than anything to find some truth amid his own and others' bullshit, and we're kept on edge as he keeps losing and finding and losing that truth again. The perfect story for our age of con artists and systemic scams."

– Pamela Erens, author of *Eleven Hours* and *The Virgins*

"*Blithedale Canyon* is a hard look at the destruction of American capitalism in the lives of the privileged and the devoured. No one here is easy to love, and yet Bourne writes each of his damaged, difficult characters with a clear-eyed complexity that readers will recognize. By the last page, readers will be asking an essential question of our American moment: Can there be any redemption without honesty?"

– Kirsten Sundberg Lunstrum, author of *What We Do With the Wreckage* and *This Life She's Chosen*

# BLITHEDALE CANYON

Michael Bourne

Regal House Publishing

Published by
Regal House Publishing, LLC
Raleigh, NC 27587
All rights reserved

Printed in the United States of America

ISBN -13 (paperback): 9781646031825
ISBN -13 (epub): 9781646031832
Library of Congress Control Number: 2021943791

All efforts were made to determine the copyright holders and obtain their permissions in any circumstance where copyrighted material was used. The publisher apologizes if any errors were made during this process, or if any omissions occurred. If noted, please contact the publisher and all efforts will be made to incorporate permissions in future editions.

Interior layout by Lafayette & Greene
Cover images © by C.B. Royal

Regal House Publishing, LLC
https://regalhousepublishing.com

The following is a work of fiction created by the author. All names, individuals, characters, places, items, brands, events, etc. were either the product of the author or were used fictitiously. Any name, place, event, person, brand, or item, current or past, is entirely coincidental.

Printed in the United States of America

In memory of my mother

# 1

"How come I only got five nuggets?" the skate rat at my register wanted to know.

It was straight-up noon, the line snaking out the double doors, machines beeping, fryers hissing, orders flying everywhere, but all I could think about as I made change and grabbed burgers and fries from under the heat lamps were the four Stoli mini bottles stashed under the passenger seat of my car. I'd popped off two before I clocked in that morning, and usually by now I would have ducked out back for a couple more, but our day manager Rajiv had written me up twice already for leaving my station without permission, and I couldn't afford another blue sheet, which is what they called disciplinary actions at Howie's Hamburgers.

The skate kid was fourteen or fifteen, loose-limbed and scrawny, acne pits deep as moon craters. Behind him his buddies were laughing. He'd passed a chicken nugget to one of them while I was topping up their sodas, and they wanted to see what I was going to do about it.

"There were six in there when I gave it to you," I said.

"Do we need to get a manager here?" Zit Boy said, doubling down. "Because I'm seriously considering lodging a complaint. I paid for six nuggets, dude."

The sad part was, I had been this kid not so long ago: the same filthy do-rag covering the same weedy splotch of sun-bleached hair, the same battered skate deck and designer-label kicks that cost more than I made at Howie's in a week. The effort it took to stay cool, to not jump over the counter and wipe that dickish grin off his face, was making my hands shake. I closed my eyes, trying to shut out the noise and the heat and the panic, but when I opened them again, he was still there, still grinning at me, waiting for me to lose it in front of the lunch crowd.

"Trent? Is that *you*?"

She had dyed her hair a streaky blonde and maybe put on a pound or two around the hips, but ten years later she was still Suze Randall. Old Pothead Suze. Except going by the cut of her navy-blue suit and the two tow-headed boys at her side, it had been a while since she'd seen the business end of a bong. She looked good. Better than good. Polished. Put-together. In her purse, you could just bet, was the key to a silver Beemer, or at the very least a frost-blue Lexus, two years past its warranty but so clean you could eat your lunch off the hood.

The skate rats drifted back from the counter, sipping their sodas, fascinated.

"What are you doing here?" I asked.

"I'm buying my kids some lunch," Suze said. "What're *you* doing here?"

Zit Boy giggled and she shot him a look that sent the four of them skittering off toward the dining area, chomping their fries and chucking each other. But now my register was free, and she had no choice but to step up to the counter. The two boys had gone still, twigging that Mom was deep in the weeds and didn't know how to get out.

"I didn't know you were back in Mill Valley," she said.

"You, either," I said. "I thought you were still in L.A."

"I was, till a year ago. Then I moved back."

I nodded, speechless. This was the first time all summer I had run into anyone from the old days and I wanted to crawl into a hole. But there was no hole to crawl into, nothing to do but stand there watching Suze try not to stare at my greasy hair stuffed up under a plastic hairnet.

Rajiv was watching us now from his seat at the drive-up window, so I said, "You know, maybe I should take your order."

Seeing Rajiv, Suze hustled through her order: two Kiddie Meal Deals with everything for the boys and a Lean Meal Deal for her, hold the Howie sauce. I rang it all up and got the drinks and the kids' food, but thanks to the special order on her veggie burger we were stuck at the counter for an extra minute. It felt like a day and a half. The last time I'd seen Suze we were both in college, sort of, me at UC Santa Barbara, Suze at Cal State L.A. Suze had dropped most of her classes and was living in Pasadena with her boyfriend Jimmy Strasser, and I had gotten kicked out of the UCSB baseball program for trying to start a mini grow-op in my closet in the dorms. Still, nothing about the kid I was back then quite added up to this: a twenty-nine-year-old white guy working the register at Howie's Hamburgers.

"They have to grow the soybeans," I said.

"Huh?"

"Out back," I said, wishing I hadn't started on this. "That's why it's taking so long. They have to grow the beans first."

"Oh, right," she said, and laughed. It wasn't funny, to her or me, but the way she laughed, the old Suze way, waving her hand in front of her face like she was putting out a fire, flashed me back nine years, to the very last time I saw her. She had called me in the dorms, drunk and babbling, saying Jimmy had cheated on her again. I borrowed my roommate's car and drove to L.A. to comfort her, just like old times. And what happened then? Jimmy called is what happened then. By eight the next morning, Suze and Jimmy were having window-rattling makeup sex and I was bombing through Oxnard on my way back up the coast.

When Suze's veggie burger arrived, I slipped it into the sack and handed it to her across the counter. The fluorescent lights were like ten thousand needles pressing on my eyeballs, and I needed that Stoli hit, bad. But she didn't move, not right away.

"I saw your mom the other day," she said. "She's with that guy now—what's-his-name, the eco-patio-furniture guy."

"That would be Stan Starling," I said, sneaking a peek at the third finger of her left hand. My pulse skipped a beat: no ring.

"Mom, let's *go*," the older boy whined, nudging her.

"Hang on, Dylan. Mommy's talking." She turned back to me. "Your mom was at some thing, a charity thing at the tennis club. In fact, I think she was running it."

She said more, but I was staring at little Dylan. The wash of freckles, that jutting jawline, the thatch of strawberry-blond hair: there was only one man on earth who could be this kid's father, and that man was Jimmy Strasser. I peeked again at Suze's left hand: still no ring.

"Is everything all right, madam?" Rajiv asked, swooping in out of nowhere.

Suze gave him the slow elevator eyes. "Everything's fine, thanks."

"She's a friend from school," I said. "We were just talking."

Rajiv was slight-built and pale, his eyes a blackish, oily color. I'm not good at ages, but if you'd put a gun to my head I would've said twenty-two. No razor had touched that delicate chin. If it weren't for the clownish Howie's manager's uniform with its blue wool-knit tie and oversized lapels, he might have even been handsome in a geeky, science-camp-kid kind of way.

"I see that," he said. "I am thinking only of our other customers, who are waiting."

"Where were you a minute ago, then?" I said, loud enough to cut through the lunch-rush din.

"I beg your pardon?"

"Some kids were hassling me at my register. They were holding up the whole line, and you didn't move a muscle. So how about you give me one minute to catch up with an old friend?"

Suze smiled, and the world's tiniest helium balloon of self-respect inflated in my chest. But then I saw Rajiv's hairless chin wobble, and I realized that, stupid, stupid me, I'd just caught my third and final blue sheet.

"It's okay," Suze said, grabbing her bag of food. "We were just leaving."

"Very well, madam," Rajiv called after her. "Enjoy your meal!"

But she was already gone, striding out toward the parking lot, her two boys half-running to keep up. Rajiv cleared his throat, gave that ridiculous blue tie a tug, and marched back into the kitchen. The kid at the register next to mine kept his head down, smirking as he made change from his drawer, but from behind the order window I heard the day cook LaShonda's hissed catcall: "*Tell* him, white boy!"

I was halfway through keying in the next customer's order when a fleck of white caught my eye on the counter next to my register. It was a business card, a fancy one, cream-colored with raised blue lettering and the embossed logo of a local real estate firm. It read,

### SUZETTE R. STRASSER, REALTOR®

and listed four phone numbers: office, cell, pager, and home.

"Close the door, please," Rajiv said, without looking up from his computer.

I did as I was told, shut the door and stood across from Rajiv's desk, watching him fill out an electronic order form, typing in numbers, stopping every few seconds to check them against a sheet he'd filled in by hand. It wasn't much, Rajiv's office, just a windowless fiberboard cubicle behind the walk-in freezer with a desk, a beat-up computer, and two battleship-gray filing cabinets. On a calendar on the wall, someone had crossed out the first twenty-five days of July 2001 like a convict counting off days. Next to that, clipboards hung from a row of nails, each stuffed with food-flecked invoices and staffing schedules. Across the corridor in the break room, kids from the kitchen crew were sipping sodas and goofing off, doing Eminem impressions. One kid called out, "Yo, won't the real Slim Shady please stand up?" in a doofusy white-boy voice, and the others answered in high falsettos, "Hey, yo! Over here, yo! It's *me*! It's *me*!" And then they all fell out laughing.

"I'm sorry, Rajiv," I said. "I was having kind of a rough shift."

He went on entering numbers, stopping and checking, stopping and checking. Next door the singing had stopped. Someone must have heard Rajiv ask me to close the door, and now they were waiting to see if the white boy was really going to get it this time. The word in the break room was that if I was Black or Mexican, like everybody else at Howie's, Rajiv would have shit-canned me long ago. There was something to this. I was the only white employee at Howie's other than Robbie, the mentally retarded guy who picked up trash in the parking lot, which made me sort of a mascot, a friendly white face for our mostly white suburban customers to pick out in a sea of dark, mostly immigrant ones. Still, I took pride in blending in, and part of me itched to give the break room a show, tell Rajiv to go fuck himself and stomp back out to my car. But that was never going to happen. I needed this job. If I got fired now, it would mean a trip to my probation officer, which would mean peeing in a cup, which, if I caught the wrong judge, could send me right back to jail. Not county lockup, either, where I'd spent four and a half safe, boring months that winter. No, this time it would be state prison.

I needed this job.

"Seriously, I'm sorry," I said. "I was getting hassled by some kids earlier, but that doesn't excuse my behavior. What I said was out of line."

I might as well have been talking underwater. Rajiv kept typing in numbers until he got to the bottom of his handwritten sheet, then he flipped it over and started entering numbers from the next page. Even the kids next door were getting restless, waiting for the show to start. At last Rajiv reached for the mouse, checked his numbers one last time, and clicked "save." Only then did he look up from the monitor, folding his hands neatly on the desk.

"Tell me," he said. "Have you ever heard of Chennai?"

"What?"

"The city, Chennai. Do you know where it is?"

"No, I'm sorry, I don't. Somewhere in India, I'm guessing."

He smiled, blandly. "It is a city of several million on the Bay of Bengal. For many years, it was also called Madras. My family still lives there, in a small town on the outskirts of the city. We are not poor. My father sells plumbing supplies. But I have four brothers, all older. So, as you might imagine, when it came time for university there was no money to finance my tuition. Are you familiar with our Institutes of Technology?"

I shook my head, trying to look like I had some clue where he was going with all this.

"They are quite remarkable," he said. "On par with your Harvard and MIT. Best of all, they are heavily subsidized, so they are nearly free. For six years I studied night and day, hoping to earn a place at one of the IITs. No football. No cricket. Only studying all the day long, learning equations. When it came time for examinations, what do you suppose happened?" He looked up, his oily black eyes studying me. "A ninety-six. Not even close. The IITs accept only those in the top one percent, if that."

In spite of myself my heart dropped a little in my chest. I had no real feelings for Rajiv, the guy was a paycheck to me, but looking around at the fanatical neatness of his office, the papers all perfectly stacked, the ballpoint pens lined up along the edge of the desk arranged by color, everything awash in overbright fluorescent lighting, I thought: *Jesus, you poor son of a bitch.*

"Rajiv, I mean it, I'm sorry," I said. "I shouldn't have spoken to you like that."

He opened the single drawer of the desk and pulled out a lavender-colored sheet of paper. It was filled out in triplicate, with my name printed neatly at the top. "I assume you know what this is," he said.

"Please, man, you can't do this to me," I said. "I told you, that girl, she's somebody I grew up with. I used to be in love with her, for Christ's sake."

I saw the flash of surprise in his eyes. I was surprised, too—surprised and stung. Rajiv leaned back in his broken-down swivel chair, steepling his long fingers under his chin.

"If you will permit me a personal observation, I don't understand what you are doing here," he said. "You seem intelligent. I understand you have had your—your difficulties with the law. Nevertheless. Only a few weeks ago I was considering promoting you to assistant manager. But this is your third blue sheet in as many weeks."

Our old manager, Mary Jo, had gone over the disciplinary policy when I was hired: three strikes and you're out. But I wasn't thinking about Mary Jo just then. I was thinking about what I'd said about Suze. Sure, we'd been tight in school and we'd had our share of drunken hookups, but when we were kids hooking up at a party was like sharing your geometry homework: it was the friendly thing to do. But love? Where had *that* come from?

Rajiv was still holding the blue sheet, his lips pursed, considering me. "This young woman, you say you once had a romantic attachment?"

"Yeah," I said. "I mean, no. It wasn't like a boyfriend-girlfriend thing. I don't know, man, it was a long time ago. I couldn't really tell you what it was."

I braced for the laugh I knew was coming. But no laughter came. He just smiled, a little wistfully, and I had a vision of him, Rajiv Srinivasan, a guy not so unlike myself, stuck in this reeking asscrack of a restaurant, trying to get through the day without putting a bullet in his brain.

"Here." He pushed the blue sheet across the desk. "Take it. It's yours."

"Seriously? You're just going to give it to me?"

He flushed with the anger he'd held in earlier out on the line. "You embarrassed me today," he said. "That was rude and unnecessary. But I can understand if you felt I was not paying your friend the proper respect. Perhaps this will teach you to show that same respect to others." He pointed to the blue sheet. "I suggest you take it now, before I reconsider."

I took it, of course. I even thanked him, sort of, mumbling the words as I stalked out into the hall to face the kitchen crew, who were seated in a silent circle around the break table, their mouths forming small Os of stunned outrage.

"Score two for the white boy," I said, tossing the crumpled blue sheet into the break room trash bin.

After I punched out, I sat in my car listening to Nick Cave and the Bad Seeds as the traffic ripped past on Highway 101, carrying all the lawyers and dot-com zillionaires to their mansions in the Ross hills. I thought of the skate rat and his chicken nuggets. I thought about Rajiv skipping cricket to study equations. Then I thought of Suze's face frozen in shock, her pale blue eyes meeting mine, and I tried to remember how much money I had on me. Twenty-one dollars. Two tens and a one, maybe some nickels and dimes. Last I looked I had $273.47 in the bank. Not even three hundred bucks, all told. Ever since I'd started up with the mini bottles, I had been dreaming of putting together enough cash to buy a pound or two of grow-room weed and head back to Isla Vista, the little college town outside Santa Barbara where I'd been living since I left home. But three hundred dollars was barely enough to get me to S.B., much less stake me to any dealable weight. Then again, my Honda was all gassed up and Highway 101 led straight as a string down the coast to Isla Vista.

This was where this fantasy always seemed to end: I was on the 101 heading south, Nick Cave snarling into the speakers, night falling, the darkened ridges of the Gabilan Mountains stretching out on either side. And then what? And then *where?* Isla Vista was the obvious call, but forgetting my probation officer and all the promises I'd made in court, I didn't know anyone in Isla Vista anymore—not anyone who would be glad to see me without a bag of premium herb. So, L.A.? Not likely. Not so long as my dad was still living in Nichols Canyon with the Human Chihuahua and their three charming young Chihuahuaettes. So, Tijuana? Guadalajara?

It was at this point, when the whole thing was starting to sound like a bad Nick Cave song, that I reached under the seat for the last two Stoli mini bottles. Skinnies, I called them. I'd gotten started on the airplane bottles on the theory that, at fifty milliliters per, how much damage could they do? Which made sense, sort of, until I found a discount liquor store in Terra

Linda that sold them by the gross. Now I was the proud owner of four shrink-wrapped flats of fifty-milliliter Stolichnaya and Gilbey's bottles stashed in my bedroom closet at my mother's house.

I shot the Stolis one after the other, leaning across the passenger seat like I'd dropped something there and was looking for it. I felt the burn of the vodka going down and a flash of something like peace along my spine, but that's about it. After a while you stop expecting to feel drunk. Instead, you get a sort of lubed feeling, like the dust's been blasted out of the engine block and the oil's pumping in the pistons again. My high school baseball coach, an old guy named Jorgenson, used to talk about getting our game faces on. We'd warm up and take infield, and as we gathered in the dugout, Jorgenson would hock up an epic lunger of tobacco spit and look around at us like Patton addressing the troops.

"All right, guys," he'd say. "Game faces."

That was how I felt as I chewed a fistful of wintergreen Life Savers and punched the key into the ignition. I had my game face on.

A good thing, too, because when I pulled up outside chez Starling high above the tree line in Blithedale Canyon, my mother's sleek black Mini Cooper was parked, top down, in the carport. Not a good sign. My mother had her weekly tennis lesson at five on Tuesdays and back then there wasn't much that could get between my mother and a tennis court.

"Honey, is that you?" she called when I came through the front door. "Come on up. There's something I'd like to talk to you about."

I radared a look at Lupita, the silver-haired Ecuadorian who cooked and cleaned for Mom and Stan, but she just shrugged and went back to chopping tomatoes. To Lupita, I was one more chore in an already crowded day. She tolerated me well enough, and so far I had won the battle to keep her out of the crime scene that was my bedroom, but she knew better than to get in the middle of anything involving my mother and me.

Climbing the stairs to the living room at my mother's new home was like entering a tree house belonging to a fantastically wealthy child who read shelter magazines. The house was four stories of redwood and glass cantilevered out over the western-most lip of Blithedale Canyon. Before my mother moved in, she'd had Stan tear out the back wall along with most of the ceiling and replace it with a row of picture windows and three long skylights. These could be opened to vent the upper floor, which meant that on a warm July day like this one, the house smelled of eucalyptus and jack pine. Down below, past the silvery treetops, Mill Valley was laid out like a train-set village, first Lytton Square and the red-brick Plaza, then Miller Avenue cutting through the valley along the Old Mill Creek until it emp-tied into Richardson Bay, a sliver of which you could see in the distance, a tiny sapphire triangle shimmering in the late-day sun.

My mother was sitting on one of two cream-colored sofas, one tawny foot tucked under her legs, sipping a mug of herbal tea, a Barbara Kingsolver novel open on her lap. Stan grew up in Albuquerque, the son of a half-Navajo sheriff's deputy, and Mom had decorated the living room Sante Fe-style, with Nava-jo rugs draped over the sofas, original Native American art on the walls, and big terracotta pots lining the shelves. Between the clay pots, the shelves bristled with serious-looking novels, though if you looked closely you would have found few signs of actual readership. My mother used books the way she'd once used cigarettes and boyfriends, as props, something to do with her hands. But that was the thing about my mother. She looked so damn good sitting there, so tan and blonde and healthy, so at ease in these opulent surroundings, that you could know all her tricks and still forgive her everything.

"You're home early," she said, setting aside Barbara King-solver. "Were you able to make it to your meeting after work?"

I did some quick math, trying to remember if I had ever told my mother when my shift ended on Tuesdays. "Didn't need to," I said. "I hit the noon meeting on my lunch break."

She nodded, giving me a pained smile that said she'd decided on principle to believe me. Earlier that summer, when I was still taking the whole twelve-step thing seriously, I had told her about every meeting and even got her to go to a few herself, until she discovered Al-Anon. So far as I knew she was still going to her meetings, but I'd quit talking about mine.

Hoping we were done, I turned for the stairs, but Mom placed her mug on the table next to Barbara Kingsolver, her chin set. I knew that look, having seen it directed at my father for most of the first decade of my life, and I thought: *Oh shit, what now?*

"Do you remember Mike Papadakis?" she asked.

"The Mr. Rogers-looking dude down at the supermarket?"

"Mister—?" She rolled her eyes. "That is so ridiculous. How'd you even get started on that?"

"You know who started me on it."

She laughed the way she always did, even twenty years after the divorce. "That is so like your father," she said. "Mike Papadakis doesn't look remotely like Mr. Rogers. He's *Greek*, in case you hadn't noticed."

"No, Ma, check him out sometime," I said. "He even wears those trippy little cardigans. You can just see him coming home at night, putting on his sneakies and riding the trolley out to the Land of Make-Believe."

"What*ever*," she said, waving my father from the room. "I ran into Mike this afternoon and we got to talking. Did you know Tam Grocery is starting a home-catering business?"

I stopped laughing. "You just happened to run into him?"

"Don't you think it's a great idea?" she said. "I mean, nobody cooks anymore. I used to be embarrassed that I couldn't boil an egg, but to you guys *coffee* is a mystery. Mike's idea is that you order your dinner online as you're leaving work and by the time you get home, there's a four-course meal waiting for you on your doorstep, ready to go on the table."

"Like Domino's Pizza for yuppies," I said.

No laugh this time, only a thin, determined smile. I was damned if I was going to make this any easier on her than I had to, but between my father and me, my mother had put in thirty long years at the Wolfer School of Impossible Men and she wasn't going to be put off so easily.

"Mike's very excited about it," she said. "They're leasing a new building downtown and he's looking for an office assistant to help with the transition." She held up her hand, cutting me off. "It's mostly administrative stuff, answering phones, taking orders, that kind of thing. But Mike said there might be some writing involved. Press releases, I guess. Descriptions of the food. Anyway, when I told him about your journalism experience—"

"My *journalism* experience?"

"You majored in it in college, remember?"

"Ma, that might carry a little more weight if I'd finished college. Or if I'd ever done any actual journalism."

"As I said, it's mostly administrative," she said. "I'm sure Mike won't give you anything you can't handle. Anyway, honey, it's perfect for you. I just know it."

"Stan set this up, didn't he?" I said.

"I don't see why it matters who set up what. It's a full-time job with benefits."

"Jesus. Don't tell me Stan's paying half the fucking salary for this, too."

She glanced in the direction of the kitchen, toward Lupita and her tomatoes. "Trent, I've asked you not to use that kind of language in this house."

This was a bit rich coming from my mother, the former rock-star groupie and suburban bar fly who used to swear like a truck driver. It was also not exactly a denial.

"Maybe you hadn't noticed, but I already *have* a job."

"Oh, for God's sake," she said. "I've known Mike since we were kids. I can't think of a nicer guy to work for. And it would get you out of that stupid burger joint."

I was up now, pacing in front of the sofa. "I told Stan to stay out of my fucking business!" I shouted, Lupita be damned. "I don't want any more of his fucking help!"

"Well, you're not going to get any more of it if you keep this up," she said, finally losing it. "If you want to embarrass me by flipping fucking hamburgers at a fast food joint, fine. But pretty soon, buckaroo, you're going to need a job that pays your rent—all of it."

That stopped me. Not the "buckaroo" part, which was plenty weird enough, but what she'd said about paying my own rent. "You're kicking me out?" I said.

Honestly, I was expecting another weary denial, more therapist-approved talk of love and support, but she just sighed. "We both agreed it would be best if you found a new place to live by September first."

I stared at the cream-colored couch, trying to remember the date. Then it hit me: It was the last week of July. I was being given a month's notice by my own mother.

"Stan's tried so hard, honey," she said. "And you've never even thanked him, not once. I think he just finally had enough. So for now I think it would be best for everybody if you tried having your own place for a while."

Still, no words came. It was a shitty thing for Stan to do, to set all this up and leave my mother with the dirty work, but the man had put up tens of thousands of dollars to spring me from jail, and to thank him, I'd sat like a sullen lump through every meal he tried to eat, played music he hated at all hours, and invited every AA gasbag in Southern Marin to his house for late-night coffee and cigarettes. Now, finally, he'd stopped trying. And I had to admire his methods: he'd given me a deadline to get out of his life, then pulled strings with his buddies at the Chamber of Commerce to grease my way out the door. For the first time in all the years I'd known Stan I felt something like respect.

"What do I have to do?"

"You'll do it?" my mother said.

"Ma, just tell me what I have to do."

"Okay. I set up an appointment for you to meet with Mike on Saturday. Eleven o'clock. He said it'd only take half an hour or so."

"He understands my situation? You *did* tell him about that, didn't you?"

Her eyes flicked away. "Mike and I talked about that. It's not going to be a problem."

"Are you sure?" I said, rubbing it in. "Because technically, it's still a felony. Most places won't hire you with that on your record, especially when it involves theft."

"I said we talked about it," she said. "You don't know Mike. He's—let's just say he believes everyone deserves a second chance."

Which made me wonder if Stan wasn't paying the whole salary for this job and throwing in half the rent on the new building, too. But it didn't matter. I was done. Anything had to be better than another day at Howie's.

"You'll need some new clothes," Mom said.

"C'mon, it's a stupid office job. How dressed up do I need to be?"

"You'll need clothes," she said again. "Don't worry, it's on me."

# 2

On Friday, I traded out with LaShonda and pulled an early-bird shift, opening up with Rajiv at six a.m. and frying dozens of sand-dollar-sized sausage patties for the breakfast rush. I'd taken the job at Howie's because, as Pete, my ponytailed ex-offender P.O., had explained to me, given my felony conviction and my flat refusal to work for my stepfather, a fast food chain was the most likely to skip the formality of checking what I'd actually been arrested for. But my mother was right. I also got a kick out of knowing that sooner or later one of the Botox Brigade at the Mill Valley Tennis Club would slink over during cocktails and ask if that really was *her* Trent she'd seen behind the counter at Howie's Hamburgers.

But now that I knew I might not be back, I felt a weird nostalgia for the place. I hated the food, hated going home every day reeking of cola syrup and beef tallow, and I wasn't going to be sending Christmas cards to LaShonda and Rajiv anytime soon. Still, in a way, it was a family there—a squabbling, screwed-up family, maybe, but a family. At Howie's, my four months in county jail was chicken feed. One of the night cooks, a pockmarked ex-con named Antwoine, had done six *years* at Pelican Bay for armed robbery—holding up a Taco Bell in Vallejo, of all things. One night in the break room Antwoine had broken it down for me, how he'd waited until he knew the night manager's routine, how much cash she kept on the premises, where she kept it, when she took it to the bank, and then he pounced. "A place like this here, without no good cash control, it's like taking candy from a baby," he said, flashing a shy, gold-toothed smile. "All you need's your nine and a man driving the car and you good to go."

At two-thirty, half an hour after I finished my shift, I was still waiting on the sidewalk in front of Howie's in my street clothes when my mother pulled up in the Mini wearing a peach-colored sundress, a pair of blue-mirrored Ray-Bans, and not a whole lot else.

"You said you'd be here at two," I said, opening the passenger door.

"And you said you were going to clean up a little," she said. "Honestly, Trent, don't you have *any* shirts that aren't full of holes?"

We drove over the Horse Hill grade in silence. The Mini was new—they'd only gone on the market that summer—and Mom was fighting the British-style transmission as she zoomed in and out of the sleepy midday traffic. I preferred her last car, a lipstick-red Porsche Boxster, but no matter how you cut it, the Mini was a step up from the Chevettes and Dodge Darts we drove before Stan showed up. Stan Starling had been sniffing around my mother as long as I could remember, going back to when she was still married to my father. Back then, he had been the long-haired, Birkenstocks-and-overalls-wearing guru-in-chief at Walden West, a hippie gardening collective that published an underground mail-order catalog known for its back-to-the-land manifestos and how-to manuals on marijuana cultivation. In the eighties, Stan shed the overalls and the druggie philosophizing, along with most of his original partners, and retooled the catalog to sell eco-friendly home and garden products for the upscale suburban market. Goodbye, advice on crossing sativa and indica cultivars; hello, beeswax taper candles and jute-fiber patio mats. When the Internet came along, Walden West added an online sales division, and for a couple years there Stan had a paper net worth north of $100 million.

I started hearing his name again around the time I dropped out of school for good in the late nineties. He was married to Wife #2 at the time, but he ditched her and married Mom in the summer of 1999. Which meant that while I was living in a crappy garden apartment on the edge of UCSB's student ghetto embezzling tens of thousands of dollars from a frat-row liquor store, my mother was trekking the Himalayas and jetting to L.A. for a day's shopping on Rodeo Drive. The dot-com bust had hit Walden West like everyone else, and for a few weeks that winter, it had looked like Stan might have to shut down or sell out to his competitors. In the end, he survived because in the end guys like Stan always survive, but Mom was back to flying commercial and shopping at Nordstrom.

She parked at the south end of the mall, and we sat listening to the ticking engine while she checked her makeup in the rearview mirror.

"Honey, I don't want you to freak out," she said, touching up the corners of her lips, "but I sort of told them you were interviewing for grad schools."

"You told who?"

"David. My Nordy's guy. I told him you're doing personal interviews."

"You lied to your personal shopper?"

"Hey, I have to live here, okay?" she said. "This guy David, he dresses half the women in Marin and don't think they don't talk."

"We don't have to do this, you know. Stan's got the whole thing wired. I could show up in that dinner napkin you're wearing and Papadakis would still give me the job."

"Oh, I don't know. You're cute, but I don't think you could pull off Nina Ricci." She was grinning now, slyly, out of one side of her mouth. "Let me do the talking. I know these people. I know how they think. Come here, let me get a look at you."

I didn't resist, just let her take my chin in her hand, turning me first this way and then that. This was as old as I was, this inspection. Before visiting my grandparents, before leaving for school in the morning, before going out in high school, I had to subject myself to this motherly once-over. Even when she was at her lowest—and my mother would be the first to admit she dipped pretty low—she always looked good and insisted that I did, too. Sometimes I wondered if what bothered her most about the last decade of my life wasn't that I'd dropped out of college and very nearly did three-to-five in state prison, but that by the time I landed in rehab I'd put on fifty pounds and quit blow-drying my hair. Now, she ran her fingers through my hair, feathering the sides, then wet the pad of her thumb to wipe an invisible smudge from my cheek. "Hey, I know," she said, taking off her Ray-Bans and setting them over my eyes. "That's better. They're guy's glasses, anyway. Go on, look at yourself."

On me, her blue-mirrored Ray-Bans were a touch too groovy: all I needed was a ponytail and a soul patch and I'd have fit right in at a poetry slam. But she was right: they transformed me, made my cheap jeans and ratty Pearl Jam concert tee look like a pose, an ironic statement. Seeing myself in the rearview mirror, I could almost believe I was a hipper-than-thou spoken-word artist applying to grad schools to please the tight-assed 'rents.

We were barely out of the car when Mom let loose a high-pitched, girly yelp, waving in the direction of the Nordstrom entrance, where a knife-slim young man in an expensive gray suit stood, hands on his waist, a cheeky smirk on his lips. This was, it took me a moment to realize, my mother's personal shopper's way of scolding her for being half an hour late.

"Sorry, David, I should have called," Mom said. "I was at the club. And Trent here was late getting back from the gym."

"I had paperwork to catch up on, anyway," he said, kissing her once, lightly, on each cheek. "You're looking stunning as usual, Sandra. Love the dress."

"You should. You picked it out, remember?"

"So I did, so I did," he said, stepping back to admire it. "Give that boy a gold star. But that's just it, isn't it? We could put you in sack cloth and ashes and you'd still come out looking like Gwyneth Paltrow's kid sister."

Gay men have always loved my mother. They get her at some elemental level, the way she wears her beauty so lightly and yet takes it so seriously. They seem to intuit what I know only because I grew up with her: how hard she works at the way she looks. My mother had spent fifteen years climbing out of the hole she dug for herself by marrying my father straight out of high school, and she understood that, if at forty-nine, her hair wasn't still full and blonde and her figure wasn't as trim as it had been when she was nineteen, she would still be answering phones at a dentist's office. She was up four mornings a week working with a private yoga instructor and spent hours in front of mirrors tweezing her eyebrows and cleansing her skin with exotic restorative creams that sold for hundreds of dollars an ounce. But all this was in private. In public, except with her oldest girlfriends, she played the role of the frisky, slightly loopy Marin trophy wife. *Ninety percent of looking good*, she must have told me a thousand times, *is making it look easy*. And also this: *When in doubt, let them think you're dumber than they are.*

She had tossed a white silk jacket over her shoulders to ward off the department-store chill, but her long, tanned legs were bare from her knees to her slingback heels. I knew, because I knew her, that as soon as we were upstairs, inside the private fitting room, the heels would come off and she would pad around the parquet floors in her bare feet, the blood-red polish on her toenails flashing under the overhead lights. It was sexy, this act, even I could see that, but it was a very particular kind of sexy, angled to please young, queer David. Around Stan's older friends my mother was quieter, more understated. She could still let loose peals of laughter or spill a glass of red wine down the front of her dress if the need arose, but more often she turned on her bedroom eyes. My mother's eyes are a strange, almost silvery color, clear as water, and when she turned them on an older man, lightly touching his wrist as she laughed at a joke, she called to mind a forties movie queen, Lauren Bacall asking Bogie for a light of her cigarette.

Now, as we rode the escalator to the second floor, I watched her flirt with David, giddy and sisterish, admiring the silk lining of his suit, brushing back his blond hair to look at the new gold stud in his left ear. Their conversation was all about me: what David had found for me to wear, what look I was going for, which fabrics would go with my coloring. But I might as well have been a sack of potatoes. David never looked at me except in the most clinical, professional way, and even once we reached the fitting room and his assistant, a middle-aged, exceedingly formal tailor named Umberto, whisked away my knapsack and sunglasses, David's first glance was always toward my mother, who sat perched like a tiny bronzed bird on a white leather armchair in the corner of the room, barefoot and cross-legged, sipping a cappuccino.

"It's law school, right?" David said.

I turned to my mother. We hadn't gotten this far in the car. She took her time, setting her cup in its dish before giving David an absent-minded nod. "That's right," she said. "UCLA, USC, UC Davis, and University of Washington. But we're hoping he'll stay right here, in Berkeley."

"So nothing East Coast, then? New York? Boston?"

He was looking at me, but all I could think was: Does UC Davis even have a law school?

"No way, Trenty's a West Coast kid," Mom said. "Aren't you, hon?"

No one had called me "Trenty" since I was five and I'd hated it then, but I could see what she was doing. She was telling me to shut up, be cool, this was her world, and my job was to let her run things.

"Good, that eliminates a lot of boring blue blazers," David said. "But still, even out here you have to go a little dressy, right? I mean, these are lawyers, after all. Or do you interview with the professors? How does it work?"

I didn't have a clue. An hour ago, I was standing over a hot grill wearing a plastic hairnet and flipping Howieburgers.

"It sort of depends on the school," I said. "Mostly you talk to lawyers, alums and stuff, but sometimes you talk with faculty, too, if they're seriously considering you."

In her white leather chair my mother smirked into her cappuccino.

"Okay, I'm thinking one good suit," David said. "A little edgy, but not *too* edgy. Hugo Boss, Joseph Abboud. But neutral. Charcoal gray, earth tones. We want these guys to see your suit, but not *see* it, you understand."

"And then we'll work our way down?" Mom asked. "To the more casual stuff?"

"Sure, but I want to get the suit settled first. That'll set the tone for the rest." He clapped his hands, once, sharply, like a kindergarten teacher starting a class. "Umberto, the suits, please?"

As poor, short-legged Umberto shambled off to gather the suits, David turned to me. "How are you set for shoes?" he asked.

"Shoes?" I asked.

"I see. I better call Jennifer in Men's Footwear. What's your instep?"

I told him 9½ wide, and while he was on the phone with Jennifer in Men's Footwear ordering what sounded like half their inventory, I shot a look at my mother. *A suit?* I mouthed.

But she just smiled, all rippled lips and glinting eyes, and turned to look out the lone window at the tidal marshlands that bordered the Bay. In the distance, across a narrow span of water, stood the faded yellow buildings of San Quentin State Prison. Every time I drove that stretch of Highway 101, my eyes were drawn to those three low-slung cell blocks at the foot of the Richmond–San Rafael Bridge, where, but for the grace of Stan Starling, I might very well have been residing. But I wasn't thinking about San Quentin just then. I was watching my mother in her whisper-thin Nina Ricci sundress and wondering whether she'd come that day with the intention of blowing more than a thousand bucks on a tailored suit, or whether she'd tricked herself into it. Whatever she intended, it was clear that I was getting a new suit and that she was going to have to hope she got to Stan's American Express bill before he did.

An hour later we sailed out of Nordstrom, our arms loaded down with two grand worth of new clothes, all of which had gone on Stan's AmEx. In the end, we'd settled on a slate-gray Hugo Boss suit, $1,200 all by itself, which I could pick up the next day once Umberto finished taking in the trousers. All that shopping and schmoozing, combined with two cups of industrial-grade espresso, had made my mother a little high, and as we strolled the open-air mall toward the Cheesecake Factory for a celebratory slice of cake we held hands like we were on a date, window-shopping and talking about old times.

At the pastry place I insisted on paying, which nearly brought Mom to tears. Several times while we were eating, I caught her eyeing me shyly over her forkful of cake, half-flirting, as if she wasn't sure how much longer I was going to go on acting like a normal human being. I danced away every time, playing hard to get. I knew that game. I knew, too, that looking at my mother, with her sun-browned face and water-colored eyes, was like looking too long into the sun: it blinded me. It made me forget the years of bullshit behind us: the weird guys, the dumpy apartments, the nights at home alone watching Letterman and smoking up her latest boyfriend's head stash, wondering if I should call the Last Ditch Bar & Grill, if I should call the Sweetwater or the Brothers Tavern, wondering who I was going to be sharing my Frosted Flakes with in the morning. But she wouldn't quit. She kept touching me, poking me playfully with her fork, teasing me about how good I looked in my new designer duds. When the waitress came to clear our dishes, my mother shot her a shrewd look. "You look like you know a little something about clothes," she said. "Don't you think that shirt looks good on him?"

Our waitress was heavy-set and chinless, with the moist, yeasty complexion of a teenage girl who has to change her shirt three times a day, but she was working for tips so she squinted at my shirt, a collarless V-neck Ralph Lauren number that made me look like I'd just beamed up from Deep Space Nine.

"That's a real pretty blue," she said.

"That's what I said," Mom said. "At the store they wanted to go with the brown, but I think this brings out his eyes." She reached over to brush a stray lock of hair from my forehead. "Trent has the loveliest green eyes, but he insists on hiding them behind those bangs of his."

"Ma, Jesus," I said, swatting away her hand.

But she just laughed, soft and flirty. She'd made a wrong turn, missed an exit somewhere, and in her mind she was still in the private fitting room at Nordstrom with flitty David ogling her sundress and feeding her espresso.

"Seriously, though," she said, turning back to the waitress. "You don't think it's too—I don't know, too jazzy for an interview?"

"Okay, that's it, I gotta hit the head," I said, standing up.

"What?" Mom protested.

"Bathroom break," I said, already halfway gone.

I had wisely stashed a skinny of Gilbey's in each of the pockets of my new chinos before we left the Nordstrom changing room, and as soon as I closed the bathroom door, I shot them both, pacing in front of the sink. I chewed through half a roll of wintergreen Life Savers, trying not to think about my mother begging our chinless waitress for a compliment, trying not to think of all of Stan's loot she'd just blown on me, but deep down where the gin couldn't reach, I felt a hard snap of rage and slammed my fists on the porcelain sink. Like that—*kerwhoosh!*—the dam gave way, unleashing a tidal wave of bullshit that flooded the room. And then I was swimming in it, sputtering, cursing, gasping for air. The bathroom door was locked so I was free to thrash and kick and throw my fists, punching myself on the side of my head, my chest, my upper arms, anywhere it wouldn't show, until the gin finally kicked in and the sour stink of my own bullshit receded from my nostrils.

I leaned over the sink, my eyes shut, my chest still heaving, mumbling: "Don't quit before the miracle. Don't quit before the miracle." These were just words, something I'd heard a guy say in a meeting once, but they were words that had worked for somebody, once, somewhere, and maybe that's why they worked for me now. Slowly, slowly, the real world seeped back in: the cool white tiling of the sink-stand, the hum of the ceiling fans, the muffled hubbub of voices coming through the bathroom walls.

I washed up with hot, soapy water. My cheeks were flushed

and the corner of my left eye was pinched in a less than totally normal way, but otherwise there was no sign of the raving maniac I had been just a minute ago. I looked pretty good, in fact. I felt good, too, and it wasn't just the 100 mls of straight gin I'd shot. That was the most unsettling thing about these episodes. I always felt weirdly refreshed afterward, like the anger inside me was a physical thing, a coin stuck in a tin can, and if I could just shake myself hard enough the noise would stop. I tucked in my Ralph Lauren shirt and brushed the hair from my eyes. The day I was arrested I had weighed 220 pounds. I looked like I'd sat on an air pump: my face, my neck, my arms, even my fingers were fat, with these sad, fleshy dimples at all the joints. Four and a half months of stale baloney sandwiches at the Santa Barbara County Jail had fixed that, but I was putting on weight again thanks to my daily diet of Howieburgers and grain alcohol. In the mirror, though, I looked disturbingly normal, just another twenty-something guy from Marin out with his mother for a little shopping on a Friday afternoon.

On the terrace, Mom was sipping her mineral water, watching the crowds drift by on the brickwork mall. At a distance, she, too, ran to type—in her case, the trim blonde yoga princess whose problems you'd pay to have. But when she turned to me I saw the private anguish in her eyes, a look as old as I am and as intimate as a hand rocking a cradle.

"Sorry about that," I said, sliding into my seat. "The guy ahead of me had his kid with him."

"Trent, look at me."

I was wise enough to bring my eyes up to meet hers. We both knew what she was looking for, and the way we played this game, I had to let her feel like she had free range to knock around inside my brain, see what she could see.

"What were you doing in there?" she asked.

"I told you, the guy in front of me—"

"For ten minutes?"

Part of me was ready to call it a day: fall at her feet and let her hold me and tell me everything was going to be all right.

But everything *wasn't* going to be all right, not if I copped to the skinnies I'd just shot in the men's room, and that old Wolfer survival instinct was chanting: *Maintain, maintain, maintain.*

"You really want to know what I was doing?" I said.

"Yes, in fact I do."

"You're not going to believe me. I was praying."

*"Praying?"*

I let the word sink in, marinate a little. "It's something my sponsor told me to do," I said. "In moments of stress, he says I should try to find a quiet place and pray."

She laughed, but it came out half-strangled. My mother had spent her entire adult life being lied to by drug addicts and alcoholics, so her bullshit detector was more finely tuned than most, but coming from me, this was such a weird-ass admission it almost had to be true.

"This is that guy you were telling me about?" she said. "The priest?"

"Ma, it's been ten years since Frank left the priesthood. He drives a cab, remember?"

This fact, the image of a defrocked Catholic priest driving a yellow cab, had cracked my mother up the first time I told her, but she wasn't laughing now. She was watching me, the look in her eyes guarded, and at the same time almost pathologically hopeful.

"You stopped talking about him," she said. "I figured you'd given up working with him."

"Well, I had, but then I called him again last week. All that Big Book thumping's hard to take, but the man knows his shit. My program was getting all out of whack without him."

She stared, fighting to hold on to her skepticism, the anger that had boiled up in her when I left her alone. If I'd been anyone but me, she would have already walked off. But I *wasn't* just anyone. I was me, her only son, and this news, that I was talking to a sponsor again and working a program, was so hopeful, so wished for, she had no choice but to buy it.

"What do you pray for?" she asked.

"It doesn't work like that," I said. "You don't pray *for* anything. It's more like you ask to be open to whatever's coming. To have the strength to face it."

"Does it help?"

"Sometimes it does, yeah. It calms me, you know? The way a drink used to."

Talking like this made me wish it were true. I hadn't been to an AA meeting in weeks, and even when I was going regularly I never had a sponsor. I'd meant to ask Frank T. to sponsor me, and I'd gone ahead and told my mother that I had, but I never followed through. I *had* prayed, though. Not just mouthing random Twelve Step catchphrases, either—actually prayed. I felt like an idiot kneeling at the foot of my bed mumbling into my hands, but I could have sworn I felt something, an easing of the pressure in my neck and shoulders, a sort of lifting. When I opened my eyes, I was still me, still twenty-nine years old, clueless and lost, but for a moment it felt real, like some invisible hand had swooped down and held me in its palm, warm and still and safe.

"Ma, I'm sorry," I said. "I shouldn't have walked out on you like that."

"I wasn't going to tell her about all the fancy law schools you've applied to if that's what you were worried about."

"I know. But you were kind of heading in that direction."

"I'm proud of you, honey," she said. "Can't I be proud of you?"

"Proud of me for *what?*"

"I don't know. For coming today. For trying." She stopped, wary again. "Trent, tell me the truth. Are you really talking to that guy again?"

It spooked me how easy it was to laugh away her fear. "I don't know how long Frank's going to put up with me," I said, "but for now, yeah, he's got me working a program again."

If we hadn't been on the brickwork terrace with crowds of people streaming past, she would have been crying. I could see the tears welling in her eyes, water on water, glistening in the afternoon sunlight. "This calls for a celebration," she said. "Stan's got a business thing tonight, so what do you say you and me go out? I'll treat you to dinner at the Buckeye, and then we can see a movie. Anything you like, I don't care how gory it is, I'll watch it with you."

"Sorry, Mom. No can do. This boy's got a hot date."

"A date?" She laughed, high and startled. "With who?"

"Afraid that's classified for now."

She was grinning, that sly lip-rippler that said she was shocked and pleased and maybe also, in a way I wasn't sure I wanted to explore, a teensy bit jealous.

"Wow, it's all just coming together for you, isn't it?" She took a deep breath. "Okay. Let the record reflect that I wasn't going to do this, not after that little performance a minute ago. But this is all such good news, I can't help it. I have to do this now."

With a twinkling of excitement, she reached into her white-leather Coach bag and pulled out a plain white envelope.

"What is this?" I asked.

"Well, I don't know," she said. "Guess you'll have to open it and find out."

She was smiling, watching me, so there was nothing to do but take the envelope and open it. I pulled out a custom-made greeting card, with a black-and-white photograph of a moonlit Muir Beach, copyright 1984 by William A. Simonds. Inside the inscription read:

> *Dear Trent:*
> *I know the last year has been hard on you—it's been hard on all of us. But I'm so proud of you today. Someday I know I'm going to be able to say "I knew him when."*
> *With love,*
> *Mom and Stan*

"Go on," she said, nudging me. "Look inside."

I turned the envelope upside down and a second, smaller envelope fell into my hand. Mom nodded for me to open it, her eyes shining, but I already knew what it was. Sure enough, when

I opened the flap I saw the distinctive mint-green coloring of an American Express card.

"Now, don't get too excited," she said. "The limit's a thousand dollars. And I've set it up so the bills come straight to me, so I'd watch what I put on that if I were you."

I barely heard her. For one extended second my heart stopped beating, and when it started again it was going double-time, like some great speedball drumroll.

"Does Stan know about this?"

Mom, wisely, punted that one. "You'll have to pay me back, every penny, and I'll cut it off in a heartbeat if you abuse it," she said. "But the next few months are going to be rough on you and this is my way of saying I'm here for you, no matter what."

Jerry Cushman, my mother's father, child of the Depression, survivor of the kamikaze raid on the USS *St Lô* in the Leyte Gulf in 1944, had a saying: *I didn't know whether to shit or go blind.* Part of me wanted to wrap my mother in a tearful hug, but a much bigger part of me wanted to throttle her. Forget the fact that, before Stan paid it off, I had been up to my eyeballs in credit card debt to the point that I had to change my phone number in Santa Barbara twice. Forget that I had already promised to pay Stan back forty grand, plus God knows how much he'd spent on lawyers and two months of rehab. Forget all that. How could she be so fucking blind? How could she have missed the flashing neon signs of the last month: the skipped meetings, the closet full of airplane bottles, the temper tantrums, the complete and utter disdain with which I regarded every last element of her life with Stan Starling?

But I said none of this. Instead, crafty little shit that I am, I started getting teary, too. "I can't believe this," I said. "Thanks, Mom. I promise, you won't be sorry."

"You're welcome, sweetheart," she said. "I meant what I said in the note. I'm so proud of you. You're gonna make it, I just know it."

And then she couldn't say anything more because she was crying.

# 3

The Last Ditch Bar & Grill had always been a local's place, a cheap, unpretentious bar where the flotsam and jetsam of old Mill Valley, the aging hippies and under-employed plumbers and carpenters, could have a beer and maybe score a decent quarter ounce in the back parking lot. Once in a very great while an actual biker gang blew in from across the Bay, and for a weekend you'd see a row of mud-splattered Harleys parked out front and a bunch of fat, white guys bitch-slapping each other on the sidewalk. But that was rare. Most of the time the Last Ditch was quiet, even a little sleepy. During my mother's long husbandless period, whenever I wasn't sure where she was, the Ditch was the first place I looked. For most of those years she was seeing a guy named Billy Simonds, a nature photographer who lived out of a converted garage at Muir Beach. Billy had a native's eye for Marin's rugged coastline and he was the only one of my mother's boyfriends I ever liked, but he wasn't well. When he was taking his meds, he could be soulful and sweet in the starry-eyed, lost-mancub way that Mom went for in those days, but when he went off his lithium, which he did on a fairly regular basis, he was impossible to be around—paranoid, sometimes violently so. During those periods, which could last a few days or for weeks on end, Mom spent a lot of time at the Ditch, where she knew the owner, an older guy named Buddy Tanner who had been in the Navy with my grandfather.

I used to love hanging out at the Ditch, especially on lazy summer afternoons after Mom had finished her day answering phones for whichever dentist or chiropractor she was working for that year. In my memory, Mill Valley was an easier place back then, quieter, more relaxed, less stuck on itself. And the Ditch was part of that. The front room was dark and smoky, the way a good bar should be, and there was always a tang of menace in the air, an undefinable scent of danger just under the usual ones of cigarette smoke and stale beer. Buddy turned a blind eye to the drug deals out back, and once, when I was in ninth grade, I watched a sixteen-year-old girl carried bodily out of the ladies' john onto the sidewalk—O.D.'d, or just drunk, I never knew. But I've never felt safer anywhere. The Ditch was the kind of place where people knew each other, and where, if you were a kid, you could sit for hours at the end of the bar drinking free Cokes while your mom finished her beer or a last game of pool with her boyfriend.

But that Friday night when I walked through the double doors a little after seven, the sign in the window read La Pequeña Cocina and the only bikers I saw wore padded lycra shorts and were cooling down after a fifty-mile round trip to Point Reyes. The tinted windows that had once hid the Last Ditch from the world were gone, replaced by sliding-glass windows lined with boxes of bright orange California poppies. Gone, too, were the warped linoleum flooring and the yacht-sized pool table where once upon a time Billy Simonds had taught me how to shoot nine ball. In their place were Saltillo clay tiles studded with rough-hewn birchwood tables designed to make the place look like it had been built by hand, possibly by a wandering band of humble Sonoran peasants. For now, though, there were no peasants in sight, Sonoran or otherwise. Instead, the room was packed with the usual suspects: young marrieds plowing through platters of nachos; tables of lawyers drinking Coronas in their casual-Friday khakis; and, at the bar, a clutch of dot-com widows nursing fish-bowl-sized margaritas, looking lonely and bored and about ten years too old for their clothes.

Suze was in a booth near the back working on a mojito. She looked younger, somehow, than she had at Howie's. Maybe it was just that she didn't have her kids with her or that she'd traded in the navy blue power suit for a simple white cotton top and jeans. But her hair was different, too: softer, less aggressively blonde and corporate-looking. When she stood up to say hello, I was flattered, if that's the right word, to see that she was wearing makeup. Not a lot: a dab of lip gloss, a brush of silvery blue over her eyes, but she'd dressed up for me, or rather she'd dressed down in a pleasantly casual, sexy way.

There was an awkward moment when we had to decide whether to hug or shake hands. In the end, we went for the hug, both of us laughing a little at our awkwardness, and then I beelined it for the bar where I ordered a near beer for me and a second mojito for Suze. The bartender was a young guy, very Marin, with longish blond hair and a gold stud in one ear and just the hint of a goatee to let you know that, no, he wasn't gay. His eyes flicked up at me as he set the drinks on the bar, giving me a light once-over. He'd been checking out the cute blonde in the back, and he wanted a look at the guy who'd kept her waiting over her mojito. As he made change and I left two crinkled bills for a tip, he flashed me a half-smirk, that subterranean 'atta boy recognized by single guys everywhere. I grinned back, to let him know—what, exactly, I'm not sure. That everything was under control, I guess.

I had waited until Thursday to call her, and from her too-bright laughter on the phone, I got the sense Suze hadn't really expected me to call. La Pequeña Cocina had been her idea, and now that we were here, sipping our drinks, I could see why. The restaurant was crowded and well-lit, with plenty of visible exits. Once upon a time, Suze and I had been two fatherless kids helping to raise each other, as close to best friends as a guy and a girl can be in high school. But now who was I? Was I a "guy"? An old pal from high school? Or was the sweaty guy behind the counter at Howie's someone she needed to stay away from?

"This place sure has changed," I said, just to say something.

"Yeah, well. Welcome to Marvy Marin."

"That's what people keep telling me."

Out of the corner of my eye, I saw what I'd missed coming in: a faux-rustic hearth stone along the back wall. I couldn't believe I'd missed it. It was a single rough shale slab topped with a blackened-iron cooking pot suspended over a pile of actual split logs, silvered with age.

"My office handles half the listings on this block," Suze was saying. "The old place that was here, the Last Ditch—man, what an eyesore. When these guys came in, rents went up like twenty percent overnight. It changed the whole block."

I nodded, pulling on my O'Doul's. I still couldn't get over that fucking hearth stone. A cook pot, for God's sake. As if little Juan and Maria had stepped out to tend the burros and any minute now they'd be coming around to serve us steaming bowls of red beans and rice. At the edge of a lonely military cemetery somewhere, Buddy Tanner was spinning in his grave.

"My mom used to come here," I said. "When I was a kid."

"Oh, right," Suze said. "Sorry, yeah. I forgot that."

We went back to sipping our drinks. I was finding it hard to look across the table without seeing the old Suze—not Pothead Suze from high school, but the little girl I used to know. Until we were in third grade, Suze and I had lived a few blocks apart in the Sycamore Flats, which is as close as you get in Mill Valley to a working-class neighborhood. Then her dad died—self-inflicted gunshot wound to the head, out behind the garage, no note or anything—and her mother moved them to a condo on Shelter Ridge, and Suze and I lost touch until high school. Looking at her now, I kept seeing the sad-eyed girl who used to chase me around the swing sets at Sycamore Park. Back then, Suze Randall was the neighborhood ugly duckling, a quiet, intense little girl with big blue eyes and a weird dad, who nobody wanted to play with. "Little Sookie," we called her. This was, I think, an eight-year-old's idea of a slave name, and that was how we treated her. "Little Sookie, clean up this dog poop!" "Little Sookie, go home and quit bothering us!" I played with her, but only when no one else was around. I wondered what those kids would make of their Little Sookie now, grown up to be a radiant, blonde mother of two.

"Hey, thanks for calling me," she said. "It's great to see you. You look really good."

"Now that I'm out of uniform, you mean?"

Suze laughed, but before she could pursue that line of ques-
tioning, I turned it back on her. "You're looking pretty good
yourself, Mrs. Strasser."

The expression that played out over her face was complicated: part good-sport grin, part something darker, closer to actual
embarrassment.

"Right, the business card," she said. "I keep forgetting it's
on there."

"Are you guys still married?"

"Funny you should ask. I'm talking with a lawyer about that
very question as we speak."

"Hey, I'm sorry. This is none of my business. Really."

"Don't be," she said. "Next month, it'll be a year since we
split up. And Jimmy's still Jimmy. He gets older, the girls stay
the same age."

"He's still down in L.A.?"

She nodded. "Shacked up with Mindy or Mandy or Cindy or
Sunshine, or whatever the hell her name is this time. But we're
still in contact, more or less. And he's been good about keeping
up with the kids. Which is something, I guess." She grabbed a
menu from the wire-frame rack at the end of the table. "Have
you had the chicken mole here?"

"Here? No, I've never been here before."

"You should give it a try," she said, flipping through the
menu. "It's not bad. They do a real mole sauce, not like that
canned crap they give you at Chevy's."

I reached for a menu. I hadn't even thought about dinner.
When we talked the night before, we'd kept it vague. "A drink,"
we said. But now I could see that in her nervousness Suze was
committing us to a full meal.

She waved the waitress over and ordered the chicken mole.
I ordered steak fajitas, more or less at random, and by the time
I saw the price—$15.95—the waitress had disappeared into the
kitchen. Dinner was going to set me back two hours at the register at Howie's, closer to three or four when you counted tax

and tip and the second O'Doul's I'd ordered. But the business of squaring away our order had calmed Suze down, and that helped me relax a little, too.

"I'm sorry to hear all this," I said. "I hadn't even heard you guys were married."

"Neither had Jimmy, apparently." She laughed, not pleasantly, throwing back another gulp of mojito. But when she set down her glass, she had grown thoughtful again. "You want to hear something funny? The first six months, I told everybody Jimmy was commuting on weekends. Every week, it was the *next* week that Jimmy was coming. For six months. After a while, people just stopped asking."

I took another long pull on my near beer, killing it. I'd shot a couple Stoli skinnies in the car before coming in, and I had another two stashed in the glove box of the Honda. Now, for the first time, I wished I could think of a good excuse to go back out to the car.

"You did warn me," she said. "'Once a prick, always a prick,' wasn't that it?"

"Something like that," I said, my face warming at the memory.

"No, that's exactly what you said. Don't you remember? It was Homecoming Week and we were getting high out at the bunkers after Jimmy took up with that awful Marina chick."

"Katarina Dunn," I said, snaring the name from thin air.

"Thank you. Yes. I'd almost managed to repress that name, but you're right, it *was* Katarina Dunn. She of the plastic fantastic ta-tas."

I laughed out loud. I had forgotten how bitchy Suze could get when she was angry and how much I'd always liked that about her. Now, the memory of Katarina Dunn, who, if I'm not mistaken, had undergone the first teenage breast-enhancement surgery in Southern Marin, opened the floodgates, and by the time the waitress arrived with our food we were knee-deep in the gory details of Suze's marriage to Jimmy Strasser. The wound was fresh, and she spoke with the urgency of someone

who had told her story a hundred times and was running out
of listeners. I listened, though, tossing in questions whenever
the flood of words seemed to dry up, partly because I'd always
thought Jimmy Strasser was a douchebag, but also because
every minute we spent trashing Suze's marriage was another
minute we put off the questions about what I had been up to
since high school.

Suze was still going strong, having killed her second mojito
and started on a third, when the waitress cleared our half-eaten
platters of food. After the waitress left, Suze settled back in the
booth, sipping her rum and lime, watching me across the table.

"So the question is," she said, "why didn't I listen to you
back in high school?"

"I don't know. Maybe because Jimmy was captain of the
all-county soccer team?"

"*And* second-team all-state, thank you very much."

"Or maybe because he looked so darn cute in those little
black shorty-shorts."

She laughed, that funny old Suze way, waving her hand in
front of her mouth like it was on fire. "He did, didn't he?" she
said. "I swear, that boy had an *ass* on him. It used to get me
all hot and bothered just watching him walk out of that field
house."

She was, I saw now, on the giddy, unselfconscious side of
drunk. One more mojito and she might have started slurring
words, but watching her, I was pretty sure she wouldn't have
another, that Suze Randall knew her way around a drink, and
that, unlike most people you could say this about, she knew
where her limit was.

"I *missed* you, Trent," she said. "What happened to you?
What the hell are you doing selling hamburgers at Howie's?"

I reached for my O'Doul's, but it was dead. I looked toward
the kitchen, hoping to see the waitress bringing a fresh one, but
the doorway was empty and I was stranded, high and dry.

"Forget it," Suze said. "It doesn't matter."

But this was just politeness. The waitress hadn't brought the check, and Suze still had half a mojito to go. I couldn't stone-wall her for ten minutes, not after we'd spent the last hour wallowing in Jimmy's extramarital affairs. All along, in the back of my mind, I had been planning how I would carry this off: joke away the job at Howie's and turn the conversation to my new gig at Tam Grocery. But now that the moment was here I could see the obvious, that for all Mom's cheerleading, I was going to be a glorified office boy at a grocery store—and I didn't even have the job yet.

"You probably heard I had a little trouble," I said. "Down in S.B."

"I heard something. No details. Just, you know, that there'd been some kind of problem."

The moment stretched, Suze across the table from me, waiting. Around us, the restaurant had turned festive: couples laughing, families talking over their Friday night dinners. It's a sound you only hear, really, when you've been outside it, out on the dark sidewalk, alone and a little high, listening to the laughter from inside. From the sidewalk, other people's laughter sounds so smug, so pleased with itself, but that's only because you're outside of it and you think they're laughing at you. I was with Suze now, drinking near beer, because I never wanted to be left out on the sidewalk again. And so from the depths of memory, I called up an old line of my father's. My dad was a big shot music executive who specialized in managing national tours for pop stars like Britney Spears and Justin Timberlake, but he'd started out as a street lawyer in San Francisco representing actors and musicians in everything from contract negotiations to pot busts. *Work with the available truth*, he always told his clients. *Never lie. Instead, tell that part of the truth—and only that part—that shows your cause in the best possible light.*

"Maybe you remember I was dealing there for a while," I said.

"Sure, but just for friends or whatever, right?"

"That kind of depends on your definition of 'friends.'"

"Oh, Trent," she said. "Drug dealing?"

But watching Suze's face I saw I'd picked my truth well. I

wasn't lying, exactly—I had been selling drugs all along, just never in enough weight to get myself hung—but in our world, the one Suze and I grew up in, drug dealers weren't prison-hardened gangsters. They were family friends. My own mother had dated the man who sold her cocaine off and on for years, and knowing Suze's mom, she had probably done the same thing.

"They didn't want me," I said. "They were after the guys up the chain. I got off with probation. If I stay clean for three years, I'm free and clear."

"And so now you're here."

"And so now I'm here," I said. "Drinking O'Doul's."

"I noticed." She raised her glass. "You don't mind if… ?"

"Not at all."

"Good, I was wondering about that." She nodded to my O'Doul's. "How long's it been?"

"Ten months," I heard myself say. "Just yesterday, as a matter of fact."

"Wow. Congratulations! I'll drink to that."

And so we did, Suze clinking her glass against my empty O'Doul's. It was a nice moment, actually, joking but also ceremonious, as if we were drinking not to my fake sobriety, but to the fact that we were there, that we'd made it. Maybe it was that, the realization that we weren't kids anymore, but adults with grown-up problems of our own that silenced us again. It was a different silence this time, heavier, tighter. Across the table I saw Suze considering me for the first time, turning me over in her mind. I wasn't "a guy," not yet, but I wasn't just an old friend from school anymore, either. A prickle of heat traveled up my spine as I realized how convenient this could be for me. My mother had given me a month to get out of her house, and three days later, here I was having dinner with an attractive, gainfully employed woman my age, who happened to have a man-sized hole in her life. I felt an urge to warn her, leave an unsigned note on her windshield spelling out all the ways a guy like me could take a sledgehammer to her life. But what can I say? I had been so lonely for so long, and for the first time in years a woman I knew and liked was looking at me in a way that suggested I might not always have to be alone.

"I know this is kind of last-minute," I said. "But I was thinking of heading downtown, maybe catching a movie."

She pulled back. It was subtle—she barely moved, really—but she took a sip of her mojito, and it was as if the invisible jet of air that had been holding us aloft for the past minute cut off, sending us both crashing back to earth.

"I'm going to have to take a rain check on that," she said. "Not that I wouldn't love to see a movie, but Mom has the boys tonight. I couldn't make her stay any later."

My first reaction—pure relief—caught me by surprise. It had been so long since I'd been with a woman I wasn't paying in cash or free drugs that the prospect of a real date, one involving popcorn and a goodnight kiss, panicked me. Still, those last few minutes, the look of open appraisal in Suze's eyes had stirred my insides, and I knew then that I would do whatever it took to make sure I saw her again.

"Let me get this, then," I said, reaching for the check.

"Come on, I can't let you do that."

"Sure you can," I said, slapping down my new mint-green Amex card. "You just did."

Suze's car wasn't a silver BMW or even a frost-blue Lexus. It was a cocoa-brown Volvo station wagon, spiffy enough to ferry her wealthy clients up and down the Mill Valley hills, but for now, at eight o'clock on a Friday night, cluttered with knapsacks and unwashed soccer uniforms. She was parked a few spaces down from my own rat-gray Honda in La Cocina Pequeña's back lot, and as we stood at the driver's-side door saying our goodbyes, I couldn't resist checking her out now that the lower half of her body wasn't hidden under a restaurant table. Suze gave no sign of catching my wandering eye, but as we talked, swapping stories of other classmates we'd seen around town, she rested her arm on the roof of the Volvo so that her shirt rode up over the waist of her jeans, exposing a thin wedge of bare midriff. From that angle, I could see that maybe old Pothead Suze hadn't put on as many pounds around the hips as I'd thought. Point made, she brought her arm down from the roof of the car and became once again a suburban soccer mom rooting around in her purse for her keys.

"Hey, you'll never guess who else is back in town," she said. "Lee Radko."

"No shit? Rad's back?"

"I've seen him a couple times now at that bistro place downtown—you know, Hélène's? He's a cook there, I think."

I had heard this same rumor from my mother, who had thought she'd seen my old partner in crime in the parking lot behind Hélène's in a kitchen uniform. But she hadn't been sure, and at the time I was still hitting my meetings and doing my best to stay away from people and places that might lead me back to where I'd been.

Suze frowned. "I gotta say, the guy's looking a little spooky."

"Spooky, how?"

"You remember the old Radko, right?" she said. "Well, he's like that, except times a hundred. He does this thing where he stares at you like, I don't know, like you're dinner and it's been a while since he's seen food. Anyway, he's been back almost a year now. Before that he was in Colorado someplace. Or maybe it was Oregon, I can't remember. You should look him up. You guys were pretty tight back then."

"That was a long time ago."

"That it was, that it was." She held up her keys, which she'd found at last. "I've gotta fly. Mom's gonna kill me. I told her I'd be back half an hour ago."

Again, there was that awkward moment: Do we go for the handshake? The hug? Suze put an end to it by wrapping me up in a one-armed, sisterly clench. I felt her lithe body against mine, smelled her rum-scented breath, but before I had time to think what to do about it, or whether I *should* do anything about it, she was in her car waving goodbye, leaving me alone in the gravel parking lot, the tangy scent of her perfume lingering in the air.

# 4

When I came upstairs the next morning Stan was in the kitchen in his tennis whites sucking down a green-tea-and-kale smoothie. For the three days since Mom told me that he wanted me out of the house, Stan and I had managed to steer clear of each other. But it was too late now, and powered by the Stoli skinny I'd shot over the bathroom sink, I sailed into the room and reached for the hand-painted Navajo coffee mug Lupita had set out for me the night before.

Stan Starling was a handsome guy, even I had to admit that, six-two and gym-fit, with a close-cropped pelt of silver hair, his skin toasted coppery brown from all those Saturdays on the tennis court. He'd always been big on Indians, and not just the Navajo. When I was a kid, during his sandals-and-overalls period, he used to come to our school assemblies to talk about the Coastal Miwok, who lived in Marin before the white people came. Stan the Blue-Eyed Indian, we called him. He would turn up a few days before Thanksgiving with handmade bows and arrows and hemp bags full of acorns he'd foraged himself on Mt. Tam. For an hour he would tell us how the Miwok had tracked deer in Muir Woods and soaked their acorns in water to leach out the tannins, all the while going on about how Indians didn't believe in owning things so they never fought or had wars like white people. We were little kids, but we weren't morons, and every year some wise-ass raised his hand to ask about Geronimo or the Little Bighorn. Me, I kept my mouth shut. Maybe it was all hippie bullshit, but I liked hearing it, how once upon a time there'd been people living where we were now who never fought or got drunk and smashed their husband's LPs in the backyard when he didn't come home for three days after a party.

The Walden West catalog still used Native American artwork, and a page at the back explained that one percent of the company's profits went to the American Indian College Fund. Even Mom laughed about that one. The key word was *profits*, which somehow after taxes and expenses never left more than a few grand for the American Indian college kids. Sometimes I told myself that was why I hated the guy so much. He'd believed in something once. Maybe it was a crock, but he'd believed in it, and now he was just another hustler like all the rest.

"Today's the big day, huh?" he said, breaking a frosty silence.

The smug chuckle he tacked onto the end of that sentence made me want to splash hot coffee all over his spotless tennis whites.

"It's not that big a deal, really," I said. "I won't be working there for long."

"I see," he said. "What's next for you, then—a presidential run?"

"Actually, I was thinking of selling sustainable home and garden products on the Internet. I always wanted to save the planet one all-weather garden Buddha at a time."

I felt instantly shitty, the way I did whenever I got into it with Stan for no reason. The man had saved my mother. He'd saved me. Why couldn't I be in the same room with him for thirty seconds without wanting to clock him with one of his rain-forest-free teakwood patio chairs? But the fact was I couldn't, so I stared him down, grinning like I'd just cracked the world's funniest joke, until he coughed up a soft grunt of disgust and shoved aside his half-finished smoothie.

"Good luck, anyway," he said, pushing back his chair.

When he slammed the front door the whole cantilevered house shook on its stilts. I stood in the silent kitchen, staring into my still-unsweetened coffee, trying to get a rise out of myself for how I'd played Stan, but it wasn't happening. Whatever else you could say about the man, he loved my mother and she loved him right back, and here I was like some jealous boyfriend trying to break them up. I was *good* at it, too. That was what got me. I could only guess at the marathon arguments that had pushed my mother to throw her only son out of her house, but she'd done it, which meant that somewhere along the line a fight had ended with: "Sandy, it's him or me."

A minute later I was downstairs popping off another skinny, then another, until I was lubed enough to laugh at my own joke about saving the planet one all-weather garden Buddha at a time.

By the time I poured myself back upstairs Mom was sitting on one of the cream-colored sofas in the living room in a floor-length Navajo robe, having her morning tea. If she'd heard the front door slam, she gave no sign of it. My mother, God love her, hadn't survived a lifetime of cokehead husbands and off-their-meds boyfriends by sweating the details. Instead, she was all smiles, topping up my coffee and wanting to know what I was going to wear for my interview with Mike Papadakis. I hadn't gotten that far yet, and for the next fifteen minutes Mom sat sipping her tea, sometimes nodding, sometimes shaking her head, as I trudged up and down the stairs modeling different outfits.

"There, that's it," she said, setting down her mug. "We have a winner."

I looked at myself, disappointed. I was wearing the squarest of the outfits we'd bought: a blue-and-white striped Brooks Brothers shirt, pleated chinos, and a pair of black oxford dress shoes. I looked like the best-dressed kid at the Math Olympics.

"So, no bowtie?" I said.

She smiled, unamused. "Fix your hair, smart ass," she said. "You look like you've been combing it with a blender. When you come back, I have a surprise for you."

The surprise was a plate of Lupita's cuernos de azucar, small, moist croissants sprinkled with cinnamon and powdered sugar, which Mom had hidden in a cupboard above the stove. Lupita only made cuernos on special occasions or for company, and I'd never seen my mother actually eat one, but we split the plate of four down the middle and wolfed them down, licking the buttery sweetness off our fingers. Now, with my clothes picked out, Mom acted as if the job interview was a formality and all we had to worry about was finding me a place to live.

"I saw the cutest apartment on the web the other day," she said, "this great little one-bedroom out in the woods near San Anselmo. Hardwood floors. Sunlight everywhere. And you wouldn't believe the view onto the back side of Mt. Tam."

"You didn't happen to get a look at what they're charging for that place, did you?"

"So maybe not that *exact* apartment. But something like that. A studio, maybe, with a garden. That was one thing I always insisted on when I was looking at apartments—there had to be at least a little green space."

"Ma, this is an office assistant's job we're talking about. And this is Marin."

"Honey, I told you we'd help with the first couple months' rent," she said. "Anyway, you're not going to be an office assistant forever."

This was what I had told Stan, and it sounded even less convincing when she said it, but just then, sitting with my mother in her sun-splashed kitchen, my belly warm with Russian vodka and buttery cuernos de azucar, it almost seemed possible. I wasn't going to be renting a one-bedroom apartment in the woods overlooking Mt. Tam anytime soon, but maybe, with a little help from my mother, I could swing a decent studio. Why not? And why *not* a garden? I didn't need much, just a patch of lawn big enough to set out a table and a couple chairs. Then on my days off, Mom and I could sit drinking coffee and laughing over how far I'd come in a few short months.

She must have been thinking the same thing because as I was leaving I felt a tremble in her fingertips as she straightened my collar and brushed the hair from eyes one last time. Downstairs, before brushing my teeth, I'd popped off another Stoli skinny and stashed one more in the pocket of my chinos, just in case. It *hurts* to drink like that, especially first thing in the morning. Your throat closes, your eyes tear up, you have to fight the body's

natural gag reflex. But two minutes later, the empties stashed in
my closet, my mouth freshly brushed and gargled, it was like it
had never happened. My body knew, of course. I still tasted the
sting of the alcohol in my throat, felt the loosey-goosey sloshi-
ness in my limbs, but my mind remained stubbornly in the dark.

"They'll never know what hit 'em," Mom said, flashing that
lip-rippling grin, and though my body knew better, my mind
told itself that what I felt pumping through me, propelling me
up the stairs to my car, was nothing more than my mother's
unbending belief in me.

It was ten o'clock, a full hour before my interview with Mike
Papadakis, when I pulled up in front of the Starbucks on Lytton
Square. This was on purpose. I needed some time to game out
what I was going to say, how I was going to explain the gaping
holes in my work history. First, though, I had some unfinished
business at the Starbucks in downtown Mill Valley.

Before Starbucks moved in, the double storefront had been
occupied by a string of clothing boutiques, most recently a
new-age maternity shop called the Dalai Mama. But before
that, for more than thirty years until my grandfather died, it
had been home to Cushman's Shoes. All that summer, when I
couldn't sleep after finishing a late shift at Howie's, I had come
downtown after the stores had closed and wandered the empty
streets, hands in my pockets, looking in the shop windows. In
the years since I left, my hometown had become an upscale
theme park of itself, the bus depot made over into a trendy
bookstore, the old head shop into an art gallery, the pharmacy
into a doggie daycare, everything everywhere cleaned up and
prettified for the tourists on their way to Muir Woods and the
ocean beaches. My late-night strolls always ended with me on
the sidewalk outside Starbucks, peering in through the plate
glass at the lacquered tables and upturned chairs. I can't say
what I was looking for, exactly, why I didn't just come back
during the day and order myself a big, sugary Frappuccino. All
I know is that in the four and a half months since I'd come

home, I hadn't been inside the place once, hadn't even walked past its doors during business hours.

Now, though, if everything panned out, I'd be working downtown, passing by Starbucks five times a day, and so after giving myself one last once-over in the rearview mirror, I patted the Stoli skinny in my pocket for luck and strolled inside. I was ready for it to be La Pequeña Cocina all over again, and in a way it was. Along one wall, where in my grandparents' day a row of captain's chairs had faced a line of fitting stools, there was now a faux-marble bar topped with a lighted dessert case and a gleaming chrome espresso machine. The old carpet, a very seventies egg-yolk-yellow shag, had been pulled up and replaced with pine flooring, dotted on this sunny Saturday morning with tables of Marinites of every conceivable shape and size and state of yoga fitness. But just beneath this blond-wood veneer, I could make out the remains of my grand-parents' store. The room was still split in two, with the same half-wall jutting out from the back that had once divided the men's and women's departments. To the right of the wall, on the men's side of the store, a narrow corridor led to what used to be the stock room, where my granddad kept his shoe-repair bench and where until I was in eighth grade I spent three af-ternoons a week stacking shoe boxes and hiding out from all my friends who had to be dragged kicking and screaming to shop at Cushman's.

I stepped in line for coffee, trying not to stare too openly, but everywhere I turned something else sent fresh ripples of recognition down my spine. Up front, between the two main doorways, the sales counter where my grandmother used to ring up purchases on the brass cash register still stood in its old place, except that now it was kitted out with leatherette stools to make a seating counter where customers could sip cappuc-cinos and watch passersby through the window. I had stood behind that counter on a hundred busy Saturday mornings like this one. My grandmother never let me near the cash register, but I still had to stand with her in a starched white shirt and clip-on tie bagging up boxes of new shoes while she handed out balloons to the kids and gossiped with their parents.

God, how I'd hated all that. I hated the whole thing: the shirt and tie, the hours I put in after school, the way my granddad was always riffling his fingers through my hair and telling total strangers what a "good little soldier" I was. Mostly, though, I was just embarrassed. My grandparents had opened the store in the fifties with a loan from the G.I. Bill, and it still felt like 1955 in there. They stocked tasseled penny loafers and patent-leather saddle shoes of a kind that no self-respecting Marin kid had worn since Annette Funicello quit wearing tight sweaters. As if that wasn't enough, my grandfather insisted on repairing shoes in the back like some old-time village cobbler. He loved the work, and I loved watching him do it, hunched over his pine wood bench, a row of shoe tacks in his teeth, bending and snipping and tapping, making a broken thing whole again. But this was the eighties. If a woman snapped a heel, she didn't take it to Cushman's to have it fixed. She drove out to the mall and bought herself a new pair. But the old guy was unbending. Even toward the end, when the store was dying and he and my grandmother started half-heartedly stocking Pumas and Adidas, he was always pushing his customers to try "a real shoe—one that'll last."

"Good morning!" the barista chirped, snapping me back. "May I take your order, please?"

She was one of those freakishly beautiful teenagers you see in towns like Mill Valley: tall and model-slim, her creamy skin as flawless as French porcelain, her electric-blue hair swept high above her head in a gravity-defying swirl. The effect was dizzy-making, like ordering coffee from the love child of Angelina Jolie and Papa Smurf.

"I'll have—how about a caramel Frappuccino? Whatever your biggest size is."

"One venti caramel frap!" she said, calling out my order. "Would you care for an oven-fresh muffin or a gluten-free breakfast treat with that?"

"No, thanks," I said. "But could you tell me, where's your restroom?"

"Down the passageway, second door to your right. Next guest, please!"

I stepped away from the counter, fingering the Stoli skinny in my pocket. Looking around at the rows of frosted blonde heads and rolled yoga mats, I bit back a familiar, simmering rage. Who *were* all these people? What gave them the right to sip four-dollar coffees and yammer about aromatherapy in the very building—the very room—where my grandfather had keeled over dead after his second heart attack? But just under this outrage, which I had expected to feel, and which, if I'm being honest, was half the reason I was there in the first place, burned something more frightening and unexpected: a slow, hot jet of memory. Spread out before me was a living portrait of Marin at its millennial marviest: black-clad venture capitalists and their fitness specialist girlfriends mixed in with tables of sun-glazed kids in Vuarnets and board shorts looking like they'd walked out of a Billabong ad. But what I *saw* was my grandma Cushman in a corduroy J. C. Penney skirt suit, her iron-gray hair rolled into a tight bun, bent over the phone next to the cash register speaking in whispers with my mother, who was calling from a hotel pay phone in L.A. where she'd been holed up for the past week.

It was so immediate, this memory, so visceral, maybe because it had happened so often. Even when things were good, my parents never seemed very interested in me. My father was always winging around the country doing record deals, and my mother was busy being that knockout blonde you see in old photos taken backstage at the Fillmore or Winterland, her arm wrapped around a shirtless drummer. If this sounds glamorous, it wasn't. We never had any money. Our fridge was always empty and I was in high school before Mom stopped buying my clothes at Goodwill. But man, did it ever *feel* glamorous. Our house was full of actors and musicians, and late in the summer when the local bands came off their tours, my parents threw epic parties in our backyard. A pickup band would play, and when word got out that Grace Slick was sitting in with David Crosby and Carlos Santana's rhythm section, neighbors piled into our yard until the party spilled out over our back fence into Boyle Park, the old ballfield behind our house. Even then, as a child of eight or nine, watching my parents dirty dancing by the fire pit in our yard, I sensed the strong erotic content of their marriage, the force of animal attraction that had brought me into being and at the same time made my presence a constant, nagging inconvenience.

And then—*poof!*—they would disappear, Dad off on one of his road trips, Mom holed up in a fleabag motel with the keyboard player from a band my father represented. This time, the day I was remembering, it was late afternoon, nearly closing time, and I was pressed against the wall of the stock room peeking around the door jamb. Granddad was at his work bench, oblivious, re-soling a pair of patent-leather pumps while the Giants game played on the radio. On the phone, I knew, my mother was drunk and crying. *Sandy, honey, you've got to get a grip on yourself,* my grandmother kept saying. *Nobody's going to call the police, but you've got to come home.*

Behind me, the men's room door swung open and a floppy-haired kid toting a skateboard nearly as tall as he was stepped out, red-eyed and grinning.

"All yours, dawg," he said.

I stared, trying to make sense of this stoned, smiling kid.

"She came back," I told him.

"Huh?" He let out a low stoner's chuckle. "Who came back?"

"Nothing, nobody," I said. Glancing back at the faux-marble counter, I scurried down the passageway and ducked in a door marked "Starbucks Partners Only."

It was just a storage room. In one corner, there was a mop bucket and some cleaning supplies, and across the cement floor were rows of silver vacuum-packed bags of coffee beans and shrink-wrapped flats of neon-colored go-cups. No pinewood work bench, no smell of oiled shoe leather, no racks of old tools. It wasn't even the same room, really. When they remodeled the building, they must have knocked out the rear wall to make more space for the dining area.

The door clicked open behind me and I saw a flash of upswept blue hair.

"Sir, guests aren't allowed——" She stopped, confused. "What're you *doing?*"

I looked at my hand, which held the Stoli bottle, now mysteriously open. The expression on the girl's face melted. She was in high school, and she'd walked in on a grown man in a Brooks Brothers shirt and two-hundred-dollar shoes sneaking a drink in the storage room at Starbucks. It made no sense, it fit with nothing she understood about how the world worked, but whatever else it was, it was very, very sad.

"I should go," I said.

But I'd scared her, and I sensed that if I touched her, she might actually scream. I feinted one way, then the other, trying to get around her. Finally, I said, "Here," and handed her the Stoli bottle. That seemed to break the spell, and with a neat pivot, she stepped to one side, clearing the way for me to bolt out the door and through the crowded café onto the street. I was a couple blocks away, motoring past Hélène's on Miller Avenue, before I realized I'd left without my Frappuccino and that I still had nearly an hour to kill before my appointment with Mr. Papadakis.

The stocky Mexican kid who came to the back door at Hélène's spoke no English and it took us a long minute of making hand signals and hollering at each other before he understood who I was looking for. Finally, though, he turned and shouted, *"¡Oye, cabrón, hay alguien!"* and Lee Radko stepped into view at the end of a long corridor.

He was huge. That was my first impression. When we were in middle school, Lee was one of those scrappy kids who was always getting his ass kicked by guys twice his size. Crazy Radko, we called him. Halfway through high school, though, just when everyone else stopped growing, he hit his growth spurt, and by senior year he was six-two and no one called him Crazy Radko anymore. He was just Big Rad, undisputed chieftain of our little crew of burnouts and potheads who hung out in the back parking lot at Tam High School cranking Guns 'N Roses and blowing bong hits in Lee's bruise-purple 1978 Chevy Impala.

A decade later he was built like a middleweight fighter—not just tall, but wide, with a bull neck and thighs like traffic bollards. He was wearing cook's whites, with a quilted undershirt that covered his arms to his wrists, but under the tight-fitting fabric he had the tapered upper body and the kind of cut muscles you only get in the weight room. He squinted, trying to see in the dim light of the corridor, then he threw his big head back and unleashed a foghorn-deep laugh.

"Fuck me dead," he said. "If it's not old Pussy Willow."

No one had called me that since high school, and then it was mostly Lee Radko, but hearing the long-forgotten name in that long-forgotten voice tapped some primal place in me, one worlds away from the back room at Cushman's Shoes, and when I opened my mouth what came out were the words of my eighteen-year-old self: "Dude, long time, no see."

"No shit, bro," he said, offering up a massive, sun-browned hand for an overhand shake. It had been ten years since senior year ended and I left for college and Lee didn't, but one hand-shake and a decade fell away, crumbled like dust, and it was just Lee and me again in the back seat of his beater Impala sucking down that last bowl before first period. He even smelled the way I remembered him, like sweat and pot smoke and something else almost sweet—maybe a cheap cologne, maybe just his natural body odor.

He said a few words in rapid-fire Spanish to the Mexican kid, who grinned at me, sidelong and shy, like my stock had just gone up in his eyes. It wasn't hard to see why. Lee still had the easy good looks that had made him a natural leader when we were kids: tousled mop of wavy black hair, deep-set brown eyes, a small, surprisingly feminine mouth. In school, some girl or other was always hovering around Lee, mothering him and trying to keep him out of trouble, but he was too much the lone wolf, too brooding and violent to ever settle on any one girl. Suze had hooked up with him once at a party at Stinson Beach, and she said it was like fucking the Tasmanian Devil. It started out fun and easy, just sort of sexytime wrestling in the dunes, but as soon as she unbuttoned his jeans, Lee started to thrash and howl, pinning her to the ground and tearing at her clothes. When he tried to bite her—Suze swore he sank his teeth into her arm—she gave him a swift knee to the balls that sent him rolling off into the beach weed, yelping like a scalded dog.

"So, what brings you back to Fantasy Island?" he asked, once the Mexican kid disappeared into the kitchen.

"Not much," I said. "Just hanging out. Chilling at my mom's for a bit."

He nodded, eyes lidded, taking this in. "You still down in S.B.?"

"Sort of, yeah. Long story. How about you? What've you been up to?"

He shrugged. "What's it look like, man? Working here, slaving over this yuppie slop."

Suze was right. The guy *was* spooky. He held my eyes and never seemed to blink. There was something else, too: a watchfulness, a squared-away quality, like he was keeping half an eye on every corner of the parking lot at the same time. I'd only seen that look once before, in the eyes of the state prisoners who hung around the weight sets at the Santa Barbara County Jail.

"I don't want to hold you up or anything," I said. "I know you got to get back to work."

"Dude, it's ten in the morning. We're deader than shit."

He had a point there. Hélène's wouldn't open for another hour at least. I looked over my shoulder at the cars passing by on Miller Avenue, wishing I could magically teleport myself there, out of sight of those staring brown eyes.

"You still get high, Wolfer?" he asked.

"What?"

"Do. You. Still. Smoke. Bud?"

When my eyes met his, he was grinning, dead serious.

"What, now?"

"No, next week, Pussy Willow."

It had been ten months since I'd even seen a baggie of weed, and that particular ounce and a half of sinsemilla had ended up, bagged and tagged, in the basement of the Santa Barbara County Courthouse, evidence in the matter of *Wolfer v. State of California*. But did I want to get high? After that shit show at Starbucks? Hell, yeah.

Lee laughed, punching my shoulder, hard. "Don't move," he said. "I'll be right back."

He ducked down the hallway, leaving me alone. I could've been on Miller Avenue, headed for Tam Grocery, in ten seconds. Five, if I ran it. There was even an AA meeting, now that I thought of it, at the Methodist Church a few blocks away. Yet I stood fixed to the spot as if by sheer force of gravity waiting for Lee Radko to return with his baggie of weed.

"Yo, we're on," he said, bulling down the corridor. "The Big Spic says I can take twenty."

When I was in sixth grade, after my father left for good, Mom went on a Zen Buddhist kick, eating vegan and driving out to Green Gulch Farm near Muir Beach on Sunday mornings to sit zazen with the monks. She talked a lot then about achieving *samadhi*, the state of no-mind. The idea, she said, was that if you sat still enough for long enough you could clear your mind of all regret and longing and exist in an eternal present, aware only of the pure fact of your beingness. That was how I felt as I stumbled after Lee, past a row of dumpsters and up a set of wooden steps carved into the forested hillside behind a rustic mini-mall called the Old Brown Store: I had achieved a perfect state of no-mind. Hottie Smurf, Cushman's Shoes, the empty storage room at Starbucks—all that was behind me now. On each step I told myself on the *next* step I would tell Lee the truth, that my mother had just dropped two thousand dollars of her second husband's money on clothes so I could interview for an entry-level office job at a grocery store, and on every step I kept going, half-running to keep up with Lee's long-legged pace, checking over my shoulder that no one had seen us.

"You ever work with spics?" Lee said, as we started up the gravel-filled stairs.

"Uh, I think the word you're looking for there is Latino, Rad."

"Whatever, they're a fuckin' hassle," he said. "The little dude you met, Migs, he's cool. But you shoulda heard that prick Arturo. Bitch can't even read the fuckin' menu and he's all, 'Man, why you got to go now? You just got here.' Like I'm some punk-ass nigger."

I probably should have paid more attention to this little exchange, but I was still lost in my perfect state of no-mind and any brain power I had left over was focused on the weed in Lee's pocket and what we were going to do with it. And what we were going to do with it was break every rule I'd set for myself the day I walked out of lockup in Santa Barbara. Forget the drinking, the skipped meetings, the trips to the bathroom to pop off emergency skinny shots. That was bad news, all of it, a plain violation of the terms of my probation and enough to get me hung if they ever called me in for a random urine test. But that was just it. No one would call me in for a random urine test, not if I held down a job and returned my P.O.'s phone calls. Not if I just stayed cool.

This, however, was clear and unambiguous evidence that I was not staying cool. I hadn't touched a pipe or bong since the September morning ten months before when I was arrested for embezzling more than fifty thousand dollars from Campus Liquors. It was a Friday morning, a week after my boss, Al Fierro, fired me, and I was coming down off an epic six-day run. For nearly a week, all the evil, mind-rotting crap I usually stayed away from—meth, coke, crack, you name it—I'd been sucking it down like there was no tomorrow. A little before dawn that Friday, I was in my apartment geeked to the gills and surfing a Russian lesbian porn site when a young ginger-haired sheriff's deputy tapped on my bedroom window and held the search warrant up to the glass. That image, the one the deputy had seen through the glass, me alone in my bedroom wearing nothing but my socks, a glass pipe in one hand, my half-engorged dick in the other, carried me through four and a half months of jail time, sixty days of court-mandated rehab, and four months at chez Starling. Now, ten months later, here I was again: chasing a high. All around me I could see oak trees and low ferns, the leafy, fresh-smelling landscape of my childhood, but with each step I came closer to falling down a rabbit hole and landing back in my dark apartment in Isla Vista on September 8, 2000, with nothing but a bag of weed and some grainy jpegs of muff-diving Russian teenagers for company.

Lee marched fifty yards up the steep stairs before he stopped, barely winded, and took a seat on a wooden landing halfway up the secluded hillside. The air was damp under the canopy of trees, and with the morning chill, it felt more like April than late July. He pulled a clean white handkerchief from his shirt pocket and set it on the slatted-wood platform, silently folding back the corners and smoothing them flat, as if the drug was a girl and he was undressing her. At the center of the cloth sat a small hash pipe, the inlaid wood around the bowl charred from daily use, and next to it, an oblong ball of tin foil roughly the size and shape of an unhusked almond. I smelled it even before he peeled back the foil, that mouth-watering, musky reek of fresh green sinsemilla. Skunk weed, we called it in high school. But the weed we smoked in high school was dry and crumbly, full of stems and seeds, and you had to spend ten minutes hunched over one of your mom's old Bob Marley album sleeves cleaning it. This was nothing like that. This was a tight snarl of tendrils and curled leaves, blackish green and sticky with resin. Grow-room weed, no cleaning necessary. Lee pinched a thimble-sized chunk off one side, tamped it in the bowl of the pipe, and handed it, mouth-end first, to me.

I lunged in the hit, holding in the smoke as long as I could.

It all felt so good, so familiar: the tart bitterness on the tongue, the hot smoke speeding down my throat, spreading spidery tentacles of stonedness out through my capillaries, filling me up like a greedy sponge. When I exhaled, I laughed so hard I started coughing, hacking and spewing like the lightweight that I was again. I couldn't stop, coughing and laughing, laughing and coughing, except the more I coughed the less it felt like coughing and the more it felt like I was trying to get rid of my head by throwing it off.

"Hey, Mikey likes it," Lee said, watching me.

I was laughing so hard all I could do was nod, which started me coughing again, gasping for air. But even if I could have spoken in full sentences, I couldn't have explained how good this felt. It wasn't just that I was high again. I was *me* again. I felt all the usual giddy, floaty, putty-headedness you get from premium weed, but mostly what I felt was comfortable. At ease. My limbs swung freely in their sockets. I could laugh without taking a reflexive look over my shoulder. I was back in my old body, and for the first time in a year, I knew how things worked.

"Fuckin' A," I said when I found my breath.

"Just wait," Lee said, holding down a lungful of smoke.

We passed the pipe back and forth a few more times before Lee knocked the ash onto the step and wrapped up the rest for later. It was only then, as we were settling back on the wooden steps, gazing through the breaks in the pine and sumac at the downtown shops, lightly dappled in the mid-morning sun, that I saw what he meant. Down there, behind the counter at Starbucks, the cute girl with electric blue hair was probably still talking about the guy she'd caught in the storage room with an open airplane bottle of Stolichnaya, but I didn't care. The high was coming on now, slowly at first, but then more and more quickly. It was like being behind the wheel of a car when it hits a patch of black ice: one minute you're thinking about whether to go for Burger King or Taco Bell, and the next it's as if the laws of gravity have been suspended and your car's spinning across the road like a top. Except this wasn't scary. This was fun: a slow, delicious sense of no longer being at the wheel of control.

"What the *fuck*?" I said.

Lee laughed. "You gotta get out more, Pussy Willow."

"No man, I'm serious. Where'd you get this shit? Can you hook me up?"

"Sure, I'll hook you up." He looked at the diminished ball of foil, placed like some sacred relic at the center of his handkerchief. "This here's Double Black Orchid," he said. "Fresh in from Corvallis, Oregon. Shipment came in a couple days ago."

I had never heard of Black Orchid, much less *Double* Black Orchid, but I liked the idea of a shipment, a trunk full of Hefty bags stuffed with sticky green buds. But that image, all those Hefty bags in the trunk of a car, had to compete with the pillowy sounds of the words Lee had used, which tickled my synapses like fingers on piano keys: *Double, Orchid, Corvallis, Oregon.* All those O's. If the words had been shapes, they would've been warm and cuddly, reddish in color and covered in downy fur like kittens.

"I saw Suze Randall the other day," I said. There was another whole part of that sentence, I was sure of it, but my mind was caught in a muddle of soft, rounded Os. What was it about *O* words that made me see them as red? *I* words were blue. *A* words, they were a bright yellow. Except when the *A* was flat, as in *absurd*. Then there was more brown in it, somehow. Was this just me or did everyone see the same colors? Or was I maybe the only one who saw colors at all?

"What about her?" Lee said.

I stared at him, lost.

"*Suze*," he said. "You said you saw Suze Randall!"

"Right, right." I fought to make my brain work. "She said she saw you in town a few weeks ago. Said you'd been living in Oregon for a while. Or maybe it was Colorado. She wasn't sure."

Lee shook his head, his grin replaced by a darker look of disgust, as if he'd tasted my words on his tongue and found them not to his liking. "Suze-fucking-Randall," he muttered.

"What, she's wrong? You never lived in Oregon?"

"Dude, I've only ever been to Oregon once in my life, and I was just there long enough to drive through on my way to Idaho."

*Idaho?* This was the summer of 2001. I could think of exactly two things people did in Idaho: grow potatoes and shave their heads and declare war on the U.S. government. And I was pretty sure Lee Radko wasn't a potato farmer. "What, you were like hanging with the skinheads up there?" I said. "The Aryan Nations or whatever?"

He fixed his eyes on me as if I was a small, inoffensive bug he was preparing to crush. "No, Pussy Willow, I wasn't, like, hanging with the Aryan Nations."

I remembered the watchful quality in his eyes in the restaurant parking lot, the wrist-length quilted undershirt covering his muscled forearms, and I scoured my brain pan to call up what I knew about the Aryan Nations: Neo-Nazis. Twelve-year-olds packing AR-15s. Calls for armed overthrow of the United States. All of it scared the shit out of me.

"What were you doing up there, then?"

"Let it go, will ya? I never should've brought it up."

He still had his eyes on me. He never seemed to blink, not once. Now that I thought about it, there'd been some weird stories going around about Lee Radko after high school. That he'd shaved off most of his hair. That if you got him drunk enough, he started raving about coons and kikes and how Hitler had it right. I was in S.B. by then, knee-deep in my own problems, and I'd dismissed the stories as wild-assed exaggeration. Suddenly, I wasn't so sure.

"Guys like you, Wolfer, you don't know shit about shit," he said. "What you hear, it's all media hype, anyway. All that crap about sending out posses to string up spooks outside Spokane. Total bullshit, man. Never happened."

His face had gone scarlet, the color of wine splashed on a carpet. It was like watching a Discovery Channel special on the Aryan Nations, except that this wasn't a bunch of baldheaded goons from northern Idaho, this was Lee Radko, one of my oldest buds from high school.

"I want you to take one huge motherfucking step back, okay?" I said. "I want you to tell me how come we're sitting here talking about stringing up spooks in Spokane."

"You are such a pussy," he said. "I'm telling you it never happened. What kind of asshole pulls an operation like that on open ground? It's asking for heat. If you're gonna do something like that, you do it on your own turf, where you control the ground, you control the perimeter. It's common fucking sense, man. But, no. Turn on *Sixty Minutes*, open the *New York*-fucking-*Times*, all you see is those ACLU hard-ons talking about, 'They hung a nigger from a tree in Spokane.' Like there's any niggers *in* Spokane. You ever been to Spokane, man? You could drive around that shithole for a week before you found anybody dark enough to worry about."

It was hard to hold on to a thought, what with my brainwaves washing to and fro battling the hurricane-force winds of dank-think, but finally I shook out a laugh.

"You're shitting me, right?"

"You wanna see the tats?" he said, hiking up one sleeve of his undershirt. The length of his forearm from his wrist bone to his elbow and beyond was a sea of blue and green and black ink, spidery lines connecting, forming words and hand-drawn Celtic crosses and fluttering Confederate flags. "See that?" he said, pointing to a fading, free-drawn skull. "Got that a couple years ago, in Coeur d'Alene. Tim McVeigh was sitting right next to me getting the same fuckin' tattoo."

I let out another tense giggle. "Timothy McVeigh was in *jail* two years ago, Lee."

He made a hard, spitting sound deep in his throat, looking out through the branches. Then, finally, he couldn't do it anymore, the strain was too much, and one corner of his lip crept impishly upward, as if tugged by an invisible string. "He was in jail?"

"He's been locked up since Oklahoma City," I said. "They

executed him a couple months ago. Don't you watch the news?"

We sat there, stunned into silence. In high school, this had been a Lee Radko specialty, endlessly elaborate practical jokes designed to fuck with your head, smoke you out of whatever hidey-hole of white guilt or rich-kid envy you'd buried yourself in. But this one seemed a little too good, cut a little too close to the bone. I caught Lee's eye, and for a split-second, behind the defiance and surprise, I saw it: a faint glimmer of fear. Then the dam broke and he fell back against the steps, howling with laughter.

"You shoulda seen your fuckin' face, Pussy Willow!" he bawled. "I had you going, dude. When I started in about those spooks, you looked like you ate a whole *mouthful* of shit."

He was right: for a minute there, he'd had me. His rage sounded so real, so personal, so alive. After ten years I'd forgotten Lee could do that, step into a role so completely you forgot what was real and what wasn't. This was one of the reasons we'd been so tight all those years. We were both bullshit artists and we shared a practitioner's appreciation for each other's bullshit. Still, I couldn't kick the sense that this time the joke had backfired, smoked Lee out of some dark hidey-hole of his own.

"Sorry, man," I said. "It's just, you know, I heard all these stories."

"I know what you heard," he said. "Everybody heard that shit. So I read some books. Big deal. It was a long time ago, I moved on."

"Okay, but what about that shit on your arms? No offense, but those things don't look professional to me."

"Fuck you, Wolfer."

I waited, checking myself, but I'd seen the ink on his arms and the jailhouse look in his eyes. You can fake anger, you can fake a lot of things, but you can't fake fear, not that kind. In Mill Valley, we had been tough kids, Lee and me, potheads and drinkers who knew how to throw a punch, but in the real world, the one outside safe, suburban Southern Marin, we weren't tough at all. We were soft and white and scared. "So, what happened?" I said. "You were dealing?"

"Nah, man. Growing. Making serious bank, too."

"In Oregon?"

He shook his head. "Colorado. I had a string of grow ops outside Denver. But then one of the houses got raided and the chick I had running the place took down the whole crew. Twenty-six months, man. Colorado Territorial, Cañon City."

"Shit, Rad."

"You have no fucking idea. That place, it's like one long race riot with bars on the windows." His eyes settled on me again. "What about you, Pussy Willow?"

"Me?"

"Last time I saw you, you were all hot-shit Mr. Baseball, going off to play with the big boys. Now, look at you. It's like you got this big fat 'I'm sorry' sign stuck to your forehead. I figure it's either rehab or the pen."

"Try a little of both."

He nodded. "Your folks bail you out?"

I started to say no, my stepfather had, but the thought of Stan Starling reminded me what had brought me downtown in the first place. Then I was up, brushing dirt and twigs off my chinos, spluttering, "Fuck! Fuck, fuck, fuckety-fuck. I gotta go, I'm late."

"Late for *what?*"

"A job interview. At Tam Grocery. I was supposed to be there at eleven."

He stared at me, laughing. "Wolfer, you dumbass, you got high before a job interview?"

I didn't have a watch, but I knew it was past eleven. And why lie? Mixed in with the panic was a healthy dose of relief. This would break my mother's heart and prove Stan right in every shitty thing he'd ever said about me, but at least I wouldn't have to put on this preppy clown suit every day of my life just to answer phones at a grocery store.

"At least put in some Visine," Lee said, handing me a small

bottle from his shirt pocket. "I mean, I hate to break it to you, but you got the full-on Nosferatu going there."

The last thing I heard as I stumbled into the parking lot was Lee's voice, which suddenly sounded a lot like Stan's, or maybe my dad's, high up on the hill, booming with laughter:

"Wolfer, you are one sorry motherfucker, you know that?"

# 5

Then I was in Lytton Square staring at the town clock outside the Book Depot, which said it was ten forty-five. Seconds earlier, I had been tearing down Miller Avenue squirting Visine in my eyes and picturing myself sleeping in my car. But that whole train of images—the screaming match with my mother, the barely suppressed glee in Stan's eyes, the long night camped out in my Honda in the Muir Beach parking lot—all that assumed I was late, that I'd already blown it. But if the town clock was right, not only wasn't I late, but I still had fifteen minutes to spare.

I collapsed onto a bench and chewed through a roll of wintergreen Life Savers, trying to talk myself out of doing what I wanted to do, which was bail on the interview. It was my day off, after all. I could drive up the coast, maybe stop for a beer at Smiley's in Bolinas. Or I could stay right here, hang out in the plaza soaking up the warm summer weather and trying to get lucky with one of the pretty girls sunning themselves in front of the Book Depot. That would be the end of chez Starling, of course. I could probably kiss my stash of skinnies goodbye, too. But if I caught a break, my mother might forget the AmEx card. Then there was that suit waiting for me at Nordstrom. I'd never even worn the thing. It had to be worth a few hundred bucks at a consignment store, right? Between that and Mom's plastic, I figured I might be able to scrounge up just enough cash to deal myself in on the next shipment of Double Black Orchid and get back in business in Santa Barbara.

All this thinking, this sorting through of options, would have been easier if I hadn't kept seeing my mother at the breakfast table laughing as she licked powdered sugar off her fingertips. I hadn't been happy, not in years and years, but I still knew what happiness looked like, and that was it. And I'd done that.

I'd made my mother deliriously happy just by getting up one morning and putting on some clothes she'd bought for me, by looking for a few minutes like I gave a shit. I *didn't* give a shit, obviously. If I did, I wouldn't have been sitting in Lytton Square, tripping my face off on Lee's grow-room weed and seriously considering selling off a brand-new suit to buy drugs. But Mom had thought I had, and that thought made her as happy as I'd seen her in years.

When I stood up, I had eaten all the Life Savers and emptied half of Lee's Visine bottle into my eyes, but none of that changed the fact that I was very, very high—the queasy, skull-frying kind of high that cranks the brightness knob on the world and melts street signs like Dali clocks. The downtown shops, the people walking past me in Lytton Square, all had a faintly epic quality, as if I'd walked into the climactic scene of a movie—a shoot-out, maybe, in a Clint Eastwood Western. As I headed down Throckmorton Avenue toward Tam Grocery, an imaginary tumbleweed skittered by. I heard hoofbeats in the distance, then the rising yips and howls of the Ennio Morricone score: *Doom-da-doo-doom, wah-wah! Doom-da-doo-doom, wah-wah-WAHH!*

"Sir?"

I turned, half-expecting to see Eli Wallach clutching a crumpled felt hat, but no. It was just a girl, all of sixteen, wearing a pale blue smock and a puzzled smile.

"You're standing on the mat for the automatic doors," she said. "They keep opening and closing."

So I was. The double doors, I realized, had whooshed open and closed several times while I was playing out the final shootout at the Sad Hill Cemetery. As casually as I could, I stepped off the black-rubber matting.

"So, um," she said, pointing to her left, "the shopping carts are over there?"

"Actually, I'm not here to shop," I said.

She nodded, waiting, until I realized I'd once again left out the second half of a sentence.

"Because I have an appointment with Mr. Papadakis!" I nearly shouted.

"Oh right, you must be Trent," she said. "Uncle Mike said I should look out for you. He's in aisle seven, restocking bread." She smiled again, gamely, showing off a mouthful of braces. "I'm Melody, by the way."

"Nice to meet you, Melody," I said. "I think I'll go find aisle seven."

I had no idea where aisle seven was, nor did I care. I just needed to get away from Melody and all those glittering teeth. But when I walked past her, I found myself in the fruit and vegetables section, which pulled me up short. In a world where supermarkets were as interchangeable as airport lounges, Tamalpais Grocery was still an actual market. It smelled like food: ripe bananas and apples, yeasty loaves of sourdough bread, that oddly sweet scent of freshly butchered beef. Like that, I was nine years old, shopping with my dad on Saturday mornings. Back then, you could draw a reasonably accurate portrait of the state of my parents' marriage by the contents of our fridge. When they were fighting, my mother lived on green apples and Tab, which she bought by the case and drank lukewarm without ice. But when they made up, my father liked to celebrate by filling the house with food. For this reason, our Saturday morning trips to Tam Grocery often had the feel of a victory lap. Dad handled the major items, the T-bone steaks and sacks of potatoes for french fries, sending me off on solo missions for the imported mustards and fresh cheeses my mother liked. As we cruised the aisles, Dad in shorts and flip-flops, his aviator shades tucked into his shirt collar, we talked about guy stuff: girls and music and baseball, and why, even after accounting for price, a Mercedes was simply a better machine than a BMW. I committed it all to memory, every word, but really I didn't care what we talked about. What mattered was that we were talking, that he was listening to me, considering my opinions in ways he never did at any other time.

"Excuse me—Trent?" Melody called from the cash registers.

"That way," she said, pointing to my right. "In with the bread."

"Right, aisle seven," I said, waving my thanks.

I felt the eyes of Melody and the other women at the check-out stands on my back as I walked the length of the store, counting aisles, but I didn't care. Any reservations I'd had about the job evaporated. I didn't care what kind of clothes I'd have to wear. I didn't care who had set up the job for me. I just wanted to be here in the mornings smelling the fresh bread, watching the racks of meat being delivered on hooks through the back. Nothing in Mill Valley, nothing in my life, was as I remembered it, but here everything looked and smelled and felt the way it had when I was nine years old, and I never wanted to leave.

I turned the corner at aisle seven and there he was: the Greek-American Mr. Rogers, on one knee stocking loaves of Oroweat multi-grain onto the bottom shelf. His back was stooped from decades of stocking bread onto low shelves, and his slicked-back hair, once a glossy black, was now flecked with gray, but he was still loose-built and lanky, his craggy face softened by his warm brown eyes, dark as worn pennies. He wore a forest-green cardigan over a starched white shirt and cheap black tie, but even more than the way he dressed, the way he moved made you think of Mr. Rogers: slow and genial and ever-smiling, as if all the world was a six-year-old who needed to be given a gumdrop.

I cleared my throat. "Mr. Papadakis?"

"Yes," he said, looking up. "Can I help you?"

"I'm Trent Wolfer," I said. "I'm here for an appointment. I hope I'm not late."

"Oh hey, Trent." His lips formed a crinkly grin, pure Mr. Rogers, and he checked his watch. "Nope, right on time. That's a good sign."

As we shook hands, his eyes lingered on mine a split-second too long and I felt an instinctive stroke of guilt: *He knows*. But he just went on pumping my hand and grinning like we were two old buddies from the war. "I'm glad you could come by," he said. "Your mom probably told you, me and her go way back."

"You guys were at Tam together, right?"

"Oh yeah. She didn't know who I was back then, but I knew her. Sandy Cushman, my God. And now, well, she's just good people, you know? Come on, I'll take you upstairs."

Mike Papadakis didn't so much walk through his store as glided, floating on a set of invisible wheels on the soles of his shoes. His long legs barely moved, but I had to run to keep up.

"I knew your dad a little, too," he said over his shoulder. "He was a couple years ahead of me in school. Musician, right?"

"More on the business end, really. I don't think he ever played an instrument."

"Right, right, I remember now. He used to drive that little sports car—what was that thing? An Alfa? Karmann Ghia?"

It was a 1957 Mercedes sports coupe, vintage even then, and my dad, car snob that he was, would have been horrified to hear someone call it a Karmann Ghia.

"He's in L.A. now," I said.

"I think I'd heard that," he said, stopping at the swinging doors that led to the storage area. "Listen, Trent, this new project, it's really Gianni's baby. So he'll be sitting in with us today if that's okay with you."

Before I could ask who or what Gianni might be we were sailing up a narrow flight of stairs to a cluttered business office. The lone window looked out onto the foothills of Mt. Tam, which made the room cheerier than it might have been, but it was first and foremost an office: scuffed floors, mismatched furniture, papers everywhere. On a row of hooks by the door hung the Grecian blue smocks of each member of the Papadakis family, identical except for their first names stitched in cursive over the left breast pocket.

"Trent, I'd like you to meet my son Gianni," Papadakis said. "Gianni, this is Trent Wolfer."

Gianni Papadakis, thank God, resembled no children's television personality I could think of. He had his father's warm brown eyes and that same weirdly elongated head, but he was three decades younger and twenty pounds heavier, his sinewy arms bulging out from under his short-sleeved Tam Grocery polo.

"Go, Eaglets," he said as he crushed my hand in his.

I nodded, grinning back, far too stoned to pretend I knew what the hell he was talking about.

"Little League," he said, hurt. "You played for the Eaglets, right? I remember you, man. You were like the terror of the league."

That's when it hit me: *Johnny* Papadakis. The Papadakises, Johnny and his sister Andi, went to Greek Orthodox schools in the city, but my last year in Little League, Johnny Papadakis had been a pudgy eleven-year-old putting in his regulation two innings a game in right field. My only real memory of him was sitting in the dugout with my teammates competing to see who could do the best impression of his sad, shambling trot off the field between innings.

"You still play?" he asked.

"I played some in college, but I tore up my knee," I said.

This was a lie I'd been telling for years, substituting *tore up my knee* for *lost my scholarship for growing illegal drugs in my dorm room.*

"Too bad," he said. "I go in more for cycling these days, but I'm in a softball league now. Just weekends, but it's good times. I'd love to get my boy started on T-ball, but you know kids these days—it's soccer, soccer, soccer."

I had no response to this. It stunned me that fat, plodding Johnny Papadakis, one-time laughingstock of Mill Valley Little League, now spent his free time cycling and had a son old enough to show a detectable lack of interest in T-ball. But what bothered me even more was that he wasn't bragging or showing off. He was just making small talk, as if he expected me to whip out wallet photos of my own kids and compare notes.

Once we'd settled in around the conference table, Mr. Papadakis nodded to his son to begin. The big picture was pretty much as my mother had described it: a home-catering company called Chef Tamalpais designed to give corporate moms and upscale singles a way to order groceries and pre-made meals online and over the phone. The Papadakises had leased a new building a few blocks from their store, and while they were remodeling and hiring staff, they would need me, the first and so far only employee of this new venture, to help manage the office.

"Take a guess," Gianni said. "What would you say will be the single largest growth sector in the grocery business over the next decade?"

I nodded, my brain clogged, any answer I might have given crowded out by munchie-fueled images of fudge brownies and rice-krispie treats.

"Okay well, the answer's pre-made meals," he said. "That, and organics. If you've been inside the new Cornucopia Foods, you've seen the future of the grocery business. Now, we can't compete with that, not head to head. But people know us. They know my dad. They knew my granddad back when he was running the store. They trust us. So, what we're doing—and this is where you'd come in, Trent—is we're taking the Tam Grocery experience, and we're making it virtual. You can buy your groceries from the comfort of your home, but not just that. We're taking my grandma's dolmades we've been serving in our deli for forty years, all the pasta dishes, all the soups and salads we make, along with a new line of gourmet pre-made meals, and we're delivering them directly to our customers' doors. They point and click and dinner is done, and it tastes as good as homemade. Better, even."

Gianni sat back, his arms crossed, picturing it: the happy family gathered at the dinner table, the freshly made food steaming on their plates, the parents relaxed and cheerful after a long day at work—and in the kitchen, the foil-lined Chef Tamalpais takeout bags discreetly stashed in the trash can under the sink.

"We're looking at a gradual rollout," his father said.

"Not gradual, Pop," Gianni said. "Strategic."

"Okay, fine. Strategic." Papadakis turned to me. "This job, we're calling it clerical because when we get this up and running, we're going to need somebody in the office. But we're a long ways from that. So for the first few months, while we work out the kinks, there'll be some office work, but you'd also be working in the deli, running a register, stocking shelves. A bit of everything, you understand?"

"You can probably tell," Gianni said. "Dad's a little nervous about all this."

Papadakis chuckled in his Mr. Rogers-ish way, and the room got very quiet. In that silence I sensed how new this all was. And how scary. These people weren't millionaires. They weren't Stan Starling. They were a local family running a grocery store. They had leased the new building, but they didn't have a website or a fleet of delivery vans, much less anyone to drive them. What they had was an idea, a brave vision inside Gianni Papadakis's head. And now, maybe, me.

"Now that you've heard a little about our new venture," Mr. Papadakis said, "why don't you tell us about yourself, why you might be interested in taking this job?"

He was serving up a nice, fat, fluffy softball, and if I hadn't spent the last hour sucking down bowls of Double Black Orchid, I could have come up with a line of bullshit with which to knock it out of the park. But the best I could do was to ramble on about shopping at Tam Grocery with my dad, and how much I admired what I called, in a moment of inspiration, the Papadakis retail philosophy.

"I don't know," I said finally. "I guess I just think you guys are right."

"Right about what?" Gianni asked.

"All of it," I said. "I grew up here. I know your customers. I *am* your customer. And I swear, I never saw anybody cook a meal the whole time I was a kid. People have more money now, but nothing's really changed. You should see my mom's friends. They have these amazing kitchens, with six-burner stoves and brushed-steel everything, and they never even go in there. It's like they're afraid of it, like it's going to bite them or something. So if there was somewhere they could go to order a decent meal they could serve on their own plates like they made it themselves, they'd be logging on five nights a week."

"I'm glad to hear you say that," Gianni said, glancing over at his father. "It's nice to get a local's perspective for a change."

"I don't know if you remember my granddad," I said, feeling the first whisper of a breeze at my back. "He used to run Cushman's Shoes, where the Starbucks is now."

"Sure, I remember Cushman's," Mr. Papadakis said. "I got my first pair of shoes there."

"That's the thing," I said. "Everybody used to get their first pair of shoes at Cushman's. My granddad had that store for, what, thirty-five years? But then the jogging thing came along, and he couldn't see it. Everyone kept telling him he needed to stock running shoes, start sponsoring races, that kind of thing. He thought it was a fad and it would go away."

"Yeah, I remember being a kid and thinking 'Where are all the Nikes?'" Gianni said.

"He thought they were overpriced," I said. "And the whole swoosh thing, he never got it. He hated change, any kind of change, and now his store's gone. All the old stores are gone. There's nothing left in town but chain stores and art galleries and you guys. So, yeah, if you have an idea for how to stay in business here, I want to be a part of that."

Gianni turned to his dad again, his eyebrows raised.

"I like what I'm hearing here, Trent," Mr. Papadakis said. "I like this passion. But just so there's no misunderstanding, this job, it's strictly entry-level. Taking phone calls, filing invoices, working down in the deli."

"It can't be any worse than what I'm doing now," I said.

"What *are* you doing now?" Gianni asked. "For work, I mean."

I wanted to smack myself. In my excitement, I had violated Wolfer's First Rule of Working with the Available Truth: Never, ever answer a question you haven't been asked.

"I'm working at Howie's," I said. "You know, out by the Strawberry Shopping Center?"

"The burger joint?" Gianni said.

"Right, I talked to Sand—to Mrs. Starling about this," Papadakis said, saving me. "You were in retail before, right? As I understand it, you were the assistant manager at your last job."

I wondered who'd dreamed that one up, Stan or my mother, but I let that slide and did my best to pretty up Campus Liquors, moving it off Frat Row and tip-toeing around its core business, which was supplying keg beer and cheap liquor to rowdy, often under-aged, college kids. From the way Papadakis prodded me along, feeding me lines, I got the clear sense that, no matter what Mom said, neither she nor Stan had felt any burning need to let him in on what I'd done to get myself fired from Campus Liquors.

"Sounds like you had a lot responsibility for an assistant manager," Gianni said. "There wasn't anyone else working there? No one under you?"

"Just part-timers," I said. "Kids, mostly, from the university. It was different when I started, because then it was still a couple that owned the business. But when she died, it was just the two of us, me and the owner. Al was getting on, and, you know, he kind of drank a little."

"Is that why you left?" Gianni asked.

"No," I said, too quickly. "Sorry, I didn't mean it like that."

He looked up from his notepad. "Why did you leave, then?"

"It was a lot of things, really." I shifted in my seat, surprised how hard it was to lie about this. "I don't want to give you the wrong idea. Al wasn't the easiest guy to work for, but he always treated me decently. And I loved his wife. He's not the reason I left."

"Trent, you're going to have to help us out here," Gianni said. "You were an assistant manager at a high-volume store, handling inventory and keeping the books, and now you're flipping burgers at a fast food place."

By then I was looking directly at his father. In the older man's soft brown eyes I saw, as if the words were written in neon, the subject he thought I was trying to avoid.

"Trent, it's okay, I discussed this with your mom," he said. "I told her it wasn't going to be an issue."

"Okay," Gianni said. "I guess I don't know what we're talking about here."

It took every ounce of self-control I had to let Mr. Papadakis dangle, deciding how to phrase what he imagined to be my deepest, darkest secret.

"As you know, Trent's mother's an old friend of mine," he said. "As I understand it, Trent's like a lot of kids around here. He took a while to find himself, and then in the last year, I guess things got a little out of hand. Drinking, mostly." He turned to me, and I nodded, conceding this. "Anyway, last fall he called her up and let her know he was ready to get some help."

"You're saying he's just out of rehab?" Gianni said.

"Son, I should have handled this better," Mr. Papadakis said. "But like I say, his mom and I go back a long ways. All she wants is to see him to get a fresh start."

Gianni looked at me and then at his dad, the expression on his face that of a man drowning in a sea of his own disbelief. "Trent, could you give us a minute?" he said.

I was suddenly glad I hadn't brought anything with me, no papers to pack up, no jacket to put on. All I had to do was stand and let Mr. Papadakis lead me to the door.

"There's a staff lounge down the hall," he said. "Fix yourself some coffee, make yourself at home. I'm sorry about this. It'll just be a minute."

For a long time after he shut the door, I heard nothing, just the creaking of footsteps and the soft shriek of a chair scraping against the floor. Finally, Gianni coughed up a low, ugly laugh. "This is the kid you were telling Pappouli about the other day, isn't it?" he said. "The one whose stepdad just happens to be Stan Starling." There was silence on the other side of the door, not even a floor creak this time. "You don't honestly believe the guy's going to give us a quarter-million dollars because we took his fuck-up stepson off his hands," Gianni said.

I didn't wait to hear his father's answer, just bolted down the hall to the break room where I collapsed onto a battered sofa. I had been concentrating so hard, for such a long time, that I had forgotten how stoned I was, and now on the break room sofa, it all washed back over me, not the first buzzy burst of cannabinoid fireworks, but the brain-dead, cotton-mouthed downslope of the high. It was all so painfully obvious now. Somewhere along the line the Papadakises had hit up Stan for money, and Stan had decided to kill two birds with one stone: get them to take me off his hands, and at the same time string them along to see if he could swing a better deal. In other words, Mom could have saved herself two grand. The fix was in. Or it was before I sucked down a big bowl of grow-room weed and turned the conversation to the subject of my recent release from rehab.

Downstairs, a tinkly Muzak version of Hall & Oates' "Sara Smile" played over the synthetic beeps of registers scanning barcodes. Which reminded me all over again of my dad. In the seventies, he'd represented Daryl Hall on an ill-advised solo project with acid rock guitarist Robert Fripp, and years later, after Hall & Oates returned to their Top 40 hair-band ways, Dad wangled me a signed copy of their *Private Eyes* album, which I'd long ago given away to some girl whose pants I was trying to get into. This was always happening with my father. I couldn't buy a bag of Doritos at 7-Eleven without hearing the voice of some eighties rock icon whose smiling mug was up on his office brag wall between Mick Jagger and Archbishop Desmond Tutu.

I wondered what my dad would think, in his office high above Santa Monica Boulevard, if he could see me now. If I knew my father, he wouldn't have given it much thought either way. We hadn't talked in years, not since I'd wrapped a Christmas-present Saab Turbo around a tree down in S.B., but I had called him the day I was arrested. His wife Caressa, the Human Chihuahua, had picked up. "You want to speak with your father, you call him at his office, not here," she shouted in her lispy *norteña* accent before the robo-voice even finished telling her she was receiving a collect call from a correctional facility.

In a way, that had hurt more than the fact that she hung up without accepting the charges. It was like she'd been expecting it, waiting for me to call from jail so she could blow me off in good conscience. I never called his office, and for ten months I had felt no desire to ever speak to him again—until now.

"There you are," Mr. Papadakis said from the break room doorway.

Before I could get a word out, he held up his hand. "Here's the thing," he said. "There's no question you're qualified for this job, and frankly, what happened last year, it doesn't bother me that much. We're a local business. If we never hired anyone with a little blot on their record, we wouldn't have any employees."

"Sir, I promise you," I said, "the whole thing last winter, it's behind me now."

"Right. See, that's sort of the issue. Gianni's concerned—he thinks you maybe looked a little *tired* this morning. Your eyes, especially."

If I had seen this coming, if I'd been on my game, I could've pulled some story out of my ass about a lingering flu bug or a rare allergic reaction to invoice carbons. But this one had caught me sleeping, and all I could think to say was the truth: "I really want this job, Mr. Papadakis."

"Maybe I'm not being clear," he said. "I'm not accusing you of anything. I'm just saying Gianni's concerned you might be on something. And I can't have that. That kind of thing, it's got no place in my business."

Just like the day before with my mother, part of me was ready to throw in the towel, thank Mr. Papadakis for his time and zip back over to Hélène's to buy out the rest of Radko's stash. But for a second there, talking about my granddad's store, I had seen a future for myself, a life I could maybe, possibly give a shit about. It had been years since I'd cared about anything that wasn't a drug or a girl, that wasn't just *more, more, more, now, now, now,* so I did the only thing I knew how to do. I looked the man straight in the eye and lied.

"Mr. Papadakis, I've been clean ten months now," I said. "I

swear to you, I haven't had a drink or a drug since last September."

"It's not just Gianni, son. Your eyes *were* kind of red earlier. I noticed it myself downstairs."

"I know, I couldn't sleep last night," I said. "I was up till four in the morning. I've worked so hard to get this far, and I didn't want to blow it. Ask my mom."

"Your mother? She was up with you?"

"Sir, all I'm asking for is a chance. If I go back on my word or if it's not working out for any reason, I'll leave that day. I promise. But please, just give me a chance to prove myself."

Papadakis smiled sheepishly, the look of a man who knows he's being played. Or maybe he was playing me. Maybe he would have done anything to get his hands on Stan's millions. Or maybe, just maybe, Mike Papadakis was what he appeared to be: a decent, uncomplicated guy who prided himself on seeing the best in people.

"You know, I remember you as a kid," he said. "You were a screw-up then, too. I used to see you running around town, you and all your little buddies. But you were there every afternoon at your granddad's store, helping out. They never had enough help in that store, and you were there. I remember that, too."

This silenced me. I had never thought of my afternoons at my grandparents' store as anything but a personal hell it was my unlucky fate to suffer. The idea that I was needed there, or that my showing up week after week displayed character—it had never crossed my mind.

"You swear to me you've been clean since last fall?" he said.

"You can give me any test you want," I said. "I had a problem last year and I went to rehab, but I've been clean since then. I swear it."

"Look, I won't lie to you," he said. "Gianni's not going to like this. He's going to be on you night and day. If I hear you're drinking on the job, or, you know, whatever, that's it, we're done. But I liked that passion I heard in there a few minutes ago. So, if you want the job, it's yours. You can start next week."

Five minutes later when I pulled out of Lytton Square, instead of heading back up the hill, I drove in the opposite direction, along Miller Avenue, away from downtown, away from Blithedale Canyon, whooping and hollering, banging my fists on the steering wheel. I spun the radio dial, searching for something to sing along with, but all I could find were loudmouth guys talking sports, loudmouth Christians talking Christ, and Ben Folds sobbing artfully over his girlfriend's abortion. Then, hold on, wait, back up: out of the oceans of static arose the three most famous power chords in classic rock: *I was baawwwn in the U.S.A.!*

Bruce Springsteen, nearly alone among major recording artists of his era, never had a thing to do with my father, so when *Born in the U.S.A.* came out, in the summer of my eighth grade year, he was all mine. I bought all his albums, even the slow, moody ones, but I kept coming back to the one with Bruce on the cover with a red ballcap in his back pocket. On those long afternoons waiting for my mom to come home from work or from the Last Ditch, he was my babysitter, my best friend, the cool, wild older brother I never had. And now all these years later when I needed him most, here he was again, that gut-bottom South Jersey howl releasing the same flood of joy I had felt the first time I slipped the vinyl LP from its sleeve the summer I turned thirteen.

Back at chez Starling, I turned my room upside down looking for something, anything, by Bruce Springsteen. My desktop computer, along with four years of downloaded music, had been stolen from my apartment after I was arrested, and all I had left were two shoe boxes of CDs and cassette tapes I'd had in my car. I dumped them onto the floor, looking for Springsteen, but all I could find was an ancient home-recorded tape of *Born to Run*, which snapped ten seconds into "Thunder Road."

Other than Lupita, who was in the kitchen, deep into the Tony Robbins life-coaching tapes she listened to when Mom wasn't around, I had the house to myself. I catfooted it upstairs and through the living room to the master bedroom. It was like something out of *House Beautiful* in there: the Navajo red of the bedsheets playing off the adobe brown of the walls, which blended with the rich mocha of the drapes. A baby-blue silk slip dangled by its spaghetti strap from the door handle of my mother's walk-in closet, a touch of clutter that looked even more staged than the iron-flat sheets or the stack of unread novels by the bed.

Once or twice that summer, when I was really feeling the walls closing in, I had sneaked into the master bedroom looking for jewelry to pawn. I never took anything, but I'd snooped around enough to know that in the bottom drawer of Stan's dresser, where another kind of guy might have stashed a bag of drugs or top-grade porn, he kept a black-vinyl flip folder of old CDs. This wasn't the Kronos Quartet crap they played when they had company or even the Joni Mitchell albums Mom kept around for those rare days when she was feeling weepy and nostalgic. No, this was the good stuff, the essential Stan, what he listened to when no one else was around.

Kneeling in the corner of Stan's closet, I flipped past Janis Joplin's *Pearl*, past The Who's *Who Are You?* and Jefferson Airplane's *Surrealistic Pillow*. Then—bingo—between *Abbey Road* and *Hot Rocks*, there it was: *Born in the U.S.A.*

A minute later I was back downstairs bawling my guts out with Bruce, pouring fifty milliliter bottles of vodka and gin down the bathroom sink. It took me half an hour to empty them all, toss the bottles into a plastic bag, and sneak its tinkling contents around the back side of the house to my car. But by the time Springsteen had crooned the last mournful chorus of "My Hometown," my closet was empty of skinnies for the first time in weeks.

I was still straightening my room when Lupita clicked off Tony Robbins and started humming one of the Ecuadorian folk songs she sang whenever my mother was within earshot. The front door opened and Stan and Mom swept into the house, talking tennis.

"Trent?" she called downstairs. "Honey, are you down there? How did it *go?*"

Like a lid slamming shut on a coffin, it hit me what I'd done. There must have been two hundred dollars' worth of liquor in that closet. I looked around at the silent CD player, at the boxes full of my childhood crap, at the empty closet, wishing I could swim down into the sewer and lap up all that trickling booze.

But it was too late. It was gone.

# 6

Six days later I punched out at the time clock next to Rajiv's office and locked myself in the employee bathroom to change out of my Howie's uniform for the last time. I'd barely slept all week. I couldn't eat, either. Food just tasted wrong to me, like someone had mixed a pinch of dog shit into everything I ate. Night after night I lay in bed sweating, my gut aching, trying to slow down my brain, get its humming little motor to rev at something closer to normal speed. When I finally did get to sleep, I always had the same dream. I was in Isla Vista sucking down an eight-ball of crack with a girl named Nadine I'd picked up in an East Beach bar the week I was arrested. Nadine was from Bakersfield, by way of the Sunset Strip, one of those hard, beaten women who wash up every now and then in beach towns like Santa Barbara. She had no car and no money, just a couple changes of clothes she kept in a locker at the Greyhound station. She'd done some modeling in L.A., she told me once, had even made a sitcom pilot for Fox. And who knows? Maybe she had. She certainly had the face for it, all cheekbones and bee-stung lips. But by the time I met her she was a stone junkie, skeletal and pale, her teeth ground down to sad little stumps, her spiky blonde hair limp and flyblown as dandelion fluff.

We partied for four nights straight, Nadine and me, leaving my apartment only to buy drugs, until I crashed and she took off with five hundred bucks and a silver Longines watch my mother had given me for my high school graduation. One night while we were waiting to score in a park near Milpas Street, on the Mexican side of town, Nadine showed me pictures of her kids, who lived with a foster family in L.A. In the photos, they were all dolled up for picture day, the girl blonde like her mom, the boy darker, half-Mexican, his black hair twisted into a cowlick. In the dreams I had, her kids were there with us, the little blonde girl and her half-brother camped out at the foot of the bed with a bag of Cheetos and a two-liter Pepsi, watching us like we were their TV. Any moment, I thought, one of them would hit the remote and—*zap!*—we would disappear. But they never did. They just went on watching like that was what they did all day, watched their mom pad around my apartment stark naked, one minute screeching at me for being a pipe hog, the next whispering in my ear that she was a horny, horny girl, that I could ride the back road this time, nice and slow, anything, baby, anything I wanted, if she could have another hit off that pipe, just one more and then we could rock it all night.

I woke up high. Not dream-high, but actually stoned: pulse speeding, fingertips stinging from the white-hot glass of the pipe, the burnt-acetone reek of crack smoke everywhere. I rolled out of bed and stood panting on the hardwood floor. The house was quiet, except that one floor above I heard the muffled plinking of a sitar and the thump of bare feet on a thin mat. My mother, doing her morning yoga. Which meant it was after six a.m. and I wasn't in Isla Vista, but at home, at my mother's second husband's house in Mill Valley. Still, it took ten minutes of pacing by the bed, drinking glass after glass of cold water, before I could clear the room of crackhead Nadine and her two kids, their wet eyes and slack faces hovering in the corners of the room until I threw open the curtains and drowned them in daylight.

I'd gone cold turkey the year before, too, but I was in jail then, facing the very real chance that I could spend the next three to five years in state prison. I was working so hard to look like I wasn't afraid, like I was cool with watching guys go down on each other in the showers and pick through their own shit for heroin balloons that I had no time to worry that I couldn't hold a cup of coffee without spilling. Now, I was in Mill Valley, living in a three-story mansion in one of the wealthiest neighborhoods in one of the wealthiest towns in one of the wealthiest counties in the United States. I was spending my days flipping burgers in the hot, grease-soaked kitchen at Howie's, which helped, because for a few hours a day the misery inside my head matched the misery of the world around me. But when my shift ended, I drove home through Blithedale Canyon, the air smelling of honeysuckles and eucalyptus, and sat down to Lupita's blackened sea bass with grilled polenta and baby bok choy, all of it tasting faintly of dog shit. Later in the week, when the nightmares tapered off, I almost missed them. Panic, fear, loneliness, despair—that I could handle. What worried me was what came next: month after month of sameness, getting up every morning, going to work, hitting my meetings, finding a sponsor, checking in with my P.O., all the parts of that daily, boring struggle to be an ordinary human being.

So in the employee bathroom at Howie's I fumbled with my shoelaces, racing to get dressed before Rajiv finished his meal break. This moment, when I would get to tell Rajiv what he could do with his Howieburgers and his blue sheets, was a small sobriety present I was giving myself. All week I had been like a kid tossing pennies in a piggy bank. Every time I stopped myself from checking the back of my closet to see if I'd missed one of those airplane bottles, every time I stood up at an AA meeting and said my name and new sobriety date, I heard it, *tink!* another coin landing in the piggy bank. All week that piggy bank got heavier, and every time I thought I couldn't take another of my mother's proud, twinkly grins, I shook my piggy bank, thinking about the moment on Friday afternoon when I could walk into Rajiv's office and watch all those pennies spill out onto the floor.

Rajiv was at his desk reading a thin foreign-language newspaper, finishing an early dinner. Rajiv's staff meals were a running joke at Howie's. He was a strict vegetarian, which meant even the fries and onion rings, which we cooked in beef tallow, were off-limits. When he first arrived, we had been running a promotion on something called a Howie's Cobb Salad, and for weeks in the break room we all did impressions of Rajiv Srinivasan picking Baco-bits from his Cobb Salad one by one like nits. But after a few weeks we'd stopped serving Cobb Salads and now he was back to his soy burgers, which he cooked himself on a special corner of the grill and ate without bread or condiments, using a plastic knife and fork.

"Yes, come in," he said, looking up from his newspaper.

When he saw it was me, he slipped his knife and fork under his newspaper. Seeing that, and knowing he must have heard me and half the day crew cracking wise over him sawing away at the soy patties like they were mini veal cutlets, knocked some of the wind out of my sails. But not enough to stop me from dumping my uniform on his desk and announcing, "I'm quitting."

Rajiv dabbed at his mouth with a paper napkin, eyeing the rumpled uniform. "So I see," he said. "Effective when?"

"Effective now. This is my last day. I start a new job on Monday."

I had expected him to bawl me out for waiting until Friday to tell him, for giving him so little time to find someone to take my shifts. I had expected him to at least look disappointed. Instead, he dropped the crumpled napkin onto his plate and offered up a limp hand for me to shake.

"Congratulations," he said. "I wish you the best of luck."

I shook his hand, of course. What else was I going to do? And after I answered a few basic questions about my new job and where I wanted my last paycheck sent, I thanked him, of all things, for being a fair boss. Then that was it. He went back to his soy patty and his foreign newspaper, leaving me to wander out onto the line. I went around in my street clothes saying my goodbyes, but the dinner rush was starting and no one had time to talk. I'd told Antwoine and LaShonda and few of the others that I was leaving, and somehow I'd gotten it into my head they might throw me a send-off party in the break room after I punched out. This was pure dreamland. When I got to the break room, it was empty, the plastic-topped tables covered with abandoned staff sodas, the tile floor littered with crushed Howie fries.

Outside, it was overcast and cool, the fog pouring in over the ridgelines, but by the time I made it to my car, my T-shirt was soaked in sweat. I was having trouble seeing, too. The edges of my vision had gone black, like I was hurtling down a dark tunnel into a gleaming void. I knew what this meant. I knew, too, that the thing to do was wait it out—sit in my car taking deep breaths, offer up a prayer to my Higher Power, and get my sorry ass to the nearest meeting. But when I got in my car I did what I'd known all along I was going to do: slapped the keys in the ignition and roared out onto the Frontage Road, Springsteen at full bawl.

I swerved in and out of traffic, running red lights, honking at the slowpokes, screaming at all the suburban fuckheads who'd never fucking learned how to drive a fucking automobile. I tried to focus on Suze, on seeing her again. Earlier in the week we'd talked about catching a movie. That was all it was, though. Talk. She'd blown me off once already that week to show a house, and I knew she had to keep her Friday nights open in case a client called. Still, as I turned onto Miller Avenue, muscling my way into the oncoming traffic, I tried to paint a picture of her in my mind, how she might style her hair, whether she'd go with the jeans-and-scoop-neck tee look, or bump it up a notch, put on heels and a dress to signal that we were officially on a date.

But I kept circling back to that break room full of dirty soda cups, me standing there like an asshole thinking somebody might be sad to see me go. Halfway down Miller, I brought my fists down hard against the steering wheel. The pain felt so good, so real, that I did it again. And again. And again. I had the presence of mind to pull over to the median strip, but I couldn't stop throwing my fists at the steering wheel, the dashboard, the car window, my own head, anything within reach. There was a weird Zen to these moments. I was screaming, punching myself, thrashing my arms and legs around, but for once I was wholly and purely in the Now. I yanked open the glove compartment, hoping to find a stray skinny under the owner's manual. No dice. The glove compartment wouldn't close, so I kicked it, to teach it a lesson. "Don't you fuck with me!" I shouted. "Don't you fucking fuck with me!" I kept kicking it, screaming and screaming, until the vinyl finally buckled, exposing the yellowing Styrofoam underneath.

I searched the car, ducking my head under the seats, opening ashtrays, digging my fingers into the crevices between the seat cushions. It was madness, all of it. I knew I'd emptied the car of skinnies the day I cleaned out my closet, but I still wriggled between the front seats to search under the piles of old newspapers and CD cases on the back seat. I found a few bucks in change, a torn wetsuit bootie, a used condom wrapper, and between the seats, a faded brass-and-feather earring that, for one jarring instant, called to mind a blonde marine-sciences major named Connie who used to sit for hours on Isla Vista Beach in a skimpy red bikini watching me surf. But no skinnies. Desperate, I threw open the driver's side door, thinking maybe I'd hidden a bottle in the trunk and forgotten about it. I hadn't, I knew that, but I had to look. I was flying around the back end of the Honda, doing about ninety, when I saw a neon sign across Miller Avenue:

## VILLAGE LIQUORS
### Beer * Wine * Spirits

I stared at the sign, too stunned even to laugh. Then I ran. If a car had been coming down Miller Avenue I would've been roadkill, but I got to the other side in one piece and ran another twenty yards along the sidewalk before I slowed my pace in the parking lot, trying to appear sane, under control, just a guy stopping off after work to grab a six-pack.

Every town in North America of any size has a Village Liquors: a single, windowless room stocked with bottles, large and small, amber and clear, of every possible brand and price point. There was some wine, too, mostly of the screw-top jug variety, and a row of brightly lit coolers of beer, half of it imported and expensive, half domestic and cheap. But like most people who did their shopping at Village Liquors, I had no time for beer or wine, and I beelined it for the vodka, which the owners,

knowing the sticky fingers of their customer base, had placed
directly across from the checkout stand.

Just seeing that shelf of gleaming bottles chilled me out. I
was stone broke as usual, down to the loose change I'd found
in my car, but I still had my mother's American Express card. I
was weighing the time it would take me to find an ATM against
the reign of terror that would come crashing down on my head
if my mother saw an entry from Village Liquors on her AmEx
bill, when a toilet flushed in the back room and a hefty guy with
bug eyes and a frog face stepped out from behind a small blue
door.

"Hey," he said, nodding to me.

"Hey," I said.

The store was empty when I came in, which had given me a
sense of privacy, as if this dimly lit room full of bottles wasn't
just a dream come true, but an actual dream, like the ones I'd
been having about crackhead Nadine. By walking in and saying hello, this guy had pierced the dream, made it real. And he
wasn't just any guy. I knew him. He was a whale-bellied, alco-
hol-ravaged version of a guy named Terry Mathis who, twenty
years ago, had spent his afternoons hitting on my mother at the
Last Ditch. Back then Terry had been a journeyman carpenter and small-time coke dealer, famous at the Ditch for going
around with a wad of bills in the front pocket of his jeans like
some scrawny, half-hippie gangster, peeling off fives and tens
to buy drinks for my mother, and if she let him, burgers and
sodas for me.

I peeked over my shoulder at the checkout stand. Terry
Mathis, all right. It had been a while since anybody could have
called him scrawny and what had been once his best feature, his
head of Jesus-blond hair that reached halfway down his back,
had thinned to a wispy friar's ruff, white as an ashed cigarette.
But I would've known that frog face anywhere. His head was
rounder and redder than it used to be, his cheeks starred with
broken blood vessels, but his eyes still bulged from their sockets and his nose and mouth still seemed out of proportion to

the rest of his face, as if they'd been made with a larger, happier man in mind.

"Help you with something?" he asked, setting aside his newspaper.

If you've ever worked in a liquor store, you've seen a million guys like me, sick and shaky from lack of sleep, eyeballing the shelves of liquor like a cat at a goldfish bowl. I stepped away from the wall of bottles, quickly, guiltily, like it was on fire and maybe I'd set it.

"Just looking," I said.

Terry nodded, considering this. "You like Smirnoff?"

"Sorry?"

"Smirnoff, the vodka. They've got a promotion going. You buy two liters of their premium product and they throw in a couple twelve-ounce cans of Smirnoff Ice."

"That's that orange-malted stuff, right?" I said. "Like beer only it's vodka."

He shrugged, as if to say: *What do you want, man? They're giving the shit away.*

A minute ago I'd have drunk orange-flavored antifreeze if I thought it would get me off, but now, looking at frog-faced Terry Mathis, I felt the deep sadness of the room: the lack of natural light, the laugh track on the black-and-white TV behind the checkout stand, the racks of chewing gum and candy that for many of their regulars would make up the bulk of the solid food they ate in a day. Throw in some windows and a bigger beer cooler, maybe a faded poster of a girl in a bikini straddling a sweating beer bottle, and you'd have Campus Liquors. How many hours—how many *years*—had I stood right where Terry was now, rereading day-old horoscopes and waiting for *Jeopardy!* to come on?

"You know, I'm a little low on funds," I said. "Maybe I'll just get some gum."

When I got home, as if in reward for a job well done, there was a message from Suze on the machine saying her last appointment of the day had bailed and she was up for seeing a movie if I could swing by her place on Shelter Ridge around seven.

When I was a kid, Shelter Ridge was where cops and school-teachers lived and where single moms ended up when the alimony checks stopped. "The Projects for white people," we called it. I hadn't been up there in years, probably not since the last time I dropped Suze off after school, and as I drove up the hill to where she lived now, a few blocks over from her mom's old condo, I couldn't get over how sunny and gorgeous it all was. This was the Projects? The units were freshly painted, with plenty of trees and open space between them, and the long row of condos that crested the ridge looked out over the Bay, past Sausalito and Alcatraz to downtown San Francisco, the tops of the skyscrapers hovering Oz-like above the curling fog.

But I was older now and I saw in a way I never had before what set Shelter Ridge apart from the rest of Mill Valley. Coming in from East Blithedale, I passed Longfellow Road and Millay Place before turning onto Kipling Drive. From there, I cut across Chaucer Court and Dickens Court to Thoreau Circle, where Suze lived. Maybe this wows 'em in Modesto or in the commuter suburbs of North Marin, but not in Mill Valley—not the part my mother lived in, anyway. In Blithedale Canyon, you could leave a Barbara Kingsolver novel on the coffee table or put on the Kronos Quartet for your dinner guests, but you didn't name your *streets* after them. And if you drove a jet-black Mini Cooper, you didn't show it off, all glossy and finely tuned, in your driveway. No, you bitched about the funky British transmission and left your sweaty tennis things in a pile on the back seat. This was the trick to being rich, Mill Valley–style, the trick I watched my mother learn and relearn every day: you had to have everything—the right house, the right clothes, the right politics, the right friends—and then you had to pretend you didn't give a shit about any of it, that truth be told you hadn't noticed you had all this money.

That was what Shelter Ridge was for: to do the noticing. And the envying. On Shelter Ridge, the units had been built at the same time, from the same plans, and the residents were falling all over themselves to make up for it, keeping their gardens just a little too neat, washing their cars a little too often, displaying their flatscreen TVs a little too prominently in their front windows. If I hadn't been raised the way I had, as a poor kid in a rich town, I might not have picked up that special odor of desperation the merely comfortable emit in the presence of the truly wealthy. But I had been raised that way, and as I pulled up in front of Suze's condo and saw her Volvo in the driveway with its "Free Tibet" sticker on the bumper, it hit me for the first time how shaky her foothold was in our hometown. The condo, the car, the suit she'd been wearing that first day at Howie's, all of it was designed to make Suze look like the kind of person who belonged in Mill Valley, which, of course, marked her as exactly the kind of person who *didn't* belong.

I parked a few houses down from Suze's condo and stared up through the gathering dusk at her bedroom window. I had showered and shaved and done what I could to clean up after the carnage of my crazed search for skinnies, but there was no good way to hide the fresh gash in the glove compartment. I'd covered it with masking tape, and if you'd never been in my car before, you couldn't have known the damage had been done that day. But *I* knew, and every time I looked at it, I thought again how demented I must have looked as I ripped apart my car on the median strip of Miller Avenue. This thought led to the next one, the one that had been buzzing, mosquito-like, around my brain ever since I caught Suze checking me out at La Cocina Pequeña, that I had no business being here, that I had no business being out with a woman at all.

For most of the years since I'd dropped out of college, my only contact with women had been drunken hookups that started around a keg in Isla Vista, and more recently, professionals. The first girl I ever paid was Mexican. She had sat down next to me in a bar on Milpas Street: short and stocky, not yet twenty, her wide, round Mayan face pitted with acne scars. After I bought her a drink and tried to chat her up in my half-assed

high school Spanish, she asked if I wanted to go *afuera*. I was
trashed, alone in a part of town I didn't know, but I said, Sure,
what the hell, I'll go *afuera*. I figured there was a patio back
there, maybe a quiet spot we could smoke a blunt, but it was
only a dirt parking lot surrounded by chain-link fencing. She
didn't say a word, just led the way between two parked cars,
where she knelt in the dirt, her eyes lowered, weirdly penitent.
"*Cincuenta dólares*," she said to the tops of my shoes. All around
us, people were getting in and out of cars, talking and laughing,
not even bothering to look away. A skinny Mexican kid in a
blaring yellow suit had been watching us from the back door
of the bar, and drunk as I was, I knew that no matter what
happened next, I was going to pay that guy fifty bucks. "Okay,"
I said. "Fifty's good."

I never went to that bar again, and for years afterward I went
to other ones like it on Milpas Street and around the harbor so
rarely I could tell myself I wasn't doing it at all. Then, one night
in a sports bar on Hollister Avenue, on the other side of town,
I met a guy who said he was an executive with a construction
firm out of Seattle, in town to bid on a contract at the airport.
We were watching the Dodgers game, buying each other beers
back and forth, getting pleasantly smashed, when out of the
blue he asked where a guy like him could find a decent piece of
ass in Santa Barbara. After I outlined his options, which weren't
all that many, he pulled a business card from his pocket. "Next
time you're in L.A., man, call this number," he said. "These
chicks, they're not hookers. They're models and actresses. College girls looking for a little fun. One of these honeys, you can
take her anywhere—dinner, a show, whatever. Then you can
take her up to your room and she'll suck you like a lollipop."

Whether that guy was a satisfied customer or a paid shill
I'll never know. What I do know is that I tossed the card in
the back of a drawer and forgot about it until a few days after
Thanksgiving. Thanksgiving was, hands down, my least favorite
day of the year. Since my father left, it had been just me and
my mother and whatever tripped-out session guitarist she was

seeing at the time, but I drew the line at Stan, and since I wasn't talking to my dad, I was on my own that year. For four long days Isla Vista was a ghost town, everybody cleared out except the homeless guys and rookie cops pulling double-time holiday shifts. I spent Thanksgiving Day at the movies, and two days later, working a murderously slow Saturday at Campus Liquors, I still felt the shame-faced hush of the movie theater as a dozen of us, all guys, all of us on our own, hung around the lobby between shows. It was a bright fall day, windless and still, one of those crisp November afternoons that once upon a time would have sent me out to the beach with a board under my arm. But that was before I gave up surfing, before I dropped out of school, before everybody I knew graduated, and I became "the guy behind the counter at Campus Liquors."

What surprised me most about what I did next was how easy it was. Later on, I went to a lot of trouble to cover my tracks, shifting money between accounts and writing up elaborate fake invoices, but that first day I just wrote myself a check for $2,500 and cashed it. On the stub, I put down that I'd used the check to pay the electricity bill, which came to about eighty bucks. When the cancelled check came back, I shredded it and covered some of the shortfall by claiming an unusually large loss from shoplifting. We were still short $1,500, and even a quick glance at the books would have turned up something deeply funky in the numbers. But by then I knew Al Fierro well enough to know that so long as there was money in the till and bottles on the shelves, he would never look at the books. That was my job.

The girl who met me outside the Beverly Wilshire called herself Lexi. She was fine-boned and willowy, her skin lightly freckled, her hair dyed black and combed straight down, goth-style, to her shoulders. According to the girl who answered the phone at the escort agency, Lexi had recently moved out west and was trying to break into Hollywood. It was winter in L.A., the temperature in the low fifties, but when she stepped out of the Lincoln Town Car, she was wearing a skintight leather miniskirt and a blue satin halter top that showed off miles of freckled midriff. I was forty pounds overweight, my skin pasty from spending so much time indoors, my hair so long I sometimes wore it in a ponytail, but when Lexi saw me on the sidewalk, she gave me a flirty smirk and planted a kiss on my cheek. "Hey, you're *cute*," she said under her breath, slipping her arm into mine.

I told her I was an entertainment lawyer, and over dinner that's what we talked about, my job in the New York offices of a major record label, the local band I'd come to L.A. to sign. These were stories I'd picked up from my dad and the details were years out of date, but Lexi listened, tilting her head to one side, tucking and re-tucking a strand of black hair behind her ear. It was intoxicating, this kind of attention. She kept her phone in plain sight and made sure I saw her "driver," a squat, burly Black guy with a clean-shaven head who looked like he could rearrange my body parts without breaking a sweat. Still, I felt protective of her. I knew her name wasn't Lexi and I had a pretty good idea what kind of films she was going out for, but I could believe she hadn't been in L.A. long. Despite her clothes and the witchy hair, she seemed naïve, almost sweet. All around us in the restaurant, real couples were out on real dates, and when Lexi had heard of a band I claimed to represent, or when her eyes lit up at a joke I told, I could almost believe I was on a real date, too, that if I was interesting enough, if I could just get her to laugh like that again, she might go out with me again, for free.

*Zap-zap! Zap! Zap-zap!*

Down the length of Suze's street the white-globe streetlamps flickered on one after another like lighted dominoes. I sat up blinking, struggling to get my bearings. I had no idea how long I had been sitting there, whether it was before or after seven. Was I supposed to honk the horn for her to come down? Run upstairs and ring the doorbell?

I hustled up the gravel steps to Suze's condo, fighting back one last image of Lexi naked in my hotel room at four in the morning, her bony butt in the air, doing a line off a framed print we'd pulled down from the wall. Between the sex and the coke and dinner and the hotel, I blew three thousand dollars that night. The next day, alone in my apartment, I told myself I was done. No more Lexis, no more ripping off Al. It was time to move on, quit my job, and get the hell out of Isla Vista. Then a month later, I did it again: different girl, different restaurant, different hotel, another three grand down the drain.

"No, *you* shut up!"

I stopped a few feet from Suze's door. The shout had come from inside, and near as I could tell, the voice belonged to Suze's oldest boy, Dylan. The sliding-glass door was open halfway, and I could see into the cluttered front room, where Suze's mother, Sharon, and Suze's younger boy stood next to a long sectional sofa. At their feet sat a brown packing box, slit open at the top, with white-plastic popcorn spilling onto the floor. I heard Suze and Dylan yelling at each other in a part of the house I couldn't see, and then a few seconds later, here they came, Dylan first, a pair of spanking-new roller skates in his arms, and Suze close behind, running as fast as she could in heels and a dress.

"You come back here right now!" she shouted.

"Fuck you!" Dylan screamed.

Suze stopped, her head snapping back in shock. "*What* did you just say?"

"Fuck you! Fuck you! Fuck you!" the little boy shouted. "Go back to your stupid boyfriend, you stupid fucking bitch whore!"

Suze's mother was up now, too, screaming. Dylan dropped the skates and tore off down the hall chased by Suze, her limbs spastic with rage. The bedroom door slammed, twice, and then the house went silent except for the muffled whimpering of Suze's four-year-old curled up between his grandmother's legs, sobbing, his fat little hands covering his head.

The skates Dylan had thrown on the floor were the old-fashioned kind with leather uppers and hard-plastic wheels. From there, the living room was a story that told itself. The skates had come that day in the packing box, and before dinner Dylan had talked Suze into letting him open the box. Apparently, he hadn't liked what he saw.

"Mom, you're going to have to handle this," Suze said, coming back into the living room. "My ride's going to be—"

But Suze's mother had seen me through the sliding-glass. She pointed, and for a sickening moment, the three of us stood frozen like cardboard figures in a crime-scene diorama. Suze wore a cream-colored sheath dress and heels, a saffron-yellow pashmina wound loosely around her shoulders. It was a good look, one that spoke of forethought, of serious time given to mental additions and subtractions, which, when I thought about it, was probably what had sent her son off.

Dylan skulked back into the room, silently taking in the wreckage. It was as if by walking in on what had happened, I'd jolted them all out of some collective nightmare, and now, the fight forgotten, they were trying to look like a normal family. Even the littlest boy had quit crying and sat up, his wet red face dumb with surprise.

"I can wait in the car," I said, jabbing my thumb in the direction of the street.

"No, no, come in," Suze said. "I'm almost ready, anyway." Before I could argue, she opened the sliding-glass door for me. "Mom, you remember Trent," she said, waving through the introductions. "From high school."

"Of *course* I remember!" Sharon Randall gushed. "It's *so* good to see you again."

It was all so awkward and weird, and at the same time so familiar, that I rolled with it, let Sharon wrap me up in a fleshy, patchouli-scented hug, as if I hadn't just walked in on her daughter's seven-year-old son calling her a whore. When we were kids, Sharon Randall had been a cocktail waitress on the Sausalito waterfront, one of those ageless hippie chicks who fill their tip jars by wearing low-cut minidresses and cowboy boots. She still had a bit of the hippie about her, with her flowing batik dress and armloads of silver bangles, but she'd hardened around the edges, congealed somehow, her face bloated and splotchy, her bottle-blonde hair fried white by the sun and chopped off in an unflattering shoulder-length bob.

"What's this Suzy tells me about you working at Tam Grocery?" she asked.

I looked for Suze, but she had disappeared back into the bedroom. "Yeah, I start next week," I said. "I'm helping out with this new online shopping service they're launching."

"Ohhh, I didn't know you were a computer programmer," Sharon said.

"Actually, this job, it's mostly administrative," I said. But then, fuck me, I couldn't help it, and I added: "I'm hoping to get into the programming side of things later on."

"Good for you!" she said. "I keep telling Suzy she needs get with the computer thing. Is that what you studied in college, computer science?"

"Nah, I mostly picked it up on my own, just, like, noodling around online." Before I could shovel any more bullshit onto that steaming pile, I turned to Dylan who was on the floor fitting the skates back into the packing box. "Hey, I had skates like that when I was a kid," I said.

This at least was sort of true. My grandparents sold roller skates at Cushman's, and one Christmas when a pair my size came in with mismatched wheels, I found them in a box under the tree. I never wore them, but I *had* owned them for a while.

"They just came today," Suze said, coming in from the bedroom. "Turns out I was supposed to get him a pair of those new heely-wheel thingies."

"Wheelies?" I said.

"See, even *he's* heard of them," Dylan said.

I watched the looks fly, Dylan rubbing it in, Suze warning him not to even *think* about going there again, and I saw a way, maybe, to make things right.

"No, man, you don't want Wheelies," I told Dylan. "They've only been out a couple years and they're still dinking around with the engineering."

"The engineering?" he said.

"Yeah, the grind plate. They're redoing it. To give it, you know, more torque."

"What's a grind plate?"

"Sweetie, Trent doesn't have time to explain it all to you right now," Suze said.

"What's a grind plate?" the kid said again.

Suze had her coat in her hand, ready to shove me bodily out the door, but I was on a roll. In the break room at Howie's, I had heard kids on the kitchen crew complain about the grind plates on their Wheelies and how you never could get enough torque out of them.

"It's hard to explain without having one to show you," I said. "But they're on the heel of the shoe so the wheel doesn't grind through to your foot."

"And they don't work right?" he asked.

"Yeah, it's been a total nightmare for the company," I said. "So for now you're better off with just the regular skate."

Dylan nodded solemnly. This is why people lie. It makes everybody feel better. I had no idea whether Wheely needed to re-engineer its grind plates to give them more torque, or even what torque was, really, but as Suze made a final pass around the room kissing the boys goodnight, Dylan was eyeing his skates like it was worth trying them on, just for a test run.

Suze and I didn't say a word, not even hello, until we were in my car, cruising along Kipling Drive toward the freeway. I was still riding the high of the Wheelies and the faulty grind plate. How many times had I watched my dad pull a stunt like that, walk into a scene of chaos and pull a story out of his ass that left everybody smiling? That was why his clients loved him. He was a drug addict and a prick, but when he was on his game it was hard to be unhappy around the guy.

"You must think I'm a shitty mom," Suze said. "Screaming at my kid like that."

I turned, seeing her, really, for the first time. In high school, Suze had always been half a tick away from lights-out gorgeous. She had the body and the look, her hair teased up in one of those big eighties waves, but there was something off about her face, a sadness in the way her features lined up that never went away even when she smiled. Her face had sharpened since then, bringing out her pale blue eyes and her full, sensuous mouth. Tonight, though, the sadness was back.

"Come on, no," I said. "I wasn't thinking that."

"Just so you know, I don't usually."

I eased into traffic, trying not to think what I was thinking, which was how much Suze and Dylan reminded me of Mom and me back in the day.

"Those Wheely things," she said. "I probably should've heard of them, huh?"

"Not really. They're still pretty new."

"You seemed to know a hell of a lot about them."

"Yeah well, I spent the summer working at a burger joint with a bunch of teenagers," I said. "I don't get it, though. Why can't you just take back the skates and buy him a pair of Wheelies?"

"I could. Except, stupid me, I bought them online, which means I pay full freight on returns. This isn't exactly the flushest time for me, so either I pay my phone bill or buy my kid a pair of Wheelies. And for this I get fifteen minutes of Linda Blair." She exhaled slowly. "Anyway, thank you. For defusing things. That was a pretty hairy situation to have to walk into."

I wanted to say *Hey, no big*. Or *No sweat, I've been there*. But I *had* been there when I was a kid, and I could see no upside in reminding Suze how that had turned out.

"Do you even know what a grind plate is?" she asked.

"I'm pretty sure there *is* one. The kids at Howie's, they were always bitching about them, so if they fix anything, that'd have to be at the top of the list."

She cracked a smile, the first one I'd seen out of her all night. "I hope you're right," she said. "Because that kid's gonna tell all his buddies at day camp about those lame grind plates and how you can never get enough torque out of them."

In the distance, across the darkening Bay, I saw the lights of

San Quentin, a smear of halogen yellow at the western end of the Richmond–San Rafael Bridge. For once it couldn't touch me. The memory of Lexi, her bare ass in the air, hoovering one last rail of coke off the hotel painting—that was gone, too.

"He's never talked to me like that before," Suze said. "Ever."

"He's only seven, right? He probably doesn't even know what the word means."

"He's almost eight. He knows what the word means."

That shut me up. Of course he knew what the word meant. I had been him once. Maybe I wasn't seven, and maybe I hadn't called my mom a whore, but I had been the kid who torched his mom when she tried to buy him off with a cool toy because she was seeing a new, sketchy-seeming guy. Suze turned away, watching the passing traffic, but I could see her face in the passenger window, and I didn't know who to feel more sorry for, her or her pissed-off kid.

I couldn't tell you what movie we saw that night if you paid me. Whatever it was, I didn't see much of it. Most of the time I was watching Suze and not the screen. At first, she seemed to be following the plot, looking over at me when anyone cracked a joke, rolling her eyes if it wasn't funny. But twenty minutes in, she slumped in her seat, her legs wrapped in a complicated knot, chewing the red-painted nail of her pinkie finger until it bled, and after that, I don't think she saw much of the movie, either.

In the car, on the long drive through the North Marin suburbs, I'd done my best to convince her that this would all blow over by morning, but the more she talked about how the fight started, how calm Dylan had been until he saw her in that clingy white dress, the more I thought of Mom and me. Every guy she brought home had to get past me. And I took no prisoners, man. If the guy had drugs, I stole them. If he spoke with a lisp or an accent, I imitated it, mercilessly, every chance I got. If he had kids, I found out who the other kid was and I told him. Mom not only put up with this, she laughed at my impressions.

If a guy she was dating came around pissed at me for screwing up his marriage, she shrugged and told him he should have thought of that before he went and screwed up his marriage. She took my side every time, which, looking back on it, was the whole point. I hated her for letting my father leave, but more than that I needed to know I still came first. And I did, year after year, boyfriend after boyfriend. Until Stan. My mother knew I hated his guts and she married him anyway, and now, when she'd had to choose between him and me, she'd chosen him.

When the movie let out, instead of going straight home, Suze and I stopped off for dessert at an Applebee's in the mall. I tried to keep it light, replaying scenes from the movie, but my heart wasn't in it, and neither was Suze's. She was talking to me, looking at me, but in her mind she was back in her living room hearing her kid call her a whore.

"Hey, I have an idea," she said, settling back into the red-vinyl booth. "How about we talk about *you* for a change? What'd you do today?"

I laughed. Somewhere between the fight over Dylan's skates and the giant slab of chocolate-mousse cake we were sharing I'd forgotten all about Rajiv Srinivasan and my meltdown in the median strip of Miller Avenue. "Okay," I said. "I quit my job today."

"You *what?*"

So I told her the story. I'd already told her about my interview with Mr. Papadakis at Tam Grocery, tiptoeing around Lee Radko and his white hankie full of Double Black Orchid, and now in the half-empty mall restaurant, I told her the rest: Rajiv and his veggie burger, my rumpled Howie's uniform, our awkward farewell handshake, the break room littered with soda cups. Except that now it came out funny. I didn't lie, exactly, but I didn't have to. Take out crackhead Nadine and the night sweats and my head-banging fit on the median strip of Miller Avenue, and it *was* kind of funny.

When I finished, Suze called the waiter over to order another O'Doul's for me and a second glass of merlot for her so we could toast my new job. The joke was getting stale by then, but even that was nice. We already had a good story about how we met and now we had an in-joke. All we needed was a favorite song and we could be a real couple. Just as I was thinking that, wondering if I could say it out loud, wrap it up in a joke somehow, Suze drifted off again. One minute she was nodding along with what I was saying, and the next she was gone, staring into the middle distance like something was written there and she was trying to read it.

"You've barely touched your wine," I said, nodding to her glass.

"I know." She reached for the glass, then made a face and pushed it away. "Maybe we should just go. This can't be much fun for you."

"You've got a lot on your plate, that's all."

"They miss their dad," she said. "That's what this is all about. I mean, of course they miss him. He's their dad. But till tonight I guess I didn't—have I told you about Jakey's crying fits?"

I shook my head. Until that moment I don't think I had even known his name.

"Well, he has them," she said. "Practically every time I drop him off at day care. Last week he bit a kid. Not hard. Not like it drew blood or anything, but the day-care people freaked. The thing is, he's a great kid. They both are. But they miss their dad. They miss L.A. and their friends and our old house and the beach and everything. They'd never put it that way, they're too young, but I can see it. I'm not blind."

"What about you?"

"Do *I* miss him?" She snorted. "The guy's a sleaze. Worse than a sleaze. He walked out on his kids."

She stopped, her gaze dancing away again. In that moment I saw how very little I knew about people, really, how much I had missed all those years I'd spent mooning around Isla Vista. I had asked about Jimmy because I wanted to hear her say she didn't miss him, that she was moving on. But I had grown up with my mother, and I'd seen for myself how, after she had been dating other men for years, her face still lit up at the sound of my father's voice on the phone.

"You've never been married," Suze said. "Not that Jimmy and me had the world's greatest marriage, but there's something about waking up in a house you bought with your own money. Your kids are upstairs, there's food in the fridge, and I don't know, your life just makes sense. That's what I miss. Feeling like my life makes sense. Knowing my kids are happy. I mean, they *weren't* happy. That's why I left. But at least then there was something I could do about it. Now, I'm running my ass off and I don't even know why. Or what for. Or when I get to stop."

I felt a short, sharp needle-stick in my side: She was right. I had no clue what it was like to be married or own a house or have kids, and what she was saying was that I couldn't help her, that I was in over my head.

"God, let's go," she said, tossing a twenty on the table. "I'm depressing myself here."

Back in Shelter Ridge, I parked across from her condo a few feet from where I'd stopped earlier that night. The lights were out in the bedrooms, but in the living room a TV flickered against the half-drawn curtains.

"Is that your mom?" I said. "Waiting up for you."

Suze smiled. "Used to be the other way around, right?"

On the stereo, very low, Springsteen was singing about how someone had taken a knife, edgy and dull, and carved a six-inch valley through the middle of his skull. I had been listening to that song all week, over and over, wondering how a complete stranger could have crawled inside my head and described my darkest, most private dreams. But now, sitting outside Suze's condo, it sounded like a communication from another planet, one with no children, no tantrums over old-school roller skates, no panicked phone calls from day-care workers. Looking over at Suze, her jaw set, her mind a million miles off, I felt again the distance between us. We were the same age and we had grown up together, but since then our lives had taken such different paths. I could see hers, the strain of it, in her face. She looked exhausted, and for the first time, a little old.

"I'm sorry to dump all this on you," she said. "I never thought I'd become that person, you know, the one who goes on and on about what a dickhead her ex is."

"It helps that your ex is kind of a dickhead," I said.

She laughed, as I knew she would, and I reached for her hand, interlacing her long fingers with my thicker, more calloused ones. It had been so long since I'd had to be tender with anyone. I was worried I'd forgotten how, that I would take things too quickly or too slowly, or put my hand in the wrong place, or worse, not have the guts to touch her at all. But in all that time I hadn't considered Suze, that she would be there with me. She took my hand in hers, pulling it close, and together we listened to Bruce sing about what it's like to be on fire.

"I should go," she said when the song ended.

I wanted to kiss her then, if only to show her that I could, that someday I was going to want more than just holding hands in a car, but some finely tuned inner antenna I didn't even know I had told me, no, it was too early for that. I squeezed her hand once, gently, and let go.

"I'll watch you to the door," I said.

She laughed, surprised. "You don't have to do that. Mom's waiting up for me."

"I know. I'll watch you to the door."

So I did, watched her cross the moonlit street and, with a quick finger wave, start up the gravel stairs. When the light came on in the living room, I turned the key in the ignition and eased back down the hill.

**W**olfer," Gianni said, poking his head in the office. "You got a minute to grab some lunch?"

I didn't, actually. It was quarter past eleven, and as I'd told Gianni when I came in that morning, I was meeting Suze at noon to look at an apartment. But Gianni Papadakis was the boss's son and this was the first day of my second week at Tam Grocery, so I nodded and said, "I was just thinking I could go for a roast beef sandwich right about now."

"Go on, help yourself in the deli," he said. "We'll meet back here in ten. Then we can talk—you know, catch up a little."

Downstairs in the deli I cleared some space on the white-plastic chopping board and started building my sandwich, running a sliced Kaiser roll through the toasting machine and picking out slabs of extra-rare London broil. The deli occupied its own separate wing of the store, housed in a former stationary shop the Papadakises had bought out in the seventies. A little before noon, the first office workers would start trickling in, and for the next hour and a half the place would be jammed, customers lined up four-deep jostling for position and shouting out sandwich orders, but for now all was sleepy and still. Behind me, Melody Papadakis was running a foot-long stick of cheese through the slicer, while the deli manager, a thirtyish bespectacled Kenyan named Henry Sironga, was on the phone going over an order of Snapple juices, his Afro-British accent so soft and musical it sounded like he was singing a lullaby about mangos and tea.

I had been called in to work the lunch rush in the deli a couple times during my first week at the store, but only as a "runner"—a sort of utility infielder of the deli section whose job it was to rush trays of dolmades out from the cold room or slice cold cuts and cheeses when supplies ran low up front. Most of that first week, though, Gianni had kept me upstairs straight through lunch, walking me through the Papadakises' maddeningly complex ordering system and getting me up to speed on the new catering operation. On my first day, after introducing me to his uncle Stavros, who ran the meat department, and his sister Andi, who oversaw the stock rooms, Gianni had taken me to see the building they'd leased, which turned out to be the old Post Office building on East Blithedale. It had been built in the thirties in the Spanish Mission Revival style, its granite front studded with four vaulted windows set off by columns and the words MILL VALLEY, CALIFORNIA carved in bold block letters over the entrance. But it had been empty since the postal service moved its main branch to a strip mall closer to the highway, and for now it was a hollow shell, its interior stripped to the bare brick, the concrete floors littered with broken glass and scraps of pink insulation foam.

But from the way Gianni talked as he led me through the building you'd have thought all they had to do was turn on the lights and move in. The business office, where we would handle phone orders and oversee deliveries, would take up most of the second floor, while the rear half of the ground floor, where they used to sort the mail, would house a storage area and an expanded deli kitchen, twice the size of the one in the old store. "This'll be the public area," he said, leading me into the high-ceilinged lobby. "There'll be a deli counter along the wall, like the one we have now, only bigger. We'll put in some tables by the window so people can have a cup of coffee while they're waiting, maybe even eat dinner here if they want. Can you see it? We'll find some old black-and-white photos for the walls, maybe commission an original mural—a view of Mt. Tam, a downtown street scene, something like that."

I told him, sure, I could totally see it. But I couldn't, not really. The building was huge, eight high-ceilinged, echoey rooms full of intricate period detail. I could picture it as a bank, maybe, or a snooty restaurant with white tablecloths and tall food. But a home-catering company? I kept my mouth shut, though. It wasn't just that the Papadakises were signing my paychecks. Something in Gianni's enthusiasm, his bottomless appetite for labor, made me think that if anyone could make the place work, it was probably him. He handled the store's finances and ordering, a job that had once required two employees, and now, as if that wasn't enough, he was his own general contractor for the renovations on the new building. That sounded insane to me until I saw how hard the guy worked. He was in the office every morning when I came in, and he was still there when I left at night, working the phones, planning menus, poring over spreadsheets. He never let up. There was always one more sub-contractor to call, one more web consultant to meet, one more set of architect's drawings to read. One morning that first week, he found a listing on eBay for a handmade glass display case from a deli in Little Italy in New York. I thought he was going to kiss me right there in the office. He printed out the photos and spent the morning bouncing around the stock room showing them to anyone who would look.

Still, in all the time we spent cooped up together in that stuffy second-floor office, Gianni had never asked me a personal question. He wasn't rude, exactly. He just watched me, the way the deputies used to watch us in lockup, not with any special interest or zeal, just waiting, knowing sooner or later we would reveal ourselves for the fuckups we really were. So, as I sliced my roast beef sandwich in half and wrapped it in butcher paper, I knew that if Gianni wanted to "catch up," it wasn't out of any great desire to shoot the shit with the help. This was a business lunch, and unless I was very mistaken, the business at hand was me.

Gianni sat hunched over a square of spanakopita and an Odwalla strawberry-banana smoothie, his forearm curled, paw-like, around his lunch as he paged through *California Grocer*. He took half a dozen grocery-industry magazines and read them whenever he had a minute to spare, poring over the articles with an intensity other guys reserve for car mags and porn. As I pulled up a chair, I caught a glimpse of the headline on the article he was reading:

# DON'T GET FREEZER BURNED!

*5 Easy Steps to Cutting Energy Use in Frozen Food Cases*

"A little light reading?" I said, unwrapping my sandwich.

"No, you know, this is interesting," Gianni said, stabbing a thick finger at the page. "Do you have any idea how much one blown coolant pipe gasket can cost you in extra fuel bills?"

"No, how much?" I said, taking a bite of my sandwich.

"Nine bucks a month," he said. "Now, maybe that doesn't sound like much, but add it up and you could buy yourself a new freezer every ten years. Which is roughly how long a new freezer lasts before maintenance costs start eating into your margin. That's the whole point of the article. People get all hung up on buying up the latest floor toys when what they really need to do is keep an eye on the little stuff: plugging leaks, eliminating inefficiencies."

Under the table, I noticed, his right leg was pumping like it was running a hundred-yard dash all by itself.

"Same goes for your employees," he went on. "Read all the studies, they'll tell you the same thing. Your single greatest source of shrinkage, it isn't shoplifting, it isn't inventory errors—it's employee theft, plain and simple."

A half-chewed ball of London broil turned to sawdust in my mouth. I tried to tell myself he was free-associating, riffing on ideas from his magazine, but I'd spent a week in close quarters with the man, and he was about as subtle as a guided missile system.

"You think somebody's skimming off the top?" I asked.

He pushed away his spanakopita and sat picking at a spinach stem caught in his teeth. "You need to understand something about my dad," he said. "He's always had a thing for reclamation projects. My granddad was the same way. Ever since I was a kid, we've been taking on people—local people, mostly—who've had a little trouble one way or another."

I set down my sandwich. I'd only taken a few bites, but I wasn't going to get any more of it, not until after lunch.

"Dad can be a little clueless," he said. "He sort of missed

the sixties, if you know what I mean. When everybody else was turning on and dropping out or whatever, he was here busting his ass, stocking shelves and sorting tomatoes. So he misses stuff."

"Like, what kinds of stuff?"

"Be honest. The other day when you were here for your interview, you weren't maybe a little under the influence? Because your eyes, they were kind of red."

"I told your dad, I was up late the night before. I have trouble sleeping. It's a condition I have."

"A condition," he said.

"I told your dad the truth, Gianni. I was in rehab before I came home, but I'm sober now. I'm an alcoholic—a recovering alcoholic."

He pulled on his smoothie, swishing the drink around in his mouth as if to cleanse his palate of the words I'd used. "This rehab facility you went to," he said, "what's it called?"

"Casa Esperanza. It's in Solvang, just north of Santa Barbara."

"How long were you there?"

"It's a sixty-day program. I was there for sixty days."

He nodded, eyes hooded, his expression almost comically intense. "How about before that?"

"Before that—I was out of work for a little while."

"Out of work," he repeated, as if we both knew *out of work* was jailhouse code for *peddling kiddie porn on the Internet.* "When we were talking last week, you made it sound like you quit your job at the liquor store. Is that the way it happened?"

"No, I didn't quit. Al fired me."

He cracked a smile, pleased we were finally getting somewhere. "What exactly was the bone of contention between you two, if you don't mind me asking?"

"I guess you'd have to ask Al."

"See now, I thought of that," he said. "But when I called Information down there, they said the number for Campus Liquors is out of service. I tried Al Fierro, too. Nothing."

"That's because the store shut down last year," I said.

"That's what I figured. The part I can't quite work out is how come when we were talking last week you never thought to mention that fact."

People think lying is about dreaming up ever more creative bullshit things to say, but it's not. To be a good liar, to serve up bullshit so it tastes like truth, you have to see the world through the eyes of the person you're lying to, know what he values and what he doesn't, so you know what sort of bullshit he's most likely to eat. It is my particular defect of character that for most of my adult life I'd only had this insight into people when I was lying to them.

"You have to understand, that store was all he had," I said. "Al had just lost his wife. He has a daughter in Florida, but they don't get along. I *was* his family, like a son almost. He depended on me and I let him down. If I had been in better shape, if I'd just been paying more attention, Al would still have that store. He wouldn't have lost his house and all the rest of it."

"He lost his *house?*" Gianni said.

"He lost everything. His house, his car, his savings—everything. Last I heard he was in some kind of assisted-living facility. Like, one of those old folks' homes for people on welfare."

"And you had nothing to do with that?"

"No, I had everything to do with that. That's what I'm saying. Al and his wife, they took me in when I had nothing, and then when they needed me, I checked out."

Give or take a few Class 1 felonies and a four-month stretch in county jail, everything I was saying was true. After his wife Verna died, Al sank into a year-long funk, spending whole days in the stock room mainlining Dewar's and spinning old Frank Sinatra records. I'd put more than my share of nails in the coffin of Campus Liquors, but during those first months after Verna's death, I was the one who kept the doors open while Al was out back warbling along with "Summer Wind." The last time I saw him, in court on the day I was sentenced, Al was in a wheelchair, breathing through a tube because of his emphysema, but the thing that killed me was that as I was being led away, I looked back at the visitor's gallery and saw him sobbing, the tears streaming down his cheeks. I had ruined him, bled him for every penny he had, but without me he was alone in the world.

"He fired me right before they shut down the store for good," I said. "I was pretty hacked off at the time, but now I wish I could make it up to him. That's why this job matters to me so much. I want to prove to myself I'm not like that—you know, that I can do better."

Gianni sat watching me the way you'd watch a mouse caught in a trap, as if at any minute he might put me out of my misery with a hammer. If I'd had a hammer just then, I might have done the job myself.

"This was when, exactly?" he asked.

"Almost a year ago. In September."

"And after that, you went into rehab?"

"Well, like I say, it took me a little while to get desperate enough. There were a few months there when I wasn't doing much but sitting around feeling sorry for myself."

Criminal records weren't online then the way they are now, but we both knew he could check this with a few phone calls. I watched him try to decide whether it was worth his time to pick up the phone.

"I'll be honest," he said. "I figured you'd be gone in a few days, just as soon as you figured out you'd have to do some real work. But you surprised me. You're doing a decent job here. Dad and I were just talking about that."

"Oh," I said, surprised. "Thank you."

He shrugged. "It's obvious you understand bookkeeping and inventory, which is more than we had a right to expect given what we're paying. And you're not afraid of hard work, which goes a long way with me. But just so you don't think I'm an idiot, I know you're bullshitting me about the first day you were here." He held up a meaty hand, stopping me. "Maybe you were high, maybe you were just hungover. Whatever. If you ever come in looking red-eyed and raggy like that again, we're done. No questions, no appeals. Got it?"

I nodded. Of course I nodded. If I was him, I would have fired my ass ten minutes ago.

"You told my dad you wanted a chance," he said. "Well, you're gonna get that chance. But no more bullshit, okay? No more 'conditions.' Clock in on time, do your job, and don't make me regret not running you out of here today. You're doing well here, Wolfer. Don't fuck this up."

When I pulled into the parking lot at the Valley Knolls Apartments fifteen minutes later, Suze was in the driver's seat of her Volvo, nodding into her flip phone. She was back in corporate mode in a white linen suit and pearls, a pair of oversized sunglasses propped Jackie O.–style on top of her head. No hugs this time, no chitchat. As soon as she set down the phone, Suze pulled those big round sunglasses down over her eyes and she was all business. "This apartment isn't on the market yet," she said as she fast-walked me to the manager's office. "They're doing me a favor by letting me see it first. I hope you brought your checkbook."

"In the car," I said, the lie escaping as easy as breathing.

"Good," she said. "If you want this place you'll have to sign the lease today."

It was weird letting Suze be my realtor. The property manager was an older guy named Rick with the blister-red face and pregnancy gut of a man who had decided to work just hard enough to drink himself to death with name-brand liquors. With her linen suit and expensively blonde hair, Suze was clearly a cut above the general run of realtors who turned up at the Valley Knolls Apartments, and it was interesting how she played this. We never talked about the apartment or the rental application Rick handed us when we walked in. Instead, while Rick rounded up extra chairs and poured us sodas from a sad little bar fridge behind his desk, she flirted with him in a gentle, almost daughterly way, asking about a picture on the wall that showed him looking tan and healthy and about five hundred years younger on the deck of one of the old Sausalito ferries. By the time we had finished our sodas Rick had forgotten all about the rental application and was escorting us across the parking lot to the apartment, wrapping up a long tale of his thirty years working on the ferries before he took early retirement.

The apartment was at the very end of the row of buildings, next to the pre-fab shed where the residents dropped off their trash. From the look of it, the unit had until very recently been the laundry room for the complex. They'd put in windows and fresh linoleum, but it was still just a long, narrow room, with a tiny kitchenette at one end and an even tinier bathroom at the other. The side nearest to the door had sunk an inch or two, as if the soil had settled there and taken the floor with it. But who was I kidding? Before chez Starling, my two most recent places of residence had been a locked rehab facility in Solvang and the Santa Barbara County Jail. The area around the Valley Knolls Apartments wasn't much, a sprawl of discount furniture shops and apartment complexes along the highway, but a few blocks up the hill the houses stopped and for five miles there was nothing but open park land, one long rolling hillside of sun-yellowed grass dotted with eucalyptus and manzanita. Which is why it didn't surprise me when Rick said they wanted a thousand a month, plus utilities.

"Trent, it's a steal," Suze hissed when Rick stepped outside to let us talk. "If this was on the Mill Valley side of the highway, it'd be another three hundred, easy."

"No doubt," I said, ducking into the bathroom, which was roughly the size of a utility closet. When I looked closer, I realized it *was* a utility closet, hastily kitted out with a molded-plastic shower stall and a doll-sized sink and toilet.

"It's small," Suze was saying. "And it could use some help in the charm department. But if you sign today, I bet I can get them to work with you on the utilities."

"Even with a break on gas and electric, this is at the top of my price range. To be honest, it's a little ways past it."

"Okay. How much were you expecting to spend?"

"Seven hundred, seven-fifty. I could maybe do eight, but the place'd have to be amazing."

She stared. We had gone over all of this on the phone, I was sure of it, but it must have sounded so delusional she had just tuned it out.

"I'm cool with roommates," I said.

"Even with roommates you're not going to find anything under eight hundred a month in Southern Marin. You'd have to go to Petaluma for that, or maybe Sonoma, and even then you'd be pushing it."

Sonoma was an hour north by freeway. I had been there exactly twice, both times to play baseball. All I remembered were cow pastures and a guy in the back of the bus plunking out the theme song from *Deliverance* on an invisible banjo.

"I'll tell Rick we're going to keep looking," Suze said.

We crossed the parking lot back to our cars in silence. Neither of us had said anything about our night at the movies, but the memory hung over us, unspoken. I wanted to reach out and touch her, take her hand the way I'd done that night in my car, but I didn't dare, not after I'd stood in that slapped-together apartment on the wrong side of the freeway and admitted it was hundreds of dollars beyond my wildest dreams.

"I'll be fine," I said as she popped the door on the Volvo. "I'll go online, check out the listings for roommates."

"God, no. Whatever you do, don't go online," she said. "You never know what kind of whack job you're going to end up with. Let me make some calls. Sometimes things show up that aren't on the regular listings. Are you free this Saturday?"

"Suze, I'm free pretty much every Saturday."

"Oh no, wait. Sorry. Saturday's no good. I'm showing houses and then Dylie's got a game."

"Soccer?"

"Right, at Boyle Park." She stopped, eyeing me. "How'd you know that?"

"A friend of mine has kids who play. What team's Dylan on?"

"Maggliore Tires," she said. "You should hear us on the sidelines: 'Goooo, Tires!' It's a big time. You should come down, help us cheer on the squad."

She laughed, then caught herself, her eyes averted. I turned away, too, staring at the pocked asphalt at my feet, not so much embarrassed as hurt that she was.

"Nah, it's cool," I said. "Mom's got a thing this Saturday. Some party she's throwing. I told her I'd help out."

This lie, its transparent vagueness, only made things worse. Our eyes met for an instant, each of us begging the other for help, before I leaned in and kissed her, hard, on the mouth. There was no warning, no thinking involved. It was like Suze was a magnet and I'd gotten too close, and—*wham!*—we were lip-locked, our bodies mashed together, fingers groping for a handhold, until the magnet switched poles again and we flew apart, stunned and breathless.

"Oh shit," I said. "Suze, I'm sorry."

"No, *I'm* sorry," she said. "That was bad. That never should've happened."

She wheeled around, checking for witnesses, and froze when she saw Rick standing in the door to his office, hands in his pockets, a look of undiluted shock on his face.

"Great," she said. "Right in front of the apartment manager."

"Don't worry, I'll talk to him."

"The hell you will. You will not say one word to him, do you understand?"

She turned back to Rick, who had ducked back inside, shutting the door behind him. Suze scanned the parking lot again to make sure we really were alone this time.

"This didn't happen, okay?" she said.

"Totally. Never happened."

"What is it with me and guys like you, anyway? You'd think I'd have learned my lesson by now." She looked back at Rick's office one last time. "I need to go. I'm meeting a client at one."

But she hesitated, and for a split-second I thought she was

going to kiss me again. I saw it in her eyes, a flash of need, a hunger. She saw it, too, how vulnerable this left her, and with a hard yank on some inner leash she slipped in behind the wheel of her Volvo.

"Wait, can I call you?" I said. "About the apartments, I mean?"

"No, I'll call you," she said, as the engine turned over. "Give me a couple days and I'll call."

She popped the brake, and the Volvo rocketed from the curb. She tooted the horn, brightly, and sped off, once again leaving me alone in a parking lot with her scent hanging in the air.

That afternoon Gianni was meeting with suppliers in the city, so I spent the rest of the day in the deli helping Henry Sironga prep for the dinner rush. Henry was the only manager at Tam Grocery who wasn't a Papadakis either by birth or marriage, and maybe for that reason he was my favorite person to work for there. He was a year or two older than me, slight-built and bullet headed, with rows of tidy dreadlocks and a knobby goatee. Think Bob Marley if he'd given up reggae and become a tax accountant. He wore squared-off rimless glasses and you could have sliced bread with the crease of his khakis, but there was an ease about him, a deep-down instinctive gladness, that made the hours pass.

While we restocked the drinks coolers and Henry taught me how to make baked ziti, he told me about the East African restaurant he wanted to open in San Francisco one day. He planned to call the place Serengit, the Maasai name for the part of Kenya and Tanzania his family was from. To bring in the tourists, the dining room would be done up like a safari lodge, with zebras and lions mounted on the walls, but the kitchen staff would be East African and the food would be strictly authentic. "Have you ever had banana roasted in its own leaves?" he asked as we sliced balls of fresh, briny mozzarella.

I shook my head. "I had bananas flambé once, I think."

He considered this. "That's the one you cook with rum and it makes a big flame?"

"My dad ordered it for me in a restaurant. It was kind of nasty, honestly."

"Yes, yes, that's nothing like this," he said, waving away bananas flambé. "These are African bananas, plantains, and you grill them over an open fire. In Nairobi, you buy them on the street."

As we sliced mozzarella he described each element of the dish: how to pick the bananas when they were still green, what temperature to broil them at, how they could be served as a savory dish with traditional Kenyan spices or as a dessert with a drizzle of honey or chocolate. I couldn't help envying the guy a little. All those years I'd moped around Isla Vista feeling sorry for myself, and here was someone my age who had spent those same years working the angles at the U.S. consulate in Nairobi and dreaming of opening a restaurant in San Francisco. I wasn't built that way. No amount of clean-time could ever make me want anything that bad, but listening to Henry talk about his Kenyan bananas got me wondering what I would do if I ever put together more than a few weeks of white-knuckle sobriety.

But even as I was thinking that, how maybe I could go to school to learn how to help guys like me, my mind drifted back to Suze Randall and the need I saw in her eyes in the parking lot of the Valley Knolls Apartments. I tried to focus on slicing the mozzarella just so, getting the proportions of oregano and basil right for the marinara sauce, but it was so damn seductive, the high of being wanted again. I had blown tens of thousands of dollars, brought a man's business to ruin, to get a woman to look at me the way Suze had that day, and nothing, not my job, not my sobriety, not even Suze herself, was going to stop me from getting her to look at me like that again.

# 8

The next morning I set my alarm for six and went for a run along the fire road that cut across Blithedale Ridge. The morning fog hadn't burned off yet, and I was freezing in shorts and an old Oakland A's T-shirt, but I was glad for the fog because it made me feel invisible. I did some half-assed toe touches at the trailhead and broke into a loping canter. I had been worried about my left knee, which I'd dinged up in high school, but fifty yards up the hill was all it took to tell me that my trick knee was the least of my problems. My lungs were on fire, and I tasted twenty years of pot smoke rising in my throat, black and tarrish, like I'd been gargling with creosote. But I knew that if I stopped I'd never get started again, so I kept running, letting that flicker of desire in Suze's eyes push me, step by creaking step, up the side of the grassy canyon.

Halfway up the hill, I broke through the fog and jogged into a bright, sunlit morning. I forgot my torched lungs and aching legs and sprinted the last hundred yards along the ridgeline, the sun warm on my face. I had the whole mountain to myself: no other runners, no bikers, no cars, just me and two red-tailed hawks circling the treetops, scanning the browned-over hillside for breakfast. Out of breath, I climbed a limestone outcropping and stood greedily sucking air. Below me, all of Southern Marin was a boiling sea of fog, the ridges peeking out from the swirling clouds like eucalyptus-topped islands. Somewhere under that fog Mom was doing a downward-facing dog to Nepalese daha and flute. Farther down the hill Gianni Papadakis was at Tam Grocery, drinking his tenth cup of coffee and reading manufacturer's specs on delivery vans. And way out there where the last wisps of fog gave way to the glassy blue of the Bay, Suze was stumbling into the shower, checking off the seventeen things she had to get done before breakfast.

And for once I was with them: up early, my mind clear, my body working again. I tried to think of the last time I'd been up this early, and I flashed on the redheaded sheriff's deputy knocking on my window in Isla Vista. The memory, the sheer out-of-the-blueness of it, froze me: the naked Russian girls going down on each other on my desktop, the half-loaded bong on the floor at my feet, the cop's big, freckled hand holding the search warrant up to the glass. For an hour, while I sat on the bed in my underwear, hands cuffed behind my back, six of Santa Barbara County's finest had trooped through my apartment digging up old crack pipes, wilted wads of cash, and finally, under the bed, the box of forged invoices I'd boosted from Campus Liquors the day Al fired me. The search had the air of a treasure hunt, the cops laughing and patting me on the back every time they bagged another piece of evidence. "Don't sweat it, buddy," the arresting deputy said as he zipped my weed scale into an evidence bag. "With the case they got against you for check fraud, nobody's even gonna notice the drugs."

I stood on the limestone outcropping, my chest heaving as I stared out at the slow-moving ocean of fog, waiting for the waves of panic to stop. Then, sore and bent and out of breath, I started back down the hill again, picking my way over the rocks and deep ruts in the road until I plunged back into the fogged-in gloom of Summit Avenue.

All day I hobbled around Tam Grocery like a crippled war vet, my left knee bent at twenty degrees as if someone had snipped two inches off my quadriceps, but two days later, when I still hadn't heard from Suze, I set my alarm again and dragged myself out of bed for another early morning run. This time I spent ten minutes at the trailhead stretching and warming up, and when I started up the fire road, I alternated bursts of speed with longer stints of walking and slow jogging. When I got to the top of the ridge, instead of climbing the limestone boulder and playing King of the Mountain, I did a few more quick stretches and headed for home.

Back at the house, as I was peeling off my sweaty T-shirt

to step into the shower, it hit me that I was actually looking forward to going in to work. I couldn't think of the last time that had happened. Maybe it never had. All week, between trips to the old Post Office to settle squabbles among the contracting crews, Gianni and I had been working with his web designers to mock up a demo of the Chef Tamalpais website. Gianni had already burned through three software designers, and with just ninety days until launch, he was down to Global Digital Partners, which as far as I could tell consisted of two guys: Theo Albrecht, its president and "chief visioning officer," and a skinny Vietnamese kid named Quan, who wrote the actual code. Theo was a year out of college, cocky and full of himself, with the startled blue eyes and downy blond hair of a newly hatched chick. I never knew how old Quan was, or even his last name, but if you had told me he was in high school I would've believed it. He weighed ninety pounds soaking wet, with mole-like eyes and a fixed expression of perpetual, crushing boredom. He was hell on code, though. Once a week Gianni sat down with Theo to go over the six million things that were still wrong with the website, and a few days later Theo would be back—sometimes with Quan, sometimes not—with a brand-new design.

When I punched in that morning, Theo and Quan were upstairs bent over the lone desktop computer, checking the ordering system for bugs. The office was like a locker room before a big game. No one spoke, and when the phone rang, Gianni waved for me to let it go to voice mail. He had promised his father he would have the site up in time for customers to pre-order Thanksgiving dinners, but now it was August and every time we tried to use the menu software, the site crashed. To make matters worse, renovations at the Post Office were weeks behind and a good hundred grand over budget—and we hadn't even put in an order for delivery vans. So a little after nine, when Mr. Papadakis sat down in front of the terminal, self-consciously flexing his fingers like a maestro at the piano, I settled in behind him, butterflies swirling in my stomach.

"Okay," Theo said. "Pretend it's November and you want to

order Thanksgiving dinner for your family. You're at the Chef Tam website and you click on the menu icon. What's the first thing you're going to order?"

Papadakis squinted over his half-rim glasses at the mocked-up homepage, which displayed the Chef Tamalpais logo, a silhouette of Mt. Tamalpais wearing a chef's toque at a jaunty angle. "The turkey," he said.

"Right, good," Theo said. "Now, here's the cool part. The menu page is designed to look like the inside of your fridge. You've got your dairy and cheeses over here. And your veggie crisper down here. And, look, when you open the door, you've got your trays of condiments—mustards, mayos, ketchups, everything. All you have to do is run the mouse over the fridge until you find the poultry section and click on the turkey icon."

The interactive fridge was Gianni's proudest wrinkle. I'd spent the past week watching him and Theo high-fiving each other over how cool it all was, but now his dad stared at the screen, which displayed an image of a golden brown turkey that had popped up when he clicked on the turkey icon in the fridge.

"How do I say what size turkey I want?" he asked.

"Well, how many sizes are there?" Theo said, looking at Gianni.

"They're animals," Papadakis said. "They come in all different shapes and sizes. Usually people order them by the pound."

"Okay, that's an easy tweak," Theo said. "We can add a field at the bottom of the page so people can say how many pounds they want—and, you know, whether they want a girl turkey or a boy turkey or whatever."

"A girl turkey or a boy turkey?"

"Dad, don't start," Gianni said. He turned to me. "You got that? Weight window at the bottom of the turkey page."

"Got it," I said, scribbling on a legal pad.

"So, here's the *really* cool part," Theo said, sounding rattled now. "Once you've ordered your turkey, you click on the picture and—presto!—it appears on your virtual dinner table."

The four of us craned in, holding our breath, as Papadakis

slid the mouse over the image of the turkey and clicked on it. For weeks, whenever anyone tried to move the turkey from the fridge to the table, the turkey had vanished or turned into a plate of boiled carrots—or else the program simply crashed and the screen went blank. Now, for five long seconds nothing happened. Even Quan shifted in his chair, coiling his midsection in a slow, yogic twist, as if he could make the turkey move by sheer body English. At last, the screen blinked and a cloth-draped dinner table materialized on the left side of the screen featuring a golden brown turkey on a silver platter. The four of us fell back into our seats, breathing audible sighs of relief.

"I like that," Papadakis said, chuckling. "That's really cute."

"That's the whole concept, Dad," Gianni said. "You're a participant in the meal. You select the dishes, you put them on the table, you decide how many portions you need. Everything." He turned to me. "What was that line you came up with the other day?"

"It's your meal, we're just cooking it for you," I said.

"That's it," he said. "All the literature talks about this. The customer's got to feel like she's taking an active part in the meal. She's got to take some ownership. Otherwise, she feels like she's not doing her job."

Papadakis nodded, not drinking the Kool-Aid yet, but not *not* drinking it, either. "'It's your meal, we're just cooking it for you,'" he said, trying it out.

"Not bad, huh?" Gianni said. "Wolfer here's got a way with these snappy little lines. What was that other one you had?"

"You buy, we'll fly," I said. "But that's just what we used to say when someone was making a late-night run to the store."

"That's what I like about it," Gianni said. "It's casual. Friendly. Like, you know, this is no big deal, we're just giving you a hand putting together dinner."

"'Chef Tam—you buy, we'll fly,'" Theo said, tracing the words out in the air.

"What do you think?" Gianni asked his father.

"I think I feel old is what I think." Papadakis turned back

to the screen. "Okay, so the magic turkey is on the magic table. Now, what?"

"You order the stuffing," Theo said.

As Theo talked Papadakis through each step, the table filled with food items: mashed potatoes, cranberry sauce, dinner rolls. Once, when Papadakis ordered green beans, the image failed to load, and when Theo double-clicked on it, the bowl of green beans turned into a pecan pie. But when they retraced their steps, the green beans stayed green beans and popped up in their proper place on the table beside the bowl of mashed potatoes, and everyone relaxed again.

Theo stepped back, letting Mr. Papadakis search the fridge for the last few items on his own. The four of us watched the cursor nose around the virtual fridge as he ordered a pint of gravy and then eight ears of corn. When he clicked on the cole slaw, I stared at the picture on the screen.

"We need to change the price on that slaw," I said. "It still says six bucks a quart."

"So?" Gianni said.

"So, that's the old price," his father said. "There's a cabbage blight on the Central Coast. It's six-fifty a quart now."

"No problem," Theo said. "We'll fix that tonight."

I made a note on my pad—*chng slaw $6 → $6.50*—but when I looked up, Papadakis was eyeing Theo over his half-rims. "We can't change the prices on our own?"

On the screen the cole slaw zipped over to the dinner table, and Theo allowed himself a silent fist pump. "They can change their prices," he said to Quan. "Right?"

"They could, yeah," Quan said. "But they'd sort of have to know code."

"Our prices change every day," Papadakis said. "I don't know code. Gianni doesn't know code. The only person here who can program this thing is Quan and he doesn't work for us."

We all turned to Quan, who sat very still, his deep-set eyes blinking at slow, regular intervals. "I could build in an app that would allow you to alter the price points," he said. "But that would be a significantly more complex product than what we've got here."

"How much more complex?" Papadakis asked.

Quan paused, his smooth face slack, as if he were processing this new data set through his own proprietary software. "Significantly," he said.

"Okay, thanks, guys," Papadakis said, standing up. "I appreciate your time."

"Mr. Papadakis, sir, this is all part of the process," Theo said. "Any time you build a new software system, there's going to be a few bugs."

"Yeah, I got that part," Papadakis said.

Theo held out for another minute or two, explaining the difference between the alpha and beta phase of a web-based product, and when that went nowhere, reassuring Papadakis he would have this new bug worked out in a matter of days—or no, actually, tomorrow. Finally, Gianni corralled Theo and Quan out into the hall and down the stairs. Even then I heard Theo explaining the rollout process, and how they'd be ready for another usability test by the end of the week. Papadakis never budged from his spot next to the computer terminal. When Gianni came back in, he and his dad stood at either end of the room, squaring off like two bull elk in the wilderness. I knew I should excuse myself and get real busy cleaning the break room coffee maker, but no one had asked me to leave and this was shaping up to be a very interesting five minutes.

"That's all you've got, isn't it?" Papadakis said. "Thanksgiving dinner. That fridge, there's nothing else in it."

"It's a template," Gianni said. "You add more items and the template expands. It's a couple weeks' work, tops."

"Would that be before or after that teenager you've got working for you builds this new 'app' that allows us to update our own prices?"

I'd never seen Mr. Papadakis angry before, and it spooked me, not just because it cut against his usual sunny Mr. Rogers vibe, but because the man looked so spooked.

"This is my fault," Gianni said. "We've been jamming against a deadline and we got ahead of ourselves. But we can fix this. I don't know where Theo found that kid, but he's a heck of a programmer. You'll see. We'll have this up by October...November, at the latest."

"You told me September," Papadakis said. "I take that back. You told me June, but that was before you decided to lease the single most expensive building in Southern Marin."

"Trent," Gianni said, "could you maybe help out in the deli for a minute?"

"Right, sorry," I said, bolting up out of my seat.

"Tell Henry you're his for the rest of the day," Gianni said. "We're done here."

"Nice catch on the slaw thing," his father said.

I wanted to acknowledge the compliment, but Gianni was at the door, holding it for me. "See you tomorrow," he said. "Nine o'clock sharp."

The next day I went for my longest run yet, two miles along Blithedale Ridge and back down a hand-cut trail through the foxtails and scotch broom. On my lunch break, I deposited my first Tam Grocery paycheck and put in calls to three people looking for roommates on Craigslist. That afternoon when Henry went on his lunch break, he left me to hold down the fort in the deli.

He hadn't been gone five minutes before I broke down and called the number for the private voice mail my mother had set up for me. "You have no new messages in your mailbox," the robo-voice said for maybe the eighth time that day. I hung up and went back to the tuna salad I was making. These hours when I had the deli to myself were the longest of the day for me. It would have been so easy to stash a six-pack of Rolling Rock in the little creek that ran behind the store. No one would even miss it, and if they did, they'd chalk it up to sticky-fingered teenagers. But I'd put together almost three weeks of clean-time, white-knuckling it all the way, so I dumped two industrial-size cans of tuna fish into a stainless steel mixing bowl and started chopping celery and green onions, trying to forget the cold beers in the cooler and Suze's business card in my wallet. As I worked, I replayed our last minute together in the parking lot of the Valley Knolls Apartments one more time, pausing the mental videotape, searching for clues to why Suze hadn't called. Had she said *a couple days* or *a few? A couple days*, that meant two. But *a few days*, that could mean anything. Or maybe she was waiting for me to make the first move. That was possible, right? Women did that all the time, said the opposite of what they meant, assuming the guy would figure it out. Except in this case, it seemed to me, Suze had made it pretty clear what she wanted, and it wasn't me. But then she'd almost kissed me again there at the end. Right? Hadn't she? Or was I making that up, too?

"Fuck it," I said out loud and reached for my billfold. I wasn't going to call her. I just wanted to see her business card, make sure it was still there, but when I opened my wallet everything spilled onto the floor: my money, the AmEx card, half a dozen slips of paper with the names and phone numbers of people from AA meetings on them. I was sorting through the pile, half-looking for Suze's card, half-trying to get it all back into my wallet, when my AA prayer card dropped onto the counter.

I had been carrying the prayer card around in my wallet since the day I checked out of rehab that spring, but I hadn't looked at it since the last time I knelt down to pray at chez Starling. The back of my neck still burned when I remembered those mornings: Me, of all people, on my knees praying to the Lord. But I'd felt something, I was sure of it. An easing. A lifting. Whether it was the hand of God or some random muscle spasm seemed less important just then than the fact that whatever it was, I'd felt it.

I found a quiet corner behind the deli counter and shut my eyes. No way was I getting down on the floor, not there, but I bowed my head, touching my knee to the stainless-steel fridge under the counter to simulate kneeling and whispered the Lord's Prayer, peeking at the card whenever I forgot a line. Then I stood very still, my eyes closed, hoping the right words would come. "Don't quit before the miracle," tumbled into my brain and I said it aloud. It was still nonsense, still just words, but I said it again, louder: "Don't quit before the miracle. Don't quit before the miracle. Don't quit before the miracle." Sure enough, I started to feel something, not a lifting this time, but a presence, a shadow looming behind me.

Then it spoke.

"What kind of miracle you looking for there, Pussy Willow?"

I whipped around to see Lee Radko, his eyes lidded, grinning at me across the deli counter. I did a quick room-check, but except for a high school girl browsing the iced teas in the drinks cooler, we were alone.

"Hey, I didn't see you there, man," I said. "Sorry I haven't been by the restaurant. It's been crazy around here the last couple weeks."

He swept his eyes over the empty aisles. "Don't know how you handle the pressure, bro."

I realized I'd left the prayer card in plain sight on the counter. I reached for it, but Lee got there first.

"'Our Father, who art in heaven, hallowed be Thy name,'" he said, reading off the card. He looked up, his dark eyes gleaming, as if he'd caught me beating off behind the counter. I melted inside as if I'd been doing just that.

"Give me the fucking card, Lee."

"No, no, hey, I might learn something here." He flipped the card over. "Check it out, there's *directions*. 'Step One: We admitted we were powerless over alcohol, that our lives had become unmanageable. Step Two: Came to believe—'"

"It's a condition of my probation," I said, grabbing the card. "I have to get my sheet signed a couple times a week. Court orders."

"The judge make you pray, too?"

He grinned, a little sloppy around the edges, and for the first time I saw how stoned he was, his eyes blood-red and bugging out of his skull. The full-on Nosferatu, he'd called it. Throw in the ripped upper body and the sea of ink pouring out from the collar of his quilted shirt, and he might as well have been wearing a sign around his neck that said: *Ex-con.*

"Look, man, I've got other customers," I said. "Maybe you should come back later."

He turned to the girl at the drinks coolers, who was holding up two bottles of iced green tea, comparing their ingredients. "Yo, Jin, you gonna be all day?" he said. "Trent here's got all these other customers he's got to deal with."

The girl was eighteen, maybe nineteen, tops. Even in flip-flops, she was nearly as tall as Lee, raw-boned and pale, with a hank of glossy black hair tied off in a careless knot. She wasn't pretty, exactly—her face was too plain for that, her limbs too stick-like and bony—but in a bikini top and faded cutoffs that showed off the twin half-moons of her ass, she was making it very, very hard not to stare.

"Trent, you met Jin?" Lee said. "Jin, this here's my old running buddy, Trent."

Behind her Nordic pallor, her face had an Asian cast, her cheeks rounded, her eyes almond-shaped, but the way she carried herself, the pearly blue of her fingernails, the hundreds of dollars she'd spent to have her shorts professionally ripped and faded to look like she'd found them in a dumpster, marked her as 100 percent Marin. And like Lee, she was high as the sky.

"Lee was just telling me about you," she said. "You guys grew up together, right?"

"Tam High, Class of '90," I said, rubbing it in.

Her laugh was a bright, explosive pop, like a champagne cork escaping a bottle. "19*90*?"

"Come on, we don't got all day," Lee said, pouring on the jailhouse stare.

"We're going to the Bolinas Lagoon," Jin said. "The great blue herons are nesting this time of year. Can you believe it, he grew up here and he's never even seen them."

Lee shrugged in a way that said, *Cool, whatever, herons.* "Give the man your order already."

The way Jin was standing, one leg akimbo, the tip of her sandaled foot tapping the floor as she studied the menu board, she looked a little heron-like herself. "Do you guys have anything without, like, meat products?" she asked.

"Sure, there's our grilled Portobello sandwich with—"

"She'll have roast beef on a roll," Lee said. "No slaw and an extra pickle."

"*Lee-ee!*" she sang out, swatting him.

"Make it two," he said. "And pour a little extra blood on hers, will ya? You know, soak the bread real good."

While I worked at the counter, unwrapping the roast beef portions and spreading mustard on the toasted Kaiser rolls, I heard ·them whispering behind me. She was telling him she'd read an article in *Yoga Journal* that said you could raise your peak energy level twenty percent just by giving up meat products, and he was telling her he'd heard about a meat product that would raise her peak energy level two *hundred* percent.

"God, you're such a little kid sometimes," she said, swatting him again.

"Not so little, maybe."

She giggled. "That's right. Class of '90."

"So hey, I skipped a few years," he said. "When I was in fifth grade, they said, 'Fuck it, that kid's such a genius, let's put him in high school.'"

"Do you have *any* idea how old I was in 1990?"

She laughed again, this time with a dirty downbeat to it, and the room went still. I made as much noise as I could pulling the sealing tape from the dispenser and dropping the wrapped sandwiches into a plastic carry bag. It didn't help. All I could hear was heavy breathing and pornographic lip-smacks, until Jin whispered: "Lee. The food's ready."

I turned around to see them joined at the hip, wearing matching blissed-out grins like someone had set off a pheromone bomb at their feet. I felt it, too, a weird potency to the air, and I realized what I should have known the moment they walked in, that they had just come from Lee's bed, and nesting great blue herons or no, that was where they were heading back to now.

I rang up the sandwiches, along with a Tazo tea and a Heineken Lee had set on the counter, trying not to watch as Jin discreetly shifted from one foot to the other, adjusting the crotch of her shorts. "Comes to $15.35," I said, eyes on the screen.

"That's it?" Lee said. "Fifteen bucks?"

"I gave you the lunch special," I said. "If you order a sandwich, the drink's half-off. Doesn't work with the beer, though."

He patted Jin on the butt. "Get yourself another tea. And hey, grab me an extra beer while you're at it."

She didn't move. "C'mon, how much tea can I drink?"

"Get me another fucking beer," he snapped. "In fact, you know what? I'm thirsty. Make it a six." He turned back to me. "Ring it up, Pussy Willow. Two Tazos and a sixer of Heine."

I didn't like it, he was hassling me, but I had other customers now—a yellow-haired surfer kid browsing the potato-chip aisle and two women in pantsuits chitchatting at the salad bar—and I needed Lee out of there before Henry came back from lunch wanting to know what was taking me so long to wait on this stoned ex-con and his half-naked jailbait girlfriend, so I rang up the extra Tazo and the five extra beers. With tax, it came to just less than twenty-three bucks.

"That's more like it." Lee patted the pocket of his jeans. "Shit. Forgot my wallet."

"Quit fucking around," Jin said softly. "It's in your other pocket."

He didn't even look at her. Instead, he fished an oblong silver ball from his shirt pocket and set it on the counter. "There you go. That oughta cover it."

The tightly wrapped ball of tinfoil was roughly the size of the one we'd smoked that morning behind the Old Brown Store: an eighth of an ounce, give or take a few milligrams.

"What the fuck?" I said.

"What, it's not enough?" He fished another foil ball from his pocket, the same size and shape as the first and dropped it onto the counter. "Sorry, man. Didn't mean to Jew you there."

We were up to a quarter ounce now, and I could smell it: that fine, skunky dank-stink of fresh sinsemilla. I checked the room again, beyond caring how freaked out I looked or how much of a kick Lee was getting out of seeing me look freaked out. The pantsuit ladies were still happily chatting at the salad bar, but the surfer kid had picked out a bag of BBQ-flavor Kettle chips and was heading for the counter.

"Get this shit out of here," I hissed.

"You wanted me to hook you up, so I'm hooking you up." He shrugged. "I figure the least you can do is front me a couple sandwiches and some beer."

The surfer kid was in line now with his Kettle chips and a Red Bull. The deli counter smelled of summer in Isla Vista: Red Hot Chili Peppers on the stereo, college kids wandering in and out of my apartment, a whole, lazy, sun-drenched day spread out in front of me with nothing to do but blaze big bowls and watch cheesy monster movies on cable.

"I'd give you the fucking sandwiches, but I already rang them up," I said. "I can't void a sale without a manager signing off on it."

"Where is he? We'll tell him you've decided to accept an alternate form of payment."

"Jesus, Lee, just give him the money and let's go," Jin said.

"How about it, Wolfer?" Lee said. "You want the money instead?"

My eyes darted down to the two foil-wrapped buds on the counter. That was all I did, just looked, but it was enough. He laughed and grabbed the plastic carry bag from the counter.

"Come by the restaurant sometime," he said. "Bring your little prayer card and we'll party."

Jin reamed him out as they left the store, but part of her, I could tell, was getting off on seeing her boyfriend push people around. She'd give him shit all the way back to his place, but as soon as they were in bed all that would matter would be the cool, easy way he'd played me.

The charge for $22.83 was still showing on the register when the surfer kid set his soda and chips on the counter. To erase a sales item all I had to do was hit "delete entry" and it went away, but to void a completed sale, Henry or one of the other managers had to enter his eight-digit pin to sign off on the error. The kid and I stared at each other, and then he looked down at the two foil balls on the counter. The obvious thing was to give them to him. He looked like he would know what to do with a quarter ounce of premium weed. But I breathed in another briny lungful of summertime in Isla Vista and swept the two balls into the pocket of my deli apron.

"You're good," I said, waving off his food.

"I'm good?"

I glanced at the two pantsuit ladies laughing as they took forks and napkins from the self-serve tray next to the salad bar.

"Yeah. Now, beat it."

"Sweet," he said, grabbing his chips and soda. "Party on, dude."

I'd watched Henry void out a sale a few times but he'd done it so quickly I missed all but the first two numbers. I closed my eyes and typed in the first eight digits that came to mind: 7-3-7-3-6-4-4-8, which, on a keypad, spelled out "SERENGIT."

Bingo. I was in. With a few keystrokes, I zeroed out the sale, erasing all signs of Lee Radko and his free lunch. If anyone ever checked the tape, they might have wondered how Henry could have voided a sale while he was on his lunch break, but no one would check the tape, not if the tray counted out right at the end of the day. And I was going to make damn sure the tray counted out right.

"Next guest, please," I said, waving the two businesswomen to the counter.

# 9

The Saturday morning meeting at the Methodist Church on Miller Avenue was an old-timers' meeting, which meant that aside from me and a few other stragglers, everyone in the room had been sober five years, and most much longer than that. It was smaller than your average AA meeting, too, just twenty or so regulars, all guys, most of them of that generation of servicemen who'd shipped out to the Bay Area in the middle part of the twentieth century and stayed after their hitch ended. The ones who weren't retired ran small, failing businesses selling office supplies or house paint, things you could buy more cheaply at the big box stores along Highway 101. Others drove cabs or worked nights at the post office or just collected disability checks. I was an outsider there, half the age of the other men in the room, with a very different life history, but I liked going because the regulars reminded me of my granddad, and because for an AA meeting it was low on the bullshit quotient. Every now and then some cokehead securities lawyer wandered in off the street, all cool and cocky in his Ray-Bans and Saucony tracksuit. I'd watch him take in that church basement full of sad old men, their faces washed-out and battered, their haircuts bearing all the signs of a lonely afternoon with a hand mirror and scissors, and five minutes later the guy would be heading for the exit, leaving us to ourselves.

I arrived early to help fill the coffee urn and set out the store-brand Oreos and coffee cake, the way I'd done after I got out of rehab. Back then, I came early every week and hung around afterward to help clean up and put away the chairs, hoping somebody would invite me out for coffee. But it had been a month and a half since I'd been to a meeting there, and longer than that since I'd showed up sober.

A few of the regulars recognized me and offered up rough,

mitt-like hands for me to shake, and at the start of the meeting, when the moderator asked if there was anyone in their
first thirty days of sobriety who cared to identify themselves,
I raised my hand. "Hi," I said, "my name's Trent, and it's been
twenty-one days since my last drink." There was a smattering
of applause, none of it especially heartfelt, and I sat down and
kept my mouth shut for the rest of the hour.

But I hadn't come that morning to talk. I had come looking
for Frank T. He was sitting, as he always did, in the front row
of folding chairs a few seats down from the moderator, a well-
worn Big Book in his lap, jotting notes in the margins with a
stubby carpenter's pencil. Frank was from Chicago, from one
of the older Irish neighborhoods on the South Side, where
he'd been a priest for thirty years. These days, he drove a cab,
mostly at night, and lived in a residence motel in San Rafael's
Canal District, the closest thing in Marin to an actual barrio. He
looked like the kind of guy who drove a cab at night: sixtyish
and balding, a little frail, a little sad, a man you could look at and
safely forget. He wore polyester Sansabelt slacks and a shabby
checked sport coat, a few inches short in the sleeves, and those
thick-soled black shoes cops and hotel bellmen wear. His long,
lean, curiously unlined face was a Picasso painting come to
life: a broken nose jammed a quarter inch to the right, his left
eyelid drooping like a fallen tent flap, one corner of his mouth
pinched in on itself like he was holding in some private joke on
the world.

A couple weeks after I'd started in on the airplane bottles, I
showed up one Saturday morning already half in the bag. For
an hour Frank stared me down across the room, one ropy vein
in his forehead pulsing in time with his heartbeat, until I gave
up and bolted for the street. I hadn't been back since, but for
weeks afterward I thought of him every time I shot a skinny,
that twisted blue vein flashing like a police siren in a car window
as he glared at me across the dimly lit basement.

When the meeting broke up, I helped put away the coffee
things while Frank talked with the moderator. I had washed out

the coffee urn, put away the sugar and the non-dairy creamer, and was straightening the stacks of folding chairs along the wall before I saw him alone. It took me another minute of stacking chairs to work up the nerve to sidle over to where he was sitting under a frosted-glass window, quietly reading a Bible.

"Frank?" I said. "Could I have a word?"

He looked up, his one droopy eyelid rising slowly, exposing an iris of liquid blue clarity. "Jesus, kid," he said. "Took you long enough."

I looked around the fluorescent-lit basement. We were alone.

"Come on," he said. "Let's get some coffee."

Frank took his coffee black, with five heaping spoonfuls of sugar. For the first ten minutes, he barely spoke and just stared at me, smirking slightly, that ropy blue vein throbbing in his forehead. It was like talking into a one-way mirror. I had the sense that everything I said, every gesture and tic, was being recorded by a hidden camera and matched against the words and gestures of other guys Frank had sponsored over the years. When he did speak, it was only to smirk a little more and agree with some totally obvious point. Every now and then he nodded, not, it seemed to me, in response to anything I'd said or done, but just to mark the passing of time.

The quieter he got, the more I talked. I told him about the skinnies. I told him about getting high with Lee Radko behind Old Brown Store, and how I'd sweet-talked Mr. Papadakis into giving me the job, anyway. I told him about my meltdown on the median strip of Miller Avenue, and my run-in with frog-faced Terry Mathis at Village Liquors. Then, because he was giving me so little to work with, I told him why I'd gotten started with the skinnies in the first place. Basically, I said, it boiled down to bullshit. I was up to my ears in it. Everyone I met, everything I touched or smelled or saw stank of it. Mill Valley was full of shit. My mother was full of shit. Stan Starling, my dad down in LA, the people I worked for—all of them, full of shit. And yes, sure, I was full of shit, too. Probably more so than anyone else.

But that was the problem: I didn't know how *not* to be full of shit. I had been raised in a bullshit world, taught from the cradle how to work with the available truth, how to shape it, mold it, and polish away its imperfections until all that remained was a gleaming golden turd, scentless and immaculate.

"So what would I hear if you told me the truth?" he asked, sipping his cooling coffee.

"I just told you," I said. "All that stuff with the airplane bottles and the—"

"No, not that," he said. "Come on, you've had the whole summer to come up to me after a meeting. What is it about today that made you actually do it?"

"But that *is* why I'm here. I stopped going to meetings. I started drinking again. I almost lost my job. I lied to my mom. I lied to everybody."

He set down his coffee, disappointed, and maybe also a little bored. I got the clear sense that I'd better come up with some truth, and fast, or he would drink off his oversweetened black coffee and vanish into the bright summer afternoon like smoke.

"Okay look, I did some time," I said. "Last year, in Santa Barbara. I stole money from a guy I used to work for down there—a lot of money, actually—and I got locked up for four months. It would've been longer except I got bailed out by my stepdad."

"Haven't you already talked about this in meetings?" he asked.

"I've told people I spent time in jail, but I never said why. I've never told anyone here about the money. When people ask, I just say it was drugs. Up here, that goes over better."

"That's what you asked me out for coffee to tell me? You stole some money in Santa Barbara and did time for it?"

I knew what he was driving at, what I was holding back: the quarter ounce of Double Black Orchid Lee Radko had given me the day before. I had stashed the two foil-wrapped buds in my Kenneth Cole lace-ups at home, waiting for Frank to tell me what to do with them. But now that I was here, sitting across from him at the Book Depot coffee shop, I wasn't so sure I wanted to hear what he was going to tell me.

"Remind me," Frank said, "how long've you been clean this time?"

"Twenty-one days."

"And how many meetings have you been to in that time?"

"Twenty one." This was a lie. It was more like five or six.

"Don't you think it's a little strange, that, as many meetings as I make, this is the first time I've seen you since you came back in?"

He grinned, that pinched half-smirk, and I knew I was fucked. But as any fuckup will tell you, knowing you're fucked and acting on that knowledge are two very different things.

"Okay, maybe I missed a day or two," I said. "I haven't been, like, anal about it."

"Trent, why are you wasting my time like this?"

I forced myself to meet his eyes. "I told you, I need your help."

"With what? Reading the meeting schedule?"

The couple at the next table, a white-haired college prof and his tiny, kerchief-wearing wife, looked up from their morning lattes.

"No," I said, lowering my voice. "With the steps. The program."

"You mean, you're"—he gasped—"an *alcoholic?*" He sat back, the ropy vein in his forehead throbbing. "You know, I was locked up, too. A lot longer than four months. Did you know that?"

I *had* known this, I realized. Of course I had. What else would explain why a man like Frank T., a Catholic priest in late middle age, would end up driving a cab at night and eating off a hot plate in a residence motel? How else to explain the itchy silence that met me every time I pressed any of the other old-timers about Frank?

"It's called statutory rape," he said. "I liked little girls. Not boys, unfortunately for me. If I was queer, I'd have made bishop by now. No, I liked girls, the younger the better. Nice, pretty Catholic girls brought up to think a priest stands at the right hand of God. The youngest I ever had was ten. You want to hear about that, what I did to that little girl?"

I shook my head, staring at the lacquered table. It wasn't just the white-haired couple beside us listening now. The whole room had fallen into stunned silence.

"I didn't think so." He reached for his wallet and dropped three wrinkled singles on the table. "Kids like you piss me off on principle," he said. "It's not just the money and the privilege. It's the way you seem to think that every crappy little thing that ever happened to you, because it happened to you, is some great crisis the world has got to solve."

"Frank, I'm not asking—"

"*Hey*," he snapped. "I let you talk all you wanted. Now, shut up and listen."

I shut up and listened.

"You've been locked up so you know what happens in prison to guys like me," he said. "I was older and a priest, and that helped. But only so much. I spent six years sure that every day was going to be my last. But I'm here. I didn't drink and I didn't use, and by the grace of God, I haven't hurt any more little girls. Now, I cannot begin to guess what is going on in that head of yours, but whatever it is, sitting here blowing smoke up my ass isn't going to make it any better." He stood, reaching into his shirt pocket for a stack of business cards. "That's my cell," he said, tossing a card on the table. "When you're ready to talk, I mean really talk, not just feed me a line of bullshit—give me a call. Any time, day or night, doesn't matter."

A minute later I was in my car speeding away from the Book Depot, away from downtown, in the direction of Village Liquors. I felt slippery, unmoored. It wasn't just that Frank had walked out on me. It was the way he'd done it, the pleasure it seemed to give him. As he left our table, twenty pairs of eyes tracking him to the door, there was a swagger in his step, a cockiness, like it had made his day to shock all those smug suburban assholes. And I was supposed to listen to him? I was a screwup, yes, and I would go to my grave seeing Al Fierro on a respirator sobbing as I was led off to jail, but I hadn't raped a ten-year-old. If I had, I wouldn't broadcast it to the world like some great blue ribbon of screwedupness. There's addict logic for you. Guys like me, who hadn't raped any children, who hadn't spent years on the streets or put our houses and cars and marriages up our noses, we were the lightweights, the wannabes, the candy asses. Men like Frank, who had ripped gaping holes in the fabric of society and done years in prison for it, they were the royalty, the big swinging dicks of Twelve-Step Land.

I was driving more slowly now, wishing I could just call a time-out, park myself in a nice, quiet parallel universe until the cravings stopped. But I was a rat caught in a maze. Every path I tried led me back where I'd started. I didn't want to go to Village Liquors, but I couldn't go home, not with that quarter ounce of Double Black Orchid waiting for me in my closet. I wasn't going to call the number on Frank's business card, either, not if it meant getting another lecture on what a pussy I was for not being a child-sex predator.

Halfway down Miller Avenue, I saw a street sign nailed to a telephone pole, pointing toward Boyle Park, and by the time I heard the warning bells telling me I was making a mistake, probably an even bigger one than asking Frank T. out for coffee, I had turned off Miller Avenue and was barreling down the tree-lined streets of the Sycamore Flats toward the old ballfield.

As soon as I pulled into the dirt parking lot behind the backstop and smelled the newly mown grass, I was twelve years old again, playing shortstop and hitting cleanup. That year, we played our crosstown rivals, the Lions, for the City Championship. Half the town turned out for the game and the park was packed with families having cookouts and spreading blankets in the grass past the outfield fences. Some of the Eaglet moms had dyed dish towels our team colors, blue and gold, and every time I came to bat, fifty people on our side of the bleachers waved those crazy towels over their heads, chanting,

"Wolf-er! Wolf-er! Wolf-er!" Climbing the clanging metal stairs to the bleachers, I heard the satisfying *tink!* my aluminum bat made when I connected with the first pitch, sending it over the centerfield fence for a two-run homer.

Then I saw the field. It was tiny. Like everything else in Mill Valley, Boyle Park was shiny as a new penny, the backstop and dugouts freshly painted, the infield turf lush and finely manicured. But it was still just a kiddie park. With baseball season over, the fences had come down to make way for a soccer field laid out diagonally across the outfield grass, with parents spread out along the sidelines cheering on two noisy clumps of seven-year-olds chasing a silver-and-white soccer ball. Suze was standing on the near sideline with Sharon and her younger boy, Jake. She was dressed for work, in slacks and a tailored blouse, but she looked relaxed holding Jake's hand and chatting with the guy next to her, who, going by the rock-like muscle formations on his calves, was either a professional cyclist or the team's coach.

I was halfway out onto the field, drawn to Suze by the same magnet pull that had thrown me at her in the parking lot at the Valley Knolls Apartments, when Coach Wonder Calves laughed at something she said and rested his hand, oh so casually, on her shoulder. I froze, staring at the two of them across the centerfield grass. What, exactly, had given me the idea Suze wouldn't have another guy in her life? And what had made me think that if she *was* single, she would want the guy in her life to be me?

Just then, a cheer went up and Suze broke away from Coach Wonder Calves. "Take it, D!" she shouted, pumping her fist. "Take it, take it—*go!*"

Even thirty yards off, through a row of cheering parents, I could pick out Dylan Strasser, who had intercepted a pass and was streaking downfield toward the goal. A different kind of kid might have looked for an open teammate, someone to pass to. Not Dylan. He dodged one defender, outran two more, then cut across midfield where there was nothing but green between him and the goalie. She was a corn-silk blonde, barely four feet tall, standing with her back to the field waving to a friend through the netting of the kiddie-sized goal. The far sideline erupted in shouts: "Scar*let!* Scarlet, turn *around!*" She turned just in time to let loose a high-pitched shriek as the ball rocketed into the net.

Dylan came tearing back up the near sideline where Suze lifted him in the air, spinning him in her arms. Coach Wonder Calves followed a few beagle-like steps behind her, but Dylan made him wait, high-fiving the rest of his team before grudgingly accepting a hug from his coach. I was watching this, thinking maybe the kid wasn't *all* bad, when Dylan turned and pointed at me. Suze whipped around, her eyes locking on me, and I saw how royally I had screwed up. This wasn't a movie theater in Novato. This wasn't the front seat of my car in Shelter Ridge. This was a public park where Suze was surrounded by her kid's friends, and here I was stalking her like some psycho from the movies.

Dylan's coach started my way, strutting across the grass. He was in his forties, with a salon-bed tan and a two-tone hair weave, but his calves alone could have kicked my ass twenty times over. I looked to Suze, silently begging her to save me from having to scurry back to my car like a roach from a folded newspaper, but she just stared, her lips still rounded in shock.

"Trent!" a voice sang out. "So glad you could make it!"

It was Sharon Randall, in a kelp-green maxi dress, waving to me from the sideline, her big grin saying, *Don't think. Just roll with it.*

"Hey, Mrs. R.," I shouted back, waving. "Hope I didn't miss too much of the game!"

"Oh no, we're just getting started," she said. "Do you know Rod?"

She meant The Calved One, who had pulled up short between Suze and me, his eyes radiating dark rays of confusion under a Maggliore Tires ball cap.

"Rod Berryman, this is Trent Wolfer," Sharon said. "Trent's an old friend of Suzy's from school. He's in software design."

"Nice to meet you, Rod," I said, reaching for his hand as if I had come there to do just that.

He shook my hand, still baffled. "You're in software design—Tim, is it?"

"Trent," I said. "And I'm more on the marketing end, really. I try to leave the serious coding to the pros."

"Really? I work in the Valley myself. Venture capital, mostly. Who are you with?"

"Global Digital Associates," I said. "We're a start-up out of Cupertino. We specialize in web-based shopping apps."

The referee blew the whistle, thank God, before Rod could ask just what kind of marketing work I did for Global Digital Associates. Suze sprinted for the sidelines, Rod stomping after her, leaving me with Sharon, who draped a many-bangled arm around my shoulders.

"Thanks," I said. "I owe you big-time."

"No, you don't," she said. "The man's a putz. Two divorces, and he's still got the house and the kids. I look at him and I see Jimmy with better lawyers."

By then Dylan had stolen the ball again and was blazing downfield with it, zigzagging through defenders like they were planted to the turf.

"Ref, where's the whistle?" Suze shouted when a kid finally tackled him.

"I don't think that was a foul, honey," Sharon said. "That was a clean tackle."

"Like hell it was," Suze said. "You're supposed to play the ball, not the man."

The other parents hung back, eyes averted, shooting each other nervous smiles. Me, I wanted to hug her. My mother never came to my games, not even in high school when scouts were lining up behind the backstop to watch me bat. This, I could see, wasn't going to be Dylan's problem.

"Open your eyes, ref!" I shouted. "Call the fouls!"

Dylan heard none of this. He was a boy in a bubble, aware only of the ball and his gift for being near it. Watching him,

I saw his dad in that streak of strawberry-blond hair and his slashing, low-to-the-ground running style, but I saw myself, too. Soccer was easy for him, the way baseball had been easy for me for so long. It never made sense to me why the other kids couldn't hit the ball as far as I could. It seemed so simple: You swung the bat and the ball flew. Soccer was like that for Dylan now. I could see it in his eyes, the way he never took them off the ball, the way he ran with his tongue curled in a corner of his mouth like it was a gear he could shift at will. It would get harder for him, the way it had gotten harder for me when I started playing college ball and realized there were thousands of kids like me hungry for a shot in a way I wouldn't ever be. But for now, for Dylan, it was just a gas, knowing that wherever he played, whoever else was on the field, no one could stop him.

"Take it, take it, Dylan!" I shouted. "Yeah—*goal!*"

I stayed where I was as the team poured onto the field to congratulate him again, but I was there when Suze came back to high-five Sharon and me. Safe in his soundproof bubble, Dylan steered clear of the sidelines, but the younger boy Jake, the little traitor, high-fived me twice.

In the final minutes, after Dylan had scored a hat trick, Rod benched him to give the other kids a chance. It was the right thing to do, coach-wise, but not a smart move, Suze-wise. She didn't say anything to Rod. Instead, she complained to me, to her mom, to the other parents, anyone who would tell her what she wanted to hear, which was that her kid was the best player out there.

When the referee blew the final whistle, and the teams lined up to do their post-game cheer, I hung close to Sharon and Suze, hoping to pass for parental, or maybe step-parental. Finally, Rod strutted over. "Some of the families are heading out for pizza," he said, putting a little extra juice on *families* in case there was any confusion.

"Aren't you two looking at apartments today?" Sharon asked. "Where was that place again?"

"Valley Knolls," I said, rolling with it. "Suze, I've been

thinking, maybe I could swing the rent if they gave me a break on the utilities."

"Hey, that's great!" Sharon said. "Suzy's so good at working these things out. I can take the boys. Jake, Dylie—come on, time for pizza!"

Jake raced off toward the car as fast as his chubby little legs could carry him, but Dylan held his eyes on Suze, doing a slow burn as his grandmother led him away.

"Dylan had a good game today," Rod said, watching them go.

"He was just getting started, Rod," Suze said.

He smiled, beaten. Up close, his tan was the telltale orange of the spray-on kind, and his eyes were weary in the way of a man who doesn't do lonely well. His kid was around somewhere, but there was no wife or girlfriend, nobody to ride shotgun while he blew his venture capital bucks on strip-mall pizza.

"Nice to meet you, Tim," he said, extending his hand.

I didn't correct him this time, just shook his hand and watched him trudge off toward his gleaming black Ferrari.

"You don't really want to go back to Valley Knolls, do you?" Suze said when he was out of earshot.

"Not unless Rick knocks three hundred bucks off the rent and puts in a real bathroom."

Around us, the park had emptied out except for a few stragglers loading kids into their cars and a maintenance guy carrying the fold-up soccer goals to a storage shed.

"Where are we going, then?" she asked.

"Good question," I said, turning for the parking lot. "I'll let you know when I figure it out."

I tried being quiet at first, and then when that got awkward, I went the other way and filled the car with talk, babbling about Dylan's game and how great it was that kids were still playing ball at Boyle Park. We were half a mile down East Blithedale, heading nowhere in particular, when an ominous silence once again settled over the front seat.

"Look, I'm sorry," I said. "I shouldn't have showed up like this today."

"I did sort of invite you, right?"

We fell silent again as we passed the middle school. We both knew that wasn't true.

"I'm glad you came," she said. "I just wasn't expecting you, that's all." She slid her eyes toward me. "Trust me, if I didn't want to be here, I wouldn't be here."

"What about Coach Wonder Calves back there?"

"Rod? He's nobody, Trent. Really. Just a guy I went out for drinks with a couple times."

"Your mom doesn't seem too crazy about him," I said.

"No, she's rooting for the small-time drug dealer just back from S.B. Go figure."

Something about this, the fact that we were joking again, broke the mood. I rolled down the window, letting the furnace-hot August breeze blow over us, while Suze rooted through the boxes of CDs and mix tapes at her feet, looking for something to replace the Springsteen album I'd been listening to for weeks.

"Seriously, you still have INXS?" she said, holding up a scuffed CD case.

"I still have *your* INXS," I said. "I'm pretty sure you left that in my car ten years ago."

"And you still have it?"

This wasn't the moment to get into how I had lost most of my music, my real music, when someone who may or may not have been a homeless crackhead named Nadine broke into my apartment the week I was arrested and stole my desktop computer and my stereo. Instead, I swapped out Springsteen for INXS, and a minute later we were belting out the opening lines of "Suicide Blonde."

I pointed the car south, skipping the freeway to take the scenic route through Sausalito. I knew where we were headed now. Suze had settled into a corner of the passenger seat, heels kicked off, shades pulled down over her eyes, sunning herself like a contented cat, ignoring the throngs of tourists licking ice cream cones and snapping pictures on the Bridgeway. It was only when we started up the hill toward the Golden Gate Bridge that she stirred awake.

"I can't go into the city," she shouted. "The boys'll freak."

"Good thing we aren't going into the city, then."

I watched her look up at the underside of the famous, red-painted bridge, waiting for her to twig. How many times had we done this, driven just this stretch of road, with just this album on the stereo, at just this hour on a summer Saturday afternoon?

"Get the fuck out!" she said, laughing. "The *bunkers?*"

All the way up the Waldo Grade she tried to talk me out of it. The bunkers were too far. We weren't dressed for the weather on the Headlands. There'd be a million tourists. But by the time we crossed under Highway 101 and started up the winding coast road, she'd settled into the seat again, those oversized Jackie O. glasses pulled down over her eyes, a sloppy grin on her face as she hummed along with Michael Hutchence.

Once upon a time, the Marin Headlands were a launch site for Minutemen and Nike missiles, and whole hillsides were fenced off with barbed wire and patrolled by MPs in unmarked black jeeps. The missiles were long gone now, the warheads buried under some mountain in Nevada, the launch pads abandoned or prettied up for school tours, but the rocky cliffs were still studded with the crumbling concrete bunkers built after Pearl Harbor to keep San Francisco safe from Japanese invasion. Most tourists never get past the first set of bunkers, with its postcard-worthy views of the Golden Gate Bridge, the whitewashed buildings of the city glittering in the background. But if you keep driving along the coast, you pass through an old military checkpoint onto a single-lane road that seems to dive headlong over the cliff. It's something else, that road. For a mile or more, you crawl like a fly across the windowsill of the world, nothing but blue sky above and crashing surf below, the air scrubbed so clean by fog and rain and wind that you can pick out the long-necked pelicans and cormorants skimming the breakers half a mile away.

I pulled in at the bunker at the bottom of the hill and killed the engine. In high school, I used to come out here two or three mornings a week when the waves were breaking at Rodeo Beach, me and Lee Radko and a car full of guys, our boards lashed to the roof. We'd stop at the bunkers for a pre-dawn bowl, shivering in our board shorts in the chill, before tugging on our wetsuits and plunging into the icy surf at Rodeo Beach. I'd brought girls out here, too, spreading an Army blanket in a dry creek bed near the edge of the cliff out of sight of the Fort Cronkhite MPs who liked to park their jeeps on the fire roads high above the bunkers, binoculars out, sweeping the hillsides for local kids making it in the grass.

This last fact silenced us as we climbed the rusted metal stairs to the main turret: The bunkers were a notorious hook-up spot. Not the bunkers themselves, which were strewn with broken bottles and twisted rebar, but the apron of windblown grass that stretched out to the edge of the cliff. The distinction between the bunkers and the grass gave us the cover to stand on the cement gun emplacement, eyes shaded against the sun, pointing out familiar landmarks. There, across the wide belly of blue, were Baker Beach and the Presidio. And there, at three o'clock, was Point Bonita, its glass-topped lighthouse set, jewel-like, on a lonely rock outcropping. Beyond that, thirty miles offshore, the white-tipped Farallon Islands jutted out of the silver sheet of sea like the half-submerged jaw of a shark.

"Feels weird to be out here without a bong and a case of Bud Talls," Suze said.

"If we looked we could probably find one of my old one-hitters," I said. "I must've lost four or five of those things up here over the years."

"Yeah well, I lost more than a one-hit pipe out here," she said. "As you may recall."

Like that, there was Jimmy Strasser again, intruding on our afternoon. I knew the night she was talking about. I'd helped her set up the whole thing: scored the beer and the drugs, led the convoy of cars out to the Headlands, and kept Lee from killing Jimmy's soccer-pussy buddies long enough for Suze and Jimmy to slip away into the tall grass. I still remembered the moment Jimmy came back to the pillbox, where Lee had rigged a beer bong out of plastic tubing and an old Clorox bottle. There had been smirks all round, some low fives from Jimmy's soccer buddies, and by the time Suze wandered in, bits of grass still in her hair, Jimmy was skulling a Tall Boy from Lee's beer bong, ten guys hooting and cheering him on.

Suze had gone silent beside me, watching a freighter pass under the bridge, hugging herself against the stiff breeze. I needed a line, a joke to zap Jimmy Strasser back to high school where he belonged. Instead, I slipped my arm around her shoulders. She leaned in against me, and we stood like that, staring out at the open water, both of us waiting for me to do what I did next, which was lean over and kiss her.

"That was nice," she said. "You always were a good kisser."

"I was?"

"When you weren't totally hammered, yeah."

We kissed again, more hungrily this time. I couldn't get over how easy all this was, no panicking, no pulling back, our bodies fitting like two lost puzzle pieces, Suze's arms draped over my hips, her small breasts pressed against my chest.

"You think it's still out there?" I asked.

She laughed, startled. "What, my virginity?"

"You never know, right?" I said, taking her hand.

I led the way down the concrete stairs to the apron of grass. The creek bed was just where I remembered it, a shallow crease of land shielded from view by a stand of wind-stunted scrub oak. I wished I'd brought a blanket, but it was too late for that. We collapsed into each other in a tuft of bunchgrass on the banks of the now-vanished river. Seven years of hookers and cheap porn had taught me to go straight for the breasts and crotch, wrestle the girl's shirt over her head and her panties down around her ankles. I hadn't been with a woman since crackhead

Nadine, and the shock of Suze's tongue in my mouth, her soft grunts and moans, tripped a memory of those ugly, drug-feuled four days. I knuckled back all thoughts of Nadine, and every girl I'd paid down in Santa Barbara, shutting my eyes and easing my hands down Suze's back where her blouse had slipped out from her slacks. But then I stopped, helpless, lost.

"What is it?" Suze said, pulling back, breathless. "What's wrong?"

"Nothing, I'm fine," I lied. "It's just—it's sort of been a while."

We lay in the grass, our eyes locked on each other, hearts beating crazily in time. I had never hurt a woman, not once in all my years in Santa Barbara, but part of the rush of giving a girl money or drugs was that I could, that it gave me that license. This was the game I played for four nights with Nadine. I filled the glass pipe and she took me in her mouth so deep she gagged, her mascara streaming down her cheeks. Then I loaded up more rock and she showed me the dime-sized divots on her ass and thighs where one of her exes had ground out half a pack of lit cigarettes. Night after night, she offered to let me hurt her, degrade her, humiliate her, and I didn't. That *was* sex for me, the urge to destroy and my refusal to give in to it. Now, I saw, I was going to have to relearn everything.

Slowly, we disentangled our arms and legs, my heart still thrumming in my chest. Under me, Suze looked wild, unsettled, her shirt rumpled, her mouth bruised from our kissing.

"You okay?" she asked.

I nodded. "I think so. Yeah, I'm good."

"You don't look okay."

"Suze, I don't know what I was thinking. I'm not ready for this. I thought I was, but I'm not."

Her eyes wheeled around the creek bed, like she was seeing it for the first time. I had remembered this place as a hidden paradise, a grassy cockpit at the top of the world, but it was just another party spot. Trampled weeds. Candy wrappers. Crushed Slurpee cups. Even a pair of girl's cotton panties, white with little red hearts on it, snagged on the low branches of a scrub oak. Suze's eyes flicked past me, across the yellow grass to the empty pillboxes near the road.

"Maybe you better take me home," she said.

On the long drive back, she sat pressed against the passenger-side door, not frightened, just separate, in her own world. A hundred times I willed myself to turn to her and apologize, and a hundred times I kept my eyes on the road and said nothing. In rehab, when I couldn't sleep, I used to calm myself by plotting out, step by step, how to break into the pharmaceuticals cabinet and O.D. They kept every tranquilizer known to man in that thing, from Xanax and Oxycontin to hardcore antipsychotics like Zyprexa and Clozaril, which they used to bring people down from severe manic episodes. There were a couple of those a week, usually right after they brought a new guy in from detox. I would lie in bed, following the key in my memory as it passed from the head counselor to the staff nurse and back, searching for a weak link, a moment when someone's attention strayed. It soothed me to game it all out, having the key in my pocket, cat-footing it into the staff room after lights out and opening up that big steel-mounted cabinet of pharmaceutical-grade oblivion.

That was what I hungered for now: an off-switch, a way out. A couple grams of Oxycontin crushed into a tumbler of Stoli. A fiery car crash. A leap from a high bridge. Blackout, gone. But I wasn't going to jump off a bridge. I wasn't going to O.D. on Oxy, either. I didn't have the balls for a move like that. Which meant it was either the drip, drip, drip oblivion of Stoli and weed, or I was going to have to learn to sit with this, face the fact that my problem wasn't the skinnies or the escorts or the foil-wrapped bud in my closet, but me.

At the turnoff to Shelter Ridge, Suze asked me to pull in at the Chevron station on Frontage Road so she could clean up in the bathroom. When she came back out, we didn't say another word until we were parked outside her condo staring up at her mother's Toyota in the driveway.

"Suze, I'm sorry," I said. "I know I keep saying that, but I am. All that back there, that had nothing to do with you."

"What *was* all that about?"

"I don't know if I can explain it," I said. "I've never been with anyone sober before. I've never done anything sober, ever. I keep thinking I know how things work, and then I don't."

"But it's been almost a year now, right?"

"No, I was lying about that. It's only been a few weeks, and I'm barely hanging onto that. Yesterday—I haven't told anybody this, but yesterday Rad came by the store and gave me a quarter ounce of weed."

"He *gave* it to you?"

"Well, no. I paid for it, sort of. It's a long story. Anyway, I haven't touched it, but I haven't thrown it away, either. It's in my closet at home."

"So, throw it out."

"I know, and I'm going to."

"All you have to do is flush it down the toilet."

"It's not that simple."

"Hey, you want complicated? Try raising two kids who hate your guts in a condo you can't afford while your husband, who's down in L.A. fucking some nineteen-year-old Pilates instructor, is talking about suing you for custody."

She turned away, her fingers pressed against her forehead, like she was holding back a gusher of rage and bile.

"Jimmy's suing you for custody?" I asked.

"No, he's not," she said. "Oh God, it's all so stupid. I got behind on my rent a little while ago and Jimmy found out. He keeps threatening to bring it up if I ever file for divorce—you know, tell the judge I can't support the kids. But he's so full of shit. He'll never do it because the judge could turn right around and make him pay more child support."

"But he could try to take Dylan and Jake."

"He could, yeah. But he won't. They're why he bailed in the first place." She turned to look at me. "I missed you this week. I don't think I got how much I missed you until I saw you today.

But I've got two kids here. My mom's paying half my rent. I can't be rolling around in the dirt with some guy. I'm in some pretty deep shit here myself."

I wanted to tell her I could help. I wanted to tell her about all the meetings I was hitting, how I was starting to think I might get clean for real this time. But it was bullshit, all of it. There was nothing I could say that wasn't bullshit. The only thing that mattered now was what I did.

"Throw out the drugs, Trent," she said.

"I will. Today."

"And stay away from Lee Radko. That guy's trouble."

"Yeah, I know. Totally."

She smiled, and in the way her expression melted I saw she'd already forgiven me, that she always would forgive me, that she couldn't help herself. I had watched her all those years with Jimmy, how he kept humiliating her and how she kept coming back, making excuses for him. I told myself I would never be that guy, but I saw now how easy Suze made it.

"Next time I see you," she said, popping the car door, "I want to hear how you flushed that weed down the toilet."

It was after five when I pulled up outside chez Starling. Through the row of cypress trees that shielded the house from the street, I could see Lupita in the kitchen stirring something in a cast-iron pan. Mom was at the kitchen island in a gauzy red dress, her long blonde hair tied back in a plaited bun. She had a glass of wine in her hand, and she was talking. She and Stan were going out that night—to a cocktail party, from the looks of it—and whatever Lupita was stirring in the pan, that was for me. Lupita would leave it on the stove, and when I was ready, Mom would sit with me in her stage makeup and her wine-colored dress, asking about my day, sifting my lies and evasions for answers to the real questions she'd stopped asking months ago.

I fished in my pocket for Frank's business card. It gave no address or job title, just his name, Francis X. Terrell, and a phone number. I pictured him drunk, his face flushed, his hair askew, whipping off his hassock or cassock or whatever it is they call that thing priests wear, in front of a ten-year-old girl. I wasn't going to call him. Not today. Maybe not ever. But I felt better knowing I could, that all I had to do was reach into my pocket and pull out his card.

# 10

"Uncle Stav, Andi—are they coming?" Gianni asked. His father slid his tired eyes toward me, looking for an ally. "Your uncle said he might drop by," he said. "If he finishes piecing out the beef delivery on time."

"Should we wait?" Gianni asked. "I figured they might want to hear some of this."

The truck that delivered sides of beef from an organic processing plant north of Petaluma had left at noon, eight hours ago. If by now Stavros and his meat room crew hadn't cut and dressed the half dozen beef sides the store went through in a week, it wasn't going to happen.

"Let's get started," Papadakis said. "If they show, they show."

All that week I had stayed late helping Gianni create a spreadsheet detailing the competing bids for a fleet of delivery vans. Originally, he'd planned to buy three vans, each painted Grecian blue with the Chef Tamalpais logo painted on the sides. But with the cost of renovations on the new building soaring, he'd scaled back to two vans and a golf-cart-looking thing for deliveries around town—and even that was looking like it might bust the budget.

It was eight o'clock on Thursday night when his dad showed up to look at our spreadsheets. Papadakis had been at the store when the doors opened at seven that morning and he looked it, his eyes red-rimmed, his shirt collar flecked with tomato sauce, but when he took a seat across from Gianni and me at the conference table, he rubbed his hands together like a guy sitting down to a hot meal. "Okey doke," he said. "What've you got for me?"

Gianni walked his father through the bids, explaining how they could shave a few dollars here and get a better price there, while I handed him spreadsheets and vehicle specs. Most of the bids were non-starters, but two—one from a dealership in Oakland, another near Fresno—had come in at $80,000 including tax and service contracts. When Gianni turned over the last spreadsheet, showing the final tally, his father nodded slowly, lips pursed, his expression unreadable.

"This is before you hire drivers, right?" he asked.

"Yeah, and that could get pricey," Gianni said. "So, if we want to go a little less aggressive"—I handed him another stack of spreadsheets, which he passed to his father—"I looked at leasing the vans instead of buying them. That gets us down to five grand a month. You pay more over the life of the fleet, of course, but it does bring down your up-front costs."

Papadakis flipped through the second set of spreadsheets, squinting through his half glasses. "I talked to Hal this morning," he said, setting the papers aside.

Hal, I knew, was Harlan Stafford, the loan officer handling the Tam Grocery account at the Savings Bank of Marin.

"Dad, if we listened to Hal, we never would have tried this in the first place," Gianni said.

"They're three hundred grand into this thing already," his father said. "If we want them to open up the credit line any more, we'll have to take out a mortgage on this building here."

I had been working at Tam Grocery long enough to know how much it meant to the Papadakises that they owned their building free and clear. A framed copy of the original mortgage, stamped cancelled on November 13, 1983, hung on the wall next to the door.

"Trent and me, we've scoured the West Coast," Gianni said. "This is the best deal we're going to get. If we have to give up a little equity to make it happen, it's worth it. A year after we open, we'll be in the black."

Papadakis chewed the arm of his half-rims, considering his son. With his glasses off, he looked a decade older, his cheeks slack, his eyes sunk into his skull, their rubbed-penny brown dulled to the color of wet cement.

"No, you won't," he said. "Forget drivers. You haven't even

hired kitchen staff yet. Even if you're turning a profit, the interest on the loan'll eat a hole in your rear end." He shook his head. "No, it's too much. Maybe next summer if the economy picks up, we can come back to this."

"Next summer?"

"It's been a tough year," his father said. "But if we have a big Christmas, maybe we can get some cash flow going, and we'll see if Hal can open up our credit line."

"There's a dozen guys working on that building. They're putting in the kitchen tomorrow."

"I know. Six weeks late."

"What do you want me to do, shut it down? Tell them all to go home?"

"Oh God, no," Papadakis said. "We'd spend the next ten years in court. No, we're going to do what we should've done from the start. We're going to take this slowly. In stages. First, we open as a deli. We can cater events, maybe even do some home delivery. No vans, no trucks, just local kids working for tips like at a pizza joint."

"Dad, I've run these numbers a million times," Gianni said. "There's no way it works without home delivery. The mortgage on the new building's too high. We can last a year, maybe two, but sooner or later we're gonna have to give it back."

"Then maybe we'll have to give it back," his father said.

Gianni sagged, stunned, taking the punch. Now I understood why we were here: Papadakis was pulling the plug on the home-catering business. The family, Stavros, Andi, and the rest, had made their decision, and Papadakis had been delegated to break the news to Gianni.

"It wouldn't be the end of the world," he said. "We've already spent a ton of money, and no matter what we do we're going to spend a bunch more. But the deli business has always been strong here, and we'll still have the store. We'll be fine."

"We are *not* going to be fine!" Gianni shouted. "Cornucopia's kicking our ass. We're losing money and market share, and they want us gone."

"Son, calm down."

Gianni pushed back his chair. "Okay, you know what? Fuck this. I need some air."

"Hey, whoa, whoa," his father said. "What kind of language is that?"

"You and Uncle Stav can stick your heads in the sand all you want," Gianni shouted. "We're dying here and counting pennies on truck purchases isn't going save us." He turned to me. "Lock up, will you? I'm outta here."

"Come back here!" his father shouted, but Gianni had already stormed out into the corridor, slamming the door behind him. After a few clattering footsteps on the stairs, the building went silent.

"He'll be back," Papadakis said to the closed door. "He just needs to blow off some steam."

But even he didn't look like he believed this. He looked like someone had slapped him, hard. I started picking up spreadsheets, wishing there was something I could do, something I could say. He was such a decent guy, so soft-spoken and kind, and here he was having doors slammed in his face and getting yelled at by his son.

"You don't have to do that," he said. "I'll take care of it. Your mom's probably wondering what the heck happened to you by now."

I set down the spreadsheets and stood. I wanted to apologize, but I couldn't think for what. "Anything else you need before I clock out?" I asked.

"A double scotch wouldn't hurt." He smiled. "No, I'm good. Go home, get out of here."

I reached under the computer desk where I kept my backpack, Papadakis's eyes still burning a hole in the back of my head.

"What do you think?" he asked. "Is Gianni right? Are we done here?"

"I don't know if I'm the right guy to ask, Mr. Papadakis."

"Call me Mike, okay?" he said. "And I'm not asking for your

business judgment. I'm asking you as a customer—a longtime customer. Thirty years ago when the chains started beating us on price, we decided to beat them on quality and service. But this new store, Cornucopia, they're different. They do what we do, but on a national scale. Gianni says we have to go after them, beat them to the punch on the next big thing."

I thought of my dad cruising the aisles of Tam Grocery in his aviator shades and backward ball cap. I hadn't seen him in years, but if I had to picture him in a supermarket, it wouldn't be Tam Grocery. It would be Cornucopia Foods.

"With all due respect, I don't think you have a choice," I said. "I think you have to go for it, all out. Otherwise, they'll crush you."

He stared a moment, then shook his head, chuckling. "Okay, I guess I asked for that."

"No, wait, don't listen to me," I said. "What do I know about the grocery business?"

He held up his hand, waving me off. "See you tomorrow, Trent. And thank you for being honest. Every day you make me feel a little smarter for hiring you."

When I came in the next morning a tractor trailer was parked in the gravel lot behind the Post Office building and a crew of beefy guys in orange reflective vests were loading in stainless-steel sinks and industrial ovens. Gianni was nowhere to be seen. Not that he needed to be there, really. The floor plan had been spec'd out weeks ago, and there were architects and crew foremen to direct traffic. Still, it was weird. Gianni had spent two years designing that kitchen, obsessing over every last electrical outlet. I couldn't see him missing out on seeing all those big cello-wrapped machines go in. But he was gone all day—no note, no calls, nothing.

I spent the day running between the two buildings, taking phone calls and signing off on bills of lading, but whenever I had a minute to myself I shut the office door and punched in the numbers for Suze's cell, all but the last one. I had been doing this all week. It calmed me, somehow, the thought of Suze saying hello, her voice rising in surprise when she realized it was me. But I never hit that last digit. After our afternoon out at the bunkers, I didn't know if Suze would take my call, and I wasn't so sure I wanted to hear what she would say if she did.

When the last delivery truck pulled out of the parking lot that afternoon, I locked up and walked the three blocks back to the main building to clock out. Upstairs, the door to the business office was open and Gianni was standing at his desk in a black spandex cycling outfit, flipping through a stack of phone messages. Wrapped in shiny spandex, his pink face glowing with sweat, he looked more toy than human, like a life-size Lego mini-figure plucked, mid-cycle, from the washing machine.

"So, the truck people called?" he said, holding up a message slip.

"Yeah, the Fresno guys," I said. "They wanted to know if we had an answer on their bid."

"What'd you tell them?"

"I said we were loading in the new kitchen today and you'd call as soon as all the machines were in."

He nodded, taking this in. "You think they believed you?"

"Honestly? I have no idea. I was just stalling the guy until you got back."

I hadn't realized how angry I was until I heard the snap in my voice. Gianni must have heard it, too, because he tossed the message slips onto the desk. "Hey, sorry about leaving you hanging today," he said. "I hopped on my bike for a morning ride and before I knew it I was halfway to Healdsburg."

"Healdsburg? That's like fifty miles from here."

"Try sixty. With hills." He grinned, proud of himself. "You should come along sometime, man. I took the back way along the Bolinas Ridge over Mt. Tam. Fucking gorgeous. No cars, no people, nothing but open road as far as you could see."

Wherever he was heading with this, it was nowhere I wanted to go. But it wasn't five o'clock yet, and technically I was still on the clock. I was curious, too. This guy in crotch-hugging spandex calling me "man" and inviting me to skip a day's work to cycle the back roads over Mt. Tam, it wasn't the Gianni Papadakis I knew.

"You didn't tell my dad about the Fresno guys, did you?" he asked.

"Gianni, I hardly saw your dad today."

"Good. Don't, okay? Not for a few more days." He was pacing now, his ankle socks leaving faint steam imprints on the hardwood floor. "Close that, will you?" he said, nodding toward the door. "I want to show you something."

I did as I was told, looking both ways down the corridor as Gianni unlocked the top drawer of his desk and pulled out a thumb-sized flash drive. He inserted it into his computer tower, and with a flurry of keystrokes, typed in his access code. Eight digits, I noted, starting with the numbers 1-1.

"I should have shown you this a long time ago," he said, clicking through screens. "These are year-end sales figures going back to 1997. You know what happened in 1997, right?"

In 1997, I'd wrapped my Christmas-present Saab around a tree coming home from a party. In 1997, I had finally, formally, dropped out of school and started full-time at Campus Liquors. It was also the last time I had spoken to my father. But I knew what Gianni meant.

"Cornucopia opened here in 1997," I said.

"Very good." He pointed to the screen. "Tell me what you see."

What I saw were four columns of figures, starting with FY 1997 and ending with FY 2000, and a fifth column of sales categories, with titles like, "baked goods," "beverages, beer," "beverages, juices." I scanned the page, searching for a pattern in the wilderness of numbers.

"Okay well, your sales are down," I said. "They're down a *lot*, every year."

"Except the deli and fine wines," he said, pointing to the relevant line items. "We're holding our own there. But everywhere else, we're down nearly twenty percent in four years."

"Twenty percent?"

"This isn't just us, Trent," he said. "The same thing's happening across the country. It's how Cornucopia does business. They move into markets where independents have thrived and they bleed their competitors dry. Then when guys like my dad throw in the towel, they buy them out for pennies on the dollar."

I turned back to the long rows of numbers. Twenty percent in four years. No wonder Hal Stafford was getting antsy about his credit line.

"Here's the thing," Gianni said. "When I turned twenty-five, I inherited a one-fifth interest in the store. Andi has the same. So does my uncle. The way it's set up, nobody can make a major decision—move money around, make a big capital investment—without the rest of the family." His eyes found mine. "You see where I'm going with this?"

I stared back. I didn't, at all.

"I own twenty percent of a business worth millions, but I'm outnumbered," he said. "I love this store. I want it to be here for my kids, same as Pappouli left it for me and Andi. But you heard Dad last night. He wants to give the new building back to the bank."

"Have you shown him these numbers?"

"Of course I have. Many times." He was up again, pacing, his sock-feet leaving more sweaty imprints on the floorboards. "You've got to understand, for guys like my dad, stocking shelves, produce delivery on Tuesday, meat on Thursday, it's all he knows. Nothing I say is going to do anything but make him come back tomorrow and work a little harder. We need a professional here. An investor. Somebody who can see this thing the way it needs to be seen."

The dime finally dropped. "*Stan?*"

"I know what you're thinking, but I've been reading up on your stepdad," he said. "The guy knows digital retail. And he knows us. We talked this summer about doing a loan."

"Yeah, and he turned you down."

"Not exactly," Gianni said. "He wanted exclusive franchise

rights if the online business took off. Now, exclusive rights, that's never going to happen. But if he came in with a bridge loan"—he shrugged, a Greek Don Corleone—"maybe we could work something out."

I stared at him all kitted out in black spandex and thought of my granddad's old line: *I didn't know whether to shit or go blind.*

"What about your dad?" I asked. "Does he know about this?"

He shot a glance at the door. "I'll talk to him. But first I need to know if there's interest."

"All right, well, trust me, you don't want me anywhere near Stan Starling."

"No, no, I know," he said. "I'm not talking about you. I'm talking about your mom. That meeting this summer, it never would have happened if it wasn't for her."

"You want me to talk to my mother…about Stan?"

"All you'd have to do is tell her I want to meet with him. That's it, just a meeting. I know if I can sit down with him, I can get him to see this the way I do."

I liked Gianni more just then than I ever had. He was so proud, so desperate to prove his dad wrong and save the family business. If there was a shred of human decency left in me, I needed to keep him the hell away from Stan Starling.

"All right," I said. "If you're serious about this, I'll talk to her."

"Will you?" he said. "Because I'm right about this. Ten years from now, people will be doing all their shopping online, not just groceries—clothes, music, household items, everything. We can't afford to miss out on that."

"I said I'll talk to her," I said.

But I didn't. Instead, I spent the weekend looking for a place to live. The first couple weeks, honestly, I hadn't looked that hard. I had moved three times since I left the dorms in S.B., and it never took me more than a day or two to find an apartment. But I hadn't been a convicted felon then. Now, everywhere I went, even the unpainted farmhouse deep in the Sonoma hills where a grow-room funk hung like fog over the padlocked barn, the conversation always ended with somebody handing me a rental application, with space for my credit history and a list of questions that ended with, "Have you ever been convicted for selling, possessing, distributing, or manufacturing illegal drugs or convicted of any other crime?" If I really wanted a place, I lied, but I had to report any change of address to my probation officer and I knew that would be the first question Ponytail Pete would ask. So most of the time I just filled out the form and shook hands all round, knowing I would never see any of these people again.

When I got home Sunday night, Mom and Stan were out and a plate of fish tacos sat waiting for me on the stove. I took the tacos downstairs to Stan's oak-paneled man cave and slapped a DVD of *Blood Beach* into the wall-mounted TV. I hadn't watched *Blood Beach* since high school when I saw it with my dad at the old Paramount Drive-In in Compton. Dad was the one who'd turned me on to horror flicks in the first place. Before he married Caressa, I spent a month with him every summer, just the two of us in his glass-walled mansion in the Hollywood Hills, and we hit a different movie every night, the cheesier and bloodier the better.

We went back to see *Blood Beach* two or three times at the Paramount, where we could duck behind the popcorn stand to spark up between features. This was the eighties, the golden age of arena rock, and Dad was up every morning at five going over stadium receipts he had flown in overnight from wherever his bands were touring, totting up grosses and bawling out road managers for shorting his clients on merchandise sales. But by four in the afternoon he'd be on the patio pounding margaritas with A&R men from the big downtown labels, his hair slicked back, his skin toasted brown, like he'd been doing nothing all day but hanging around the pool pronging the topless blonde sunning herself in the deck chair beside him.

God, he made it all look so easy. The cocaine helped, of

course. So did the amphetamines he popped like breath mints. But there was an animal strength to the man, a dog-like persistence that enabled him to sink his professionally capped teeth into whatever he wanted—a girl, a stadium deal, a new act he wanted to represent—and hold on until his target flopped to the ground in exhaustion.

That was what was so great about our movie nights. If we went to a Dodgers game, he always brought clients, and the few times I tagged along on his scouting missions to the clubs on the Strip, he forgot I was there the minute we passed the stage door. At the movies, there were no girls, no sweaty-palmed A&R guys, no shouting matches over merch sales, just the two of us stoned out of our minds in his white-on-white Mercedes in some dirt lot in Compton watching a badly shot movie about a mutant worm gnawing the legs off bikini-clad babes under the Santa Monica Pier. He was off-duty on those nights, just himself, a guy who liked to get high and watch low-budget spatter flicks. In the car, sharing a big, syrupy Dr. Pepper, we cracked each other up over the half-assed plots, the ketchup spurting from severed limbs, the actresses who kept looking off-camera to read their lines.

But without the drugs, without my dad, *Blood Beach* was just another lame monster movie. Fifteen minutes in, while the two leads were talking on the pier, the microphone boom dropped into the shot. Stuff like that always made my dad laugh, but when I turned to point it out to him, he wasn't there. I was alone in the dim, wood-paneled room. A minute later, when the mic dropped into the shot again, I hit the remote and popped the DVD out of the machine.

I wandered the empty house, pinballing from room to room, wishing my dad was someone I could call out of the blue. All these years later, I still knew his phone number, but even if I could get past Caressa, what would I say? That I was lonely and scared? That I had no idea what I was going to do if I couldn't find a new place to live? That all I wanted to do was break out the quarter ounce of Lee's weed I'd somehow never gotten around to throwing away? I couldn't say any of that, not to my dad. My father hated weakness. Fat people, ugly people, people who couldn't sing or cut a record deal, they were just boring. Weak people disgusted him. *I* disgusted him. He had never said it, not in so many words, but he didn't need to. It was why he left all those years ago, why I hadn't heard from him since I drove his stupid second-hand Saab into that tree. I was weak. Weak. Weak. Weak.

The phone rang in the kitchen. I was about to let it go to voice mail when I remembered a couple I'd met in Petaluma that morning who had converted their garage into an extra bedroom. They lived an hour from Mill Valley and I would have to share a bathroom with their teenage son, but the garage conversion wasn't legal, which meant that in the half hour I spent with them checking out the room and going over the house rules, nobody had mentioned a credit report.

By the time I got to the phone it had stopped ringing, but I hit *69 and waited, mentally running a towel through my hair, working up a story about how I'd just jumped out of the shower.

"Trent?" a throaty voice said in my ear.

In the background, just above the whoosh of wind and the mosquito-like whine of a car engine, I heard a riot of guitars and horns backing Christina Aguilera, Lil' Kim, and P!nk on "Lady Marmalade."

"Who's this?"

I heard a hard, bright champagne pop of laughter. "Your fairy fucking godmother, dude! We're coming to bust you out."

"Jin? Wait, you're coming *here*?"

That set off another run of cackles, and I heard the jostling of the phone being passed from hand to hand.

"It's your lucky day, Pussy Willow," Lee said. "There's a big rager in Sausalito, and you're invited."

"What're you talking about?" I said. "How'd you even get this number?"

"Dude, you live with your mom. How hard could it be? I'm

doing you a favor here, so get your hands off your dick and tell me how to get to Ralston Avenue."

"No fucking way. I've got to work in the morning."

"Makes two of us," he said. "Just tell me how to get to your mom's place. We've been driving around this shit for like half an hour now."

This didn't smell right. Why would Lee Radko call me at ten o'clock on a Sunday night to invite me to a party in Sausalito? But he seemed to know I would say yes. And he was right. Parties were drugs and beer and every kind of thing that would send me right back to the Santa Barbara County Jail. But parties were also girls. And fresh air. And new faces. Staying here cooped up in my mother's second husband's empty house, that was just going to end up with me in my closet hunting for that quarter ounce of Double Black Orchid.

I was weak. Weak. Weak. Weak.

Jin's car was a bubble-gum-pink convertible VW Bug with chrome rims and a padded roll bar, the word "BAADGRRL" spelled out on the vanity license plate. I was still arguing that the back seat was too small for me to ride in when Jin slammed the car into gear and we roared off, trailing Lil' Kim. Lee passed me a cold Heineken, which I set unopened on the floor of the car while he hunched over in the front seat, trying to light his hash pipe in the wind.

When the pipe came around to me, I sat back in the seat, holding the still-smoldering pipe. It was the same one we used the day we got high behind Old Brown Store, a finger-length lozenge of burnished oak with a miniature pot leaf carved into the stem. It sat warm in my palm, like a live thing, a small, purring animal.

The first hot jet of smoke I took in caught me by surprise and I coughed it right back up. The next one I held in. It felt so good down there, warm and delicious, like that first sip of coffee in the morning. I flashed on Suze Randall, pulling off her Jackie O. sunglasses to tell me to stay away from Lee Radko, but it was too late. I sucked down another hit, then another, hacking and spewing like a guy just in from the TB ward.

"Gimme that, you fucking pipe hog!" Lee shouted, turning around.

I let him have it. I was done, anyway. I lay back, the wind whipping my hair, feeling the drug seep into my bloodstream. I'd blown it, again. Let myself down, again. In a few hours, I would be wracked with guilt, looking for somebody to confess to. But for now I was high, sprawled across the back seat of a pink convertible VW Bug headed to a party in the Sausalito hills. My long, depressing weekend of looking at unfurnished rooms I couldn't afford, that was gone. Gianni Papadakis and his crackpot scheme to save Tam Grocery, that was gone, too. All of it, the promises I'd made, the lies I'd told, they were wiped away, erased from the hard drive, and I was free to stare up into the star-spackled sky, comforted by how little what I'd done mattered to all those billions of tiny suns spinning out into infinity.

We pulled off the highway and started up a steep, winding private road to Wolfback Ridge, a double row of redwood-and-glass mansions high on a rocky bluff overlooking Sausalito. It was a traffic jam up there, secondhand Beemers and Porsches jockeying for parking in the narrow pullouts, and we ditched Jin's Bug to walk the last hundred yards. In all my years in Marin, I had never been on Wolfback Ridge, but this I'd done a thousand times, walked high and bleary-eyed along an unlit mountain road past cars full of teenagers pounding beers and sparking final bowls before heading into a party. When Lee said we were hitting a party, I'd pictured the backyard of a house near the water, women my age, music playing on speakers hanging from a tree branch, maybe even a pick-up band. Not this. Not a high school party. But it was a warm August night, balmy in a way it almost never gets in that part of Marin, and I was pleasantly toasted, so I kept walking, riding that fluffy white cloud of Double Black Orchid.

The party was at the last house on the street, three stories of cantilevered decks and soaring windows like some giant, red-wood-shingled pterodactyl poised to take flight. All the houses up there were like that, built to look cool to people on drugs. Wolfback Ridge was where the rock stars lived, or at least where they'd lived until they were priced out by the investment bankers and tech geniuses.

"Where you think you're going?" said a neckless giant in a Tam High football jersey, No. 62, stepping up to Lee. "This is a private party."

"Out of my face, shithead," Lee said, waving him off.

Two more football players, Nos. 73 and 64, joined the first one, forming a thick, unsmiling wall. These guys were security, the Marin-kid equivalent of hiring off-duty cops to watch the door of your nightclub.

"Guys, guys, chill," Jin said. "We're friends of Larissa's. She invited us."

"She invited *you?*" No. 62 said to Lee.

"We're bringing the entertainment, asshole," Lee said, brushing past him.

Jin popped off another of her champagne-cork laughs and hustled up the stone path after him, leaving me alone on the driveway surrounded by glassy-eyed teenagers.

"How about you, man?" No. 62 asked me. "You here to entertain us, too?"

"Not if I can help it," I said, slipping by. "I'm just looking for a ride home."

Inside, I roamed the mansion's maze-like halls, ducking into darkened bedrooms and scanning the crowded patio for Lee. That was one very weird house to be stoned in. One upstairs room was stocked with eighties action figures: Han Solo and Chewbacca from *Star Wars*, the *Ghostbusters* gang, Dream Glow Barbie and Ken still pristine in their boxes. In another bedroom, tropical fish swam in aquariums made out of candy-colored iMac monitors, and all the appliances—lamps, clocks, picture frames, even the light-switch covers—were built from old Nintendo and Sony PlayStation game consoles. Every now and then a kid poked one of PlayStations to see if it would light up or staged a sex scene between Chewbacca and Princess Leia, but mostly they just talked and laughed and broke things. I envied them, in a way. It's fun to be that heedless, to know that everything you touch is expensive and rare and not give a shit. Mostly, though, it just made me feel tired. And sad. And old.

I gave up looking for Lee and found a spot on the porch overlooking the yard and beyond it, the blue-black expanse of the Bay set against the lights of the San Francisco hills. There was a pool back there, a blue oval lit up like a Day-Glo Easter egg, but nobody was swimming in it. Instead, the crowd swarmed around two kegs on the trampled lawn. I didn't want to be around when the beer ran out and the real mayhem started. I didn't want to be there, period. All weekend I'd been dreaming of calling Suze, the moment when I could punch in the last digit of her phone number and tell her I had a new place to live. But here I was homeless and high at a high school kegger party in some rich guy's ugly house in the Sausalito hills, waiting for Lee Radko to sell out his stash so I could catch a ride home.

"Kinda makes you wish you brought a swimsuit, huh?" he said, sliding in beside me at the railing. "Except it looks like Blondie down there forgot hers, too."

I had been half-watching the girl he was talking about. She was chunky and blonde with lots of pale orange freckles, and she had either fallen into the pool or been pushed. Now she was splashing around the shallow end, her tube top and jeans wet-welded to her skin, her clear-plastic heels bobbing in the water behind her.

"Somebody oughta go down there," he said, "help that poor girl out of her wet things."

"That girl's shit-faced, Lee. *And* she's in high school."

"'Don't ask, don't tell,' right? Isn't that what the man said?"

"Right up until they impeached his horny ass. When'd you start selling coke to high school kids?"

He fixed me with that jailyard stare. "What makes you so sure it's blow?"

"You've been gone less than half an hour. Nobody sells out a weed stash that fast."

He shrugged, granting me the point. "Maybe you heard of this new law they got, Prop 215? Little Johnny can go to his doctor, get a note saying he needs five grams a month for his anxiety issues. Makes it hard for the little guy to compete." He nodded toward the pool. "Check it out. Blondie's lost her top."

Below us, the chubby blonde was wearing only her jeans now, shrieking in mock outrage as three football players tossed her wet tube top over her head, playing Monkey in the Middle. A crowd had gathered around the edges of the pool, the girls looking on in undisguised horror, the guys just staring, unable to take their eyes off the topless girl's flopping white breasts.

"One of your many satisfied customers?" I asked.

He nodded. "Tell her you're with me and I promise she'll take the rest of it off."

There was a scream and a splash as a second girl, a redhead this time, sailed into the pool. The real party was starting now. In a few minutes, the pool would be full of kids, mostly girls but some guys, too, play-scrapping and tearing at each other's clothes.

"I hope you know what you're doing," I said. "A coke bust, that's some serious time. Especially if it involves minors."

"You'd know all about that, wouldn't you?"

I thought of what I had told Frank about how much easier it was to let people think I'd been busted for drugs. Even now, when it would have made things easier, I couldn't bring myself to tell Lee about the theft, about looting a man's business so I could party with a bunch of overpriced hookers.

"I'm not doing that anymore," I said. "I'm retired."

"Retired, my ass. I saw you hitting on that pipe tonight."

"That was a mistake. It's not going to happen again."

"Whatever. This here's a straight-up business proposition. Jin knows where the parties are. Who's looking, how much they'll pay, all that. But I need a real partner on this shit, somebody I know, somebody's got my back when I go on buys."

I picked out Jin at the edge of the patio in a black leather miniskirt and heels, a plastic beer cup in one hand, a cigarette in the other, looking bored out of her skull. When I was a kid, girls like Jin had seemed so exotic, with their older boyfriends and grown-up jobs. Now I knew better. They were the future crackhead Nadines of the world.

"You didn't need to bring me here," I said. "I would've said the same on the phone. I'm not going anywhere near this shit."

He turned away, his mouth a thin angry line. "Okay, I'll make it easy on you," he said. "You front me a grand or two, I'll pay you back with interest."

"You want me to play bank?"

"I'm trying to get back in the game here, Wolfer," he said. "Not this kiddie bullshit. The real thing. My connect in Oregon, he's moving to Canada. Dude's got a whole fucking island up there, just him and a few other guys. Gets his power off a generator, enough to run six ops around the clock. He wants me to come up there, help out with the harvest."

I hated how much I liked the sound of this: a private island off the Canadian coast, no Gianni, no Stan, no sharing a shower with a pimple-faced teenager in Petaluma, just suitcases full of cash and all the premium dope I could smoke.

"You're really getting out of here?" I asked.

"As soon as I can put together fifty grand," he said. "So, whatever you got, I'll take it. These Mexican fucks I'm dealing with, they're sitting on kilos and I'm buying by the ounce."

I thought again of the converted garage I'd looked at in Petaluma. This was the last weekend in August. If I didn't find a place to live by next week, I would be camping out in my car.

"Sorry, man, no can do," I said.

"What the fuck? You'd just be playing bank. You wouldn't even have to touch the product."

Before I could start in again about hitting my meetings and staying clean, he threw up his hands, done.

"Yo, Jin!" he shouted. "Up here!"

She looked up from her spot near the pool, searching the

darkened balcony. When she saw us, she waved, relieved. "Where'd you go?" she shouted. "I've been looking everywhere."

Lee waved back, grinning, and mimed two fingers walking down the stairs.

"I got a few more eights to unload," he said to me. "If you change your mind, let me know. This here's a gold mine, dog. These little skanks, it's like they've never *seen* cocaine before."

# 11

The next morning when my alarm went off, all I wanted, all I could think about was getting high. I had barely slept and my head was pounding like someone had taken a power drill to it, but I shrugged on a robe and cat-footed it up the stairs looking for an apple and a paring knife. I hadn't smoked an apple pipe since sixth grade, but I still knew how to make one. You core the apple, unscrew a mesh screen from the bathroom sink, and press it into the cored apple: instant hash pipe. I paused at the top of the stairs, my ears pricked for sounds from the master bedroom, and ducked into the kitchen—where I nearly ran headlong into my mother carrying two steaming mugs of green tea, one for her, the other for Stan.

"Hey, you're up early," she said.

"I'm going for a run," I said, thinking fast.

I stopped there, out of ideas. The apples sat in a lacquered redwood bowl on the table, a pyramid of pale green Granny Smiths and speckled red Fujis.

"You were out pretty late last night," she said, handing Stan his tea.

"Yeah, I decided to hit a movie after I got back."

"Without your car?" Stan asked.

I shrugged. "My date's ride was nicer than mine."

The lie lay there, turd-like, next to the fruit bowl. For thirty years, you think your lies are so smart, so wickedly sly, until one morning it hits you that you've been getting away with it all this time only because it would be so much easier on everyone if what you were saying was true.

"You're being awfully mysterious about this girl," Mom said.

"It's just, it's still kind of new," I said. "I'm not sure how long it's going to last, you know?"

"I like the sound of that," Mom said, unfurling one of her slow, lip-rippling grins. "That there's a chance it might last."

I smiled back, giving her nothing. "Any caffeine in that?" I asked, nodding to her mug.

There wasn't, and without Lupita around to help, it took us five minutes of opening cabinets and fumbling with kitchen gadgets to get a kettle going, grind the beans, and spoon coffee into the French-press coffee maker. By the time I filled my mug with Columbian Roast, my morning run and my late-night movie date had been conveniently forgotten.

"You hungry?" Mom asked. "There's bagels around here somewhere, I think."

"I was thinking of keeping it light, maybe just have an apple."

The room quieted as I plucked a yellow-flecked Granny Smith from the bowl and rummaged in the cutlery drawer for a paring knife.

"You didn't find any apartments this weekend, did you?" Stan said.

I stopped looking for the knife. I didn't care for the way he'd put the question, like he already knew the answer.

"I found plenty of apartments," I said. "They didn't want me or my lousy credit history."

"Honey, I told you, I can co-sign the lease," Mom said. "We'll help with the first couple months' rent, too, if you need it."

"It's not enough, Ma, not in Marin," I said. "I need more time."

"How much more?" she asked, her eyes finding Stan.

"I don't know," I said. "A couple weeks, maybe a month."

"A *month*?" Stan said.

"Look, if I'm not wanted here," I said, "I can have my shit packed in an hour."

"Be my guest, pal," Stan said. "I'll help you pack."

"Hey, hey, guys!" Mom said, standing between us. "No one's going anywhere, not today."

"We had a deal, Sandy," Stan said. "One month and he was out."

"You heard him," she said. "He just spent the weekend looking for apartments."

"Bullshit!" Stan roared. "He's been lying from the minute he walked in here. He didn't go to the fucking movies last night. He was out partying. I was still up when his buddies dropped him off. You should've heard them out there, laughing and shouting, high as kites."

I grabbed a paring knife from the drawer and a Granny Smith from the bowl and stormed down the stairs, leaving the stunned kitchen behind me. The obvious call was to eat the apple, get dressed, and go to work. After all, I still had a job, and in a few hours, after Stan and my mother finished killing each other, I might still have a place to live for another couple weeks. But even as I shucked off my robe and pulled on my khakis and a pale blue Tam Grocery polo, that power drill was boring into my skull, and I needed that Orchid hit *now, now, now.*

I rooted through the piles of dirty clothes and old CDs in the closet, anger bubbling up in me like steam in a kettle. I had a minute, maybe less, before I blew, started whaling on myself, rolling on the floor, howling, punching my head, my neck, my arms, my chest, anything I could reach. At the back of the closet, I found my new dress shoes and jammed my hand into the left shoe where I'd stashed the quarter ounce of Double Black Orchid. It was empty. I reached for the right shoe. Again, nothing. I tried the left shoe again, then the right.

"Looking for these?" Stan said from the bedroom doorway.

I jumped back so fast I slammed my shoulder against the closet door, sending a flamethrower of pain down my right arm.

"Lupita found these last week," he said, holding out the two lumpy foil balls for me to see. "I was wondering how long it would take you to figure out they were missing."

"You sent the fucking *maid* to spy on him?" Mom shouted from the hall.

"He's using again, Sandy," Stan said patiently. "Can't you see that? He's been doing it all along. Lupita found a bunch of those little airplane bottles in the garbage."

"You had that bitch go through his trash?"

"Mom, please, stop!" I shouted.

"If you wanted to kick him out, you fucking prick, why didn't you just do it?" my mother screamed, beating him with her tiny fists. "Why'd you have to bring the fucking help into it?"

"Stop, okay? Just *stop!*" I shouted. "He's right. I came down here looking for that weed he's got right there in his hand."

She was crying now, her finely featured face red and crumpled. In the space of five minutes, her whole carefully constructed life, the work of decades, had been blown to smithereens.

"We'll take you rehab right now," she said. "We can charter a plane and have you in Santa Barbara by noon today. Nobody has to know. I'll work it out with the Papadakises."

"Ma, I'm not letting you charter a freaking jet to take me back to rehab," I said.

"Well, you're sure as hell not staying here," Stan said.

"Fine," I said, blowing past him. "I've slept in my car before. I can do it again."

Behind me, I heard my mother screaming at Stan to get his filthy fucking hands off her, and then I was out the door, jogging to my car, carrying my dress shoes in my hand. I flew down the mountain, my feet bare on the pedals, slaloming down the twisty single-lane road, spraying rocks at every turn. I had no idea where I was going, what came next. If I begged, Lee might let me crash on his couch until we hit enough of his kiddie parties that I could afford a place of my own. But even in full panic, adrenaline pumping through my veins, I knew how that would end. Inside a week, I'd be dipping into the product.

At the bottom of the hill, I turned toward downtown, driving aimlessly past the shuttered shopfronts. I didn't know where I was headed until I turned onto Throckmorton Avenue and pulled into the employee lot behind Tam Grocery. It was still early, and the employee lot was empty except for Mr. Papadakis's homely brown Celica. Inside, the lights were on, and I could smell the loaves of fresh sourdough stacked by the back door. I heard voices, too—Murray, who ran the overnight crew, and Mr. Papadakis talking inventory as they broke down boxes in the stock room. Any minute now, the morning crew would start trickling in, first the meat-room guys, then the checkers and Henry's deli team, everyone turning on lights, counting out tills, and stacking newspapers in preparation for the first wave of morning shoppers.

I cut around back and let myself into the deli kitchen. The ovens were on, racks of fresh rolls and croissants cooling on the countertops, but the big room was empty. I loaded a toasted onion bagel with cream cheese and Scottish lox, and took it upstairs. After a week of late nights with the delivery van specs, the office looked like a tornado had hit: chairs facing every which way, the floor unswept, unfiled invoice carbons and spreadsheets piled on every available surface. I gave myself ten minutes for breakfast, browsing the latest *California Grocer*, before I attacked the stacks of paper, starting in one corner and working my way across the room, sorting and filing as I went. In a few hours, I knew, I would have to start calling the landlords I'd met over the weekend. I had a pretty good idea how that was going to go, so for now I was happy to have a task, something to do with my hands. At Campus Liquors, even when the bank account was nearly zeroed out and the phones were ringing off the hook with creditors wondering what had happened to their money, I kept a neat office. This was a habit I picked up from my dad. No matter where he'd been the night before and no matter how late he'd stayed there, he started the day by clearing his desk and filing every piece of paper he didn't plan to throw out.

That's what I did now, checked every sheet of paper, deciding what needed to be tossed, what needed to be filed, and what needed to be set aside for Gianni to read later. Once I had the room more or less in shape, I sat down with the weekly sales report. This was a Monday morning ritual for Gianni. After he'd tallied the weekend receipts and walked the cash across the street to the bank, he spent an hour combing through the week's sales figures, checking inventory levels and having me call in rush orders of whatever we'd run out of over the weekend.

That Monday, a week before Labor Day, we were down to half our usual backstock of soft drinks and a single pallet of charcoal. Grabbing a pen, I jotted a list on a sticky pad:

Labor Day → rush orders?
Soft drinks/juices/iced teas
Charcoal/lighter fluid
Beer, imported/domestic
Boxed wines, red/white
Pre-packed deli salads
Ketchup/mayo/mustard
Buns, hot dog/burger
Paper plates/plastic utensils

My list was crude and probably half as long as it needed to be, but I liked gaming it out, thinking through the calendar the way I used to for Spring Break and Grad Week at Campus Liquors. I tore the sticky note off the pad and pressed it onto the stack of inventory sheets on Gianni's desk.

Half an hour later, I was filing the last of the delivery van spreadsheets when the door clicked open and Gianni strode in, his backpack over one shoulder.

"Hey," he said, surprised.

His eyes made a slow circuit of the room. It was spotless, every sheet of paper either filed away or stacked on his desk awaiting his review. I had even swept the floor.

"Guess I'm going to have to start coming in earlier," he said, stowing his pack under his desk. "Dad tell you about Theo and Quan?"

"No way," I said. "Already?"

"Yep, he called them Friday when I was out. Gave them a month's pay and tore up their contracts. Effective immediately."

I looked to the open door, wishing I had spent even one minute of the last hour preparing for the question I knew was coming next.

"Gianni, my mom's been out of town," I said. "One of her

friends got married and they had this girl's weekend down in L.A."

He nodded slowly. "When does she get back?"

"Tonight, I think. But you'll have to give me a couple days. I need to pick my moment."

I was about to shovel on another load on top of that one when his eyes landed on the sticky note I'd pasted onto the sales report.

"What's this?" he asked, picking it up.

"I was looking at the inventory checklist this morning—"

"And what, you figured you'd do my job?"

But then he turned the page, then another, and another. He flipped back to the sticky note I'd tacked to the front sheet. "Hey, this isn't half-bad," he said.

"Thanks," I said.

"You forgot sunscreen," he said. "And bug spray. But I'm impressed. Most people wouldn't think of the condiments. If you run out of ketchup on a holiday weekend, you might as well shut down the store." He tossed the report onto the desk. "What am I going to do with you, Wolfer?"

I stared at him, lost. I'd thought he was pleased.

"Look at yourself," he said. "Your eyes are red, your hair's a mess—and what'd you do with your socks? Who comes to work in designer shoes and no socks?"

I stared at my Kenneth Cole lace-ups, my hairy ankles peeking out from under my khakis.

"I meant what I said about the rush orders," he said. "I should've been on this weeks ago, but I've had my head up my ass with the new building. So thanks. That was a good catch."

I nodded, too embarrassed to form words.

"I know you think it's a bad idea, me asking your stepdad for a loan," he said. "I get that. But I don't see any other way to keep this store from going under. So, I need your help."

"Okay."

"Okay, what? You'll talk to your mom?"

"I'll talk to her," I lied. "Maybe not today, but I'll talk to her."

He shook his head. "I wish to hell I knew what was going on in your private life, man," he said. "I've said it before and I'll say it again: You have a future here if you want it. But you've got to want it. I can't want it for you."

The phone calls to the landlords went pretty much how I thought they'd go. Every place I had seen, either the room was rented or the landlord wasn't taking my calls. I even called the grow house in the Sonoma hills. *Sorry, room's taken. Nice meeting you. Click.*

After I clocked out at five, I drove up to chez Starling one last time to pick up my clothes, sneaking in downstairs while Tony Robbins droned on in the kitchen. It took me three trips, tossing everything I owned into boxes and humping them across two neighbors' backyards to my car, until the only thing in the closet was that ridiculous, unworn Hugo Boss suit.

I made several slow laps along Miller Avenue, out past the high school and back, just to keep moving, to keep from drawing attention. When it got dark, I figured I could head up to the fire roads on the back side of Mt. Tam where the local cops wouldn't go. But then what? How was I going keep from being seen? Where was I going to shower in the mornings? All it would take was one park ranger wondering what was up with the beater Honda parked in the bushes, and I'd be at a police station peeing in a cup and trying to explain to Ponytail Pete why I was no longer welcome at my stepdad's house.

After an hour of aimless, anxious driving, I broke down and stopped at Howie's for a Double Meal Deal Deluxe and a shake. The place was packed, the kitchen crew jamming for the dinner rush, but I didn't recognize anybody behind the counter. No LaShonda. No Antwoine. Even Rajiv was gone—back to India, somebody said, but no one knew for sure.

I set out along the Frontage Road with my warm bag of food, telling myself I was looking for a spot to pull over and eat. But I knew where I was headed. At the base of Shelter Ridge, I cut over onto Kipling Drive, then up past Chaucer

Court and Dickens Court to Thoreau Circle. The lights were
out at Suze's place and her driveway was empty, as I knew it
would be. On Mondays, she'd told me once, Sharon picked up
the kids from day care so Suze could tour the houses going
on sale that week. I drove to the end of the block and pulled
a U-ey, edging in close to a cement retaining wall a few car
lengths from Suze's driveway.

I slit the Howie's bag along the seams, draping it over my lap
like a tablecloth, and ate my dinner, alternating bites of How-
ieburger with sips of chocolate shake. I had no business being
there, I knew that. But I was the moth and Suze was the porch
light. All day, one way or another, I had been thinking about
her, wondering where she was, who she was with, picturing her
doing this or that. Making dinner here, for instance, with Sharon and the boys. Hamburgers, real ones she grilled herself out
on the patio. In a better world, one where I wasn't such a freak,
I would be back there with her in an apron and a backward
ball cap, flipping burgers and waving the smoke from my eyes.
Then afterward, if it was still light out, I could take the boys to
Hauke Park and throw the ball around, maybe show Dylan how
to swing a bat.

That was never going to happen. I knew that, too. Whatever shot I'd had at a normal relationship with Suze, I'd pissed
it away that day at the bunkers. I balled up the greasy burger
wrapper and reached into my wallet for Frank T.'s card. I had
done some asking around after our coffee at the Book Depot
and learned that he lived at the Motel Filkins, a bombed-out
former Travelodge along the freeway in San Rafael. The Motel
Megan, they called it around AA. As in, Megan's Law. As in, if
you were a registered sex offender recently released from San
Quentin, the Filkins was on a very short list of places in the
North Bay where you could get a room.

I had spent enough time shopping for drugs and sex in SRO
motels in Santa Barbara to know what I'd find at the Filkins:
junkies in the parking lot, drug deals in the stairwells, porn
shoots down the hall. Frank or no Frank, I wouldn't last a week

at a place like that without getting high. But then I wouldn't last a week camped out in my car on the back side of Mt. Tam, either. All of which put me on a six-seater Gulfstream with my mother jetting down to Solvang for two more months of morning affirmations and equine therapy.

I never saw the cocoa-brown Volvo glide past me in the half-dark. One minute I was staring at Frank's card, trying to decide what I would say if I called him, and the next Suze's Volvo was parked in her driveway, the two boys spilling out the rear doors, gathering up backpacks and extra pairs of shoes. Suze looked great, as always, in a charcoal gray skirt and heels, but what hit me this time was what a mom she'd become. The boys were whining, Dylan especially, trying to get out of cleaning up a mess he'd made in the back seat, but Suze waited him out, her arms crossed, tapping the toe of one foot, until he collected a fistful of food wrappers and walked them to the trash bin at the bottom of the driveway.

When she saw my car, she pulled up short, instinctively eas-ing Jake behind her to put herself between me and her little boy. I thought, just for a second, about slamming the key into the ignition and peeling out of there, never to be seen again. Instead, I popped the car door.

She nudged Dylan. "You guys go on in, watch some TV."

He looked at me, then at the front door, like he was trying to make up his mind if it was safe to leave his mother with me. "Can we watch cable?" he asked.

"*Go*," she hissed.

Dylan waved to his baby brother and the two of them gal-loped up the stairs, their oversized backpacks bouncing on their backs. Once they'd cleared the top step, Suze turned back to me, shading her eyes against the slanting evening sun.

"What are you doing here, Trent?" she asked.

I opened my mouth, but no words came. What *was* I do-ing here? Why wasn't I at a pay phone dialing the number on Frank's card? For that matter, why wasn't I in the detox ward at Casa Esperanza spilling my guts to the intake shrink?

"I got kicked out," I said.

"Kicked out? Of your house?"

"Honestly, it's a good thing. I needed to get out of there. I was making them miserable."

She was close enough now that she could see through the car windows to the row of cardboard boxes lining the back seat. I had only been driving around for an hour or two, but already it looked like the bargain bin at the Salvation Army back there.

"I fucked up, Suze," I said. "I need a place to crash tonight."

She was still looking in through the car window. "You started drinking again? Is that it?"

"No, I got high. With Lee. It's a long story."

"I'll bet."

In the scrape of pity in her voice I heard just how desperate I sounded. And how scared.

"I know this isn't cool," I said. "You've got two kids, you're in the middle of a breakup. It's totally not cool. But I don't have anywhere else to go."

"There's really nobody you can stay with? Couch surf a little while?"

"I don't know anybody here, Suze. Not anymore."

She looked up at the living room again, where a TV now flickered in the window. I didn't say a word. There was nothing to say. There wasn't one good reason why she should say yes.

"Okay," she said, finally. "But just for a couple days, that's it."

"Thank you, Suze," I said. "I'm serious. I don't even know what to say."

"Say you'll be out in a couple days," she said.

Upstairs, the boys lay sprawled across the sofa like they'd crash-landed there from space, eating Cap'n Crunch cereal and watching *SpongeBob SquarePants* at car-alarm volume. Neither of them took his eyes off the screen when Suze shut the door behind us.

"Guys, you know my friend Trent," she said. "He's going to be staying with us tonight."

"What's wrong with *his* house?" Dylan asked the TV.

"He's sort of in between places right now, honey," Suze said. "Trent's an old, old friend—"

Dylan dropped the remote, stood up, and marched to the bedroom, taking his cereal bowl with him. For one jittery second, Jake sat frozen on the sofa caught between his mom and his brother before he grabbed his cereal bowl and scampered off after Dylan.

"That went pretty well, wouldn't you say?" Suze said.

"Maybe you're right," I said. "Maybe I should just crash in my car."

"No, go grab your stuff," she said. "I have to deal with this, but you're staying."

In my car, I tossed what I needed into a paper bag and turned on the radio to wait for Suze to finish talking with her boys. I still could have bolted. Probably *should* have bolted. Left a note in Suze's mailbox and gone looking for a pay phone to call Frank. Or I could have called my mother instead, like I was secretly afraid I would, bawling my eyes out, begging her to charter a jet to fly me to Solvang. But I stayed right where I was, hunkered down in the front seat of my Honda listening to lame nineties rock, waiting for the kitchen light to come on. When it finally did I carried my shopping bag full of clothes and shaving gear up the stairs, knowing that, just this once, I was exactly where I wanted to be.

The TV was off and Suze was in the kitchen tearing into a tomato-and-avocado sandwich.

"How'd it go with the boys?" I asked.

"Oh, I'm an evil, raging bitch." She shrugged. "I'm making some tea. You want a cup?"

I've never been a big tea drinker, but it gave us something to do, Suze putting the kettle on the stove to boil, me searching the cabinets for mugs and setting them on the counter. Suze's kitchen had a reassuring suburban smell: white bread, overripe bananas, sugary cereals. Once upon a time, someone had tried to make it over to look like my mother's kitchen in Blithedale

Canyon, all blonde-wood highlights and brushed-steel appliances, but that was years ago and now there was a big dent in the
fridge and the knobs on half the cabinets were missing. And
the place was a mess. Not dirty, exactly, just lived in: the floor
unswept, coffee grounds sprinkled over the lip of the sink, like
whoever lived here had better things to do than wipe down her
counter eight times a day. As we settled in over steaming mugs
of peppermint tea, I felt comfortable, at home in a way I never
did in Lupita's spotless kitchen.

"I thought you were going to stay away from Lee," she said,
blowing on her tea.

"I did, for a while."

"Right. Until you didn't," she said. "This is how my dad died,
you know."

Her eyes held mine across the table, eerily calm. In thirty
years, Suze and I had never talked about her father, not once.
Even when he was alive, she and her mom tiptoed around him
like he was a human landmine and one wrong look could trip
the wire.

"I mean, in the end, yeah, it was a gun out in the garage," she
said. "But for ten years before that it was booze and pills, until
finally he was shooting up in the bathroom. I used to walk in on
him nodding out on the fucking toilet."

"Jesus. You never told me that."

"We never told anybody. That's what I'm saying. He died
because we didn't talk about it. Because he wouldn't let anybody
help him."

"I was in rehab for two months," I said. "Detox, therapy, the
steps, the whole nine yards. And then two months later I was
right back here, using again."

"So, that's it? You tried it once and now you're all done?"

"No, that's not it," I said. "Rehab isn't the problem. The
problem is me. I'm tearing up my mother's life, Suze. Mine,
too. If I go down there now, I'll spend two more months riding
horses and conning the therapists, and the whole bullshit cycle
will start up all over again. Nothing will change, except maybe

this time I'll figure out how to break up her marriage for real."

Suze was silent, sipping her tea. She'd seen enough of my mother and me back in the day to believe everything I was saying. I was the one in shock. I kept hearing my mother yelling at Stan, telling him to keep his hands off her. Her life had been so good. She was married again. Happy again. She had money, a house, friends, all of it. And then I got arrested in Isla Vista.

"So, what're you going to do?" Suze asked.

"I don't know," I said. "I want to stay here. I want to try to make it work."

"Make what work?"

I was quiet a moment, thinking how to put it into words. "This morning, after Stan kicked me out, I didn't have anywhere to go, so I went in to work early," I said. "I was there for a couple hours—catching up on filing, sorting invoices, that kind of thing. I even wrote up a rush order for the holiday weekend. It's hard to explain, but it felt so good doing that. I was helping out, you know? Doing my part. Being useful for once."

She eyed me over her teacup. "I thought you hated that job."

"Yeah, I probably said that," I said. "The guy I work for, Gianni, he can be a prick sometimes, but I like what they're doing over there. I like what *I'm* doing over there. This morning, writing up those rush orders, organizing the office, I was good at that. Down in S.B, before I screwed up everything, I was good at that, too. It's like there's some tiny speck of hope for me, you know?" I stopped, hearing myself. "Fuck me, I sound completely insane."

"No, I hear you," she said. "I do. I wish I could feel the same way, honestly."

"What're you talking about?"

"Nothing," she said, waving it off. "Forget it. I'm just tired."

She was still smiling, but something in her eyes, the way they kept darting away, reminded me of the night I'd walked in on her oldest son calling her a whore.

"Hold on, rewind the tape," I said. "Something's up. What is it?"

Suze used to smoke when we were kids, and she did that thing ex-smokers do when they're uncomfortable, searching the room for a non-existent pack of cigarettes. When she didn't find one, she turned around, checking the doorway for crouching seven-year-olds.

"I got a call this morning," she said. "About my car."

"Your car?"

"The Volvo. The one I bought when I left Jimmy. The one I'm, like, five months behind paying off."

A weight of pity dropped in my chest. I knew the calls she was talking about. For years down in Santa Barbara, I couldn't pick up the phone without hearing some pissed-off guy in a call center yelling at me about my Visa bill.

"Can't your mom help you?" I asked.

"She's already covering half the rent on this place. The collection people, they're calling *her* now." She looked for those imaginary cigarettes again. "There's a lot you don't know, Trent. I haven't sold a house all summer. The agency's been great, letting me take phone shifts, pick up a little extra cash around the office. But if I lose that car, I'm done. I can't work. I can't stay here."

I reached for her hand across the table. I was just trying to be supportive, a friend, but she pulled back her hand like it was on fire.

"Trent, no," she said.

"You're right, you're right," I said. "Sorry, my bad."

She pushed aside her mug and stood. "I'll put some sheets out for you," she said. "We get up pretty early around here so if you have an alarm you might want to set it."

I nodded. "Sure thing."

"And the boys, they like to watch cartoons while I'm getting ready for work. So if you could clean up around the sofa before they get up, that'd be great."

She stopped in the doorway, that great magnet pull of need tugging her in my direction. My drug of choice came in fifty-milliliter bottles. Suze's, I saw now, was guys like me.

"Are we going to be okay here?" she said. "You and me? This?"

"I think so, yeah."

"You think, or you know? Because if you're not sure, you can walk right out that door."

Like that, the magnet switched poles, turning us back into two ordinary people in a room. Suze looked me up and down, asking with her eyes if what she thought had happened had really happened. Then, without another word, she turned to go find my bedding for the night.

# 12

**T**hree days later, I was halfway up a ladder in the Post Office building, double-checking the aluminum flashing around a ceiling duct, when a truck pulled up outside carrying four thousand dollars' worth of office furnishings. Until then it had been a quiet week. Too quiet, really. Theo and Quan were gone and there was no more talk of the Magic Fridge or the Chef Tamalpais website, but the work went on at the new building, the same small army of plumbers and pipefitters installing eight-burner stoves and industrial sinks in the kitchen while, out front, carpenters hammered walls of pre-built shelving into place. But now here they were, two sweaty delivery guys wanting me to sign off on half a truck's worth of rugs, desks, and swivel chairs we weren't going to need anymore.

When I called Gianni out onto the loading dock, he got into a shouting match with the driver and then, by phone, with the driver's boss at the warehouse. Gianni and the driver were still going at it, their faces inches apart, when Mr. Papadakis came hustling in from the street, his food-smudged work apron tossed over one shoulder.

"You're going to have to take all this back, okay?" he told the driver. "There's been a change of plans. We're not setting up an office here, after all."

"Dad, let's just take the damn furniture," Gianni said. "We're going to need it at some point."

His father smiled tightly, his eyebrows saying, *Let's try not to have this conversation here, huh?* "I'm really sorry," he told the driver. "Somebody should've called you, but I'm not signing for this."

"As I was just explaining to your son," the driver said, "this contract carries a twenty percent cancellation fee. If we leave now, you owe us eight hundred bucks."

Papadakis narrowed his eyes, sizing him up. "You're Ed Whalen's kid. Tom, right?"

"Todd," the driver said, flushing. "How do you know my dad?"

Papadakis laughed. "I've been doing business with Ed Whalen for forty years and you look just like him. Have him give me a call. I'm sure we can work something out."

"All right, but I'm not promising anything," Todd Whalen said.

"Just have him call me." Papadakis looked over his shoulder at the kitchen full of men in hard hats trying to not to stare too openly at the family drama unfolding in the middle of their job site. "Awful big for a deli kitchen, huh?" he said, winking at me. "You think you could give Henry a hand with the lunch rush? Gianni can hold down the fort here."

He didn't have to ask twice. The last two nights I had been out late looking at apartments and up again at dawn to be out of the house before Jake and Dylan rolled out of bed. I would have given anything to curl up under one of the industrial sinks and take a nap, but I put away my tools and jogged upstairs to drop off a morning's worth of delivery receipts. In Gianni's original plans, the second floor was to be the nerve center of the catering operation, with offices for the two of us and a larger bullpen area for the delivery drivers and dispatchers. I didn't know what they were going to do with it now. Use it for storage, maybe. The carpentry crews had sprayed blue lines on the floor where the interior walls were supposed to go, but for now it was just a big, brick-walled room lit by bare, forty-watt bulbs.

I was sorting invoices at a sawhorse worktable near the door when I heard Gianni's heavy tread on the stairs. A moment later, his husky frame filled the doorway.

"You talk to your mom?" he asked.

No *Hello*. No *Hey, sorry about the scene on the loading dock*. Nothing. He wasn't looking well, I have to say: a good ten pounds underweight, his cheeks still pink from all the shouting, his usually immaculate store-issue polo untucked and wrinkled at the collar.

"You mind closing the door?" I said.

He shut the door behind him. "So. Did you?"

I was starting to wish I had. Yes, Stan was a capital-A asshole. And yes, if he ever loaned the Papadakises money, he would probably end up taking over the whole company. But who was I to say that was a bad thing? Maybe you needed a Stan Starling to take on Cornucopia Foods.

"I don't know if you know this, but Walden West almost went under last year," I said.

"Yeah, but he survived," Gianni said. "The company's fine."

"Stan survived, but money's tight right now. He's not looking to acquire. Maybe it's for the best. You can't be at war with your own family."

"I'm not at war with anybody," he said. "I'm living in the real world. I showed you those numbers. If we give this building back to the bank, sooner or later Dad'll have to sell out."

"That's not going to happen. You guys have been here for fifty years. People love this store."

"God, you sound just like him." Gianni's eyes roamed the empty room, like he was looking for a small dog to kick. "If we shut this down, you're out of a job. You do get that, right?"

"Hey, you're the one who keeps saying I have a future here."

"*If* there's a future here." He shot one last murderous look around the room and reached for the door. "People liked your granddad, too, and look what happened to him."

The lunch crowd was five deep at the deli, everyone waving numbered slips of paper, so for the next hour I put Gianni and Stan out of my mind and ran my ass off, ferrying tubs of baby corn and cucumber slices out to the salad bar and slicing meats and cheeses for the deli case. There was a Zen to this, too. I couldn't save Chef Tam. I couldn't find a place to live. I couldn't silence the voice in my head telling me to sneak out back with an ice-cold sixer of Rolling Rock. But I *could* run a ten-pound stick of American cheese through the auto-slicer. The machine ran fast, lopping off a wafer-thin slice every two seconds, and it took all my attention, all my focus, to stack each new slice on the pile, slap down a sheet of wax paper, and square the edges before the next bright orange slice curled down off the blade. *Stack, slap, square. Stack, slap, square.* Over and over, the three-count rhythm like a drumbeat, ruling my movements, soothing my speeding brain.

I'd filled a tray with sliced Swiss and American cheese and was stacking it in the deli case up front when, through the crowd, I saw a flash of yellow hair outside on the street. I looked again: a woman, blonde and yoga-trim, in a strappy sundress and blue-mirrored sunglasses, was bending over to admire—or pretending to admire—the bottles of olive oil in the display window.

"Where are you going?" Henry shouted after me.

Outside, the midday sun was beating down, the street buzzing with tourists and office drones on lunch-hour errands, but the sidewalk in front of the deli was empty. No tousled blonde hair, no mirrored shades, no whisper-thin summer dress. It had only been a flash, seen through a pane of glass, but the artful messiness of her hair, the dancer-like way she held herself: It was my mother, I knew it.

"Everything okay?" Henry asked when I came back in.

"Yeah, I'm good," I said. "I thought I saw somebody I knew."

But my hands were still shaking when I made it back to the kitchen. This wasn't the first time I thought I had seen my mother that week. A couple days earlier, I'd seen a black Mini parked across from the Post Office building, but I hadn't been sure. Now I was. If she had come looking for me, she was doing it behind Stan's back, which, the way we played this game, meant the next move was mine. One swipe of my mother's black AmEx card, and I could rent any apartment I wanted. A couple more, and I could fill it with furniture and kitchen gadgets. Maybe I could even get her to talk to Stan about Tam Grocery. All I had to do was shed a few tears, tell her how sorry

I was, make her believe I'd turned over a new leaf. All I had to do was play the game the way we had always played it.

I reached for a colander of freshly stemmed tomatoes waiting to be cut. It took four slices per tomato, then you could sweep it aside: *One-two-three-four, sweep. One-two-three-four, sweep.* That same Zen, that same mind-emptying rhythm.

I had seen my mother do this so many times with my dad, especially toward the end. When they fought, she sulked for days, downing endless cans of Tab and telling me, tearfully, this time was different, this time she'd finally had it. But it never lasted. One way or another, she always ended up chasing after him, haunting his hangouts, stalking his girlfriends. One time, she even brought me along. "Hi there," she told the tiny blonde backup singer who answered the door wearing one of his white dress shirts, "I thought you'd like to meet the son of the man you're fucking." For years, this had worked. For years, my father kept coming back, drug-sick and ashamed, promising to stay, to make us a family again. Until one summer he went on tour with his secretary and never came back.

*One-two-three-four, sweep. One-two-three-four, sweep.*

For twenty years, I'd hated him for leaving us. For twenty years, if he gave me money, I blew it. If he bought me a car, I got drunk and wrapped it around a tree. But what if leaving us was the best thing he'd ever done? It hadn't looked that way when Mom was doing tequila slammers off the bar at the Last Ditch. But look where she was now. She'd picked herself back up, started looking after herself again, eating right, working out, taking night classes at College of Marin. None of that would have happened if he hadn't moved to L.A. and found Caressa. If he hadn't stopped coming back.

*One-two-three-four, sweep. One-two-three-four, sweep.*

I was slicing the last of the tomatoes, the chopping board covered with their glistening red flesh, when Henry poked his head in the door.

"I think your friend's back," he said. "She wants to talk with you."

"She *does?*"

Henry laughed, soft and musical. "If you're busy, I'd be happy to take her off your hands."

Which weirded me out almost as much as having to go outside to face my mother.

"Thanks, I'm good," I said, pulling off my apron.

Following Henry out onto the deli floor, I reminded myself: No tears. No lies. No black AmEx cards. I would thank her for coming, tell her I was all set for now, but that I'd call as soon as I found somewhere permanent to live. But before I could say any of this—before I could be sure I *would* say any of it—I stepped through the kitchen doorway and saw Suze Randall on the other side of the deli case, her tight smile giving off a *Something's up, can you talk?* vibe.

"I hope it's okay, me coming by like this," she said.

I checked the front window, but I saw nothing but plateglass and olive oil.

"No, hey, it's great to see you," I said. "I think I can take five. Let's go around back."


The meat-room crew at Tam Grocery were mostly Guatemalan, and on sunny days, they took their lunches in the employee parking lot, chain-smoking stubby brown Guatemalan cigarettes and sneaking shots of *chicha*, a corn-based homebrew that smelled like something you'd use to strip paint. But I could see why they liked it back there. Even now, in the heat of the day, it was cool in the shade of a small grove of redwoods, the Old Mill Creek trickling by a few feet away. But before I had time to clear the ashtray full of butts the meat-room guys had left behind, Suze handed me a sheet of paper.

"What's this?" I asked.

"A rental listing," she said. "The Park View Apartments, just off Miller Avenue."

After a month of apartment hunting, my eyes went straight for the price: $1,000. "Hey, this is near Sycamore Park," I said, going with the positive. "Our old 'hood. I'd kill to live there."

"I know, the rent's kinda steep," she said. "But I know the

guy Randy who runs the complex. I told him about you. He might be willing to work with you on price."

I slipped the paper into my back pocket. "Cool, thanks. I'll call him tonight."

We looked at each other, neither of us seeming to know what came next. She had given me the rental listing, and I'd taken it, but her pasted-on smile told me she hadn't taken an hour out of her day just to bring me a rental listing for another apartment I couldn't afford.

"Jimmy called," she said. "About an hour ago. Dylan's been calling him, apparently."

"Dylan?"

"He walked away from day camp this morning, him and Jakey both. The camp people called a couple hours ago, completely freaked. I was driving around looking for them when Jimmy called. They'd walked all the way to Mom's place and called him from there."

"Oh shit," I said, seeing where this was going.

"You should've heard him, Trent," she said. "On and on about what a shitty parent I am, how he was gonna have to fly up here, take me and the kids back to L.A."

"What's he going to do, move you in with his hot little yoga chick?"

"Hot little Pilates chick," Suze said. "The point is you can't stay. It's freaking the boys out. I can't have them wandering all over town looking for a phone to call their dad."

Suze looked panicked and pissed off and tired, but behind all that, I saw a half-crazy glimmer of hope in her eyes. I knew that look. Oh man, did I ever know that look. I'd seen it in my own mother's eyes for fifteen years after my dad left.

"What else did Jimmy say?" I asked.

"What do you mean?"

"This morning, on the phone. What else did you guys talk about?"

"Nothing," she said. "Look, if this place doesn't work out, I'll call around again, see what else is out there. But it could take a few days."

"Suze, for Christ's sake, he's living with another woman."

"I know that! I'm not a fucking moron."

A woman loading groceries into her Land Rover looked up from her cart: we were shouting. I backed off, fixing my eyes on the ashtray full of cigarette butts until the woman went back to her shopping bags.

"Where are the boys now?" I asked, quieter now.

"With Mom," she said. "I'm taking the rest of the day, and we're all going to go someplace, maybe the beach." She sighed, beaten. "Trent, it's different when there's kids involved. And lawyers, and support payments. Jimmy and me, we aren't even divorced yet."

"So file the papers."

"I want to, believe me. But I'm not hacking it here. It's not just the money. I left because of the boys and now they're in even worse shape than when I left."

"Would it make it any better to go back to Jimmy?"

"No, of course not."

"Then file the papers," I said. "Look, I'm sorry for screwing all this up. And I'll leave. Tonight. But please don't go back down there."

She looked away, pain radiating off her like an odor. I wanted to tell her that I would help her, that I'd have her back if Jimmy drove up from L.A. to take the boys. But what was I going to do? I didn't even have a place to sleep that night.

"It's been five minutes," she said. "You better get back to work."

The Park View Apartments were a seventies-era stucco-and-glass complex running nearly a full city block along the north side of Sycamore Park, across from the swing sets where Suze and I used to play before her dad died. I was early for my appointment with Randy so I found a bench off to one side of the park and sat watching some kids play touch football. I'd waited all afternoon, but my mother had never come back. I wasn't sure how I felt about that. On the one hand, she was my mother and I missed her. On the other hand, I knew myself. I knew her, too. Her guilt—for raising me without a father, for running around after men all those years, for leaving me alone in Santa Barbara until I called her one day from jail—was a musical instrument I'd spent a lifetime teaching myself how to play. If I wanted money, I hit one note. If I wanted her to keep it from Stan, I hit another. If I wanted her to look the other way while I hid hundreds of mini bottles of vodka and gin in my closet, there was a whole symphony I could play.

As soon as I saw Randy J. waiting for me in the alcove entrance to the Park View Apartment complex, I knew what Suze had told him about me. I'd seen him in meetings, always wearing the same sad flannel shirt and saggy jeans, a pair of granny glasses wrapped around his ears like he was going to break into "Imagine" right there in the basement of the Strawberry Rec Center. When he saw me, he did a double-take, too, then smiled, a little sheepishly, like he'd lost a bet with himself. The last time he'd seen me, I had been wearing a filthy Howie's uniform and stank of beef tallow and Russian vodka at noon on a weekday.

The apartment he showed me was even smaller than the one at Valley Knolls, just a single room with a windowless bathroom tucked into a corridor at the back. You could cross the main room in five strides, and you couldn't stand to your full height at the far end because of the slope of the roof, but the floor was glossy heart-of-pine and the windows looked out onto Sycamore Park. I slowly circled the room, touching the toy-sized kitchen appliances and looking out the windows at the park, where the same gang of kids was still playing touch football.

"Does it always get this much light?" I asked.

"The windows are south-facing so, yeah, you get sun most of the day," Randy said. "Warms the place up in winter, too. I never used the heater except maybe in January."

"You lived here?"

"Yeah, until just a few weeks ago," he said. "When I moved in, this was a storage room. Concrete floors, exposed insulation, no windows. Nothing. I fixed it up from scratch in exchange for rent. But look, here's the cool part." He opened a sliding door to what I'd assumed was a closet and pulled down a narrow single bed. "Ever see *An American in Paris?*"

I shook my head, staring at the unsheeted bed that reached six inches from the refrigerator.

"Check it out sometime," he said. "Gene Kelly's a painter living in Paris after the war. He lives in an artist's garret with a bed that drops down from the ceiling. I thought about doing that here, but the ceiling isn't strong enough, so I put this in. It's called a Murphy bed."

"But where do you put the—"

"Furniture?" He laughed. "I had to get creative there. The chest of drawers is built right into the wall here. Then I got a table from Salvation Army and cut it in half. When you put it against the wall, see, it's only a couple feet wide, but when you open out the flap, it seats four people." All of a sudden, shy, quiet Randy J. was like an overgrown kid bouncing around the tiny room showing off his home-improvements. "It's in storage now, but I'd throw it in with rent for the right tenant. I can't tell you how many times that thing got me laid."

I was picturing this myself: inviting Suze over for dinner, and when we were finished eating, folding down the table flap and pulling out a freshly made bed.

"Okay, this place rocks," I said. "But there's no way I can do a thousand a month."

"Your friend said that might be a problem," he said. "Are you at all handy? Plumbing, carpentry, anything like that?"

"I can do your books. If you've got any overstock you need inventoried, I'm your man, but carpentry and plumbing, I'm hopeless."

I expected him to flash another sheepish grin and say he was sorry, maybe another time. Instead, he said, "I remember when you first came in. You were so pissed about being back here, having to live with your mom and all that. All you could talk about was getting back to—where was it again?"

"Santa Barbara."

"Right, that's it. So, how much time do you have now?"

"Tomorrow, it'll be sixty days," I lied.

"Congratulations, man. Those first two months are a bitch. You working with anybody yet?"

"You know Frank T.?"

He looked up, his jaw working in surprise. "The priest guy?"

I was playing with fire here. I *wasn't* working with Frank T., not yet, and AA is a very, very small world. But it was this place or the back seat of my car.

"The man's a hard-ass, but that's what I wanted," I said. "No bullshit, no easy landings."

"Is it true what they say, you know, about the…?"

I nodded and let that addict logic work its magic. If I was in bad enough shape to seek help from a child-raping ex-priest, then I must be a serious guy, someone worth knowing.

"Could you swing nine hundred a month?" he asked.

I had done this math a thousand times. Even if I spent half my take-home pay on rent, that was just seven hundred a month. Without regular cash infusions from the First National Bank of Mom, I could sell my car and eat all my meals at work, and nine hundred dollars a month would still be a pipe dream.

"No chance you could bring it down to eight hundred?" I said.

"Let me ask you: If I ran a credit check, what would I find?"

"Nothing very good, I'm afraid."

"That's what I figured," he said. "In that case, nine hundred's as low as I can go, and even then we'd have to keep it on the down-low. My boss, he's one of us, he'd understand, but the other residents, they'd be pissed if they knew."

I looked around the small, bright room. This was madness. I could live in somebody's garage in Petaluma and keep my car. But I'd been looking at garage apartments in Petaluma for weeks. I was a broke ex-con with bad credit. Even if I lied about my criminal record, no landlord in his right mind would rent me a room without my mother's name on the lease. Unless I got creative.

"Any chance I could move in tonight?" I asked.

"Tonight?" He looked surprised. "I mean, sure, I guess. The place is just sitting here empty. But that'd have to be on the down-low, too. Officially, I'm on the lease till September 1."

"It's cool, I'll keep it quiet. I'm kind of wearing out my welcome on a friend's couch, if you know what you mean."

"I *do* know what you mean. You can crash here for the next couple days, but I'll need first and last month's rent before the weekend's out."

"Deal," I said, reaching out to shake on it.

I spent the night on the Murphy bed, no sheets, no pillow, just an old sleeping bag Randy dug out of storage. I was up and down all night, pacing the small room in my boxers, doing the math and then doing it again, trying to talk myself out of the half-crocked plan I had dreamed up while I was talking to Randy J. But the minute I rolled into work the next day, I picked up the phone and called Hélène's. I sat on hold a full minute listening to "The Blue Danube" before Lee Radko's husky growl came on the line: "Kitchen."

"I can get you twelve hundred," I said. "I can have it for you today."

He just laughed. "Good morning to you, too, Pussy Willow."

"Sorry, man, I'm at work," I said. "But if you're still up for the arrangement we talked about, I can put together twelve hundred bucks, maybe a bit more."

I heard the clatter of plates, the hiss of meat hitting the grill. A few feet from the phone, two cooks were shouting at each other in harsh, guttural Spanish.

"This line isn't cool," he said. "You got a cell?"

"No, call me back at the store. Use the business line. It goes directly to me."

I set down the phone. Outside, it was a hot summer morning, moms in Range Rovers running errands, couples sharing lattes in front of Starbucks. Below me, a twiggy blonde in parachute pants strutted toward Yoga Madness, a rolled mat slung over her shoulders like a papoose. None of these people, I was going to guess, were financing drug deals to pay their rent.

At last the phone rang. "So, you want to get back in the game?" Lee said.

"Nope, I'm just playing bank here," I said. "I'm the money guy."

"Okay. How much is this gonna cost me, money guy?"

"I was thinking twenty points."

He snorted. "Try ten. And all the product you want at cost."

"No way, I'm not going near that shit. I don't even want to see it. I'm loaning a buddy some money here. What you do with it after that, that's your business."

"Then ten's as high as I'm gonna go. I'm doing all the work and all you're doing is handing me a wad of cash for the weekend."

This was the math that had kept me up half the night. Ten percent of $1,200 was just $120. Even if he paid me back by Monday morning—a pretty big if right there—I still wouldn't be able to cover first and last month's rent. This was the point that any rational human being would have hung up and called his mother. But then no rational person would have called Lee Radko in the first place.

"How about I go in with you?" I asked.

"Full partners?"

"No, just selling," I said. "What if I go with you to a couple of these kiddie things and help unload the product?"

"That's different." His voice had dropped an octave, grown softer and warmer, more relaxed. "If you came with, I could give you five eights for $1,200. After that, the profit's all yours."

Five-eighths of an ounce was seventeen grams, give or take, and down in S.B. a gram went for about $100. If Marin prices were the same ballpark, I could walk away with $500—more than that if we stepped on the weight. Not bad for one night's work. Of course, if it went wrong, I could spend the next five to seven years in jail.

"Make it seven eights or we forget the whole thing," I said.

I sensed Lee pacing by the dumpsters behind Hélène's, calculating how much he made per gram after he stepped on it, and how much better this math got if he started with more weight.

"You can get me the cash today?" he asked.

"By noon," I said. "I'll walk it over on my lunch break."

"Then I can do three-quarters of an ounce. That's a fucking gift, man, and you know it."

I turned away from the phone, pumping my fist. It *was* a gift. He was supplying the connect and the customers. All I had to do was show up with some cash. "Can you use more than twelve hundred?" I asked.

"I can use everything you can get me, bro. What'd you do, jack the Greek's payroll?"

"No, but it's a thought," I said. "Give me a couple hours. I'll put together as much as I can and I'll have it to you by noon."

I took an early lunch and cashed my paycheck for $722.35. I drew down another $477.65 from checking, and took a cash advance of $500 on my AmEx card, which as I had hoped, my mother hadn't cancelled yet. That brought it up to $1,700. I had all but zeroed out my checking account and my mother's AmEx, which meant that, at least through the weekend, I'd have to live on staff meals and the loose change in my pockets. The thing that really worried me, though, was the drawdown on the AmEx card. That looked fishy. But as long as I paid the money back, I could tell my mother I'd used it to help pay rent, which was even sort of true.

None of it felt real, though, until the teller handed me that fat envelope stuffed with fifties and hundreds. In Santa Barbara, I had been small-time. I sold weed and Ritalin and sometimes a little Vicodin and Oxy if people asked for it. Cocaine was a different ball game, especially if it involved minors. If just one kid got pulled over for DUI and ratted us out to keep his license, I could spend half my thirties in state prison.

I thought again of that flash of blonde hair in the deli window. The obvious move was to call her—and tell her what, exactly? That I'd rented an apartment for hundreds of dollars more than I could possibly afford, and that, to pay for it, I'd cleared my bank accounts to buy into a drug deal that could put me in jail for most of the next decade? *Save me, Mommy! Save me from myself! And oh, by the way, don't tell Stan!* The thing was, she would. All of it. Front me the rent money, plus hundreds more for furniture and kitchen crap, and never breathe a word to Stan. I'd hate myself for taking the money, and I'd hate her even more for giving it to me, for lying to Stan and funneling me more of his cash. But she was my mother. I could bleed her dry just like I had Al Fierro, and there was nothing Stan or anyone else could do to stop me.

By then I was already halfway to Hélène's, my feet carrying me where my brain didn't want me to go. Lee met me at the back door and walked me behind the dumpsters to count out the cash. "You sure you don't want to go all in on this?" he asked, shoving the wadded bills into his checked kitchen pants. "You'd make a fuck of a lot more than a few hundred bucks."

This, I knew, was the point of the gift. Cash Lee could get plenty of places, and if it came down to it, he could talk Jin into helping him unload the blow. What he wanted was a partner, not just on the buys, but to help him cut and weigh the product, maybe even carry a cell and do house calls. But I couldn't worry about any of that now. That was my rent money he had in his pocket. If he got jacked on the buy or decided to bolt for Canada, I was sixteen flavors of fucked.

"That's $1,700, Lee," I said. "I'm going to come out of this with close to a thousand bucks."

Lee shot me that prison-yard stare, which made me wonder all over again if it was such a wise move to give every dime I had to a convicted felon who was saving up to skip the country.

"Whatever you say, Pussy Willow," he said.

# 13

O n Monday night, Frank T. was in his usual spot at the six o'clock meeting a few seats down from the moderator, a Big Book open on his lap. I sat in the back and kept my mouth shut, but after the meeting broke up and I finished stacking chairs, he was waiting for me on a church pew near the door, rereading the passage we had been discussing that day.

We took our coffees to go this time, sharing a bench on the red-brick plaza surrounded by high school kids smoking clove cigarettes and practicing skate tricks in the gauzy late afternoon sunlight. It was Labor Day, the last day of summer, and the plaza was packed. I didn't recognize any faces, but I'd probably sold cocaine to a few of those kids. We had hit three parties that weekend, one on Friday night and two on Saturday. Each time we were in and out in less than an hour, kids lining up ten-deep outside the bathrooms where we set up shop like they were waiting for the ice cream truck. First thing Sunday morning, I had settled up with Randy J., handing him $1,800 in wrinkled tens and twenties, some of them probably still coated with a fine layer of coke dust.

Naturally, I said nothing about any of this to Frank. Instead, as we sipped our coffees, I told him about getting high on the way to the party on Wolfback Ridge and my fight with Mom and Stan and how I'd had to beg Suze to take me in. I leaned hard on that last part, figuring the more pathetic I sounded, the easier he'd go on me for using again. But Frank, as usual, was giving me nothing to work with. He sat very still, fiddling with the lid of his coffee cup, those liquid blue eyes boring into me, recording every word for later decryption and analysis.

"I don't know what's wrong with me, man," I told him. "Everything was fine. I was going to work, hitting my meetings, just putting one foot in front of the other. Then a buddy calls me out the blue and next thing you know I'm getting high in the back of some chick's VW Bug."

"Let me ask you something," he said, taking a sip of his oily coffee. "When was the first time you got high—alcohol, marijuana, whatever, when was the first time?"

I flashed on a memory of a singer for one of my dad's early bands, frizzy-haired and summer tan, handing me a joint. We were at Stinson Beach, a bunch of us around a fire pit, guitars out, singing, and a cheer went up when I took in the hit without coughing.

"I don't know," I said. "Maybe five or six?"

"Five or *six*?"

I laughed. I'd shocked him. Just a little, but still. "I grew up around musicians, Frank," I said. "Somebody was always passing me a joint or letting me have a sip of their beer."

"Okay, so when was the first time you remember using on your own—not somebody giving it to you, but you picking it up yourself?"

I had to think about that one. "I guess I started getting into my dad's stash when I was nine or ten," I said. "I mean, he never really tried to hide it, left it in the bottoms of drawers and stuff. I got into his coke, too. Didn't snort it, just sort of rubbed it around my gums the way I'd seen my mom do." I smiled at the memory of all that magic, glowy numbness in my mouth.

"And you've been using ever since?"

"Well, yeah," I said. "It was everywhere when I was growing up. It would've been weirder if I wasn't getting high."

"So, maybe it's not such a big mystery why you keep using. Maybe you're just a person with feelings who's never really had to feel them before."

I turned away, watching a shirtless kid with buzzcut hair and eyebrow rings practice an old-school skateboard trick called an M-80, flipping his board over and over, flipping and missing, flipping and missing, each time coming closer to nailing the trick.

"Could we maybe skip this part?" I said. "All the head-shrinky childhood stuff. I thought we were going to talk about the steps, about being powerless over alcohol or whatever."

"Is that what you want?"

"See, there you go again. I had a therapist in rehab. I'm not looking for a new one."

He studied me a moment. "I don't particularly like you, Trent," he said. "I don't think I've made any secret of that. And sure, it's the money and the privilege, but mostly it's how much you remind me of me. When I was a young priest, even before I took my orders, I knew what I wanted. I knew it was wrong, too, and I still did it."

"And what, you're saying I'm like that? I want to screw little girls?"

"No, I'm saying you know the difference between right and wrong. You have a moral sense. You've drugged it into submission, but it's there. That's what makes people like you so destructive. Me, too. We know what we're doing is wrong and we do it, anyway."

I watched the skate rat trying to flip his rig, feeling the strangest mix of flattered and insulted. He'd put his finger on the thing that frightened me most about myself, that I could know what I was doing was stupid and wrong, watch myself lie and steal and sell drugs to children, and still not be able to stop.

"With those girls," I said, interested now, "you knew what you were doing?"

"Of course I did," he said. "My M.O. was to make the girl believe she was seducing *me*, that she was so bad, so rotten with sin, she could make a man of God betray his vows. Later on, they ended up on the streets of my own parish, a lot of them, turning tricks, getting high. I helped them then—ran off their pimps, got them into rehab, whatever it took. And then I went back and did the same damn thing to the next one in line. For thirty years."

We were surrounded by teenage girls, I realized, some as young as twelve or thirteen, dressed for the beach in crop tops and shorts.

"Do you still have those feelings?" I asked.

"About girls?"

We were both watching the same girl now, a sunburned brunette with a ski jump nose and a dopey grin at the edge of the crowd around the M-80 kid. One look at her, the way she kept checking the other girls' faces and copying their reactions, told you she was the new kid, the wannabe, the one nobody would miss if she disappeared.

"Every day," Frank said. "It's like a hunger, only worse, because if you're hungry, you just eat. If it was just booze I wanted, I could drink. I mean, really, who'd give a shit if an old fart like me died of alcoholism? But what I want, I can't have that. It destroys too many lives."

"So, what do you do?"

"I do the work," he said. "I see a shrink twice a week. I go to my meetings. I meet with a sponsor. I speak at jails. I speak to victim's groups, which believe you me is the most miserable experience you can possibly imagine. And then sometimes I talk to guys like you, who make me feel just the tiniest bit less insane."

I watched the sunburned girl, cheering on the skate-rat kid who'd finally managed to flip his board. She was safe for now, though she had no idea she'd ever been in danger.

"You really want to stop?" Frank asked.

"I do, yeah."

"Then you need to look at this stuff. You've been high your whole life. Since you were six. That doesn't go away because you go to some meetings. It takes time. It takes work."

"I know. I'm ready for that."

"No, you're not," he said. "You're still sitting here blowing smoke up my ass."

A mouthful of coffee went down the wrong way, and I coughed.

He laughed. "Do you think I can't add and subtract? A week ago you were ready to sleep in your car and now you're living in a place right here in town. Where's a broke kid like you going to find that kind of money?"

"I've been picking up a little cash on the side. Helping out a friend."

"This friend, he wouldn't happen to be the guy who got you high the other night?" he said. "The one selling cocaine to teenagers at this party?"

I watched that pinched smirk form on his lips. Some bullshit artist I was. I'd given away the whole game and not even realized it.

"You're still on probation, am I right?" he said.

"You think I don't know that?"

"Hey, hey, calm down. I'm just asking you a question."

But I couldn't calm down. "I could go away for years for this and I did it, anyway," I yelled. "That's what I was trying to tell you before. It's like I'm fucking crazy, Frank. Like some part of my brain is missing."

He said nothing, just waited. I wanted to scream. I wanted to take a swing at him, break his fucking nose for him all over again. But he was so calm, so unfazed, like sitting on a park bench hollering about missing a part of your brain was the most normal thing in the world, was even in a way progress. And that calmed me. Because in a way it *was* progress. All my life I had felt like an essential piece of me was missing, a part most people took for granted, but I'd never said it out loud before, not to the shrinks, not to my mother, not to anyone, and now I had.

"That talk you wanted to have about powerlessness?" he said. "I think we just had it."

Behind us someone had broken out a boombox and the skate chicks were dancing to Blink-182. I thought again about my mother and Stan. About Suze Randall and her boys. About my dad, too, how long it took him to leave and how much damage he'd done before he did.

"Are you going to be at the six o'clock meeting tomorrow?" I asked.

"I could be," he said. "One thing, though. This girl who put you up last week—Suze, Suzy, whatever her name is. If we're going to do this, you need to stay away from her."

"What? Why? She's got nothing to do with this."

"She has two kids and she's in the middle of a divorce," he said. "You're the last thing she needs in her life right now."

I turned away, my face warming all over again.

"See you tomorrow," he said, pulling himself up. "Good work tonight."

I did see Frank the next night, and the night after that, too. He was working so we didn't go for coffee, just chatted in the open doorway of his cab until the dispatcher called with his first run of the night. But each time the dispatch call came through, Frank thanked me, like I was the one doing him a favor by staying after the meeting, and each time I felt a little better, a little less crazy, as I watched his cab roll away down Miller Avenue.

Not that I was telling him everything. I left Suze out of those conversations, letting slide the box of old dishes she'd dropped off at my new apartment and the time she called me from her car to kill a few minutes between showings. I didn't tell Frank about the messages Lee left me at the store, either. I hadn't returned those calls, and now that I'd paid off my rental deposit I figured I didn't need to. If I kept my spending down and picked up a few weekend shifts at the store, I was pretty sure I could make my rent in October. But I didn't tell Frank about the calls. I didn't tell anyone. I just erased the messages and got back to work.

Gianni was gone all day Wednesday, meeting with wholesalers in the city. He was back the next day, but he wasn't his usual chatty, cocky self. The construction crews were still working at the Post Office, and I was over there half a dozen times that day signing off on deliveries and answering contractor's questions. Gianni never showed up once. He took phone calls and browsed his grocery magazines, but whenever I left, I came back to find him staring out the window, his eyes dead in their sockets, like a horse sleeping standing up.

"You have a car, right?" he asked that night as I was packing up to go home.

"Sure, yeah," I said. "It's a beater, but it gets me where I need to go."

"You ever thought about doing deliveries?"

"You mean, here? For Chef Tam?"

"Yeah, no, you're right. Forget it. That stuff's for teenagers."

That did it for me. I hated seeing him like this, moping around the office, reading old trade magazines and dreaming up ways to run the catering operation on the cheap. I also thought he was right. Without Chef Tamalpais, sooner or later Cornucopia Foods was going to make his father an offer he couldn't refuse, and then we would all be out of work.

The next day, on my lunch break, I parked myself a few doors down from a vegan restaurant just off Lytton Square where Stan Starling ate lunch five days a week. I had only been waiting a few minutes when he strode out onto the sidewalk, blinking in the midday glare. He was with two younger guys, finance types from the looks of it, but with a hip Left Coast vibe: skinny suits, earrings, one with a splash of platinum blond in his gelled black hair. They were shaking hands at the curb, Stan in full sales mode, his bleached white teeth flashing in the sun, when he saw me. I waved, but he went right on slapping backs and cracking jokes as he steered the two suits in the direction of their chauffeured Mercedes. He waited until the car had rounded the corner before he turned and walked over to me.

"The answer's no," he said.

I laughed. "You don't even know what I'm going to say."

"You want money, and you can forget it. The Bank of Stan's closed, pal."

"I want money," I admitted. "But not for me. For the Papadakises."

He scanned the crowded sidewalk, like he was searching for the bank of hidden cameras that was going to turn this all into a reality TV show from hell.

"Where are you living these days?" he said. "If you don't mind me asking."

This was my mother talking, not him. I'd kept an eye out for her all week, but if she was still staking out the deli, she was getting better at disguising herself.

"I have a little place just off Sycamore Park," I said. "I moved in last weekend."

He raised one immaculately manicured eyebrow. "Here? In Mill Valley?"

"Yeah, my friend Suze set it up. Stan, I know you and I haven't always—"

"Save it," he said. "I already talked to your buddy over at the store, and I'll tell you what I told him: This deal, it's not for me."

"That was this summer," I said. "You could get way better terms now."

"No, you're not listening. I talked to him a couple days ago. The little fucker made me drive all the way into the city to take the meeting so his dad wouldn't find out."

I remembered the note Gianni had left on his desk saying he was meeting with wholesalers in the city. Of course he'd gone to see Stan. What had made me think he would take my word for it that I had?

"You know what he wanted?" Stan asked. "A quarter million dollars guaranteed by his own personal ownership interest in the store. Which, unless I'm out of my fucking mind, is worth a lot more than a quarter million dollars."

I nodded, silenced. Gianni Papadakis was twenty-eight years old, with a wife and two kids. Aside from his salary, which wasn't much, his one-fifth interest in the store was all he had.

"You don't think it's a little weird he's doing all this behind his dad's back?" Stan asked.

"Papadakis is old school," I said. "The whole family is. But if you were giving him a loan, he'd tell them. He'd have to."

"Well, before he did that, he'd have to open the kimono a little."

"The what?"

"The kimono. The books. Before I start handing out that kind of money, I need to see numbers. Not just some bullshit bank prospectus, either. Real numbers. Sales figures, bank loans, property records."

"I could get you that," I said.

He cocked his head, interested now. "You could?"

It hit me, a split-second too late, that if Gianni hadn't shown Stan the sales figures he'd showed me it was probably because he didn't want Stan to see them.

"I mean, he showed me some numbers," I said. "It was a while ago, though. They're probably really out of date."

"But you could get more?"

"I'm not going to break into the guy's files if that's what you mean."

"As I recall, you have some expertise in this area."

Across Lytton Square, I could just make out the rustic, barn-style façade of Tam Grocery. I wished I was there now, finishing up my lunch break in the back parking lot watching the meat-room crew sneak shots of their lighter-fluid homebrew.

"What's your angle on this thing, anyway?" Stan asked.

"No angle. I'm trying to help Gianni. I want this to work."

"Bullshit. You're the most selfish prick I ever met. You don't wipe your ass unless it's going to get you something."

The truth, I could see, was getting me nowhere, so I reached deep down and pulled one of those great gleaming gold turds out of my ass.

"What if I told you I'd like to take over part of the business someday?"

"You?" He snorted. "What do you know about running a business?"

"Doesn't matter," I said. "They're bleeding money over there. If they don't get some cash soon, they'll have to give that new building back to the bank, and in a few years they'll have to sell out to Cornucopia. So if I help bring in this loan, which Gianni himself couldn't get—they'll have to cut me in on something, won't they?"

"You know who you sounded like just then?" he said.

I knew who I sounded like. The tone, the cadence, the wise

guy diction, all of it was lifted from a hundred overheard pool-side phone calls to nervous A&R execs. But I wasn't channeling my father. I was channeling Stan. If he was in my shoes, this was exactly how he'd play it.

"Well, that's all very nice, but I'm not doing shit until I see some numbers," he said.

"I can get you numbers," I said.

"I'm not going behind the old man's back, either. That's not how I do things."

I nodded as if we didn't both know this was how he'd been doing business ever since he cut his original partners out of Walden West.

"So, you'll think about it?" I said.

"I don't know, I really don't." He smiled, showing off that mouth full of professionally bleached teeth. "But it just might be worth a quarter-million bucks to watch you fuck up somebody else's life for a change."

I came in to work early Monday, hoping for some time alone with Gianni's computer, but he was already there, staring out the window as if he hadn't moved since I clocked out on Friday. He was like that all day, his movements slow and clumsy, like a toy whose batteries had run low. Finally, just as I was finishing up my shift, I talked him into touring the Post Office building with his architect and the construction manager, which bought me half an hour alone in the office.

Getting into the desk drawer where he kept the flash drive was easy. I'd "forgotten" my keys when we walked over to the new building so Gianni had to lend me his. The hard part was hacking the flash drive. If Gianni had ever written down his eight-digit pin, it wasn't in his desk or the filing cabinets. I'd spent Friday afternoon quietly making sure of that. That weekend, I'd sat down with a legal pad and a touch-tone telephone keypad to crack his pin. All I had to go on were the two 1s I'd seen him type into his computer the day he showed me the sales figures. On a telephone keypad, the numeral 1 doesn't correspond to any letters, which meant the numbers didn't spell out a word like Henry's did. It had to be a number, or partly a number. After hours of scratching out every combination I could think of, I convinced myself the number I was looking for was a date, with the digits 1-1 standing for the month of November, followed by two digits for the day, and four more for the year. Somebody's birthday, maybe, or a wedding anniversary. But whose? Gianni's birthday was in May, and I couldn't see him getting married in November.

I started with his kids. Gianni had two: a boy, Nikolas, who was four, and girl, Ava, who was three. I plugged the flash drive into the USB port and typed in the eight-digit string for the first day in November 1997, the year Nikolas was born: 1-1-0-1-1-9-9-7. A dialog box popped up: "ERROR. ACCESS CODE INCORRECT." I'd expected this, and tried the number string for the next day: 1-1-0-2-1-9-9-7. Wrong again. My plan was to key in all thirty combinations for November 1997 and start over with November 1998, the year Ava was born. But after just five tries I got a new error message:

WARNING!
Access Code Incorrect.
Further Unsuccessful Attempts Will Cause
System to Automatically Lock Down

Well, shit. I checked the clock over the door. I had been back all of five minutes and already I was nowhere. Worse than nowhere, because I still had twenty-five combinations to go for November 1997, and I didn't know if that was the right year or if the pin was a date at all. I was about to power down the desktop, hoping a reboot would give me five more shots at his pin, when my eyes wandered down the wall to the framed Savings Bank of Marin mortgage certificate, which, as I remembered now, was stamped cancelled November 13, 1983.

I didn't think. I just whipped around and keyed in 1-1-1-3-1-9-8-3. The screen froze, and for one heart-stopping second I was sure I'd locked down my boss's computer. Then the screen refreshed, and I was in.

I clicked through screen after screen, looking for anything that might be a year-end balance sheet, but the document menu was a sea of incomprehensible abbreviations. Some I could figure out, like "invt07.01," which was a spreadsheet of inventory orders for July 2001. Others were harder to make sense of, like "wfps10.99," which, when I opened it, turned out to be a two-year-old prospectus Gianni had written for some bankers at Wells Fargo.

I checked the clock again. Ten more minutes had passed, fifteen total since I'd sat down. A full walk-through of the Post Office building would take thirty minutes, but what if Gianni got bored? What if he forgot something and came back to get it? I tried to remind myself I was doing this for Gianni's own good, to get the documents that Gianni was too pig-headed to hand over to Stan on his own. It didn't help. Gianni would kill me if he caught me snooping in his files. No, first he would fire me, *then* he would kill me. I scrolled through the document menu one last time, searching for something, anything, I could give to Stan. Three-quarters of the way down, I stopped on a file titled "pyrl08.01."

I stared at the flickering screen, hating how my mind worked. "What'd you do, jack the Greek's payroll?" Lee had asked. "No, but it's a thought," I'd said. Luckily, as embezzlement schemes went, hacking the Papadakises' payroll would have been an act of epic stupidity. At Tam Grocery, paychecks came out of the printer autosigned, but I'd watched Gianni inspect each check against a spreadsheet of staff salaries. Of course, I could always go into the file and change the figures on my paycheck before it was printed, but the spreadsheet was programmed to automatically calculate hourly pay rates. Even an extra hundred bucks a month would bump my hourly pay by sixty-two cents—just the kind of detail Gianni would never miss.

Nothing was stopping me from cutting a check for a *vendor*, though. That, after all, was how I'd stolen most of the money from Campus Liquors. I had created fake vendors for real products the store carried, like craft brews and chewing tobacco, and paid their fake orders using checks I made out to bank accounts I'd set up for myself. This scam would be even easier to pull off at Tam Grocery because the Papadakises did business with literally hundreds of mom-and-pop vendors. How hard could it be to create an account for, say, a purveyor of locally produced honey, and mock up fake invoices for a couple hundred dollars a month? Then, I could open an account in the name of the phantom beekeepers and cash the checks. So long as I kept the vendor obscure and the payments small, no one would ever check to see if the honey was actually on the shelves—and I could forget all about Lee Radko and his kiddie coke parties.

Behind me, the doorknob jiggled once, then again.

I reached for the mouse and started frantically zeroing out screens. There were more open than I'd realized, five or six at least.

The door rattled again. "Trent? Are you in there?"

"Who is it?" I called.

"It's me—Henry."

One screen. Another screen. Almost done. "Be right there!"

I closed out the last screen, yanked the flash drive from the computer, and bolted across the office to unlock the door. Henry was in the hall, flipping through a ring of keys.

"Why'd you lock the door?" he asked.

"No reason," I said, waving him in. "I was just catching up on some rush orders."

"You need to lock the door to make rush orders?"

"Sometimes, yeah."

His smile had curdled on his lips. Something was off, but he wasn't sure what. I didn't really care. I just wanted him gone so I could lock the flash drive back in its drawer and go home.

"There's someone downstairs to see you," he said.

Panic needled up my spine. "Who?"

Henry laughed, still eyeing me. "Someone very blonde. And very pretty."

Suze was waiting for me in the cheese aisle in low heels and that white linen suit I liked, her sunglasses tucked into the collar of her blouse. She had been downtown, she said, running some errands, and realized I was probably just finishing my shift. Was I up for a cup of coffee?

"What about work?" I said. "Don't you guys preview houses on Monday nights?"

She laughed, her face darkening. "We do, yeah. I kind of blew it off tonight."

I looked over at Henry, who shrugged. *Hey, man, don't let me get in your way.*

"Give me a minute lock up upstairs," I said. "I'll be right back."

A few minutes later, as Suze and I passed the taxi stand on Lytton Square, I willed myself not to look for Frank T.'s boxy yellow Crown Victoria. It wasn't there. At that hour, Frank's well-upholstered Irish ass would be planted on a folding chair in the basement of the Methodist Church, which is where I would have been if I had any fucking sense. But that was just it: I had no fucking sense. Upstairs in the business office, I'd locked the flash drive in the desk drawer and powered down Gianni's computer, but there was no way to erase the fact that someone had logged on using his pin while he was three blocks away touring the Post Office building.

"So, I did it," Suze said, halfway across the square. "I filed the papers for the divorce. I just came from the lawyer's office. There's still years of legal bullshit to go through, but I filed the papers. They'll serve him tomorrow. It's over. *We're* over."

I stopped walking, trying to process what she'd just said. I wanted to sweep her off her feet and dance a victory jig right there in the middle of Lytton Square, but I remembered what Frank had said about staying away from her and hung back, my hands jammed in my pockets.

"Hey, wow, I can't believe you finally did it," I said.

"'Hey, wow, I can't believe you finally did it'?" she said. "Seriously? I'm getting a *divorce* here, asshole. Partly because of you. Because of what you said the other day."

I was blowing it, I could see that, but I didn't know how not to. I didn't know how to be her friend when all I wanted to do was find my car and drive her home to my place.

"Fuck coffee," she said. "I need a drink. No, I take that back. I need to get drunk."

"Sounds fun. I'll tag along, make sure you don't break shit."

"Okay, yeah, forget I said that. We'll do dinner instead. It's on me. I owe you a dinner, remember?"

We ended up at El Paseo, a lamp-lit Spanish restaurant strung out along a brick-lined alley between two downtown streets. I'd walked by it all my life, and once in high school Lee and I broke into the kitchen and stole two gallon-sized bottles of cooking wine, but I had never eaten there. The food, it turned out, was delicious: oysters and gazpacho followed by a tableful of tiny plates of seafood and local meats seasoned with garlic and paprika.

Over her third glass of wine, Suze broke the news that she'd sold a house that weekend. The price was $900,000, small potatoes by Mill Valley standards, but after taxes and agency fees, her cut would come to nearly fifteen grand. Her boss at the agency had agreed to advance her half her share so she could pay her back rent. The rest she would get when the deal closed in October.

"I can buy clothes again," she said. "And shoes. And go to a real hair stylist."

"And file for divorce," I said.

"And file for divorce." She laughed, high and fluttery, halfway to hammered. "Seriously, though, I think I'm breaking my losing streak here. This couple I sold to, they must have looked at fifty houses, but now they're referring me to their friends."

"To picky yuppies," I said, raising my near-beer.

"To picky, loyal yuppies," she said, clinking my glass. "Long may they spend."

We drank, our eyes holding one another's. The red wine had raised the color in her cheeks and sent her eyelids to half-mast. In the lamp light, she looked like a happy, sleepy child.

"How about you?" she asked.

"Me? I'm good. I don't really need a hair stylist. Or a divorce."

This time her laughter was only dutiful. "I talked to Randy the other day. He says you're paying nine hundred a month for that place."

"He told you that?"

"I brought him the tenant, right?" She was quiet a moment, turning her glass by its stem. "He says you paid the deposit in cash."

Clearly, the wine had gone to her head less than I'd thought. Suze knew how broke I was. She also knew, or thought she did, how I used to pay my rent in Santa Barbara.

"I really wanted the place," I said. "I didn't want the guy thinking I'd give him a bad check."

"And you just happened to have eighteen hundred bucks lying around?"

"I'm not a big fan of banks, Suze."

This wasn't really an answer, and maybe for that reason, she backed off long enough for us to order dessert, a molten chocolate torte with two spoons. But she circled around to the topic again as we wound our way back through the nearly empty Lytton Square toward her car.

"I'll have a little cash left over when this deal closes," she said. "So, if you ever—"

"No way, you've got lawyers to pay and car payments to catch up on," I said. "Don't worry, I'm good. I'll just pull some weekend shifts at the store."

"Okay, but I mean it. I know what it's like, especially around here."

We had reached her car, and she turned around, her heavy-lidded eyes looking up into mine. She hadn't said the words "drugs" or "Lee Radko," but they were there in her worried frown, and I did the only thing I could think to do, which was to stop her with a kiss.

"Slow down there, Mr. Wolfer," she said, flustered. "Technically, I'm still a married lady."

The obvious comeback was *Not for much longer, Ms. Randall,* but I couldn't pull the trigger. What if she took it the wrong way and pushed me away again? And then there was the money, the eighteen hundred dollars in cash I'd magically found a week after I showed up at her house with everything I owned in boxes in the back seat of my car.

"I should go," she said. "The boys'll be waiting up."

I almost congratulated her on signing the divorce papers, but that just sounded weird, a guy congratulating a woman on getting a divorce. So I watched her settle in behind the wheel, wishing I was better at this, that I'd spent my twenties going on regular dates with regular women, that I'd spent my twenties doing pretty much anything besides stealing tens of thousands of dollars from a frat row liquor store to party with high-end hookers. But that *was* how I'd spent my twenties, so there was nothing to do but step back onto the sidewalk and wave as she drove off down the hill toward Shelter Ridge and the two little boys waiting up for her.

# 14

I was up early the next morning, doing calf stretches in Sycamore Park before six a.m. I was turning into one of *those* people, the kind who rise with the sun to go running three mornings a week. I took it slow at first, jogging a block and walking a block, all the way to East Blithedale before I opened it out into a full run. At that hour, the lights were off in most of the houses and downtown was deserted, storefronts empty, doors bolted shut, only a few stray cars nosing along the darkened streets. On Throckmorton, a produce truck was parked in front of Tam Grocery, rear doors open, Mr. Papadakis halfway up the loading ramp with a clipboard. I waved, but he didn't see me, which was fine by me. If the loan from Stan was ever going to happen, I would have to take another shot at Gianni's flash drive. Just the thought of it, the risks I'd have to take to find the store's financials, the lies I'd have to tell Gianni to find time to search for them, made me feel unclean.

I stepped on the gas, winding through Lytton Square and back down Miller Avenue, trying to outrun my real fear, which wasn't getting caught downloading the store's annual balance sheets, but the freedom that hacking Gianni's access code had given me to steal. I stole from Campus Liquors because I was lonely and sad and hornier than a ferret on meth, but also because I could. The way Al Fierro was hitting the scotch toward the end, I could have grabbed a thousand bucks straight from the till and he wouldn't have noticed. But I liked cooking up new scams, imagining myself outwitting the accountants he would eventually have to bring in to explain the store's shrinking cash flow. That was how I taught myself double-entry accounting, by stealing, and even now as I jogged past the Methodist Church and La Cocina Pequeña, I couldn't stop my brain from scheming how to siphon money out of the Papadakises' bank account and into mine.

Back at my apartment, I was still in my robe, toweling off from the shower, when the phone rang. The line had only been connected the day before and I had to dig through piles of dirty socks and underwear to find the phone.

"Hey there," I said. "Did you know this is my very first call at this number?"

"Are you watching this?" Suze asked.

"Watching what?"

"Turn on the TV. There's been an attack. In New York. They've hit two buildings."

"What're you talking about? What buildings?"

"The Twin Towers. They think somebody flew planes into them." Her voice cracked, and I realized she was crying. "God, all those people. There's got to be thousands of people in there."

A single moment of panic can clarify everything, separate what matters from what doesn't. Suze could have called anyone that morning: her mother, Jimmy, a friend from work. But she had called me.

"I'm coming over there," I said.

"Trent, no, not now. The boys are here."

"Five minutes," I said, setting down the phone.

"One of the towers has fallen," she said, opening the sliding-glass door for me. "It was just on TV. We watched it go down."

"I know, I heard it on the radio," I said.

Suze nodded, her eyes glassy from crying. She was barefoot, in shorts and a faded Dodgers T-shirt, her hair still wet from the shower. When she hugged me, burying her face in my chest, she started crying again, these deep, gushing sobs. Later, she told me that while I was driving over, she'd called Jimmy and they'd gotten into a fight because his new girlfriend, who supposedly had a place of her own, had picked up. But I didn't know that then. All I knew was that she was hugging me in front of her kids, sobbing into my chest, and she didn't care what they saw.

For the next hour, the four of us sat on the sectional sofa watching the cable networks toggle between images of the smoking buildings in New York and Washington and the stunned anchors in the studios. No one spoke. Suze had unplugged the phone after her fight with Jimmy so it didn't ring. Jake lay curled up on Suze's lap, greedily sucking his thumb. Once, not long after I came in, he asked in a quiet voice, "Why's everybody crying?" but when Suze could only tell him, "Baby, I can't explain it. It's just really, really sad," he nodded, silently working his thumb in his mouth.

When the second tower fell, around seven-thirty California time, Suze started crying again—more of those deep, gushing sobs. "All those people, those poor, poor innocent people," she kept saying. Dylan watched her from his corner of the couch, embarrassed and angry, but maybe also a little relieved. He was seven, and he hated me the way only a seven-year-old can hate, but even he seemed to get that his mom needed a shoulder to cry on that morning.

She was still weepy when the first reports came in of the plane going down in Pennsylvania. CNN didn't have video yet, just an unconfirmed report that a jet had crashed in a field near Pittsburgh, but it pulled me up off the couch. I started for the kitchen, but when I got there, I kept on going out onto Suze's backyard. I was in my socks, wearing the same ratty gym shorts I'd thrown on when Suze called, but I marched out the rear gate and around the side of the condo, checking under the eaves and behind the garden hose, sighting down between the fence lines. I have no idea what I thought I'd find down there. Terrorists, I guess. Crazy thoughts kept running through my head: *Where can I find a gun? Where's the nearest fallout shelter? Will the army still take me with a felony on my record?*

I saw another guy, also in T-shirt and shorts, wandering in the tall grass behind the condos, dazed and wary. I didn't need to ask if he'd heard the news from New York.

"I heard they're shutting down the Golden Gate Bridge," he said.

Together, we turned toward the bridge, hidden from view by the ridge to the south of us.

"They're afraid somebody's going to take it out?" I asked.

"They don't know how many planes are still in the air," he said. "One of the jets that hit the Towers was headed for San Francisco. I just heard it on TV."

I had heard this, too. I had also heard that there might still be more planes out there full of terrorists ready to martyr themselves for Allah. I stated the obvious: "We're at war."

He nodded, still staring in the direction of the bridge. "We're thinking of heading inland."

"Where?"

"I have no idea, man. But we've got a two-year-old. If anything happened, even if it was just fallout from an explosion, I don't want her breathing that in."

Across Richardson Bay I could see my old high school, and beyond that, a cottony bank of fog riding the ridgeline. No planes in the sky, no sirens going off. Just another quiet, suburban Tuesday in Southern Marin. I saw myself as I must have looked to this stranger, shoeless and sleep-deprived, peeking under the eaves for crouching jihadists. Buy a gun? Join the army? What was I thinking? This time a year ago, I had been in jail in Santa Barbara bunking with a guy who had stolen his sister's TV to buy a fifty-dollar rock of crack.

Back at Suze's condo, Sharon was in the kitchen pouring cereal for the boys while Suze stood in front of the muted TV, talking to her boss. I had completely forgotten about work, about all the details of my daily life, but when I checked the time-stamp on the TV, it was just five minutes past eight.

I called the store from Suze's kitchen. The office line rang and rang, and when I tried the main number for the store, it rang a dozen times or more before Stavros Papadakis picked up, wheezing like he'd run a five-minute mile.

"Hey, this is Trent," I said. "Are we open today?"

"Open?" he said. "Are you fucking kidding me? How soon can you get in?"

Twelve hours later, when Gianni finally sent me home, I drove straight to Shelter Ridge. I never asked Suze if I should, and she never asked if I would. I had a brief, panicky moment when I caught Dylan's scowl as I let myself in through the sliding-glass door, but before he could send up the alarm Suze strode in from the kitchen, little Jake on her hip. "You better call your mom," she said. "She's called a couple times already."

"She called here?"

"Twice," Suze said. "Call her, Trent. The last time, she sounded kind of frantic."

My mother. Yes. Shit. She'd left a couple messages for me at work, but it had been such a wild day, customers clearing the shelves of batteries and bottled water, and once those ran out, anything nonperishable they could get their hands on: powdered milk, oatmeal, canned meat and fish, blocks of cheese.

"Where the hell've you been?" she said when she picked up. "I've been calling all day."

"I know, I'm sorry. I was at work. How'd you know to call here?"

"Stan mentioned the girl's name, said she helped you find your new place. I called there, too. I talked to the manager of your complex. He said it looked like you'd left in a hurry."

I felt a fresh wash of guilt at the thought of my mother begging poor Randy J. to check my apartment for signs of life. Then I did some quick math and realized that it had only taken her a matter of hours to work out that if I wasn't returning her calls, and I wasn't at my apartment, the best place to find me was at Suze Randall's house.

"I'm sorry I didn't call," I said. "It was pretty crazy at the store today."

"I'll bet," she said, calming down a little. "So, are you okay?"

"I'm fine. Just tired. How about you?"

"I'm good. Stan's in L.A. He was supposed to fly back today, but they grounded all the flights. He met some guys at the airport and they rented a car somehow. He called from the road about an hour ago. They should be getting in any minute now."

"I'm glad to hear that," I said. "I'm really sorry I didn't call. I didn't know you were alone."

We were quiet on the phone. I knew we should be talking about the tragedy, comparing notes on what we'd seen on TV and the rumors of a second attack planned for the Golden Gate Bridge. But I was my mother's son, and I knew that despite the panic of that long, strange day, and all my brave thoughts that morning of buying a gun and joining the army, we were back to thinking about ourselves. Which for now, for my mother and me, meant our relationship to each other.

"Suzy Randall," she said. "She's the one you were always mooning over in high school. The one with a boyfriend—Johnny, Joey, something like that."

"Jimmy. They're divorced now. Divorcing, anyway."

"I see." Another long, strained silence. "You're staying there now, is that it?"

"I don't know, Ma. We haven't really talked about it."

For a year, ever since the day I broke down and called her from jail, my mother was all I had. I had needed her, desperately, and now I didn't. This realization hadn't hit me until that moment, but my mother had known all day, ever since she called Suze's home and heard her say that I would call her back.

"I heard kids," she said. "When I called earlier."

"She has two boys. One's seven, the other's about four."

"Seven and *four*?"

"Almost five. Look, I should go. I'm sorry I didn't call earlier. And I'm sorry I didn't call after I left that day. I didn't think you wanted to hear from me."

"It's okay," she said. "I checked on you a few times down at the store."

"I know. I saw you."

"Not every time, you didn't."

She was quiet on the line, letting that one sink in.

"Okay, I'll let you go," she said. "I'm glad you're safe and sound. I love you, honey."

"I love you, too, Ma. Call me if Stan gets held up, okay? I'll come over and hang out."

"That's all right, he'll be here any minute. And even if he isn't, I'll be fine."

That night, after the boys went to bed, Suze and I stayed up late watching that eerie tape loop of Flight 175 plowing into the South Tower over and over. Sharon sat up with us, ducking out to the patio every few minutes for a smoke, until it became clear that I wasn't going home and Suze wasn't going to make me. Sharon gathered up her things and hugged Suze and me goodnight. "Take care of her, babe," she whispered in my ear as she let go.

After she left, I helped Suze clean up, switching off lights and setting glasses and dirty cereal bowls in the sink.

"You want me to sleep out here?" I said.

She was standing in the kitchen doorway, the only light in the room coming from the TV.

"Is that what you want?" she asked.

"Not really, no."

"Good. Me, either."

Her bedroom was smaller than I'd expected and half-empty, just the bed and a few pieces of secondhand furniture, but it smelled strongly of her, of cocoa butter and hairspray and her tart, citrusy perfume—orange oil, maybe, mixed with vanilla and flowers.

"You're sure this is going to be okay?" she asked, watching me.

I pulled her to me and kissed her. Seconds later, we were tearing at each other, unbuckling belts, peeling off shirts, fumbling with buttons and zippers and condom boxes. We had left the bedroom door ajar, and as we fell back onto the bed I cupped my hand over her mouth to keep from waking the boys. This only made her buck more violently, her eyes bright with fear and arousal. Some part of me, the part that panicked that day at the bunkers, had known this all along: Suze *liked* being held down. It turned her on. A fresh panic bubbled up in me, a fear that I wouldn't be able to stop, that I would keep pressing and pressing, twisting her head back until I hurt her. But instead of stopping me, this thought turned *me* on, driving me onward, the rage in me drawing off her fear, the fear in her drawing off my rage, in a weird, scary, deeply erotic loop. For five long minutes, we threw ourselves at each other, blindly, recklessly, my hand pushing her head back into the pillow, her heels digging into my back, until a gigantic bomb exploded inside me, and all that rage, all that fear and need and panic spilled out in a single, brain-emptying rush.

"Holy shit," I said when I could form words. "Why didn't we do that before?"

"We did," she said, laughing, still catching her breath. "A bunch of times."

"Not like *that*."

"Not like that, no. But not so bad, either. You just don't remember."

I rolled onto my back, my chest still heaving, my skin still electric, wondering if this could possibly be true. I remembered a lost night in a hot tub in Tam Valley. Another in the back of a station wagon on Panoramic Highway. Maybe two or three more in bedrooms and pool sheds at parties. I was lights-out drunk every time, which for me had always been the explanation. Then I thought about what my mother had said: *Suzy Randall. She's the one you were always mooning over in high school.* Maybe I had it backward. Maybe Suze and I hadn't had sex all those times because we were drunk. Maybe we got drunk all those times so we could have sex.

"This is the easy part, you know," she said.

"Yeah? What's the hard part?"

"Tomorrow morning."

Next thing I knew daylight was streaming in through the

curtains and *Ren & Stimpy* was blaring full blast in the living room. When I looked up at Suze's alarm clock, it read 8:31 a.m.

I was pulling up my rumpled office khakis when the door clicked open and Suze bustled in wearing a terry-cloth bathrobe, her hair wrapped in a towel.

"Shit, I thought you left already," she said.

I hazily recalled Suze shaking me awake and telling me I needed to go before the boys came out to watch TV.

"Sorry, I think I fell back asleep," I said. "I need my shoes."

"Your what?"

"My shoes. They're out by the TV."

She swore again, then stood listening to a cartoon car crash in the next room. "Wait here," she said. "I'll get the boys up and out and then you can go."

"No, look at the clock. I'm already running late."

Before she could answer, a heavy object thudded against the bedroom door. *"There's* your stupid shoe, dickhead!" Dylan shouted.

The house was quiet just long enough for me to realize that someone had muted the TV before a second size-9 ½ Kenneth Cole dress shoe bounced off the door.

"Okay, okay," Suze said, fighting to stay calm. "I'll handle this."

"No, Suze, his beef's with me."

"And he's my kid. I need to handle this."

She was right, every atom in my body knew this. I didn't have enough fingers and toes to count the times one of my mother's boyfriends had tried to teach me a lesson and ended up being one of my mother's many ex-boyfriends. But for the first time I understood what was going through those guys' minds. This wasn't about me sleeping with Dylan's mother. This was about territory. He was claiming it, and if I wanted to stay in Suze's life, I needed to take it back.

"I need my damn shoes," I said, starting for the door.

Dylan was hunkered down behind the sofa like a soldier taking incoming fire. Jake stood a few feet away, naked from the waist down, his thumb jammed into his mouth, trying with all his might not to cry. All my forward motion ceased. I could scream at Dylan, and if he had said just the right words, in just the right snotty tone, I might have even smacked him, though I would've regretted it the rest of my life. But I couldn't do anything that would make his baby brother cry.

"Go away, asshole!" Dylan screamed. "Nobody wants you here!"

"No need to shout," I said. "I'm standing right here. I can hear you fine."

He stood up. "My dad's gonna come up here and kick your stupid fucking ass!"

"Okay, but can I get my shoes first? And my socks. They're right over there, by the sofa."

He stopped, thrown. The whole point was to make me yell back. The point was to get me to lose it, tell him I could kick his dad's candy ass with one hand tied behind my back. Instead, I was doing what he asked, I was leaving.

"I'm calling my dad!" he yelled again, but the fight had gone out of him, and I was free to walk over to the sofa to grab my socks. The anger that had propelled me out of the bedroom had evaporated, lifted like mist, and what remained was a very old, very familiar sadness. I'd spent half my childhood where Dylan was now, and I knew what he probably already knew himself, which was that if his dad gave enough of a shit about his mother to come up from L.A. to kick my ass he would have done it weeks ago.

"So, is school back in session today?" I asked, pulling up my socks.

"None of your beeswax, A-hole!"

I laughed. The kid had a point: It *wasn't* any of my beeswax. "Look, I'm not your dad," I said. "I get that. I'm not trying to be."

He glared at me, silent. I was breaking the rules by saying it out loud. He was suspicious, but we had an audience now, Suze leaning against the bedroom door frame with little Jake at her side, his thumb firmly lodged into his mouth. With them watching, there was nothing Dylan could say that wouldn't sound lame and kid-like.

"I like your mom, though," I said. "I'd like to see her again. But that's up to her. And you. You and Jake there. This is your house, and if you don't want me here, you're going to figure out a way to get rid of me. I totally get that. I don't blame you, honestly. She's your mom."

The boy's small, red face was a knot of primal rage, but for the moment I'd neutralized him. I would've given anything to look at Suze, to see how she was taking this, but I knew enough to quit while I was ahead.

"I better go," I said. "I'm going to be late for work."

The rest of that week, I put in twelve-hour days at Tam Grocery and spent my nights sitting up with Randy J. watching CNN. Every night there was a new report of an Arab guy pulled off a flight in Boston or suspected terrorists picked up trying to flee across the Mexican border. Nobody wanted to get on a plane. No one wanted to cross a bridge. But in Mill Valley, three thousand miles from Ground Zero, it was mostly a TV show. All week people filled their shopping baskets with batteries and distilled water, but outside, on the streets, the weather was Indian summery and kids hung out front of the Book Depot café flirting and smoking and flipping their skateboards. After a day or two, the schools opened again. People started going back to work. Suze's clients wanted to look at houses again. "This is the new normal," the newscasters kept saying, and when they said it, their ties askew, the studio makeup failing to hide the exhaustion in their eyes, it sounded scary and profound. But the next morning, jogging past the dog-walkers and ponytailed supermoms in stretchy black yoga pants, things seemed—well, pretty normal.

Late that Friday afternoon, I was in the dairy cooler restocking butter and margarine when Gianni poked his head in the door. "Your girlfriend called," he said. I stared, drawing a blank.

"Suze—that's her name, right?" he said. "You better call her. It sounded kind of urgent."

She had calmed down by the time I called. She had left the boys alone in the kitchen for, she swore, a total of five minutes before Dylan tossed a ripe banana down the disposal and turned it on. No one was hurt, but the sink was backed up and she couldn't afford a plumber to unjam the disposal. I started to tell her the truth, which was that I barely knew how to operate a garbage disposal, much less repair one, when it hit me that I had just spent the week watching CNN with a man who could teach me how.

"You're going to have to give me a little time," I said. "I'll need to borrow some tools."

It took us most of the night and half a dozen phone calls to Randy J. to get it done, but after I had pulled the last shred of mashed banana peel from the disposal blades with needle-nose pliers and scooped decades' worth of coffee grounds and congealed bacon fat from the grease trap, there wasn't much question about where I would be sleeping that night.

I was up at six the next morning, out on Suze's driveway doing my deep knee-bends and calf-stretches. In New York, firefighters were still picking through the rubble, but in Marin, it was another crisp fall morning, the first rays of sunshine spilling over the east peak of Mt. Tamalpais. I ran a three-mile loop to the high school and back, trying to decide what to tell Lee who had called the day before saying he wanted me to come out for a poolside rager in the Ross hills. He'd been to the house before, he said, and it was a quick, easy score.

Gianni had been sitting five feet away when he called so I had pretended he was a produce supplier in Merced. "Yes, yes, Mr. Radko, we'll look at our records and get right back to you," I told him, but I didn't like the sound of it. It was one thing to roll up on a party full of strangers, but to go back to a house where you'd been before was just asking to get hung. But as I ran along the old railroad right-of-way back to Shelter Ridge, I kept doing math problems, trying to square how much I owed Randy at the end of the month with how much money I had in the bank, which was basically nothing. I had put in fourteen hours of O.T. that week—almost two full days, at time and a half—but after taxes, it wouldn't even come to a hundred and fifty bucks. It wasn't enough, not when you added in the phone deposit and the utilities hookup fee and all the random household crap you never think about like cutting boards and shower curtains.

I stood at the bottom of Suze's driveway, blowing hard, trying to focus on stretching my glutes and quads. Maybe I could go back to being Lee's money man, loan him everything I had, and take my ten percent. But Lee would never go for that, and, anyway, it wouldn't pay enough to make it worth the trouble. I had to do something, though. In two weeks, I would owe Randy nine hundred dollars, plus another hundred or so for utilities. A few extra overtime shifts weren't going to cut it. I could hit up my mother, but I still owed a thousand bucks on the AmEx card, and after the way I'd left two weeks ago, I doubted I could count on her to float me beyond that. But without her, it was either throw in with Lee Radko or start creating fake vendor accounts at Tam Grocery.

All the lights were out when I let myself in upstairs, but when I ducked into the kitchen, Dylan was at the counter pouring himself a bowl of Cocoa Puffs.

"Hey," he said, startled.

"Hey yourself," I said.

I would have given anything just then to be able to pull a line of patter out of my ass, whip out some cool nugget of Cocoa Puffs lore, but I knew how tough this kid could make things for me, so I kept my mouth shut as he stirred his cereal, watching the milk turn cocoa-brown.

"I'm gonna watch some TV," he said.

"Your mom's still sleeping, you know," I said.

He stopped at the doorway. "Yeah. So?"

"So, maybe you could keep the volume down?"

The second I said it I knew I'd blown it, given him the opening he'd been waiting for.

"Right, *Dad*," he said, shutting the door behind him.

When the TV came on in the next room, playing an old *Scooby Doo* episode, the volume inched upward, first to the level of a shouted argument, then to that of a siren, then to some final level at the very top of the speakers' range where sound becomes a physical thing, like twenty feet of water pressing in on your eyes and ears.

When I threw open the door, the two boys were on the couch, Dylan with his Cocoa Puffs, Jake with his hands down the front of his PJs, watching the show, which wasn't Scooby Doo, but me, their mother's sweaty new guy screaming noiselessly into the fire hose of sound pouring out of the flatscreen. If I could have heard my own voice, if I thought I could wrestle the remote away from Dylan without strangling him, I never would have thought of Billy Simonds, my mother's old boyfriend. But in that moment I was helpless, which flashed me back almost twenty years to Billy and my mother holed up in her room with a pot full of peyote tea.

I was eleven or twelve, stuck at home with nothing to do but listen to the two of them giggle and sing and have very loud, athletic sex. When I couldn't take it one more second, I slapped the Bee Gees' *Spirits Having Flown*, the single cheesiest album ever pressed into vinyl, on the stereo and cranked the volume. Three songs in, the synth riffs on "Love You Inside and Out" rattling the windows, the bedroom door opened and Billy sauntered out, barefoot, wearing a filthy orange sarong, and sat down beside me on the sofa. That was all he did, just sat. He didn't yell the way my mother's other boyfriends did. He outlasted me. Out-Zenned me. Sat there on our thrift-store couch nodding along to Barry Gibb's nut-squeezing falsetto, smiling that serene mescaline smile, until the song ended and I turned off the stereo.

I wasn't wearing a sarong and I wasn't flying on four hundred mills of Zacatecas mescaline, but I willed myself to stop yelling and wait the boys out. Jake was the first to peek over his shoulder at the bedroom door, but soon Dylan was doing it, too. I tried not to watch them, tried to quiet my mind, empty it of all needs and desires, but what slipped in was how much I missed Billy Simonds. I had never thought of Billy that way before, as someone I could miss. Mom had dated him off and on for four years before he went after his therapist with a pen-knife and ended up at Atascadero, the state hospital for the criminally insane. I hadn't seen him since, but now that I thought about it, Billy was as close as I'd come to having a dad after my dad left.

By then, Dylan had pressed the remote and the TV was playing at a more normal volume. I knew better than to thank him. He didn't say a word, either, just sank low on the sofa watching Scooby and Shaggy duke it out with a pirate ghost. But as I headed for the shower, I sent up a silent word of thanks to Billy Simonds, wherever he was.

When I came back from the shower, Suze was sprawled out across the bed, two pillows piled over her head. I was combing my hair in the dresser mirror when she turned over and tossed the pillows aside. "What was that all about?" she asked. "It sounded like they were slaughtering small animals out there."

"The boys were watching *Scooby Doo*," I said. "They had the volume on a little high."

If you listened, you could just hear Fred and Shaggy arguing in the next room over whether it was safe to enter the haunted ocean liner.

"You were sleeping," I said. "I asked if they'd turn it down."

"And they did?"

I dropped the comb into my kit bag, smiling to myself.

"Sorry, I can't stay," I said, leaning in for a kiss. I meant it as a quick peck, but she hooked her arm around my neck and pulled me in for a long, drowsy kiss.

"Mmm, you smell good," she whispered.

"Yeah well, you've got quite the collection of designer soaps in there."

"And you went with vanilla-bergamot. Nice."

I checked the door. The volume was too low for what we had in mind, and, anyway, if I was going to meet up with Lee I needed to hit the bank before the lunch rush started at Hélène's.

"What's the hurry?" she said. "The boys have already seen you, right?"

"I need to run some errands. And there's a meeting I should probably hit."

"At eight o'clock on Saturday morning?"

"I told my sponsor I'd meet up with him before the meeting."

This was a lie. Frank would be at the meeting, but we hadn't talked about getting together. I had plenty of time. And I'd forgotten the morning-after smell of a bed where two people have had sex the night before. The sheets, the pillows, everything, reeked of it. Of us. Suze pulled me in for another kiss and I slid a hand inside her nightshirt, cupping my palm around her sleep-warmed breast.

"Might be time to think about losing those jeans," she whispered in my ear.

We were at that place where our bodies were no longer our own, where the usual human needs—for air, for food, for water—are overcome by one all-consuming need to get laid. In a minute, I knew, one of us would rip open another condom package and we would lose ourselves in each other, become again that crazed, bucking thing on the bed. I wanted that, badly, but I kept thinking of Dylan in the living room hearing it: the suppressed giggles, the clotted moans, the rhythmic squeaks and squeals of bedsprings, the running soundtrack of my childhood.

"Maybe we should slow down," I said, easing my hand out from under her shirt.

I was hard as a rock and she was naked under her nightshirt, all of which was making it impossible to think straight. But I couldn't sleep with her now, not if I was going to run off and do a drug deal. Then there was Dylan and Jake, who had pretended not to watch me slip into their mother's bedroom wearing nothing but a towel around my waist.

"You grew up with this, too," I said, nodding toward the living room. "It's not right."

"I hate to break it to you, but those two, they're part of the package."

"I know, I know. Look, it's my day off, right? I'm free all afternoon."

She shook her head. "Dylie's got a game. How about after that? Dinner, maybe? I could ask Mom to take the boys."

I liked that idea, a lot. The problem was Lee and his kiddie party in Ross. What was I going to do, scarf down my meal and tell Suze I was keeping an early curfew?

"Can I get back to you on that?"

She looked at me the way my mother used to, searching my face for the answer my words weren't telling her, but I was giving her nothing to work with, just an open, friendly smile.

The topic of the ten o'clock meeting that Saturday was the same one it had been every day since the morning of the attacks: where everyone had been when they heard the news from New York, and how no one—not their ex-wives, not their druggy kids, not the sketchy Arab-looking guy behind the counter at the 7-Eleven—loved America as much as they did. I had been hearing this all week, and I'd even told a version of my own story of running out behind Suze's condo in my socks wondering where I could get my hands on a rifle. That morning, though, I wasn't feeling it. I had until the banks closed at two to decide what to do about Lee and his kiddie party, and the more I thought about it, the simpler the math got. If I quit driving my car, cut all non-essential expenses, and ate three meals a day at the store, I might just make my rent in October. On the other hand, if I spent a few hours with Lee and some spoiled rich kids in Ross, I could pay my rent early, drive my car whenever I liked, and take Suze to any restaurant in town.

I was stacking the last of the folding metal chairs when Frank T. laid a weathered hand on my shoulder. "I'm driving today," he said. "If you want to talk, it'll have to be in my cab."

He'd parked in the median strip of Miller Avenue, and that's where we set up shop, him in the driver's seat, me riding shotgun. He'd brewed a thermos of mouth-puckeringly sweet black coffee, which I pretended to sip from a plastic cup as we picked up where we'd left off earlier in the week, working the Second Step. I had read the Big Book chapters he'd asked me to read, and I told him before we even got in the car that I was ready to take the step. But that wasn't good enough for him. He wanted to talk about it, break down how I had come to believe that a power greater than myself could restore me to sanity. And then it was like the meeting all over again: I was looking at him, talking to him, answering all his questions, but in my head I was doing math problems, calculating how much I could make that night if I zeroed out my bank account, and how much more I could make if I hit one of those payday loan places in San Rafael.

"You do realize I'm on the clock here," Frank said.

I had no idea how long he'd been watching me across the front seat. Going by the pulsing of the big blue vein in his forehead, it had been a while.

"Frank, I'm sorry," I said. "I guess I'm a little out of it this morning."

"Well, I've got a cab to drive. Maybe we should try another day."

"Do you really believe in all this stuff?" I asked.

"All what stuff?"

"This. God. Higher Power. Whatever you want to call it. Do you really believe in all that? After the things you did?"

"Believe me, God had nothing to do with what I did to those girls."

"Okay, see, that's where you lose me. I mean, if it helps you sleep at night, fine. But objectively? It's kind of bullshit. All the good stuff, that's my Higher Power looking out for me, but all the bad stuff, that's on me? It's like something a little kid would come up with."

He stared out the passing traffic, his droopy eyelid at half-mast. He was getting tired of me. *I* was getting tired of me. What I needed to do was shut up and go find Lee Radko.

"Maybe you're right," I said. "Maybe I should just go."

He punched a button on the dashboard, slamming the locks on all four doors shut.

"'Faith is the substance of things hoped for, the evidence of things not seen,'" he said. "Ring any bells for you?"

I shook my head. He'd spooked me with the auto-lock thing, and all I could think about was getting the hell out of his car.

"It's from the Book of Hebrews," he said. "I'll give you the *Reader's Digest* version: By the time Hebrews was written, three or four decades after the Crucifixion, the early Christians in Judea had started to doubt the divinity of Christ. The Apostle Paul wrote them a letter, and what he told them was, basically, you're coming at this all wrong. Jesus was a mortal man. He had a mother. He bled like we bleed, died like we die. But he was also God and was therefore perfect and immortal. Now, does that make any sense? No, it makes no sense. But it doesn't *have* to make sense. It's the work of God. We don't need to make sense of it. We don't need to explain it. Our only job is to believe. To have faith."

"But that's what I'm saying. I don't."

"Sure you do. Every time you're in trouble, every time you're about to do something stupid, you come looking for me. Have you ever asked yourself why that is?"

"I'm here because I think you can help me."

"I fucked little girls, Trent," he said. "I'm the last person on earth anyone would ever come to for help. You're not here because of me. You're here because you want what I've got. Because whatever it is, you think it might save you, too."

I thought again of the mornings at chez Starling when I'd knelt at the foot of my bed and prayed. He was right. On those mornings, I had believed. I felt it in my body like a physical thing, the lifting and the lightening, the scooping up and the saving. It lasted only a few seconds, but it was there. It was why I was sitting in Frank's cab now.

"What is it you've done this time?" he asked.

So, I told him. I left Suze out of it, but I told him everything else: Lee and the kiddie party in Ross, my paycheck and how far it was from covering my rent, my mother and the money I still owed on her AmEx card. I even told him about hacking Gianni's pin code and all the ways I'd dreamed up to rip off the Papadakises.

"You were gonna clear out your bank account, go all in on this deal, is that it?" he asked.

"Yeah. I was going to hit the bank as soon as I left here."

"This bank, what time does it close?"

"Two."

Frank owned a watch and I didn't, so he showed me his. It wasn't even noon yet.

"Can I come with you today?" I asked. "Just for a couple hours, that's all. You can tell people I'm a trainee."

"Till two o'clock?"

"Till two," I said. "Then I can take it from there."

We rode around together the rest of the afternoon, Frank and me, making airport runs and cruising Highway 101 up and down the county, picking up fares as they came in from the dispatcher. Between runs, we talked about money, what I could to do earn more of it, where I could cut back on expenses if that wasn't enough. By the time he dropped me back at my car, a little after five, I felt emptied out, cleansed in the way I did after one of my head-smacking episodes, like somebody had turned me upside down and shaken me until the crazy fell out.

At work, I used my employee discount to buy the ingredients for *enchiladas con pollo*, the only real meal I knew how to make. Suze had talked Sharon into taking the boys not just for pizza and a movie but for a full-on sleepover at grandma's, so for once we had her place to ourselves. While the pan was in the oven, we fell into bed, then gorged ourselves on still-steaming enchiladas in front of the tube, the two of us wrapped only in a thin sheet pulled from the bed.

Five days after the attacks, Lower Manhattan was still a smoking ruins and the count of the missing was up to five thousand people. In Arizona, four guys had rolled up on a Sikh man in a turban at a gas station and shot him dead. Another guy in a turban had been shot behind the counter of a corner grocery in Dallas. Seeing all this on the news, I was sure we would invade Afghanistan in a matter of weeks. Suze hoped we wouldn't, that we could solve it through the UN, somehow. I listened to her work it out in her mind, how a neutral third country—France, say, or Switzerland—could send troops to Afghanistan and root out the terrorists without an invasion. I had no idea if this made sense. I didn't really care. This was all so new to me, that I could sit with a woman in front of the TV, naked under a single bedsheet, and just want to talk.

We talked for hours, until some time after midnight, back in the bedroom, her eyes fluttered shut and I realized she had fallen asleep in the middle of a sentence. I lay awake a long time after that, watching her sleep. She hadn't made it to the salon yet, I guess, because the dark roots were starting to show near her scalp, and up close, I could see age lines starting to form under her eyes and at the corners of her lips. Earlier, out in the living room, I had seen an angry red slash I hadn't noticed before across her abdomen, just below her belly button. A Caesarean scar, I guessed, but I wasn't sure. I wanted to see all of it, every scar, every dent and wrinkle and imperfection. I had known her as a little girl, with big blue, startled eyes and a gap in her front teeth, and now I wanted to know her when she was old, when all that was left of her was wrinkles and a few tufts of gray hair.

# 15

The old man squinted, struggling to place me. "You're Jerry Cushman's kid, right?"

"Grandson," I said. "Jerry Cushman was my grand-dad."

But he hadn't heard me. "Good man," he said, nodding to himself. "Ran a damn fine store. Too bad you didn't take it over."

Gianni's grandfather, the one they all called Pappouli, lived in a retirement community in Terra Linda, but he showed up at the store every few weeks to run his hands through the produce bins and gossip with the long-time employees. Every time we had the same conversation: He asked if I was Jerry Cushman's son, I corrected him, and he told me what a fine businessman my granddad was. Pappouli wasn't dotty, exactly, but his mind seemed to work in grooves, and one of those grooves was that I was the son of his old Sunday golfing buddy, Jerry Cushman.

It was a little after six on Monday, and Gianni, Stavros, and I were carrying Pappouli's wheelchair up the back stairs to the break room where the Papadakises were holding a family meeting. When he was running the store, Pappouli had been lanky and tall, his torso stretched out like a human stick of taffy, but now, pushing eighty, his chest caved in, his legs shot through with arthritis, he'd shrunk several inches and weighed about a hundred pounds. Still, it took the three of us several minutes of sweating and cursing to get him up the narrow stairs, stopping to rest on every third step. Finally, we cleared the top step and Gianni wheeled him into the break room where Andi and her husband Brian sat with Henry Sironga on the sack-gray sofa, forking in eggplant moussaka.

"Perfect timing," Mr. Papadakis said, waving us in. "We're just getting started."

"I thought this was a family meeting," Gianni said, surveying the room.

"It's a managers' meeting," his father said. "Come, sit. Have some dinner while it's still hot. Trent, why don't you grab those charts you made for me?"

I ducked back into the business office to pick up the spreadsheets I had copied off at Kinko's that morning. I had hacked into Gianni's flash drive the week before and printed out three years of year-end balance sheets, but now thanks to Mr. Papadakis, I had even more recent sales figures, along with a copy of Gianni's internal projections for the online catering business, which I had never even thought to look for. It wasn't everything Stan wanted, but it was a lot more than he'd ever get on his own.

"What's Melody doing here, then?" Gianni asked, pointing to Stavros's daughter. "And Pappouli. They're not managers."

"I asked Henry to come, okay?" his father said. "Here, he *is* family."

"Maybe Gianni's right," Henry said, setting down his food. "Maybe I should let you guys discuss this among yourselves."

"Henry, sit," Papadakis said. "How about we just get started? Everybody please take a look at the packets Trent's passing around."

For a moment, as I handed around the last of the packets, the room was quiet, the only sound eight people turning pages.

"What is all this?" Andi asked. "I thought we were here to talk about Thanksgiving."

"Well, we are, in a manner of speaking," her father said.

"What's with all the sales charts, then? And Gianni's projections for the new building?"

"Mike, just spit it out," Stavros said. "All the charts in the world aren't going to make this any easier."

"Okay, okay," Papadakis said. "But, look, before we go any further I want to recognize that our country was attacked last week. It happened far away from here, thank God, but people in our community were frightened and they turned to our store in their time of crisis. And everyone stepped up. Everyone. I think we all have good reason to be proud of how we handled ourselves this past week." His expression turned grim. "But we also have to face some facts. We just had one hell of a week, one of the busiest weeks we've had in years, but the store's been in a slump for a while now. We have to make some changes, adjust our priorities. We need to get the new building open before Thanksgiving, and we've decided to put Henry in charge of getting the deli up and running."

Andi shot Gianni a look, but he just nodded back, his tight-lipped smile saying, *See? Told ya.*

"You got a little over-extended, that's all," Stavros told Gianni. "We need you here, running the office, managing the financials."

"Why can't he do both?" Andi said. "He's *been* doing both for the last two years."

"And he'll go right back to doing it as soon as we get the catering operation up to speed," her father said. "But for now we think it's better to let Henry run things day to day. He's done a heck of a job with the deli here. That's why I brought these sales figures. I want you to—"

"I'm not letting you do this," Gianni said.

The room hushed again, all eyes on Gianni—all but mine, which zeroed in on Henry. Gianni, I knew, had hired Henry when he was still driving a delivery truck for his cousin who had sponsored his immigration application and then took all his wages. Now, Henry looked like he was ready to hop the next flight back to Nairobi.

"I own a piece of this business, too," Gianni said. "So do Brian and Andi here, and we have some numbers we'd like to show you." He handed me a blue manila folder he'd stuffed into the back pouch of his grandfather's wheelchair. "Pass this around, will you?"

This stack was thinner than the one his dad had given me, just a dozen sheets of paper stapled together in eight separate packets. At the top of the first page, the title read:

## CONSTRUCTION BUDGET, P.O. BUILDING,
## JUN-SEPT. 2001

"While you two were sitting around drinking ouzo with Pappouli," Gianni said, "I was here running the numbers for the new building. What you don't know is I've been cutting costs all along. Just a month ago, we were looking at overruns of a hundred and twenty thousand, maybe more. As of last week, it's down to a little over sixty grand."

"You cut your overruns in half?" his father said.

"Look for yourself," Gianni said. "Start on page three, line six. Those are the track lighting fixtures we're using in the lobby. Our contractor wanted us to source them from his guy in the city, but then Trent here got to talking with one of the electricians who knew a supplier in the South Bay selling the same fixture for thirty percent less." He turned to me. "Remember that?"

I did remember, actually. One of the electricians wiring the kitchen had pitched for Novato High back in the day, and I'd homered off him twice. I had no idea who the guy was, but he recounted the two at-bats for me pitch by pitch like he'd faced down Barry Bonds.

"This is what happens when you're your own general contractor," Gianni said. "You can cut costs, switch materials, go with cheaper subcontractors. There's literally dozens of those kinds of savings all through the project."

Everyone was flipping pages now, me included. When I made it to the final page, I saw for myself that, as of Friday, September 14, the Post Office renovation was $61,839 over budget.

"We're still sixty grand in the hole," Gianni said, "but the overage is trending down, not up. If we can keep a lid on expenses from here on out, we can bring the project in on time and within the contingency. Which means we might still be able to open as we planned—not just as a deli, but as a full-service catering operation."

"Where are you going to find the cash to run a full kitchen?" his father asked.

"I'll find it," Gianni said.

*"Where?"*

"Christ, son, why don't you let him try?" Pappouli said.

Honestly, I'd forgotten the old man was there. So had everyone else, I think. Gianni and his father swung around to look at him in his wheelchair, his ruined face twisted in outrage.

"Did you hear what he just said?" he said. "He saved sixty thousand dollars, by pinching pennies. By being smart."

Henry chose that moment to bolt for the stairs, his face tucked into his chest.

"Henry—wait, we're not finished here," Papadakis called after him.

"Let him go," Pappouli said. "He's right. This doesn't concern him."

"You stay out of this!" Stavros shouted. "You agreed to this. This was half your idea."

"That was before I saw what the boy was doing with the new building," Pappouli said.

Henry was gone now, his shoes clattering down the stairs, with Melody just a few steps behind, but the older Papadakises were too busy screaming at each other to notice. Brian, Andi's husband, caught my arm and tugged me toward the exit. As I was leaving, I turned to see Pappouli sitting up in his chair, his watery eyes caroming between his grandson and his two angry sons, and I knew Gianni had already won over the only audience that counted.

Melody and Andi were waiting at the bottom of the stairs, and the four of us stood huddled together in the dimly lit storeroom, stunned into silence, listening to the shouts from upstairs.

"Did you guys know about this?" I asked.

"Gianni showed us those numbers last night," Brian said. "The guy's a friggin' genius when it comes to budgets. And thank God. Stavros just wants to sell his share and park his fat ass on a beach in the Bahamas."

Was this true? Was Stavros looking to sell the store and retire?

Was that what this was all about? I barely knew Brian, who was the store's beer and wine buyer, so I searched the eyes of the two women, who stared back shell-shocked but not disagreeing.

"They're going to be up there a while," Andi said to me. "Why don't you and Melody help out in the deli for a bit and then we can all go back upstairs when they're done."

Half an hour later, after I'd helped Gianni carry Pappouli down the stairs for the drive back to Terra Linda, I found Andi and Brian upstairs breaking down the steam table. I pitched in, stacking the folding chairs onto a rolling cart and circling the room collecting discarded spreadsheets. While Andi and Brian ferried the disassembled steam table, piece by piece, down the stairs, I loudly sent one copy after another through the office shredder—all except one, which I stashed in an unmarked folder at the back of the filing cabinet where I'd put the other documents I had stolen for Stan. But I couldn't help myself, and before I stuffed the folder into my pack, I opened the spreadsheet to page three, line six, where Gianni had logged the reduced price for the lighting fixtures. And there it was, in black and white:

| Item | Qty | Est. Cost |
|------|-----|-----------|
| Trck light fixt | 20 | $279/per |

| Final Cost | Est. Total | Total |
|------------|------------|-------|
| $169/per | $5,580 | $3,380 |

The discount was steeper than I remembered, but then Gianni had negotiated the final price. All I'd done was tell him about the supplier in the South Bay. Running a finger down one side of the page, I could see that, on every fourth or fifth item, Gianni had saved a few dollars—three hundred on PVC pipe here, another eight hundred on stainless-steel kitchen hoods there.

At the bottom of the page, my eyes landed on the line item for the flooring in the main lobby. The lobby had been the source of endless battles between Gianni and his architect. The architect had wanted to use stained white oak for the flooring, but in August, with the project deep in the red, Gianni had switched to a cheaper composite. According to Gianni's budget, this one change had slashed the cost of flooring materials nearly in half, from $6,519 to $3,724.

But that wasn't what caught my eye. Just under the line item pricing out the flooring materials was a second row of figures for the flooring installer, Santiago Custom Flooring:

```
                         Item
      Santiago Custom Flooring (floor install - lobby)
```

| Qty | Est. Cost |
|-----|-----------|
| Labor 16 hrs | $55/hr |

| Actual Cost | Est. Total | Total |
|-------------|------------|-------|
| $55/hr | $888 | $888 |

I remembered the Santiagos, the sixty-something Filipino couple Gianni had hired to install the lobby floor. Benny and his wife, Alma. Originally, Gianni had wanted the job done in a single day, but Benny had taken one look at the lobby, spacious enough for a decent game of half-court basketball, and told him it was a two-day job, take it or leave it.

Two people, two days. Thirty-two hours, not sixteen.

I knelt down and fingerwalked through the bottom drawer of the filing cabinet until I found the folder I was looking for: Invoices P.O. Building, Aug '01 (labor). Two weeks ago, I'd signed off on the invoice for thirty-two man-hours of work by Santiago Custom Flooring, but I searched the file front to back, then again back to front, and I couldn't find it. I'd filed the pink customer copy myself, but now it was gone—maybe stashed at the back of a filing cabinet at home, or just as likely, put through the shredder.

I checked Gianni's budget again, panic fizzing through my brain. I knew what I was looking at. I had pulled scams like this at Campus Liquors, paying suppliers one amount, claiming a different amount on the books, and pocketing the difference.

Of course, Gianni wasn't bilking his family to party with hookers at the Beverly Wilshire. Still, it added up to the same thing: he was cooking the books.

I ticked through the file drawer again until I found a second folder, this one labeled Invoices P.O. Building, Aug '01 (mtrls). Midway through the folder I found an invoice for 1,900 board feet of white-oak-veneer composite wood Apparently, Gianni hadn't had time to deep-six that one yet. On the invoice, the price was $4,724—a thousand dollars more than he'd claimed in his budget.

Like a bomb exploding in reverse, a million jangling details fell into place, forming a whole where before there had only been questions I'd never thought to ask: Why was it that a grocery store that posted millions of dollars in annual sales had just one person, the twenty-eight-year-old son of its owner, handling all its finances, including its taxes? Why was it that this same person also oversaw the company's big, new expansion project? Why was it that, before I broke into his flash drive, no one besides Gianni, not even his dad, had access to the store's financial records? And how was it exactly that a store that had lost twenty percent of its annual sales in the last four years wasn't also laying off twenty percent of its employees?

Slowly, calmly, I slipped the invoices into their folders and set the folders back in the filing cabinet, taking care to leave them exactly as I'd found them. Downstairs, I punched out and cut through the empty stock room to my car in the employee lot, still running numbers in my head. Gianni's construction budget wasn't a *total* fiction. I'd helped him get the discount on the lighting fixtures myself. That was real. So was the money he'd saved by using composite wood instead of white oak. But I'd watched him blow thousands more, through delays and indecision and mulish perfectionism. Which meant the numbers for the Post Office renovations weren't the only ones he was fudging.

An unbreakable rule of embezzlement, one I'd figured out early at Campus Liquors, is that you can't short your vendors.

If you start chiseling even small amounts off their bills, they'll call your boss, who will then ask to see the books. So you have to pay your vendors what they're owed, the real figures on their invoices, not the fake ones in your budget. For me, at Campus Liquors, this had never been a problem since I was paying our vendors less than I said I was. But for Gianni it was a huge problem. He was paying his vendors thousands more than he was claiming in his budget, and that money had to come from somewhere.

Which could only mean the store's general operations budget had a sixty-thousand-dollar hole in it. But, in fact, the hole was probably a whole lot bigger than that. Gianni hadn't been honest month after month, year after year, and then one day decided to steal sixty grand to finance a white-elephant building project. That wasn't how this kind of theft worked. At first you stole impulsively, in small amounts. You told yourself it was really a loan. You told yourself you'd put it all back. You promised yourself you'd never, ever do it again. Then a few weeks later you took a little more. Then you took a little more, and then a little more, and a little more, until one morning you sat down with the books and realized you'd stolen so much you couldn't afford to stop stealing.

That was where Gianni was now. If he had to give the new building back to the bank, or if the Papadakises sold out to Cornucopia, someone—a corporate accountant, an IRS inspector, maybe Mr. Papadakis himself—would look at his books and figure out what he'd done. That was what had been on his mind the day he skipped work and spent the day bombing up and down the back roads to Healdsburg. That was the reality staring him in the face all those afternoons he'd stood at the office window like Han Solo frozen in carbonite. That was why he'd broken his own rule and showed me the files on his private flash drive.

He needed Stan's money, and he needed it *now, now, now.*

I was sitting in my car, the key in the ignition, engine off, gazing out at the little redwood grove behind the employee lot when Mr. Papadakis's Celica pulled into the empty spot next to mine, Gianni behind the wheel. He hopped out, motioning for me to roll down my window.

"Thanks for staying late today, buddy," he said. "You were a big help."

"Hey, no problem," I said. "Happy to do it."

"We've got some long days coming up," he said. "We're way behind in hiring and we have to get that building open by Thanksgiving. We can do it, though. I know we can."

I told him I thought so, too, absolutely, you bet, and watched him bound on in through the service entrance, his feet barely touching asphalt.

# 16

S tan showed up at the Park View Apartments the next night, a Tuesday. I had asked him to come by late, around ten, and I used the hours before he arrived to read over the documents I'd copied off the day before. Gianni was a better thief than I expected. He hadn't panicked the way I had in Santa Barbara. Whatever cash he'd sucked out of the store's budget, he'd done it slowly and carefully, spreading it out across a number of departments. Without the original invoices, there was no way to know which shortfalls were real and which were fake. I had signed off on a lot of those invoices myself, and I couldn't tell which was which.

"Nice," Stan said, taking in my tiny, bare-walled apartment. "Throw in some toilet paper and a hole in the ground and you'd have a first-class outhouse."

"I like it," I said. "It's mine."

That was it for the pleasantries. No mention of my mother or the attacks in New York or her panicked phone calls of the week before. But then Stan and I didn't have to be pleasant with each other. This was a drug deal, just with paper changing hands instead of substances.

"You have documents for me?" he said.

I handed him the folder on the table. "One thing," I said. "Whatever you do, you can't ever tell him you've seen these files."

"Don't worry, pal," he said, flipping through the spread-sheets. "I'm probably violating twenty statutes just by looking at these things."

I nodded, filing that little fact away. "You think you're really going to do this?"

"Hard to say," he said, already eyeing the door. "Your buddy

Gianni called me the other day, wanting to know if I'd reconsidered."

"What'd you say?"

He smiled, back in salesman mode. "I told him I was waiting for some internal numbers to come in, see where I stood."

I waited until I was sure he was gone, then threw a change of clothes and my shaving things into my backpack and drove to Shelter Ridge. I had done this the last two nights, too, showing up after Suze put the boys to bed and leaving before they woke up. I never asked if I could come, and she never invited me, but when I arrived the sliding-glass door was unlocked, Suze on the sofa in sweats and a T-shirt watching the news.

She had cleared the house of every last drop of alcohol, even the half-rancid cooking wine next to the stove, so I poured myself a soda from the fridge and settled in beside her to catch the latest from Ground Zero. When the newscast signed off at eleven-thirty, we watched a few minutes of Leno, so refreshingly boring after two weeks of atrocity porn, and then Suze started switching off lights around the house. I set the dishes in the sink and checked the doors, front and back, to make sure they were locked, the way my dad used to do. Then she took my hand and we headed for the bedroom as if we'd been doing it all our lives.

Stavros and Mike Papadakis still weren't talking to each other, and neither of them were talking to Gianni, who spent his days upstairs at the Post Office building interviewing kitchen staff. I let all of it sail right over my head. I had done what I could do, and instead of worrying about it, I controlled the things I could control. I hit my meetings. I ran three mornings a week. I called Frank T. every day. And in the afternoons when things got slow, I holed up in the deli walk-in, touched my knee to one of the shelving units, and whispered my little prayer: *Don't quit before the miracle. Don't quit before the miracle. Don't quit. Don't quit. Don't quit.*

That's where I was that Thursday afternoon when Henry called me from the kitchen.

"You need to tell your friends they can't keep showing up here like this," he said. "I'm not your private answering service."

My pulse skipped a beat, the way it had that first day I saw Suze at Howie's Hamburgers.

"Sorry," I said. "Next time I'll tell her to come by after work."

"Not *her*," he said. "Her, I don't mind. This guy looks like he just stuck up a liquor store."

Through the window in the kitchen door, I saw Lee Radko in the beer aisle in black Ben Davis jeans and a muscle tee, his prison tats forming angry technicolor sleeves up both arms.

"Who is he, anyway?" Henry asked.

"His name's Lee," I said. "I've known him forever. We went to school together."

"Well, you need to get rid of him. He's scaring off our other customers."

Coming down the beer aisle, I caught a whiff of that old sweat-and-pot-smoke Lee smell, but when he turned, his pupils were as big as dinner plates. He cracked a sloppy stoner's grin, but the eyes don't lie: he was dipping into the product.

"Friendly guy you work for there," he said.

I shrugged. "Henry's cool. A little uptight, is all."

"I know how it is," he said. "Spook, spic, it's all the same. You gotta let 'em feel like they're in control, right?"

"What do you need, Lee?"

"You were too busy to party with us Saturday night," he said, grabbing a six-pack of Heineken from the cooler. "I figured I should drop by, see what's eating up all your time."

"Sorry, man, I should've called. But I'm done. No more kiddie parties for me."

"I thought you needed the coin. Rent and all that."

Behind us at the deli counter, Henry was ringing up a sale, doing a miserable job of pretending he wasn't watching our every move. "Let me call you, okay?" I said.

"Right," Lee said, looking over his shoulder. "Can't have Kunta Kinte over there listening in. He know about your big drug bust down in S.B?"

This time I didn't have to check whether Henry had heard. As loud as Lee was talking, the whole store had.

"You need to go, now," I said.

"I'm not gonna narc you out to your boss, Wolfer," he said, low again. "I need you. And you need me. This weekend, it's Homecoming. At Tam *and* Redwood. You know what that means, right? Parties from here to San Rafael, dozens of them."

Finally, I understood why he was here. My high school had never been a sports powerhouse, but we knew how to party. Same with Redwood High, where the kids were, if anything, even more rich and spoiled than we were. If Lee was going to feed all those hungry teenage noses, he needed a partner.

"Even if I was up for that, which I'm not, I don't have the cash," I told him.

"So find it," he said. "A night like this, you can double your money. More than that, if you're willing to work for it."

"Good luck, Rad."

He grabbed my arm. "This could be your last shot, man. If I hit it big, I'm out of here."

"Hope you like Canada, then," I said, shaking him off.

"Fuck you, Wolfer," he called after me.

"Back at ya, Radko," I said, walking away.

But an hour later, upstairs in the business office, what he'd said was still working on me like a pebble in the shoe of my mind. I didn't have the money, that much was true. But I could get it. It wouldn't even be stealing, really, like the fake vendor scam. This would be borrowing. Every weekday, Gianni counted up the previous day's receipts and put them in a bank pouch, which he kept in the stockroom safe until it was time to make the daily bank run. But on weekends, when the bank was closed, the register pouches were counted and logged, then pushed through a slot at the top of the safe to wait for Gianni to process them Monday morning. If he was skimming directly from the daily receipts, as I was starting to think he was, it had to be those Monday morning receipts he was faking.

But two could play that game. On a busy Friday, the deli

took in three or four thousand in cash. All I had to do was offer to close out the deli on Friday night. Then I could count out the till, log the correct figure on the tally sheet, and walk out with the pouch in my backpack. As long as I got the pouch back into the safe before Gianni came in on Monday morning, I had two days to do anything I wanted with the money. And if something went wrong, if I somebody noticed the pouch was missing or if I mixed up the count, I could always play my hole card: I knew Gianni was cooking the books, and I could prove it.

But it would never come to that. It would work. I just needed to call Lee, tell him I was sorry for harshing on him, and I could turn three grand into six overnight. With a score like that, I could pay my rent for a year and never have to pull an overtime shift. I could buy real furniture. And clothes. And a stereo. Maybe even a laptop so I could download music again.

I picked up the phone and punched in ten digits from memory. The line buzzed twice before it clicked in my ear.

"Not a great time, kid," Frank said. "I've got a fare."

I heard the hum of the cab's engine, the soft burble of his passenger giving directions from the back seat. I started to put the phone down, then stopped. Started again, and stopped.

"Trent, you there?" he said.

This wasn't about the money, I knew that. It had nothing to do with paying my rent or filling a laptop with free music. It was about what I'd seen in Lee's eyes, those two big black dinner plates. He was sitting on a nice, fat bag of uncut cocaine, and I could get a piece of it, for free.

"I'm thinking about using," I said.

A long, scratchy silence. Had he hung up? Was he still there?

"My buddy just came in, wanting me to go in on a deal with him," I said. "He was wired, Frank. I could see it in his eyes. It made me want to get high, too. Like, right now."

"Where are you?" he asked.

"At work," I said. "But, hey, I'm not going to *do* it. I mean, I called you, right?"

"I can be there in twenty minutes. Meet me outside, in front of the store."

I started to tell him he didn't need to do that, I could take care of myself, that we could talk after the meeting that night, but he'd already hung up.

I was still wearing my blue work apron and my nametag when Frank pulled up in front of the store in his yellow Crown Vic twenty minutes later.

"I'm sorry you came all this way," I said. "But I'm fine. Really. It was a false alarm."

"Shut up and get in the car," he said, throwing open the passenger-side door.

"Frank, I'm still on the clock. I haven't punched out yet."

"Get in the damn car," he said. "We're gonna be late."

I saw Lee again, the twitchy way he'd looked at Henry, and I got in the car. Frank pulled away from the curb and sped through Lytton Square toward Miller Avenue.

"Where are we going?" I asked.

"We're hitting my old meeting in San Rafael." His lazy eye found me across the front seat. "Should be interesting. You're the featured speaker."

The meeting was at a halfway house in a neighborhood of warehouses and seedy apartment buildings less than a mile from the prison. The meeting was huge, close to a hundred guys, most of whom wanted nothing to do with us. They played cards or shouted into contraband phones, anything to drown out the hand-holding and the God-talk. But the thirty men in the tight circle of chairs at the front of the room were hungry for sobriety in a way you don't see at your average AA meeting. You could smell the prison on them. These were the snitches, the punks, the guys three rungs down the chain who ended up doing the time for the boss. Prison does terrible things to men like that. One look and you knew they'd do just about anything not to go back.

Frank was a regular there, and I watched him work the room, remembering names, laughing at unfunny jokes, doling out hugs and words of encouragement. I saw the priest in him then. I also saw how he'd gotten away with it for so long. This was a room full of men who had been abused as children, many of them by priests. They should have hated his guts, and maybe some of them did, but with a handshake, a sympathetic nod, a word in a man's ear, he bent that anger, turned it into its opposite: admiration, respect, love. Around the edges of the room, where his powers didn't reach, guys went on dealing cards and shouting into cell phones, but the circle of chairs hushed when we sat down, thirty pairs of eyes turning to me, waiting to hear what Frank's newest sponsee had to say.

He spoke first, introducing me, and then I spoke for most of the rest of the hour. Qualifying, it's called. I had done this in rehab, but that had been for show, to make the counselors and shrinks see that I was getting it, that I was ready to go home. Here, in front of these men, who were basically me without Stan's lawyers, I just told my story, starting with my arrest in Santa Barbara, right through to that afternoon, seeing those big black holes in Lee Radko's eyes. When I talked about sitting at Gianni's desk dreaming up ways to steal the deli receipts, thirty heads nodded in recognition, and a little of the sting of it leached out of me. After I finished, a guy told a story about stealing his own daughter's car to pay off a drug debt, and I watched some of the sting of it leach out of him, too. One by one, the stories poured out, kids abandoned, jobs lost, beatings taken, each a secret held too long, and now, here, in this cheerless day room a fifteen-minute walk from the state penitentiary, spoken aloud for all to hear.

Frank and I stuck around for an hour after the meeting ended, shaking hands and giving out phone numbers to guys whose release dates were coming up. Then he took me for a late dinner at Denny's and dropped me back at the store, where my car was still parked in the employee lot. I was still buzzing, high from all that truth-telling, when I made it to Suze's place, where she was sacked out in front of the tube, snoring. I carried her to the bedroom and tucked her in under the sheets. I woke up hours later to the sound of someone crying. I wasn't sure what it was at first. It sounded like an animal, a dog or a cat, maybe, trapped behind a locked door. By the time I dragged myself out of bed to see what it was, the house was quiet again, nothing but the distant freeway hum, but in the bathroom doorway, I saw the top of a child's blond head: little Jake, fast asleep on the floor, his thumb lodged in his mouth like a key in a lock.

I looked around at the dark house. Twenty steps and I would be back in the bedroom with Suze. And then what? Was I really going to wake her up out of a sound sleep because I was too much of a wuss to carry a four-year-old back to bed?

I lifted him up, hugging him to my chest as I eased his PJs up to his waist. I had never held a sleeping child before, and I was unprepared for the soft, warm heft of him, the instinctive way his arms locked around my neck. "Shh, shh," I whispered, bouncing him in my arms. "Back to bed now." I caught my reflection in the mirror, a grown man in a T-shirt and boxers holding a sleeping child to his chest. Then I was out in the hall, heading for the boys' room.

Coming back from tucking Jake into bed, his little-boy smell—feet, pee, baby powder—still in my nostrils, I couldn't get that image in the mirror out of my head. The bouncing thing, where had that come from? My mother had never liked small children, and no one else I knew had kids. Had I seen it on TV, in a commercial somewhere? But it felt so natural. So obvious. I had this sleeping child in my arms, and the way to keep him from waking was to bounce him in my arms. It worked, too. Jake had wriggled some as I was tucking him in, but then he'd made a contented little sigh and turtled under the covers, dead to the world.

I popped the lock on the sliding-glass door and stepped out onto the lawn, hugging myself against the pre-dawn chill. Was this it, the miracle I had been waiting for? This little patch of grass, this darkened street, Suze warm in her bed, her boys softly snoring in the next room. Was this the answer to the prayer I'd been making all week in the deli walk-in? If I could just get through the next few months, if I could stay clean and pay my rent, if Suze finalized her divorce and started selling houses again, maybe it wouldn't seem so crazy for us to talk about moving in together. I couldn't say any of this out loud. I couldn't even let myself think it in Suze's presence. But out on the cold, dark lawn, I let myself picture it, coming here after work, a bag of groceries under my arm, cooking up a pan of enchiladas while Suze watched TV with the boys.

I'm not sure how long I stood out there, seeing myself in the bathroom mirror bouncing that little boy, before I noticed the car parked, its interior light on, high on the rise where Thoreau Circle meets Emerson Drive. It was an eighties-model Ford or Chevy, low to the ground, with primer paint on the hood and the driver's side door. Not a car you see a lot of in Mill Valley, yet there it was at the top of Thoreau Circle, its driver silhouetted against the morning sky.

I'd heard somewhere that repo men sometimes worked in pairs, one scouting, the other in the truck waiting to be called in. But Suze had paid off her debt on the Volvo weeks ago. Anyway, what kind of repo man drove a beater Ford covered in primer paint? I knew just enough about repo men to know they were the most car-obsessed people on the planet. This guy was just lost, idling at the intersection while he checked his map. Still, I waited, my bare feet freezing in the dew-soaked grass, until the interior light cut out and the car pulled away down the hill.

In the bedroom, Suze was awake—half-awake, anyway—her puffy eyes tracking me from the bed. "Everything okay?" she asked.

"Yeah," I said, rifling the pockets of my jeans for my keys. "Go back to sleep."

"You were gone a long time."

I had come back in with the half-assed idea of pulling my car in behind hers so it couldn't be towed. But to explain this would be to explain that I had just stood on her lawn in my underwear imagining that a random car I'd seen half a block away belonged to a repo scout come to take her car. Which, in all likelihood, would mean neither of us would get any sleep before the alarm went off in an hour.

"It was just Jake," I said, crawling back into bed. "He was in the bathroom."

"Jakey?" she said, raising her head. "Is he okay?"

"Yeah, yeah, he's fine," I said. "He got up to pee and I guess he fell asleep while he was on the toilet. I took him back to bed."

She giggled. "He fell asleep on the pot?"

"I guess, yeah," I said. "He was on the floor when I got there. Like, in a pile. I don't think he hurt himself. He was totally cashed out."

I slid my hand over her hip and felt her ease into my touch, the way a cat will do sometimes when you stroke its back.

"Dylan used to do that," she said.

"Sleep on the bathroom floor?"

"No, walk in his sleep. Once, I found him in the kitchen at like four in the morning fixing a PB&J." She pulled her feet away. "Hey, your feet are cold."

"Sorry," I said. "I went out for a minute."

"You went out? Just now?"

Her face was so close it took up all my vision, her eyes two glowing moons. I thought about the beater Ford I'd seen idling at the top of her street. Even if it was nothing, I needed to tell her. I needed to ask the simple question: *You paid off your car loan, right?* But what can I tell you? Her smell was all around me, honey-vanilla soap mixed with sleep and sweat and girl-skin.

"You left your sprinkler on," I said. "I had to turn it off."

"You turned off my lawn sprinkler?"

"It was on all night. It was wasting water."

Her hand began a slow southward run toward my boxers. "You didn't, like, take out the trash while you were at it?"

"Next time I'll take out the trash," I said. "Definitely. Maybe do a load of laundry, too."

"Now you're talking," she said. "If I ever start a porn site for moms, it'll be one clip after another of naked guys folding laundry and changing poopy diapers."

She had her hand on my cock now, her fingers wrapped

around the shaft. We kissed, open mouthed, as I eased my thigh between her knees, pressing until I reached her pubic bone. She shivered, once, then opened like a flower, a cloud of musk rising from her middle.

"Tell me there's still a condom in that box," she said.

"It's cool. I can pull out."

"You can what?"

"Pull out. Before I finish."

"Shit," she said, rolling off me. "I thought we still had a few left."

"We did," I said. "We've sort of, um, been going through them."

This sent us off on a run of soft giggles. The night of the terror attacks, the twelve-count box of condoms in her bedside table had been full. Ten days later, it was empty.

"Okay, the good news is I have an emergency stash," she said.

"Where?"

"That's the bad news. They're in my purse, in the kitchen."

We lay still a moment, our arms and legs intertwined, breathless with need.

"What're you waiting for?" I said. "I'm fucking dying here."

She laughed again, throwing back the covers. "Don't move. I'll be right back."

I shimmied out of my T-shirt and boxers and lay naked under the sheets, listening. I heard the patter of Suze's bare feet in the next room, doors opening and closing. No truck engines. No tire screeches. The whole thing was ridiculous. The guy was lost, looking at a map. Still, I was just about to leap out of bed and run for the window when I heard Suze at the bedroom door.

"Found it!" she said, holding up a gold-wrapped condom. "Thank God for gay receptionists. They hand these suckers out like candy."

The night before, she'd tied her hair back in a French braid, and now with a few quick, practiced motions, she loosened the plaits and shook out her shoulder-length hair.

"So, maybe this isn't the greatest time to bring this up," she said, "but I've—I'm thinking about going back on the pill."

I sat up, propping a pillow under my head. The expression on her face was blank, unreadable.

"Not because of you," she said. "Or okay, not *just* because of you. I went back on after I had Jake, but I stopped when I moved up here, and now my body's going a little wonky without it. My doc says if I'm starting to have sex again maybe it's simpler to just go back on."

"You talked to your doctor? About us?"

"She's my gynecologist. I saw her last week and she asked." She shrugged. "If you're a girl, you talk about this stuff with your doctor."

"And she told you to go back on the pill?"

"She said I should think about it. I *am* thinking about it. I was thinking about it just now when I went to get this." She held up the condom, embarrassed. "Sorry. Talk about buzzkill."

"Come here," I said, lifting the sheets. She set the condom on the bedside table and slipped in under the covers, her head resting on my shoulder. I pulled her close, the two of us clinging to each other like the bed was a river and we were about to be washed away in its current.

"What are we doing here, Trent?" she asked.

My first impulse was to crack wise, joke us back to the gold-wrapped condom on the bedside table. But I remembered the meeting the night before, how good it had felt not to lie.

"I think I'm falling for you," I said. "That's what I'm doing. How about you?"

She looked up, flashing a reluctant smile. "Maybe, a little."

"A little?"

"Don't, okay? This is hard enough as it is."

"What's so hard? I'm feeling pretty fucking great. I'm like the king of the world here."

"Well, you're not broke, with two little kids, hooking up every night with a drug dealer fresh out of the slammer."

"I'm not a dealer, Suze," I said.

"Okay, an *ex*-drug dealer."

"No, I mean, I wasn't dealing down there," I said. "Or, I was, in small amounts, but that's not what I got busted for."

"What did you get busted for then?"

I should have shut it down right there, gone back to how we were falling for each other and how crazy that was. But I *wanted* to tell her. I wanted to put it out there the way I had at the meeting the night before, no more secrets, no more bullshit and lies.

"I took some money," I said. "A lot of money. About fifty grand, all told."

She stared, her eyes bright with alarm. "Fifty thousand *dollars?*"

"You know, maybe we should get dressed," I said. "I want to have this conversation. We need to have this conversation, but not like this."

"Were you spending it on drugs, is that it?"

"No, Suze. I was *making* money selling drugs."

"Then, what? What the hell'd you do with fifty grand?"

I closed my eyes, letting out a long, slow breath. Part of me had always known it would come to this, not what I had taken, or how, but what I'd spent it on.

"The truth?" I said. "Most of it I spent on escorts."

The night before I'd talked about getting locked up, about ripping off Al Fierro, even about my four nights with crack-head Nadine, but I hadn't said a word about the escorts, not to Frank, not to the guys at the halfway house, not to anyone. Now I saw why. Suze edged back on the bed like whatever was wrong with me might be contagious.

"I was drinking then, okay?" I said. "Getting high every day. I was dying down there."

"But fifty grand on freaking hookers?"

"I didn't spend all of it on that," I said. "Some of it I smoked, or it went up my nose. Look, this is a really long, complicated conversation. We need to—"

"I don't get it," she said. "You're a good-looking guy. "

"What's that got to do with it?"

"You paid these women, right?"

"Sure, I paid them. That's how it works, but it's not like I started seeing escorts because there were no other girls in Santa Barbara."

"Then, why? Explain it to me. It doesn't make sense."

This had been a mystery to me, too. Pretty girls came by the store every day, sorority pledges on rush dares, high school girls waving IDs altered with pocket knives, flirting with me across the counter, asking my name, bending over the candy display so I could see up their skirts. I was fat, pale, and depressed, but it wasn't that I lacked opportunity.

"Because they didn't talk back," I said. "Okay? That's why."

"They didn't *talk*?"

"No, they talked. If I paid them enough, they talked to me like we'd been dating for years. But they weren't real to me, you know? And I wasn't real to them."

"And you liked that?"

"Not really, no. But it seemed appropriate, somehow."

I had told too much truth. Or maybe it was the wrong kind of truth, the kind you can't take back. Suze was up now, pacing at the foot of the bed, wrapped in the bedsheet.

"Oh shit, I'm sorry," I said. "I never should've brought this up."

"No, I'm glad you did," she said. "I mean, I look at you and I see this sweet guy I grew up with who's caring and loving and great with my kids, and then you tell me about this *other* guy, who stole tens of thousands of dollars to blow on hookers and God only knows what. And, I don't know, I've got two kids here."

She said more, a lot more, but I didn't hear it because there was a squeal of brakes outside the window. A truck engine idled a moment, then roared to life, reversing up the driveway.

"Did you hear that?" I asked, jumping out of bed.

"What?" she said. "Hey, I'm *talking* to you here!"

I ignored her, pushing aside the curtains to look out at the driveway where a green-and-gold tow truck was backing in behind Suze's Volvo.

"Come here," I shouted. "They're taking your car."

"My car?"

"Yeah, the repo guys, I think they're here."

She was out the door first, tugging on a terrycloth robe as she ran. By the time I made it to the front steps, still hitching up my jeans, the black-clad driver was hunched over the back of his rig rolling the wheel-lift under the Volvo's rear bumper.

"You can't take that car!" she screamed. "We had a deal. I have until October 15."

"You're talking to the wrong guy," the driver said. "Call your lender."

"I *did* call them," she said. "I'm a realtor, I'm waiting for a deal to close. I told them I could pay it off next month. I talked to three different guys. They promised this wouldn't happen."

"Ma'am, all you're doing right now is waking up your neighbors," the driver said. "Take my advice. Go inside, get dressed, have some coffee, and call your lender. Your car will be waiting for you at Marin Salvage and Tow in San Rafael."

With a violent wrench, he yanked the lever that activated the truck's hydraulic lift, and in seconds the car's rear tires were two feet in the air, ready to be rolled away.

"You're making a big mistake, buddy," I said, stepping into the driver's path. "She talked to her lender. She had a deal."

"Trent, please, stay out of this," Suze said.

"Hey, I'm talking to you!" I shouted, ignoring her. "Put that car down, now."

The driver stopped, drawing himself to his full height. I hadn't realized just how big he was, a walking refrigerator in black coveralls and a filthy white T-shirt.

"I'm only going to say this once," he said. "I get hired because I don't get physical and I don't cause headaches. But if you put a hand on me or my vehicle, I *will* get physical, and that won't end well for you, okay?"

I stepped back, my hands in the air where he could see them.

"Thank you," he said, brushing past. "You two look like decent, bill-paying folks. If there's been a mistake, I'm sure you can work something out that'll make everybody happy."

He slammed the driver's side door, mashed the truck into gear, and eased down the steep driveway. Suze and I didn't say a word, didn't look at each other, just stood at the bottom of the stairs watching twenty-five thousand dollars of glass and steel roll past us onto the street. After checking his side mirrors, the driver hit the gas and chugged slowly up the rise and out of sight.

Up and down the street, lights were coming on in kitchens and bedrooms, and in a few of the houses, human-shaped shadows stood pressed close to the windows. The driver was right. This would be the talk of the neighborhood for weeks.

"We'll call them," I said. "Whoever you talked to at the collection agency. It's a mix-up, that's all. Some kind of clerical error."

"No, it's too late," she said, her voice raw from shouting. "I owe four thousand dollars on that thing and I don't have it."

"You'll have it next month, right?" I said.

"What am I supposed to do till then, run my clients around to showings on the fucking bus?"

"Mom?"

We both swung around to see Dylan at the top of the stairs in his Spider-Man pajamas, Jake's chubby pink face peeking out from behind him.

"Baby, you need to go back inside," Suze said.

"What happened to the car?" he asked.

"Inside, D.," she said. "I mean it. No more talking."

The boy looked at the bare patch of driveway where the Volvo had been, then turned and led his baby brother back inside.

"Suze, let me help you," I said. "I can get some money from my mom. It'd be a loan, but you could pay off your lender. You could get your car back."

"I'm giving you exactly one minute to get off my property," she said.

The thing that scared me was how calm she sounded. There was no arguing with that calm.

"No, I'm going to help you, okay? I don't care what you say. I'm going to get that car back."

"If you're not gone in one minute, I'm calling the cops," she said. "Do you hear me? Go. I don't want to see you here again, ever."

I have no memory of the drive from Shelter Ridge to Blithedale Canyon. One minute I was gunning my Honda away from Suze's empty driveway and the next I was crashing through the door at my mother's house, blowing past a yelping Lupita in the kitchen. My only thought was finding my mother, who was downstairs in her yoga studio, midway through a morning sun salutation with her instructor, a bald, underfed guy in his twenties. When I burst in, they jumped apart, like I'd walked in on them having sex.

"I'm sorry," I said, gasping for air. "I know this isn't a great time, but I need to talk to you. It's important."

"Derek, could you excuse us a minute?" she said, reaching for a hand towel.

Derek coolly ran his eyes over me. "I can wait outside," he said.

"That's all right, we're almost done," Mom said. "How about we pick it up on Monday?"

"Monday, then." He bowed, formally, his hands pressed together at his chest. "*Namaste.*"

"*Namaste,*" my mother said, dismissing him.

"Ma, I need money," I said as soon as he was gone. "For Suze. They just took her car. She'll pay you back when her deal closes, but she doesn't have a car and she can't work."

"Whoa, whoa, slow down," she said. "You're not making any sense. Who took her car?"

"A repo guy," I said. "She owes four thousand on the car, but she just sold a house. As soon as the deal closes, she can pay off the note, but for now she's broke. She had a deal with the collection agency, but I don't know, there was some kind of mix-up and they came for it, anyway."

"Wait, you were there?" she said. "You saw all this?"

This, I realized, was the only thing she'd heard. I watched the rest of the story blossom in her mind, my bed head and wrinkled clothes filling in all the parts I had left out.

"Four thousand dollars," she said. "That's a lot of money. Especially for a girl you've only known a few weeks."

"Ma, I've known Suze all my life. We grew up together."

"Right. And as I recall, she kept breaking your heart with this Joey character."

"Jimmy," I said. "I'm not asking for her. I'm asking for me. I already owe you more money than I can ever repay, but I'm back on my feet now. This is the last thing I'll ever ask you for."

"And that's why I'm saying no, honey," she said. "This isn't good for you. *She* isn't good for you. The last thing you need right now is a single mom with two kids and a life she can't afford. I've been there. I've lived that life. You don't want any part of it, believe me."

"But I *do* want to be part of it," I said. "That's exactly what I want. Being with her, it's the only thing I've ever wanted."

She flinched like I'd thrown something at her. It surprised her almost as much as it did me, and she covered it by mopping sweat from her forehead with the hand towel.

"Do you have *any* idea how worried I was when you left here two weeks ago?" she said. "Do you have even the slightest fucking clue? I was down at that stupid grocery store every day, and when I saw you there, talking, laughing with the people you work with—I don't know, it was like I could breathe again. Do you hear what I'm saying?"

Her voice cracked, and she covered her face, furious at herself for crying, for losing it.

"Sandy, honey," Stan said from the doorway.

"You can shit all over me all you want to," she said, ignoring him. "You can shit all over my marriage and my friends and how I choose to live my life. All I care about is getting you through this alive. In one piece. So, if you need money, if you need to go back to rehab, if you need anything at all, call me. But stay away from that girl, you hear me? She'll drag you down, and then one day you won't be able to get back up."

"Sandy, baby, let's go upstairs," Stan said, reaching out for her.

"Get out of my way, Stan," she said, blowing past him.

Stan and I both knew what was coming, and when it came, when we heard that first howl of pain, like she was being ripped apart by wild animals, neither of us could do anything but stare at our feet. I still hated the guy, and he still hated me, but in that moment, hearing my mother sobbing in the next room, we were united.

I did no real work that day. Gianni was at the Post Office building interviewing delivery drivers, and I sat at his desk, a folder of unfiled invoices in my hands. I knew what I was supposed to do. I was supposed to call Frank T. and take an early lunch to hit the noon meeting. But I didn't call Frank. I didn't hit the noon meeting. I just stared at that folder full of invoices, trying to pretend I didn't know exactly where I could get my hands on the four thousand dollars it would take to spring Suze's Volvo from the impound lot at Marin Salvage and Tow.

A little after one, I picked up the phone and punched in ten numbers from memory.

"Wolfer Associates," a young woman answered, her voice breathy and British. "This is Mr. Wolfer's office."

"You're new," I said.

"Beg pardon?"

"I'm Pierce Wolfer's son, Trent," I said. "I don't think we've spoken before."

She laughed, a run of soft, glittery peels. "No, I don't believe we have. I'm Vanessa. Were you hoping to speak with your father?"

"I am indeed, Vanessa. If he's around."

This was straight out of the Pierce Wolfer playbook: always

flirt with the secretaries. My dad would have spent another minute with her, making a game of guessing where she was from by her accent, and if that went well, asking why she left England and what she thought of L.A. My father could do that, pick up women over the phone. The memory of this, how he used to wink at me while he was chatting up David Geffen's personal assistant, made me feel small, the way I always did when I thought of my dad.

"Hey, hey, how's it hanging, champ?" he said, his voice booming down the phone line.

"Hey, Dad," I said. "Thanks for taking my call like this. I know how busy you are."

"Well, it's not every day my kid calls me out of the blue. I don't hear a little voice telling me this call is coming from a correctional facility. That's gotta be a good sign, right?"

"Right, yeah," I said. "Look, I'm sorry, I should've called you months ago. It's just, after what happened, I wasn't sure you wanted to hear from me."

"You want money, don't you?"

This time it was unmistakable: I heard dislike in his voice. Not just disappointment or boredom or disgust. Actual dislike. The man didn't like me. I wondered, suddenly, if he ever had.

"It's not for me," I said. "I met a girl here and she's—"

"Christ. How long's it been? Four years? Five? The one time I hear from you in all that time, you call my wife from fucking jail. And now what? You knocked this girl up, is that it? You want money for an abortion?"

"Dad, no. Come on. Nothing like that."

"No, wait, I know. *She's* in jail this time and you want me to bond her out."

I sat stunned, tears stinging my eyes. His voice was still in my ear, grinding at me, spinning out all the ways I was going to waste his money, but I was no longer listening. I owed this man nothing, and he owed me nothing in return. He'd stopped being my father twenty years ago.

He was still talking when I hung up.

# 17

Lee was waiting for me by the dumpsters behind Hélène's in an old army-surplus jacket and aviator shades. When I pulled up, he looked both ways to see if I'd been followed, then dropped heavily into the passenger seat.

"You're late," he said.

"You said noon," I said. "It's like three minutes after."

"Whatever, let's roll," he said, looking over his shoulder again. "These dudes, you definitely do not want to keep them waiting."

"Where are we meeting them, anyway?" I asked.

He didn't answer, just barked directions: right on Miller Avenue, then left onto Camino Alto, toward the freeway. I wanted to bark back at him, tell him to chill the fuck out, until he pulled off the shades and I saw his eyes, like two black billiard balls about to roll out of his head.

"You bring the cash?" he said.

I nodded to the glove compartment. He popped the latch and dug through stacks of yard-sale flyers and unpaid parking tickets until he found the fat white envelope near the back.

"Fuck me," he said, laughing, holding up nearly four thousand dollars in wrinkled twenties and fives and ones. "You took all this straight from the till?"

"Not took," I said. "Borrowed. They'll get it all back after we make our haul."

"I gotta say, I underestimated you there, Pussy Willow," he said, stuffing the cash back into the envelope. "You are one devious little motherfucker."

"So, tell me about this meet," I said.

"Okay, so there's two of them, Manny and Tebo," he said. "Manny's the boss. He handles the product, makes all the decisions. Tebo, he's just muscle. You carrying?"

"Am I what?"

He turned on me, goggle-eyed. "Tell me you're not going to bitch out on me here."

"You said these guys were cool. You told me you've dealt with them before."

"I *have* dealt with them before." He opened his fatigue jacket, where the butt-end of a nickel-plated nine-millimeter peeked out from his inside pocket. "Rule #1 of dealing with crazy Mexican fuckers," he said. "Always be carrying."

Neither of us spoke as I pulled onto the freeway. I was angry now, mostly at myself. In a lifetime of buying and selling drugs I had never carried a weapon, and now I was walking unarmed into a drug deal carrying thousands of dollars in stolen money. A sour taste of fear boiled up from my gut. There were just so many ways this could go wrong. Gianni could come in over the weekend to get a head start on the week. The Homecoming parties Lee was counting on could fizzle out, leaving me with thousands of dollars of Mexican cocaine I couldn't unload. And now this: we could get robbed. Half a dozen times the night before, I'd run to my tiny bathroom to puke, until there was nothing left in my stomach, and still that sour taste filled my mouth, telling me I was going to get caught, I was going to jail.

As we crossed the Horse Hill grade, San Quentin prison came into view like an old friend, its long, barred windows glittering in the afternoon sun. How many of the guys on the other side of those high yellow walls had been where I was now, doing a drug deal they knew was stupid because they needed the money, because they couldn't think what else to do?

"Care for a taste?" Lee said, waving a small brown medicinal bottle.

"Put that shit away," I said. "This highway's crawling with cops."

"Shit's uncut, man," he said, loading up the aluminum dipper with pinkish white flakes. "Straight from Manny's top shelf. Smooth you right out."

"I don't need to be smoothed out," I said. "I just need to make some money."

"Right, save your lady friend. Your damsel in distress."

I watched him take the bump. I didn't even like cocaine, really. It gave me headaches, made me twitchy and paranoid, but right now, I knew, it would douse the taste of fear in my throat like foam from a fire extinguisher. I checked the mirrors for siren racks, trying to push from my mind the *other* way this could all go wrong: me holed up in a hotel room with a hooker and four thousand dollars of uncut pink-flake cocaine.

"I don't even know if she'll take the fucking money," I said.

"Oh, she'll take the money. They always take the money." He took one last bump, screwed the cap back on the one-hitter, and stashed it in his jacket next to the pistol. "So, then what?" he said. "You guys shack up, knock out a bunch of little Trent Jrs.?"

"I have no idea, man."

"You got to watch out for that shit. I told you about the chick brought down my operation in Colorado."

I turned to look at him. This was news. "You guys were like a couple?"

"You don't have to look so fucking surprised," he said. "Yeah, we were a couple. Almost a year. Living together, talking about getting hitched, all that shit."

"Until she gave you up to the cops."

He shrugged. "She had a kid. Tony. It was either snitch me out or let the kid rot in foster care. She moved to another state, changed her name, the whole bit. Except, the dumb cunt, she gave her address to her brother, whose ass I saved about a billion times in Cañon City."

I fixed my eyes on the dry, brown San Rafael hills, knowing Lee was watching me, getting a perverse kick out of me picturing him lying in wait for his ex-girlfriend, crouched in a corner of her double-wide trailer in some godforsaken town in Wyoming or Arizona, listening for the crackle of tires on the driveway, the click of her key turning in her front door.

"I left the kid out of it," he said. "He was cool. Little Tony. All about his Monday night wrestling. The Rock, Stone Cold Steve Austin. But that bitch took three years of my life."

We drove on in silence after that, me keeping my eyes on the road, trying not to think about what Lee had done to that girl, Lee tossing his little brown bottle from hand to hand, looking over his shoulder fifteen times a minute to see if we were being followed. The sour taste of fear never left my mouth, and I never stopped thinking about the four thousand dollars in small bills in the glove compartment and how glad I would be when this weekend was over and I could put them back in the stock room safe at Tam Grocery.

"Here," Lee said, a few minutes south of Novato. "Take this exit."

"Seriously?" I said. "These guys live in Ignacio?"

"I have no idea where they live," he said. "This is where we *meet*. There's a spot we use out by the old airfield. It's better that way. No cops. No nosy neighbors."

We pulled off the freeway into downtown Ignacio, a part of Marin I had never been before. During the war, the army had built an airbase along the Bay, but the base had been closed since the seventies, and now it was deep suburbia, mile after mile of featureless office parks and tract homes. Out here, it was a nice, lazy Saturday afternoon, families grilling on the patio, watching ball games on their flatscreen TVs. We crossed a man-made lake called Bel Marin Keys, where the houses spidered out over a murky green lake on low-lying spits of land, complete with private docks and power boats. Where the lake ended, we crossed a plank-wood drawbridge, its steel side rails rusting under pale blue paint. On the other side, the blacktop disappeared, replaced by a double-rutted track filled in with crushed seashells, bleached an eye-wincing white.

"Hang a left here," Lee said, his eyes still on the side mirror. "Not far now."

I turned onto the dirt track, seashells crunching under the Honda's thin tires. I was sweating now, bile burning a hole in the back of my throat. I had no idea where we were. The tidal flats around us had at some point been converted to agricultural use—wheat, maybe, or alfalfa. Whatever it was, it had been shorn to stubble, the fields little more than mud and plant stumps. In the distance, I could see the mirrored blue of the Bay. Other than that there was nothing. Not a tree, not a stump, nothing, just the harvested fields and the dirt road and us.

When we came to another fork in the road, I pulled the car to a stop.

"What the fuck?" I said. "Where *are* we?"

"Hey, what'd I say about bitching out?"

"I'm not bitching out. This is insane. This is your idea of neutral ground? Look at this place. They could come at us from anywhere."

"You need to man up, Wolfer," he said. "When this is all done, you're gonna be a rich man. You'll be able to buy that chick's car out of hock three times over. Till then, I need you to shut the fuck up and let me handle this."

I stared out at the stubbled wheat field, a yellow tractor rusting ominously at the far end, like the farmer had knocked off for lunch sometime in 1986 and never come back. I did not like this. It didn't feel right. But what was I going to do? This was Lee's deal. His connect. His drugs. His parties. If I bailed now, he would just go on without me, and if I wasn't careful, he might just take my four grand with him.

I shifted the Honda into gear and inched forward, taking the leftward fork in the road. I could smell the Bay now, salt and sand and rotting kelp. Gulls and terns wheeled overhead, their dark wings silhouetted against the cloudless blue.

"Here," Lee said, pointing to a narrow pullout. "This is it."

It looked no different than half a dozen other pullouts we'd passed, but I eased off the main road and killed the engine. Instantly, a chorus of buzzing insects rose up behind us, loud as a band saw. The fields, which had looked so dead from the windows of a passing car, were a hive of activity: iridescent blue dragonflies hovering over the broken stalks, brown and black songbirds flitting from fence post to fence post. Any minute now, I knew, we were going to get eaten alive by mosquitoes.

"Dude, you're sweating," Lee said.

He was right. We had been parked less than a minute, but already the back of my shirt was soaked through.

"Sorry, man," I said.

"It's cool. But wipe it off, huh? Don't want these dudes seeing you looking like you're gonna shit yourself."

I used my shirt to wipe the sweat from my face. When I was done, I checked the seashell track behind us. All was empty and still, the only sound the distant cawing of gulls over the open Bay. I thought, in spite of myself, of a million horror flicks I'd watched with my dad. If this was one of those movies, I would turn around and see waves of zombie farmers armed with scythes and pitchforks marching across the wheat field to eat our brains.

"What time is it?" I asked.

Lee checked his watch. "Twelve-thirty."

"What time are they supposed to get here?"

"About twelve-thirty."

Reaching into his jacket, he pulled the semi-automatic from his pocket and aimed it at a spot between my eyes. At first, my brain refused to process this information. I looked around like an idiot, still half-expecting a pair of Mexican gangbangers to jump out from behind the fence posts.

"The keys, Wolfer," he said. "Hand 'em over."

"Lee, no way. You can't do this to me."

"Just give me the fucking keys."

The rational part of my brain knew he wasn't going to shoot me, that no amount of obsessive side-mirror watching could guarantee he hadn't been seen with me. But there's nothing rational about having a gun pointed at your head. Slowly, slowly, the snub-nosed pistol working on me like some magic force field, I reached for the ignition and handed him the keys.

"Now, get out of the car," he said.

"You're stealing my car?"

He laughed. "This shitbox? No, man, you'll get your car back. It'll be parked behind Hélène's, same place you picked me up. And by the time you get there, I'll be halfway to Canada."

"That money, it's not mine," I said. "I'll go to jail. I'll be in there for years. I'll be lucky if I *ever* get out."

"You are such a pussy, you know that?" he said. "You could have made some real money on this, bought that bitch anything she wanted. But, no, you had to treat me like dirt under your fucking feet. Now, get out of the car. Move."

I begged him to let me keep the money, even just *some* of the money, but he kept waving that silver nine-millimeter at me, telling me to shut up, telling me get the fuck out of the car, until I popped the door and stepped out onto the seashell roadway. Lee climbed over the gear shift into the driver's seat, taking the wheel.

"I don't think you're coming after me," he said. "I don't think you have the stones for that. Even if you do, that money's stolen and you were looking to do a drug deal. But in case you get any ideas, if I go down for this, it won't be you that gets hurt. It'll be Suze. If it takes me ten years to get to her, I'll get to her. Are we clear?"

I saw again the desolate trailer where his ex had moved with her little boy, heard the door latch click, followed by her screams of panic as she felt the knife on her throat. I nodded.

"Well, then," he said, shifting my car into gear. "Good doing business with you, my brother."

He had chosen his spot well. There were no cars out there, no people. It was an hour before I saw a house, nearly two before I found strip mall with a pay phone. By then, I already knew what I was going to do. I never gave any real thought to going after Lee. I believed him when he said he would hurt Suze. We hadn't been close in years, but I knew him. He had that violence in him. Anyway, what good would it do? No matter what happened, I was going to jail. Even my mother couldn't save me this time. I had stolen four thousand dollars, and I was still on probation for stealing fifty thousand dollars in Santa Barbara—I was going to jail for a while. But maybe, I thought, if I played the few cards still left to me just right, some good could come of all this.

There was a Peet's Coffee in the mall, and I went inside to ask for a phone book. You could still do that then. I thought about calling Frank, to have him drive me back to Mill Valley, but I knew if he tried to talk me out of what I wanted to do, I would probably listen. So I called a rival cab company and opened up the white pages, looking for the listing for Gianni Papadakis.

Half an hour later, the cab dropped me off in front of Gianni's house on La Goma Avenue in the Sycamore Flats, a block from where my grandparents used to live. I knew the house well. When the first Mr. Papadakis lived there, it had been a bright lemony yellow. Now it was painted lettuce green, with an extra bedroom in the side yard, but it was still a one-story stucco bungalow, one of hundreds just like it built during the war. If I had to guess, I'd say Gianni's Pappouli had bought the house around the time my own granddad had, and unlike him, had paid it off decades ago. Gianni had built on the extra bedroom and repaved the driveway, adding a new brick walk from the garage to the front door. But in every other way, it was the same house I'd skated past on my way to school on the nights I slept over at my grandparents' place.

Gianni's wife answered the door, their little boy Nik hanging off her pants leg. I was still explaining that I worked for her husband when Gianni called from a back room, asking who was at the door.

He had been building a new bed for his son, he said, one of those Ikea things that come in pieces, and he looked sweaty and frustrated, but he led me around the side of the house to an overgrown rose garden with a rusty wrought-iron table and chairs. It was like stepping into a time warp, back to the seventies before everyone in Marin hired gardeners and stocked their backyards from Stan Starling's catalog.

"Look, if this is about your stepdad," Gianni said.

"This isn't about Stan," I said. "Not exactly."

"Okay. Then what can I do for you?"

I looked back at the house where his wife, olive-skinned and heavy, stood watching us from the kitchen window. I waited until I saw her step away from the window.

"I took money from you," I said. "From one of the register pouches. About four thousand dollars, give or take."

He coughed, dropping into one of the battered garden chairs. "You what?"

"I was going to put it back, I swear," I said. "I was going to use the money over the weekend and put it back before you opened the safe Monday morning."

"You were going to give it *back*?"

"I have a friend," I said. "A guy I grew up with. He was going to invest it in a side business he's got going. It's a long story, a very, *very* long story, but the short version is he took the money. It's gone, all of it."

I hadn't realized just how insane this sounded until I tried to explain it with Gianni's wife pretending not to watch us through the kitchen window.

"I'm going to take the fall on this," I said. "I'll turn myself in. Today, if you want. I'm not hacking it here. I haven't been hacking it, really, since I left rehab. And, well, I stole your money, that's the bottom line. But I need to ask you for a favor first."

"A favor? Are you fucking kidding me?"

"I know about the books, Gianni. I know you've been fudging the numbers to pay for the new building. I wouldn't be surprised if your dad's figured it out, too. He's a sharp guy, and I know he's suspicious. But if he hasn't, all I have to do is tell Stavros."

"What're you even talking about? I have no idea what you think you've found."

"I saw the invoices, the ones you forgot to shred," I said. "You faked the numbers on that construction budget, and I'm going to bet you moved some money from the general budget to cover your losses. If your uncle knew that, he'd shut down Chef Tam tomorrow. Even if he didn't press charges, you'd be gone, forever."

He said nothing, just sat in his patio chair, staring up at me. I can only imagine what he was thinking then. He had been so careful, so discreet, and now, here, in his sunstruck yard, with his wife and kids just a few feet away, he realized he had been caught. And by who? By a thieving office assistant he was paying nine bucks an hour.

"What do you want?" he asked.

"Four thousand dollars," I said.

He blinked slowly, dumbfounded, like I was speaking a foreign language.

"This girl I've been seeing—you spoke to her once on the phone—she just had her car repossessed," I said. "That's why I took the money. I was trying to help her out, get her car back."

"You stole four thousand dollars, and you want me to give you four thousand *more?*"

"Not me. My friend. Suze. I want you to pay her impound fees."

"Even if I wanted to give you—give *her*—that money, how am I going to do that? If you've seen the state of those books, you know how tight things are. I can't be handing four thousand dollars to some total stranger."

"So, take it out of the money you're getting from Stan."

This was the one real hole in my plan. I didn't know if Stan had offered him the loan. I was pretty sure he had, but I didn't know. One look at Gianni's face, his jaw slack, the color rising in his cheeks and the tips of ears, told me I'd guessed right.

"Were you going to tell your dad about that loan?" I asked.

"Of course. I already did."

"Did you say how much the loan was for?"

He was silent, caught again.

"Whatever you were setting aside to clean up the books, take four grand off the top," I said. "If you do that, I'll go quietly. I'll plead guilty. No trial, no investigation, nothing. You won't have to show the books to anybody. If you don't, I'll make sure every forensic accountant from here to L.A. gets a crack at that flash drive of yours."

A few minutes later, Gianni walked me back around to the front of the house and we shook hands on his freshly paved drive-way. Our deal was simple: I would plead not guilty until I saw a copy of the cancelled check from Gianni to Marin Salvage and Tow. Once I saw that he'd paid Suze's impound fees, I would change my plea to guilty and start serving my time.

"Fine, whatever," he said. "Get the hell out of my sight."

And then there was nothing left to do but walk back to my apartment and call the police. I knew these would be my last minutes as a free man, probably for years, so I took my time, wandering along La Goma to Sycamore Avenue and past Amacita Avenue, where my grandparents used to live, peeking in windows, stopping to puzzle out the secret paths between the houses. For years afterward, serving out my time first at North Kern State Prison and then at San Quentin, I wanted to shout at my younger self: *Run! You're going to lose everything! Find your car, throw everything into the trunk, and run!* But I had already lost everything I cared about. There was nothing left to run from.

# EPILOGUE

Four years, two months, and twelve days later, I handed a slip of paper to a C.O. in the Discharge Office at San Quentin Penitentiary and she handed me a bin containing the clothes I was wearing the day I was arrested. On top of the pile was a neatly folded UCSB Gauchos T-shirt, still stiff from the sweat I'd poured on it that day on the salt flats east of the Bel Marin Keys. Under that was a pair of jeans, my beat-up New Balance sneakers, a belt, and a zippered bag containing my wallet, my mother's expired AmEx card, and three dollars and twenty-six cents in cash.

In California, inmates are supposed to be discharged at noon, but with all the paperwork, it was almost two when the C.O. unlocked the last gate that led to the prison's parking lot. It was stupid to expect Suze to be there, I knew that. She had never visited me inside, and the one time I called after my arrest, she hung up as soon as she heard the recording saying I was calling from a correctional facility. But in the past couple years she had started answering my letters. Her first letter was just a short note thanking me for helping her get her car back and asking me to respect her privacy. But that Christmas she had sent me a card showing her and her two boys outside the new house she'd bought in Petaluma.

After that she answered all my letters. Sometimes it took her months to write, but she always did. She was flipping houses now, she told me, buying tract homes in North Marin and Sonoma, spending a few grand to pretty them up, and reselling them to young professionals fleeing the crazy housing market in San Francisco and Southern Marin. Dylan was in the fifth grade now, Jake in the third. She had been engaged briefly to a mortgage broker in Novato, but it hadn't worked out. Beyond that, she said almost nothing about herself, but in her letters, which I read over and over, ten, fifteen, twenty times, she never mentioned another guy, not once.

San Quentin is one of the oldest prisons in America and by 2005 the place was falling apart. The paint on the exit gate was flaking off and the hinges were rusty, forcing the C.O. to push hard, throwing her shoulder into it, to release me from the dark tunnel. Then I was out in the parking lot, the bright sun glaring off windshields, seagulls lining the prison's high walls, waiting to swoop down when the inmates were called in from the yard.

"Trent, over here!" a voice called out.

I swung around, still blinded by sunlight, and I saw my mother waving to me across the lot. Beside her, heavier now, his cheeks sunken, his hair ash-white, stood Frank T., a proud, crinkly smile on his lips. Mom had almost reached me, calling my name, her arms stretched wide, when I saw Suze leaning against the hood of a cocoa-brown Volvo station wagon. No kids, just her, dressed like she'd come straight from work in heels and a pinstriped skirt suit. She'd tinted her hair dark again, the way it had been when we were in high school, and she was smiling. She raised her hand to wave, just that, a little wave, saying hello.

# ACKNOWLEDGEMENTS

I have used my hometown, Mill Valley, California, as the setting for this novel and filled it with the sights and sounds and smells of my childhood—the ballpark where I played Little League baseball, the crumbling World War II–era artillery bunkers where we partied in high school, the eucalyptus-scented hills where my parents still live. Everything else is fiction. No one in this novel exists outside my imagination, and so far as I know, nothing that happens in the book ever happened to anyone in real life.

I would like to thank Martha Witt and the late Christina Meldrum, who read early drafts before the book was finished, as well as Claire Cameron, Hannah Gersen, Kirsten Lunstrum, and Henry and Nancy Bourne who read later drafts, in some cases more than once. In addition, I would like to thank Jaynie Royal, Pam Van Dyk, and everyone at Regal House Publishing for their belief in this book and for their hard work in getting it into print.

Last but definitely not least, I would like to thank my wife Eva and my son Luke. This book literally would not exist without you two. Thank you.